Right In The Teeth

Gary McClintock

Slipped Collar Publications

Slipped Collar Publications

Rock Island, IL 61201

slippedcollar@gmail.com

ISBN: 978-0-9994472-3-9

To   Kristie

My shelter from the wrong dreams

JE NE PARLE PAS
THIS EITHER

The elegant old building had ornate sandstone curlicues climbing both stories of its façade that the lawyers in charge had hired sandblasted clean, the façade scoured just that last summer, so even on a rainy late afternoon at the end of October, all that bright yellow nouveau twirl jumped out on the dingy street of muddy umbers like a fluffy show dog rutting through crusted garbage cans, a dog wagging its tail through the stink. The other buildings the near side of the street were decayed brick holding shops that seemed tenuous in every way. The last cobbler. The tavern with yet another owner drinking the profits. It would be seven years before the city knocked down the warehouses across the street to give a view of the river. Mostly I frequented the junkshop at the other end of the block until finally I left town in the middle of a blizzard the last days of December. But I had been working for the lawyers and the final time I entered the restored sandstone building it was a week before 1988 election day. There were probably forty people already seated on metal chairs about the long cafeteria tables I had set up at the start of the campaign in the big room on the ground floor at the back of the building. A couple gangly electricians talked loudly to each other about a grinding tool that kept sputtering out at their tractor works. They would photograph better than I could have hoped, no matter which way the camera was placed, in their blue sweatshirts printed front and back in the identifiers of their labor union, whose endorsement had as always gone to the opposition. Their mutiny might make news. I walked past a banker from the chamber of commerce combing his receding hair with hands so soft with flab they probably never came quite clean, not for mortgages, not even for the weddings of his daughters, certainly not for the television cameras. He had likely been foreclosing farmsteads all day. Perhaps he would sit on his hands like a mischievous child if I mentioned double-digit mortgage rates he made even his daughters pay. I remembered his daughters often sat on their hands. I had known his daughters in grade school.

At the far end of the table there were five slender but not young women with fresh haircuts and sleek but practical dresses competing to be the most chic within faith. They were from the same church. The very tall blonde one would steal the scene but it was unlikely she would be asked to speak about morality once again. She had been on local television at least twice the previous month exhorting the need to protect the children with conservative votes. This night the crew coming was network television. It was early evening. There were identical white telephones on the tables in front of everybody but there didn't seem to be anybody reciting the script I had written to repeat precisely when canvassing voters. Every voter in the congressional district had been telephoned at least three times. The smallest of the chic women was telling anyone who cared to listen she never watched the evening news anyway. I walked over to speak to a couple guards from the new prison.

"I told you before you can't wear your uniforms on television."

"But we paid for our uniforms out of our own pockets."

"It doesn't matter," I explained yet again to these smug bastards so keen for their authority. The prison had been the only place hiring rather than firing those last several years. The two guards thought they were the chosen people, the ones not slaves. "You can't wear anything that somehow represents state government."

The two prison guards stared at me because I was supposed to be too small not to be afraid of their bulk. They were unimpressed with the black suit I hadn't had pressed in three weeks. I wondered what they would have thought of the punk gear I had worn a decade earlier to the university lectures on film theory. My hair needed washing too but I knew I wouldn't be on camera. I had last written a poem years before in a Paris apartment at the top of a dilapidated building that had once been the magnificent mansion of a wealthy banker. There had been curlicues on that building too. I had written that last poem in bed the same day the tin drum arrived in the post.

"Even if we take all the offices?"

"I'll sell you shirts if you want."

The last thing these two wanted was to part with twenty dollars each for a flimsy t-shirt advocating their candidate in patriotic colors certain to run at the first wash. The shirts had not been a success. I had done much better with the coffee mugs depicting the candidate shaking hands with Ronald Reagan. I had drawn the image on the mugs from a not quite suitable photograph then added small amounts of gouache for color. This was before computers were even much conversation let alone a sophisticated tool for adjusting images. On the mugs I gave Reagan his rosy red cheeks. We all understood the point of the October evening was to ensure the legacy of that great president now his tenure was at its end.

The coffee mugs made a fine souvenir of victory though at seven dollars not so fine as pillage.

"It's just dumb because we've done everything there is to do," said the lawyer who chaired the campaign, my boss. "They want to put us on the news working the phones but there is next to no one left to call, no one at all really, is there?"

"I'm just going to call my own home over and over," someone responded.

The election was such a sure thing that no one even considered calling the same voter yet again, as though tongues would swell and ears would chafe, the winner seemed so obvious, why jinx it. I also thought it obvious the two prison guards were thinking this night was their last chance to knock me into place. A beating too seemed a sure thing.

"Just hang your uniform jackets in the closet over there in the hallway where you came in," the chairman said to the guards. "Then stay seated so no one sees the stripes on your trousers."

The chairman was the brother of the war hero running for a first term in Congress in replacement of a twelve-term Congressman who had taken a job at the White House but late in the administration. The war hero had already held the seat thirteen months in appointment from the governor. He too was chosen. But everyone rightly suspected the war hero himself wouldn't be there for the television crew because he wasn't important enough for a network interview. He was too vain to show without an interview. Anyway the television crew was only after something with cacophonous voices and hands darting so the war hero's younger brother would substitute in the news footage. They looked almost identical anyway, those brothers, broad and plodding beneath soup bowl haircuts. We all understood the issues.

"Kelly, give them t-shirts," directed the chairman.

After a bit more shillyshallying the guards removed their jackets as they had been told. They were large men somewhere near the end of their thirties and didn't seem properly built for their profession, not tough enough I mean, even though the new prison they guarded was only for petty criminals, drug smokers and car thieves, not real gangsters. The one going fat seemed to have trouble catching his breath. The other one wore thick glasses. Still I was no match for either in a fistfight. Finally the unrepentant fascist always at the law office no matter the time of day spoke for her sons, I mean the mother of the two lawyers, a very small woman with a large ball of henna hair, dyed, over sickly skin, warts, a face that always seemed twisted by choice rather than nature, the lips snarled, the eyes not quite synchronized. Months earlier I had given her the list of dead voters to call but no one had risen from the grave.

"You must telephone before the television people arrive else they won't take pictures. We must seem busy. Busy! They come for action. It must seem action if not news."

The mother of the two lawyers was doing my job. In my directorial debut I wasn't going to force anyone play right into the camera but the mother of the two lawyers had been young in a Germany where everyone knew how to take an order. Of course I exaggerate. I wasn't going to be allowed anywhere near the camera even from behind. The mother of the two lawyers continued screeching. The banker flipped a telephone directory. The three chic women obediently picked up their telephones to place calls to nowhere. The guards pushed past me to snag donuts before getting back at dialing.

"You don't want to piss her off again."

A week ago the mother of the two lawyers had shouted at my face that I was too small to, in any fashion, represent her son. I pointed out we were on telephones. She said it carried into my voice. Hitler Jugend. The guards were impressed by the mother of the two lawyers but they never completely conceded her authority. They didn't put on the free t-shirts I gave them either. I found myself imagining the guards fetching an extra frosted donut, on a little silver tray pushed down the cellblock on a little silver trolley, for that notorious nutter downstate at the real prison who had tried to return a strangled schoolgirl to where he had snatched her over at our local ice cream parlor, returning her because the girl was the wrong flavor, so the nutter had confessed. Obviously it couldn't have really been donuts on carts up at the state prison. I had been filling myself with extravagant visions of what other people did for a living ever since obtaining the piddling associate degree in computer science only to put that career on hold to work the election. I had appropriated the cellblock vision from Truffaut's The Bride Wore Black though I could no longer remember the much better ending I had invented for that movie the first time I ever saw it.

"She should ship you to a concentration camp rather than just up the stairs away from the cameras."

Nuit et Brouillard. La Nuit Américaine. Movie titles played against each other through my thoughts. *Ma Nuit Chez Maud.* I was going to miss having a stupid actor president. The absurdity had seemed oddly protective in the way sitting in a dark theater makes anything possible. All the same it had been jolly to desecrate my own dead mother by turning conservative for the election.

"At least you'd get rid of that hair," said the other guard.

The whole election I had been letting my hair go long but not punk with the anticipation I would have to clip it all off before starting work with computers after the first of the year. I had a job waiting. Everyone else's fantasy was that my looks had done me in. The crowd in that room felt somehow secure in their choices by having around an underling about to be humiliated by a thirtieth birthday with nothing like success in sight. To the chosen it felt not all a bad thing to have left youth behind.

"You two just try to keep your zippers up for the cameras."

I was careful to take three steps sideward before turning my back on that pair of shiftless protectors of the social order. The fat one had hit me between the shoulder blades once before, after I said something too clever for his rugged ears, something like, do movies about women in prison ever make you think you've missed the boat? There were no women at his prison.

"Unmögliches verlangen."

The mother of the two lawyers was holding a telephone receiver towards a couple people not calling, as though the receiver were a weapon.

Ask the impossible.

I was glad the guards had never followed me up the stairs to the private law offices because among the mediocre corporate artworks hanging framed on one wall in the stairwell was an original theater poster for *Das Cabinet Des Dr. Caligari*. No. It had not come from the mother. I recognized the horizontal frame. Cesare carrying the girl to the peak of a jagged path. It equaled movie posters I had seen in museums overseas and it was the object I planned to steal that night while I still had the chance. With computers everything is called an object no matter its inherent sexual value.

Don't get me wrong. It was simply that there was no reason not to steal the poster. Obviously the lawyers didn't know what they had since the poster was hanging opposite the windows in the stairwell where all that sunshine through the summer after the renovation couldn't have done it any good. I had my own civic order to protect. I just couldn't figure a plan how to successfully get the poster out of the building without being seen by the mother of the lawyers. *Knavery's plain face is never seen till used.* The hair length is noticed though.

Upstairs I went into the largest of the offices and sat down in its plush leather chair, the one behind the oak desk, the chair set too high for my legs. The telephone on the desk had buttons instead of a rotary dial like all the very old phones I had obtained free for the big room downstairs and I sometimes think I wouldn't have bothered with that poster if I had found good use for that office telephone. There was nothing to stop me from dialing Perth or Paris at the war hero's expense. It was his desk. I very much fancied that robbery while I swung my legs below the desk, but all the actors and directors and costumers and editors and screenwriters I had briefly met in university, students who might actually now be making success in foreign places, were long gone from my address book, all their numbers I still kept discarded for better.

In that last year at the university I had thought images neither more nor less practical than bookkeeping, whatever that disparagingly meant, knowing only I abandoned one interest after another so long there was a replacement, true for art, true for friends, acting without fear though there burrowed my skin some sense the future was withheld, not elusive, but genuinely denied in the way it was not meant to be denied the young, not in my day anyway. I did not yet comprehend the limitations inherent in my small body. In that one year I churned out no end of montages from scraps found in the school editing suites, or bits pillaged from eight millimeter studio movies bought cheap at the charity shops, discarded and damaged reels, Star Wars, Spartacus, My Fair Lady, no end of crap, plus the occasional family footage probably not meant to have been donated. I received shockingly good grades but all the students easily understood I was speaking to the false superiority of movies no one else thought false. At graduation I handed out no forwarding address. By that election day years later I knew it had been a mistake to think that a mantle of failure could be counted on to scramble what was merely a pathetic stagnation. There had been no derangement of the senses called for by poets. Punk attitude had not worked. Still it wasn't until later in Paris that I entirely stopped writing poetry.

The campaign's list of important donors was sitting open on the desk. I had met them all but there wasn't one I wanted to give another thought now the cash flow was over. I would not phone them. I was not thinking about financing a damned thing. Instead I was listing the new tiles of the office floor already permanently stained in several places, naming the spots, like dangerous shoals given exotic nomenclature on an ancient navigational map, the twelve lawyer archipelago stain, the reef scruff of the accountant's deniability, blue skids west of the next divorce whirlpool. Here be monsters.

"The earliest book on the art of screen writing was first published in 1931."

"Not true." The professor wasn't used to challenges on basic facts university students couldn't possibly know. "The library where I grew up had one from the 1920s on how to write for the silent pictures. It had photographs of the Keystone cops and the Perils of Pauline and Fatty Arbuckle wooing another skinny girl."

"Here you are then."

The beautiful small woman speaking to me came into the office with a certain sway to her hips registering her own expulsion from the telephone tables below. I had gone back home after university determined to find that book on screenwriting. The library had discarded it. I had not found it at the junkshop at end of the block either though that shop for generations had been full of books libraries a hundred miles around no longer wanted. I had best known the beautiful woman come into the office from that freshman year I spent in Catholic college there in the big city on the river. Davenport. The big city. In that comfortable chair I remembered the long uncomfortable commutes with my mother dropping me on her way to clerk in the county building. Naturally I could also remember Alice in almost every day around our small town because she had been only two grades ahead of me at the new public school I attended after my mother moved the household thirty miles downriver at the end of the year I finished grade school. Grade school had been parochial school. The school with the banker's daughters. Now the beautiful woman's red hair was long and her skirt was short, and when the woman sat on the edge of the desk, her bare knees were practically in my face.

"You don't mind if I use the phone, do you?"

For no good reason I was surprised to watch her punch a number I recognized rather than one of the faraway places I had been contemplating. There was a pause. I think she got an answering machine because she started to speak but then cut herself off while giving me a challenging look that faded towards contriteness. She hung up the phone.

"I believe he's the best candidate to run for office there's ever been out of this congressional district," she said. Then she stumbled a bit expanding on her explanation for being in the office though she knew I knew perfectly well. I had once driven her in the campaign's car to the discreet new airport hotel across the river. She must have told the hero not to ask me to do that again. "You know, despite the trust fund, I was raised to be a liberal Democrat just like you, but this is different, isn't it, times are very changed."

I noticed Alice didn't call herself a union Democrat, which is what I rightly should have been called, at least in terms of family, given my mother. I was sitting in the war hero's chair admiring the view up the skirt of someone who wasn't his wife. His wife had gone to all the rallies but never once had come near the bank of telephones. This was his tart. She had turned so a fall of hair obscured her face.

"I suppose I'll even have to vote for him now because you say so."

This made the tart laugh. At college I had known her face covered in freckles but now it was a painted mask with a bleached white foundation covering all imperfections and lips painted a color even more red than her hair. I was tumbling thought on how to fit all her lower shapes and upper colors together into a villanelle when what was wanted was a canvas in oils. No. A camera. It was a movie face. She had been acting in a movie being shot in Hamburg of all places when she met the war hero visiting his distant relatives. No canvas. No camera. I hadn't either anymore. My sisters had cleared out the house when my mother died. It was no longer discomforting to know I would never write another poem.

"You were telling me in the car you went on later to study in Iowa City."

It had probably been a federal offense when I took her across to Illinois but I too had wonderfully discreet deniability given I had not put a hand on her. In fact I had never put a hand on her. The greater deception is that I merely learned what I could my senior year in rather scattershot fashion from the cinema classes at the university not very far west. I never reminded anyone I originally went to study poetry.

"I took painting classes then cinema classes."

"I was so enthralled by that ridiculous class we had together I went on studying languages."

She turned so I could see her face now without the hair in the way and without the phone in the way and without my attention all on her knees. I remember her the first time I saw her with the war hero. It is unfortunate. That year of the election I had been losing my memories of everything that occurred prior some point I never could quite identify, as though only by erasing the past could I absolve the nothingness I had become, a canister of celluloid left unexposed to light, free of image, somehow more insidiously blank generation than I had ever believed possible when a punk. I was especially losing memory of faces because I no longer even sketched in pencil. I never borrowed a camera. Alice had wrangled me the dogsbody job with the campaign but for just what reason had never become clear. This time I laughed.

"All verse leads to Verlaine," I said.

"You don't look any less a poet," she responded while playfully tugging on a length in my hair tumbling over an ear. "But I really preferred the other."

"Yes. Yet this too is enough to keep a poet from landing a real job."

At the Catholic college in the year I first met Alice my hair had been short spikes dyed blue while her hair didn't even cover her ears. We met in an introductory poetry class where an insane nun kept pushing her lectures towards poetry in French, preferably Verlaine, but if not Verlaine, then Lamartine, if not Lamartine then Mallarmé, then finally onto Queneau and Prevert, across two semesters. Languages hadn't been offered at the little high school of our small town. But of course Alice had had a much better education leading up to that college class. She had travelled for whole summers at a time when a girl and had disappeared an entire year in high school to live right smack in the heart of Montparnasse. In the poetry class her French had been advanced if not so impeccable as it would be later in the foreign movies. She was never dubbed over.

"Voulez-vous jouer?"

I took from my jacket the old deck of playing cards I had bought a couple hours earlier at the junkshop. The memory of *Les Jeux Sont Faits* came rushing towards me like something with teeth rising quickly through dark seawater that was the floor. The class had translated some part of the screenplay and the nun had shown us the black and white movie itself at the end of the second semester. I remember making an inane comment to Alice after the movie, something about the clothes the actors wore, or maybe even the hair styles, how only an existentialist demand could make Paris that ugly. It wasn't the Paris of the backlots.

"Un soir, j'ai assis la Beautée sur mes genoux."

Alice laughed.

"Et je l'ai trouvée amère? You still memorize Rimbaud?"

"It's the only line I remember."

"Tant pis," she said. "But I hope you don't mind if I sit in a chair instead."

I didn't dare quote the Baudelaire I had been obsessively reading since the first day hired for the campaign, as though the two were married, poetry harnessed to a world defined winners and losers, foes anyway, the blessed against the damned, forever exchanging places in a musical chairs played with jazz. I would never have taken the job on the campaign if I had never felt derangement in it. I could have moved straight onto computers. Alice knew how to get at me even after all that time away.

Je me pris à songer près de ce corps vendu
Á la triste beauté dont mon désire se prive

Alice pulled up one of the chairs from over by the wall and sat at the end of the desk so we were kitty-corner each other. She began sorting out the cards to play Euchre because that was the game everyone had played between classes at the Catholic college that one spring. It did almost seem we were waiting on a class to commence. I took the joker from the discard pile and began to draw on it with the best pen from the desk. It was my first drawing since the madhouse.

"Honey, I think you're supposed to mark cards on the backside."

"I'm giving her thigh a strategically placed tattoo of the Arc de Triumph."

The playing cards were an old risqué deck with color illustrations of naked women in cheesecake poses on the card faces. And though the deck must have dated back almost to the time of *Les Jeux Sont Faits*, the cards were good as new, mint even, giving off a crisp slap each time Alice dealt, like a beckoning to a bit of rough sex, but just a very little. I tried not to listen. Instead I drew on the busty strawberry blonde joker while we played. I told Alice about how I got fired from the job I got after university. The one after Paris.

"She had a tattoo of a pouncing tigress like this coming over her shoulder and a chain of flowers twined all the way around her waist then upwards under the tigress like a climbing vine."

"Georgia O'Keefe complained her flowers weren't supposed to be taken for vaginas."

"But you remember Apollonia Whitton?"

"Of course."

"Bookstore turned video place."

"Run like a hobby."

After university then Paris then the other, I felt almost lucky to have gotten a job managing a video rental store for an old woman who seemed to drink coffee to chase boredom. This was down in the hometown. For five years I wasn't expected to think too much but always work long hours. Still it was a very good job in its way since the woman let me bring in videos you couldn't get anywhere else, movies even I hadn't seen before, like *Cléo de 5 à 7* and *Alphaville*, *Les Bonnes Femmes* and *Le Genou de Claire*. *La Mariée Était En Noir*. *The Bride Wore Black*. Over time because I was manager I was contacted by many different pirates offering no end of movies not legitimately available on videotape. *Zéro de Conduite*. *Le Salaire de la Peur*. Apollonia Whitton also sold vinyl movie soundtrack albums with their big bold covers, though these were years being taken over by compact discs, and I'll be damned but every time she played *An American in Paris* on television in the shop on Sundays, she'd also sell three copies of the album to the after church crowd. The actual French movies didn't rent much.

"Is that what it looks like?"

"Been a while since you've seen one?"

Then one day after church a curvaceous young woman, aged thirty or so, pulled up her blouse to show the tattoos across her belly, then hiked her blouse all the way up her back for me to see the tattoos there stretching from neck to buttocks. This was in the days before every girl about had tattoos mocking even the best pale flesh. Then the tattooed woman flexed her shoulder blades to make seated lovers hump over her spine. That was real fun. You can learn a lot from Lydia but I wouldn't have gotten fired if I hadn't pulled up the blouse from the young woman's large breasts to have a peep at the handprints outlined there like diagrammed instructions. That was that. Apollonia Whitton had always forbidden pornographic movies in the shop. In the end, the amount of my first three unemployment checks just about covered what I had promised the tattooed woman for coming into the shop to display her flesh. See, I had danced with her tattoos a couple times before in some ratskeller of a club in the city up river, where the idea to strip for the church crowd came in conversation, after many drinks, with me never really getting at the tattoos otherwise, never to the finish anyway, it turned out. In fact it had been a while since I'd seen one. The computer training had ended in the spring.

"You need to add the Tour Eiffel on her other thigh."

"Hearts."

"Are you kidding?"

"Left and right bower."

Actually, Alice never let me finish my story, never let me tell how Apollonia Whitton had keeled over dead the evening of that same afternoon, as though my drawing on the joker depicted all there was to know about revenge, the blame accorded me anyway in our small town because Apollonia Whitton had been on her way to the bank with the shop receipts, what should have been my responsibility. It was as if Alice interrupted because she had her own story to tell me after years of waiting for me to hear it. That wasn't so strange. Maybe she thought I was the only one who would appreciate it since I was the only one from that poetry class not scattered to the winds. She claimed to have never gone back home even to visit but I knew that to be merely an embraced ideal. I had seen her once at a distance down the street from the video store. That summer she had come back home for more than the war hero. But no pirated movie ever matched that poetry within language class for stretching an imagined future out before me in something other than maps of the unknown. I think it had been the same for Alice acting in movies despite the nun giving us *Les Jeux Sont Faits* to rein in all that romantic coffee table rubbish most students lurched into a poetry class, giving us existential absurdity no different to the flesh from a medieval mystery play, giving us even the heaven without promise found in that movie, quite the thing for a nun to do. I remembered Alice had announced right at the start of that class she was off to Paris again come summer. Since then she had learned languages all right but not chasing an easy degree through classes where she already knew more than the nuns teaching. She had learned languages on the ground in preparation for the next movie. Spain. Italy. Germany. Even Denmark. In the car that one time over the river she said she still wrote poetry.

"It's still the same."

"How's that?"

"I was hooked on him even before I got there."

"Who's that?"

"The movie producer I fell in love with I met on the plane to Paris."

"I think that I once tried to say I loved you, but I muffed it, using *vous*, like that stupid old Nat King Cole song."

I was giving the joker a rancid face from a Picasso. Another of the movies I had gotten into the video store was the documentary where Picasso works on glass so you can feel yourself in the painting from the other side. I suddenly felt it too was a heaven without promise.

"That wasn't you, was it?"

We went on playing cards while Alice proceeded to tell me a rather quotidian story about spending three years in Paris with an independently wealthy flaneur movie producer of some sort who taught her how to dress from a Champs-Élysées fashion house and to swear like a Seine bargeman. Alice said that at the Louvre he had taught her an especially vulgar phrase in front of Delacroix's Mort de Sardanapalus and an even worse phrase, with rude hand gesture, in front of Titian's Concert Champêtre.

"He really wanted a barbarian American for a girlfriend."

"Did he make you piss in the street?"

Alice thought it was a funny line but she didn't laugh. Instead she recounted that her favorite memory was riding down the Champs-Elysée late at night in a new sports car with the top down three minutes before the flaneur wrecked the car. I smiled back. From there Alice told about a chateau the flaneur's family owned on a beach of pebbles that rubbed off green on your skin and about the charred hamburgers the flaneur made her fry him out of that flavorless bœuf sold in the supermarchés.

"Il etait un peu fou. A bit crazy, you know?"

"In that video store where I worked I saw a movie about a looney Vietnam veteran."

"A French movie?"

"It turns out the French veterans of the 1950s were just as crazy as the Americans of the 1960s. At least in the movies."

Alice didn't like me implying her new boyfriend the politician lawyer was crazier than her boyfriend the hamburger flaneur. But I wasn't really trying to torque her off. I thought, the one guy wanted her to be a barbarian and this guy wants her to be a whore, so what's the difference in centimes? Maybe some green coloring on intimate parts of the skin? I didn't care. Alice threw down her cards without finishing the hand. She must have been used to concessions.

"It sounds like the television people are done."

We had been hearing the New York City accents talking too loudly to each other downstairs almost since Alice had come into the office. There was never any question but she had been scooted out of the way too. We looked up to see the politician's brother, the chairman, flashing the overhead lights on and off by flipping the switch at the door.

"We have to get going before it gets too late for those drinks at the hotel."

Out in the corridor the brother had to twice pull shut the office door behind us to get the lock to click into place and when he pulled at the door the second time he eyed me a bit as though wondering if I might have monkeyed the works with some old burglar trick. The hilarious thing was that he then didn't make me lead the way down the stairs. Instead he rushed off at some New York voice he had yet to impress enough that evening. I was left on the stairwell with Alice.

"Take this for me."

I pulled the frame holding the movie poster off the wall to hand to Alice.

"I can't take that."

"Who else could?"

"No."

"Take it then tell him you want me to drive."

Alice understood instantly I meant she should leave the poster in the car when she and the brother went into the hotel. It was my willingness to drive her across the river again that threw her off before she could harden. The brother would come back alone to be driven home. It wouldn't matter to him when I said I would keep the poster to give Alice later. Finally Alice walked down the stairs holding the poster against her thigh. Of course the mother of the two lawyers had to ignore her. At the bottom of the stairs Alice gave me a quizzical look as though she were wondering how I had hung onto punk attitude without the colored hair I had worn in the college. Perhaps I should have told her more about the ugly things that happened to me after my own time in Paris instead of that nonsense about losing my job years later. Over time I would do that in letters I was never often certain she received. Then we were outside.

"What do you guys want?" asked the lawyer.

"We just want to talk to this fairy for a minute."

Again in their jackets, the two prison guards were standing blocking the stairs above the sidewalk.

"Move. We don't have time to talk," commanded Alice.

The two prison guards were too stupid not to have out their cellblock voices when they meant to beat me up. Alice couldn't miss that menace. The lawyer brother didn't miss it either but he was amused by the possibilities until he saw the television crew over by a van with their camera still out. He meant to turn back to the building but Alice pushed us right past the guards and out into the lot towards the parked cars. A couple evenings later on the television news the politician's brother was misidentified as the war hero certain to win his safe district. And there was his whore working the ridiculously valuable poster of *Dr. Caligari* as a kind of wedge against the guards. But nothing happened. After the broadcast, I mean. There was no scandal to propel me from somnambulist into a protean life. I was stuck with computers.

INTIMATE JOURNALS

Before, at the university not this community college, it wasn't the ones raped in the garden I encountered but the ones who had always sought to please, the conformists plucking relevancy like wildflowers, weeds of wisdom, the hothouse weeds forever against incantation, potions, nevertheless keen for the garden poisons. But here I am looked at, wondered, wondered what went on in the garden that I should have to pay to be here, ranked lower than the welfare women, young women here on orders from the state but paid their stipends, busheled their food stamps. I talked once about being hungry all the time. The gorgeous mulatto girl looked at me with sympathy she quickly surmised needed caution, angry at herself for being caught off guard, suspicious at intelligence that suffers degradation, imagining any number of horrors for me to not imagine herself, herself in my hands. Still she talks to me every day. She likes that I am not like all the others.

Sans me résigner par trop cependant.

The movie distribution company whose catalogs I illustrated all through high school and the summer after is long gone, together with the factories now just brick carcasses lining the river, lining the moonbeams, all else, long gone together as far as I can tell with any means to see those old George Méliès movies the company distributed, the best seller that moonshot, but on a whole the other seller more defining, defining all the bits darker in the night, *The Cabinet of Dr. Caligari*. No fanciful trips to the moon for our generation. Nope. Nothing magical left unless it is to speak for the dead. We children found our own way to Dr. Caligari and now I sit here marooned on a filthed planet where this generation has figured out how to murder John Lennon but not Ronald Reagan. The failure of the somnambulists. The failure of the moon to breed sufficient madness for the minds of my generation.

Soit! le grandiose échappe à ma dent.

The teetering old man near ninety, still teaching accounting across shaking hands, worries himself sick he missed chances at theft, all those balance sheets, looks at me, certain I steal food from the cafeteria, the grocery store robbed blind the time the power cut out, the time he saw me, steaks and ham stuffed down my trousers, he tries to remember a balance sheet he might have cooked to avoid this podium many times carved with vulgarities, fuck this place, eat shit, for the old man too many echoes, wonders if I carry a knife in the winter jacket I swiped off the bus, obviously not mine, two sizes too large.

It is of course a hustle I recognize the first day, before the first day, at registration, but it comes on with the certainty of television behind it, advertisements selling the dream of a job suitable to butter and eggs and even iced tea, a slight chill in the air from the certainty, not a life with a beach full under the sun. I mean the advertisements promise no warmth. But better than the beach, right, the house with a staircase leading up from the long sofa and twin recliners, the bookcases empty but certain to someday be filled with choice, you rising from the recliner each bedtime having somehow forgotten again what is at the top of the stairs though the light switches just fine, the wife not taking your hand but pledging to be up in only a few minutes, a bit in the sink yet to clean, you hesitate, dreading a life that recounts what last was scrubbed, dusted, swept, vacuumed, mopped, so many words when cleaning even the words for cleaning can never end.

The community college sent the director of the data processing department to California to look at the latest technologies, only he returned to discover the college would instead be using an obsolete mainframe donated by the manufacturer the college most serves, donated in his absence, once he was gotten out of the way. Welders and machinists and draftsmen and electricians all come out of the college for the benefit of that one manufacturing corporation, takes them all, wants more. But the computer programmers for the corporation are always gotten elsewhere with better training to it. Their own computer but it will make no difference in hiring.

Community college not entirely unlike the old used bookstore promise, the shelves with possible hidden treasures, but you buy the book never certain it is the best to be had, probably in your hands just a castoff hurried to be rid of the weight of it, pulled away the time of the professor, the student, the transient, the mother to be, words to be forgotten by all shapes of minds. You know you too will find out it is worthless but too late. You won't get your time back.

The only computer language any of us will likely be hired for is taught by a woman who doesn't know it, so I leave programs where they can be stolen, a path towards my own destruction but the desperation in the eyes of the welfare women going untaught but graded is more than I can stomach, wretched confusion, like women caught on a sinking boat, life rafts reserved well in advance by the heiresses and their nannies. I find it all too simple. I leave behind program listings and in exchange on the unswept floors of hallways I discover abandoned copies of murder mysteries read only at beginnings and endings so leaving me crave the murders between. I sit on the floor waiting for class reading then rereading from a murder mystery open on my lap the brutalization of the next innocent girl. I decide I will leave behind no more programs that work. Let the women fail in the midst of the fraud they recognize even more clearly than I recognize.

I suddenly see the college sells paradise that is really just factory work, factory work of the information age, plastic replacing brick but the same, the only job going say all the newspapers, television reports, which is why the corporation the other side of the river cannot hire me, not only because they teach nothing wanted here, but because knowledge bordering truth is gained against the rip currents at beaches never seen, that understanding it is just factory work is a truth that ruins me, condemns me.

The two brothers across the hall in my apartment building brag about their wages for pulling apart the abandoned assembly lines, all pulled apart for scrap like pocket battleships from the losing navy, while the old men on the floor below us sit looking through their loose change cans, trying not to see the *for sale* signs slapped in the front of every third house, some blocks every yard, the toadstools of this year coming up abundant for the competition in poisons, proud toadstools, humiliated sale signs, the old men unaware that for them the old machines leave behind not even the treasure of a wheat penny, a buffalo nickel, a dime of real silver, the minor treasures of their boyhoods. No treasure for them anyway.

The madness of the women runs towards stupidity. But the welfare women all have names suitable to the paradise being advertised them, sold them, their names a madness too I suppose, Dawn, Joy, Charity, as though Mavis has more sense than to attend such classes. They wear the most beaten clothes these college women, the trousers tight to the legs not just the ass, the sweatshirts loose but ripped at a shoulder, not really in need of a wash but seeming it somehow, every color taking on gray, the run of their ideas the same, all exclamation points torn apart, shattered, broken like glass rods. Still they shout. They argue in the hallways. There is always a ruckus among them. It is just they have nothing to say that isn't rubbish.

The twist of desperation seen on the welfare women is not even hinted across the many faces of the great beauty, the most beautiful woman in the college, the one with the business suit teaching about business suits, but her face cruel at the sight of the children parked in the daycare run by the college, all red noses atop coughs, uncovered, one mitten lost, dreams lost in the maps posted on daycare walls, nothing of dreams, local maps only, the bus routes and the names of streets with ties to history forgotten. McKinley. Pershing. I see in this woman instructor so many duplicitous faces I try to look only at her clothes. At her tits. The children go running out the door certain they want no further instruction.

Here is it is instructors not professors. Experience rather than learning being the claim but what gets taught isn't the experience because that would be violently harsher than the promises advertised by the college.

At first the money seems good to the women, government money anyway so it hardly weighs against the day, but then there isn't the money some month so sex is offered, casually, a matter in habit. I explain I have rent too though I never explain it is just a room what with full houses renting for almost nothing now. I am below poor. Only the mulatto girl do I help without at first trying to negotiate cash payment. *Sorcière au flanc d'ébène.* I take on her voice for the COBOL program, almost demure at moments, full of silences I find can be coded, strange runs of despair then statements that do nothing, nothing towards the goal anyway. The programs eventually work. Still I do not look for a new paint box among all this all town being abandoned. Still I do not look for a camera among all this all town for sale in the driveways, the garages, the rented tents of the auctioneers. I bring nothing from the past not even when the mulatto lies nude awaiting a line of verse not forthcoming. Paints. Camera. All gone thanks to my sisters while now within the movement of the stars time is stolen right before my open eyes. The moon continues it cycles alone.

The cadaverous instructor from back home drives sixty miles each day to dissemble assembler instructions like parsing a montage, the baby carriage down the steps, shot for shot, test under mask, insert character under mask, a call to noble behavior from the riffraff, move long, branch and link, take this from my knees, branch and count register, move inverse, better if he would teach us the ancient algebras, the princely virtues, teach us teach us teach us how he married the aged heiress of uncertain health, the public museum walls covered in the paintings her grandfather collected, Matisse portraits, Laurencin portraits, a Utrillo view of Montparnasse where the faces unseen behind doors are promised to be much like my own, defeated, enflamed. The heiress is distantly related to Alice.

I am thirty miles upriver from home. Back home the great art collection built on buttons, a binary too, buttoned, unbuttoned, wealth from the river clams once in abundance but not seen since I was a little boy, the swimming beach having the last of the clams then, the beach so hot it burned my feet, large ugly clams never with a pearl the rumors said had once been in the river clams, little boys killing the last of that species before going to work at the ketchup plant, the only local job going once a boy stopped believing the romance of the river, onto zippers rather than buttons, the new technologies. There are computers for in homes now and like lots of people the mulatto girl believes just owning a computer means streets of gold, teeth of gold. She looks to me for something after image replaced blood after I showed I could still draw, crap portrait in crayon but she loves it all the same, couldn't find a sign of her own misery in it though the drawing is on a bit of ruled paper torn from a notebook.

Another night class with the beautiful woman in the business suit lecturing platitudes. She manages human resources of some sort. Here in the night class she shifts her tight skirt in anticipation of further adventures this rough side of the river afterwards. There are always strange happenings on offer under the bridges. She has never heard the verse I only ever heard sang by the tragic chanteuses at the Théâtre des Champs Elysées, the verse the welfare women know by instinct, the verse never recorded, the third verse where the mother and her three children go to sleep beneath the bridge without bread, sleep to forget their pain, *pain au chocolat*, pain anyway until the final exams end the dreams more certainly than another outrage beneath the bridges.

Une voix de la lune, ardente et folle, crie:
« Amour... gloire... bonheur! » Enfer! c'est un écueil!

Situationist for an hour in bed again with these three huge rubber masks mailed by Robbie years ago when I worked in the video store. I reread her letter. Her letter all about the play she made her students put on, masks from the play I've never heard of, cannot find a copy of even now in the college library between classes, Robbie having lost maybe the copy she writes she has enclosed, but never did. She was churning out introductory art history at a soon to be bankrupt private college teaching Renaissance and Abstraction to bored farmgirls. Only seventeen miles down the highway from her own mother's shabby little mobile home where the rent was always overdue. The masks take most my bed. I lie among them reading more Baudelaire rather than again the letter, just before sleep stopping to poke my fingers through the eye slits for the Ear, somehow amused at the dissonance I find in an ear with eye slits, then do the same with the Nose. Tonight the masks embody Baudelaire's theory of correspondences of the senses. In her letter Robbie again mentions one of my paintings she likes so much but remembers a coffin that was a refrigerator in the picture. The masks were meant to ask a small reconciliation after fighting all that last year at university when I made movies instead of paintings. The best of the masks is the Mouth with its large lips a bright red pucker, bucked teeth pushing through, as though in a perpetual move to kiss. I wrote Robbie back about the refrigerator but it hardly mattered it wasn't a coffin since my sisters had burned that painting. It could be whatever Robbie wanted.

The lesbian among the welfare women pays me to tutor her little boy in mathematics, at first I think because I am best in the class, but then I see the boy, third grader, eyes ruined at birth, eyes behind thick glasses on a distorted face, genetic problem maybe, a slight child never healthy, so I recognize I was hired because the boy, so in need of a father, will see in me, small, glasses now sometimes for reading, a figure perhaps even he in all his disfigurement might attain. The lesbian has money for lessons because her lover is a machinist across the river in the one surviving concern among all the closed factories. The lover passes through the kitchen without speaking though it is apparent this is because the boy is barely tolerated too.

Programming moved out of its room after a burst pipe. Sitting in a science laboratory where there are benches and stools rather than desks, Bunsen burners snaked up through the benches in case I decide to burn my books, give in to that temptation, nowhere better to put us for temptation, frog guts rotting on the benches from the previous class hour, the stench overwhelming but in its own way recognizable to the future, the card that will turn over, a rotting queen of diamonds hoping it's major arcana but settling for smaller, a principality without monuments where the tide washes in offense every day in the name of progress, certainly not fortune, the lighthouse beaming a red shaft threatening not warning. I want to roll around on the bench naked to make it my beach. Let the college trolly in the dissected corpses of the unidentified, the discarded, the huddled refuse of the indigent at death, trundle in the greater stinks of the suicides, the old women choked, the little school skirts thrown from cars after worse, the ageless hipster beat girls with too many pills, bring them to measure against my naked rot that I might learn from this book I dare not burn, dare not burn for either, bring them closer until I want for nothing, suck all the blood from me then move me to atop the stone of Bix Beiderbecke for the crows to peck, the family tomb, just another stench in a town where he was offered no wife, the wind blowing all wrong against then through his spewing lungs but never his horn, love saying, isn't that more than enough for you?

This one welfare woman so much smarter than the rest, very smart, a pretty face over a body crumbling ruin after four children, but her great shock of hair a wildly defiant premature gray from madness coursing through the roots, the hair on end, all riotous thoughts arriving as ceaseless discourse. Of course most of the welfare women are crazy. But this one in asking help with a program says she hasn't time to write the program herself for reasons she won't state but lingers about in hints as though perhaps it is important to know. She carefully maintains her story of misfortune. She talks and talks. The doorknob to her apartment is below my knees like a cruel joke but once inside you step down to where the doorknob is correct height. There is a third floor of the house above and the junkie couple that live there walk through the narrow kitchen on their way out to score. They haven't a door of their own. The welfare woman says the couple wants no door of their own because they want no address. In that too there are hints but the myriad possible vices numb my curiosity. On the kitchen floor is a bowl with cat food but no sign of a cat, instead the bowl crowded with huge beetles come up from the river for the winter, perhaps to stay forever in this house, forever warm. The house is on one of the islands that floods every spring. I could tell the welfare woman did not poison the beetles because she ached for mercy too. Beside the bed are swayed stacks of novels the welfare woman read for a literature degree abandoned years ago the first time she got pregnant, the stacks now curved to fall, like spines deformed from hard labor without rest. I notice her body is too much like her old books though she is younger than me and when I spread her legs she asks if I will take her for soup afterwards. Later over cheap beans with no sign of ham I give her my share in the crackers served.

The library here has a biography of Baudelaire that takes seriously those few acquaintances who after his death claimed Baudelaire died a virgin. The implication apparently is Baudelaire caught syphilis not from the mulatto whore he loved for twenty years but from writing dirty poems in his youth. Still it is an appropriate book for this place where most everything asserted is implausible falsehood. It is not a book I want to even page to its end. Instead between classes every day now I ask for a book the library keeps behind the information desk though I am the only person to ask for it in over ten years. The book is entirely photographs over the names of jazz bands and sometimes their lineups if the lineups are even known. No titles to songs. No mention of styles. In the book are the only surviving photographs of the early forgotten jazzmen from New Orleans. The street photograph from Storyville is reproduced from a postcard featuring the most famous of the many whorehouses, with an arrow drawn on the postcard, where the piano players upended ragtime but weren't allowed the same with the mulatto girls reserved for the white men. Seated at a piano in an accompanying photograph is a nattily dressed very dark black man whose real name has long been forgotten together with almost all the features of his face. This book too is not paged to the end. Fifty years of jazz but it is the early photographs I keep taking out the book to see. They are all bits of faces struggling not to be forgotten. I find myself imagining the masks from my bed appropriating the images from the book into some combination making not sense but rhythm. I give the book sound.

Plonger au fond du gouffre, Enfer ou Ciel, qu'importe?

Nowhere does the book suggest the ragtime players died virgins like Baudelaire because they weren't allowed to touch the girls.

ARRIVAL

I entered the large meeting room that first morning with a certain sense of aggrandizement I had assumed within the performance I was giving. It surprises me to remember so much from long ago but memory unreels a vivid old movie across days played rather than lived. Aggrandizement was my bulwark against being comic. I had already passed down the aisle where a programmer in each cubicle stared intensely at a lumpish tube with screen of green letters. Fingers danced noisy keyboards. Tap tap tap. It sounded an aisle of Dick Powells with one Ruby Keeler at the end. The green tubes were what once was commonly known as a dumb tube, a 3270 mod 5, to be exact, connected to a mainframe computer perhaps two or three states away, creating a great tug of war, each end trying to pull any semblance of intelligence away from the other. I would soon discover a programmer could get quite the ping slapping the metal casing of the tube. Piece of shit. Piece of shit. Come to Iowa and we'll make eight bits into a byte right through your balls. Piece of shit. This was in the days before the latest something-something megahertz laptop connecting routers and networks and webs and clouds that promise never to rain. This was in the last days of those terpsichorean technologies projecting green like envy.

The narrow meeting room was crowded with a long white wooden table and rolling wooden chairs painted glossy red. Across the far wall from the door there was a chalkboard covered in a diagram I wondered if I should be trying to memorize before someone kept it secret from me. If I was already Dick Powell it was Dick Powell from the later film noirs all full of suspicion. The lone credenza at the far end of the room was covered over with gifts that obviously had been opened but had their wrapping paper clumsily reapplied. I seem to remember a couple had been rewrapped in newspaper but I'm not sure it is truth. Headlines and obituaries. It certainly was plenty suspicious. I fought the sensation that everything seen was clue to the future, fought the sensation by taking a seat in a practiced gesture, hitting my spots.

"He ran away when?"

"He never showed up for the wedding at all."

"Then why did she open the presents all the department managers gave?"

"Nothing better to do that night."

The five young men all laughed until the one woman among the programmers stepped into the meeting room.

"It is idiotic to get married so late in life."

The young woman said this with a certainty that she would never be tempted to do the same once past forty. The nameplate on her cubicle read Lulu like some animal name from one of the musicals I had left on television over the weekend, where Chee Chee was the monkey and Gub Gub was the piglet, a terrible movie shown in the pan and scan rubbish that was the norm in those days, the images violently cropped, talking nose movies, meaning there were always shots where all that was left were two noses facing across the dialogue. I had not yet been introduced to anyone.

"And the fiancé was actually named Bush?"

"True."

"Do you suppose he made marriage promises to women everywhere he gave a speech?"

"He gets to break promises to everyone now."

The five young men all laughed again. I had seen the signs still in the window of the shop across the street that had been the newly elected president's campaign headquarters a month earlier. Bush Bush. I imagined him making promises to women in all the hinterlands wherever it was necessary to secure votes, like one of the missionary explorers once through those parts, run out of trading beads but was still desperate for directions to the next portage, past the next headwaters, desperate but knowing that sin against the ungodly savages is not a sin against glory. It seemed a modern corporate idea. I looked at the woman to stop my imaginings. She was no taller than me and had extremely translucent skin beneath a blonde bob that at the ends went against the cut into stump bristle.

"Dorothea attempted to judge her own worth by opening the presents."

The boss had already made it clear I was to understand this Lulu was not a goat staked out to attract new programmers. She was the best programmer he had so I was to leave her alone no matter how attractive I might find the challenge. She was officially untouchable. The large heavy boss had a whole rehearsed speech about leaving Lulu alone he delivered in undertones that seemed like warnings meant to imitate my inner voice. One of the television musicals? No. At first I thought the typical voice over from a film noir but then thought more like Orson Welles rehearsing Othello. I was meant to hear the warnings like a soliloquy to put money in my purse and money only. Perhaps I was too new to threaten overtly. The boss now came into the meeting room and sat near the door at the head of the table in the only padded chair. It was a large black chair that seemed to envelop even his huge frame in the blackface Orson Welles was missing in rehearsal. He introduced me.

"Kelly lived in Paris for a year after college."

"Why on earth did you come back here?"

"The money ran out."

Lulu was the only one that laughed at the line delivered for tough guy cynicism.

"How did you get money in the first place?"

"I had a grant."

"You were born under a wandering star."

I gave the boss a hard look to let him know I too had been watching the musicals instead of the big games over the preceding holiday weekend. I had arrived in Des Moines the week after Christmas 1988 driving a small car not especially overloaded though it contained everything I owned. For bed I had a futon with the duvet actually a wool quilt that had come off the family farm thirty years earlier when the farm was sold at auction. The quilt shed like a lamb seeking comfort from being born out of season. The black and white television I had cozened in the front seat of the car I had pitched in a dumpster before ever taking it up to the new apartment. It was a big decision. For replacement I went out that weekend before the job started to purchase on credit the largest color television I could lift by myself, arguably even more than I could lift myself, since I had had to hump it up to the apartment a few stairs at a time, all three flights. I had previously kept the credit card only for emergencies.

"He's a lifer here now," joked Lulu. Everyone laughed.

The new television sat on the floor the level of the bed. The old black and white television had been smaller than anything for sale that weekend in the electronics store but it had funneled me into certain movies with an odd sense of promiscuity. For no particular reason the public station associated with the community college I had attended near the river was forever repeating old imported comedies, not just the obvious Ealing suspects, but equally funny movies from Rank and especially British Lion, all these movies feeling somehow the same in their comic sensibilities, gentle, tweaking the social order without being rebellious, taking the viewer with charm between chuckles. It was a sensibility that had served me well with the welfare women but had so surmounted me the two years of computer study that it necessitated I approach work with a mask. It wasn't I already understood business to be a plague of banalities scrambling for intelligence. I needed restraint not merely the repulsion I eventually learned through necessity. The stolen poster for *Dr. Caligari* I hung on the wall over the futon.

Exilé sur le sol au milieu des huées
Ses ailes de géant l'empêchent de marcher.

The third movie was Paint Your Wagon. Lee Marvin's singing head came in and out of the picture cropped to fit the television screen as though he were bobbing for apples between verses. There had already been no end of shots where all I saw of cowpokes talking were their noses. Jean Seberg had a nice nose. Lee Marvin sang about being born under a wandering star but showed little chance he was a second coming chosen by the heavens. I think he might have made a good Christ. Certainly he wasn't born a singer. In my years at the video store I had watched five thousand movies bowdlerized by format. Perhaps I already felt bowdlerized from watching too many constraining screens all day long.

That weekend before the start of work I had spent the last of my cash on decorative blocks and pine planks the lumber yard had sawed into lengths four and five feet at my request. I was in and out of the apartment to fetch the many stones and boards from the car. The television was on. I hadn't turned it off since getting her to the apartment the day before. Still I threatened her all afternoon with return to the electronics store if she didn't come across with something better to watch than musical after musical. The local television channel did at least save the story of ménage à trois until coming on evening when I might have a sit. It was during this last musical I broke my tooth on the fried chicken legs I had bought for supper. Because of the broken tooth it wasn't until much later I thought about the third movie somehow reinventing the two men lustful for the same woman out of the previous two movies where one man refused to notice the beautiful woman at all while in the next movie the man fell at first sight.

"I've done a survey of all the mouths in the office and was wondering if you could give me the name of your dentist."

Lulu was back in her cubicle from the meeting room before I got a chance to plead for the reference. The tooth was killing. Lulu was swiveled quickly to face me when she saw me coming. On her great green-screened tube she had stuck one of those little convex mirrors meant to improve visibility when mounted with glue on an automobile side mirror. My own cubicle I had tried not to imagine an animal stall though the keyboard there was oddly sticky and the hard-plastic mat beneath the padded chair issued effluvium that was something other than manure but not by much.

"You've looked at my teeth?"

"It's not as though I stuck in fingers."

In fact the survey hadn't had to be anything more than superficial because the teeth of the other programmers in the aisle were a great nasty jumble of angles and stains. Still Lulu felt somehow especially violated. I believe she gave me the name of her dentist to get me quickly out from her cubicle more than any other reason. She certainly was not flattered. She certainly was not empathic. I was meant to be immured in my own cubicle at the far end of the aisle where the heavy steel door to the back stairwell radiated winter chill. The boss was good enough to let me out for the dentist that next afternoon. I liked him all the more the second day because he was a bit drunk after lunch, liked him for that only, since I fought any idea that the job had saved me from drowning myself, from worse, from going on the way things had gone after Paris.

"I knew Jean Seberg from back home," he said to me in his office when I came to ask for the time away. "I even dated her a couple times."

I had lied about once living in Paris almost two years because back then a lost year remained lost if you said you had been overseas.

"Really?" I rubbed my thumb across my lips as though to comfort a fouled tooth but the boss didn't catch the movie reference. I doubted he had ever watched a French movie even to see an old friend. "How'd that come about?"

"She and her parents lived in the house next door to my grandparents."

The odd thing was I could tell it was a confession of sorts from days when he longed to be a beat in some jazz club. It was just unfortunate he was telling it to someone now trained in writing 370 Assembler because I instantly calculated the math didn't work. I had read the biography of the boss printed in the bank's new annual report being handed about the office that very first workday of the year. Standing there, it occurred to me perhaps the boss was dissembling on his age to the bank. But his official age put him a good three years too young to have dated Jean Seberg before she went off to Hollywood then France. All the same I absolutely believed she had been next door.

"I lived a couple blocks over from her grave."

On the drive to the dentist's I kept trying to remember what big number Jean Seberg had had, if there had even been one, perhaps caught only in fragment that evening building bookcases, but all I had in my head was the song from the first musical that day, the song where the actress at thirty means to pass for younger while singing about wishing she were a man. It was the most dishonorably shallow appraisal of Lulu I could muster. Then in the dentist's office I'll be damned if there wasn't music throughout and the dentist was playing the Miles Davis soundtrack to *Ascenseur pour l'Échafaud*. I could feel nothing but suspense through the numbed side of my mouth.

"Your teeth are in bad shape."

"First time for insurance."

"We'll put the new crown in with gold so it lasts right forever."

Looking at the canvas on the wall in front of me before the drilling began I had mentioned I had studied painting originally. The dentist asked me if I had a gallery because his son the painter had had two shows though still in college. I had been wrong about the music being Miles Davis besides. Every time the vacuum tube took the side of my cheek, I imagined some voice out of Baudelaire rather than Lee Marvin, Marvin beneath the floor tiles gathering gold dust, Baudelaire somehow nearer, his inheritance frittered away on the mulatto woman. In the worst pain I knew it was Jean Seberg below the tile. Dead. Buried. Spit out. Only of course it was a modern dentist so there was a vacuum rather than a bowl to catch my dribble. I suppose it isn't possible for even the most modern jazzman to blow a vacuum yet that is how the music took me before I was out of there.

"This trouble report document gives a description of the problem but not a clue where to begin solving it."

"Someone else will show you everything."

Lulu had stopped by to ascertain I had actually gone to the dentist, then lingered oddly, as though the slump one side of my face attracted her intuitions, promised insight into something more than my character. She leaned a hip against the entrance frame to the cubicle while thumbing through a sheaf of papers butted against her breasts. She handed me three folders each containing another trouble to be worked with all haste. Each trouble represented an accumulating sum tracked in minutes to dollars the bank had lost. It occurred to me that the mirror on her great green tube allowed everyone passing to see Lulu but in some semblance distorted, face cropped too, a reflection meant to be never seen whole.

"What church do you attend?"

She knew perfectly well the answer but didn't need worry she would ever see me again in the church where she had seen me just the morning before. It wasn't merely I could hear her disinviting through solicitude. I had sat through the Mass untroubled I was soulless while thinking about the making a movie from what I found earlier in the church. I needed a camera. In the crypt there had been tables buried in bargain clothes and a few other odd donations I watched the white people plunder through before people of all different colors pushed their way forward. Coming second has more meanings than any single soul dares count even on pretty fingers.

"I haven't been to church since my mother dragged me."

"Really?"

I didn't tell her the first movie I ever made was also about teeth gone wrong, the movie a few minutes of animation beginning with the Baron Munchausen sailing towards the great sea monster, its mouth suddenly jumping open to take the ship, then the cut to miniature figures a different scale being surrounded by the giant teeth in the mouth I had constructed from a large antique wooden barrel built over with papier-mâché. The figures were toys from childhood not so different in size from the ceramic saints for sale at greatly reduced prices in the crypt and exactly the scale of the plastic bishop in his miter. The bishop was so like other action figures I thought he must have come from a recent movie I had missed. Maybe something about the Inquisition. I bought the bishop for a quarter plus for another quarter a voluptuous blonde female figure slightly larger but completely nude that the bishop could venerate in some pagan fashion when she wasn't his scullery girl. In my movie made when in high school the Baron Munchausen defeats the Turks by means less prosaic than having their fleet flounder in a storm. In flying atop the cannonball he so turns jealous the goddess of the moon she forever reverses the tides to flow only outwards away from land. Take that, Turks. Take that, Méliès.

"I suppose the trick to salvation is to choose the church with the best synchronized swimming."

This made her laugh. In the crypt she had been the only woman slim enough in winter to finger through the table of beach gear. The swimsuits had looked like they all had been donated decades ago because the patterns were those my dead mother had favored when I was a boy. I had forgotten fashion recycles then returns. Over the years I would often picture that beach gear when remembering. In my cubicle Lulu pushed her laughter into a cynical three bars something like the vacuum of dental jazz before turning away.

"I've dated her four years without ever sleeping with her."

The boss and I were sitting after my first work week at a booth in the corner of the tavern just down the street from the office. I was quiet across my only beer but the boss had turned lamenter half through his second whiskey. I thought he must mean he had never spent the night because he had a wife waiting. No. He wasn't married. For years he had taken Lulu to the movies almost every night without ever much getting hands on her unless there was a dance afterwards. He complained she would absolutely not touch in a movie no matter how romantic. He was a big redheaded yeoman with some kind of scraggly beard perhaps once meant to be bohemian but that probably was a fashion passed down his paternal line the last twenty generations. I failed to heed his desperation. It was a beard that brought to mind every good Shakespeare adaptation in the movies but what this boss delivered next came straight from a lesser comedy.

"You know what the programmers call her behind her back?"

"Other than Lulu?"

"Not that. I named her that. You know her real name?"

"Louisa."

"Louisa Will."

"That I know."

"Louisa Noshewont."

"What?"

"Lulu Noshewont. They call her *No She Won't* because her surname is *Will*."

"I get it now."

The waitress had just brought the boss a third but again he hadn't noticed this woman his own age had tried to chat him up. All the programmers in the office were under thirty. It came a bitter surprise to arrive at work start of the next week only to find there was a new boss.

RIGHT IN THE TEETH

"RIGHT IN THE TEETH"

FADE IN:

INT: IT FITS INFORMATION TECHNOLOGY OFFICE -
MORNING - TEETH

A set of chattering teeth atop business documents
atop an office desk. The teeth chatter.

CREDIT SEQUENCE

Credits roll over the chattering teeth that grow
larger as they bounce forward.

PULL BACK as the teeth come to a slow halt.

DENSHAG, the chief of Information Technologies is
seated behind his desk, engrossed in a blonde
FASHION DOLL, the toy doll dressed in a fetishist
costume, bustier and skirt, very high heels, the
doll like a decadent Barbie. At forty Denshag
has the misplaced energy of a man risen in
importance too fast for his own understanding.
He frequently fidgets though he has perfectly
managed hair and curled moustache and wears an
expensive business suit. In a child's school
chair before the desk sits the hunchback IGOR
POOLICKS. He is pushing thirty but is slovenly
dressed in a ragged suit that bunches in
uncomfortable places. His hump is absurdly

44

accentuated by being pushed out over the low back on the very small chair.

Denshag bends the doll forward and begins to lift her skirts from behind.

> DENSHAG
> (to doll)
> How is that, baby, does that do what you want? Am I the biggest you've ever had? Tell me again. Scream it to me, baby.

Suddenly remembering Igor, Denshag straightens up the doll.

> DENSHAG
> (to Igor)
> Oh, um, just a picture of the wife.

> IGOR
> She makes a lovely statuette.

> DENSHAG
> She makes a lovely rump roast, also, every night for dinner, every night, though there have been computer programmers who've worked here for years without ever being invited to take a bite.
> > (waits for Igor to
> > respond but nothing)
> You've probably guessed that this statuette...
> > (clearly borrowing the
> > word with pleasure)
> ...cannot spread her legs. It is deliberately built not to allow that.

> (again no response
> from Igor)
> Therefore it becomes important that
> computer programmers hired here
> accept sexual rejection on unusual
> economies of scale.

IGOR
> Is that a question, Mr Denshag?

Denshag rises in his chair to better view Igor's
hump while moving a hand to his own back to chase
his itch.

DENSHAG
> I don't think it's a question in
> your case, Mr...Mr Poolicks, is it?
> > (picks up résumé)
> Igor Poolicks. But let's see if
> your résumé history substantiates
> the defeated and humiliated man
> you've become. Eh, Igor, eh?
> > (reads silently a
> > moment)
> You've not held much work in the
> years since you left university.

IGOR
> I played piano three years of
> weekends in a jazz dive that did a
> brisk trade with vomiting German
> tourists.

DENSHAG
> At least one of the computer
> programmers already here is skilled
> in vomiting.
> > (gets bit heated)
> In fact, I have to keep my desk...

INSERT - LIVE ACTION

Real wingtips on real legs clicking heels.

BACK TO SCENE

                    DENSHAG
                  (continuing)
          ...right next to the kitchenette
          just to keep things from swirling
          out of control.

PULL BACK to reveal for the first time the room
is a kind of cramped shotgun shack with entryways
without doors at either end of an oldstyle office
plan. Denshag's large desk is isolated at one
end. There are three shallow small cubicles with
walls tilted first out then back in myriad crazy
angles that somehow don't topple. There is a
computer monitor with keyboard atop each table
within each cubicle indicating the programmers
must sit facing the far end of the room but there
are no chairs. At the far end of the room facing
the programmers is a lectern with a huge rotting
ledger atop it.

There are no windows.

At center of the room, establishing a false oasis
between the two work areas, is a kitchenette
comprised of nothing more than a raised table
with one stool and, against the wall in rear, a
small sink beneath a couple hanging kitchen
cabinets. On the raised table is an ancient
coffee percolator with its plug hanging off the
floor.

DENSHAG AND IGOR

Igor stands when Denshag comes from behind the
desk. Denshag leads Igor a few steps towards the
far end of the room.

> DENSHAG
> (pointing to the
> raised table)

The toxins computer programmers are
prepared to ingest never ceases to
amaze the company rat catchers.
> (back to résumé)

So what did you do during all these
gaps in time when you weren't
playing...
> (emphasizing words
> with repulsion)

...playing jazz piano.

> IGOR
> (desperate for job)

I never meant to imply that playing
the piano in a darkened room in any
way put me under the malicious
influence of foreigners. I'm
certain the proprietress of the dive
can be found sober enough at some
point to validate my never having
gone near the men's toilets.

> DENSHAG

I'm sure. But it is corporate
policy here at IT FITS to not
question previous employers about
their capacity for commerce or for
urination.
> (again reads silently)

You probably know recent studies
show that the criminally insane with
a talent for music invariably have
also a talent for numbers. Can you
count without a drummer?

IGOR

When I was a child the music teacher
was very impressed that I could work
out scales on a sheet of paper. It
was simple mathematics to me. When
she put me in front of a piano she
was horrified to see I had no idea
how to translate the sheet music to
the keys. Afterwards she would bark
like a dog whenever I got too close
to the piano.

DENSHAG

It's a pity that résumé histories
don't concentrate on childhood
failures to overcome adversity
          (writes on *résumé*)
But a résumé leaves so little room
for anything except trauma in the
workplace.
          (looks up smiling
           more teeth than
           possible)
Well, then there is merely some
paperwork to complete, before you
begin your computer programming.

Denshag leads Igor back to the child's chair then
sits on edge of desk. He proceeds to hand form
after form to Igor.

                    DENSHAG
This first form is a list of
required dietary supplements for
which your blood will be screened
once a month.

Igor pats about himself for a pen. He cannot
believe his luck yet feels it slipping away for
lack of a pen.

                    DENSHAG
                 (continuing)
This is a list of appropriate
workplace attire. You work for the
company. You wear the company. As
an employee of IT FITS -
          (proclaiming company
          motto)
The Second Skin Your Skin Abides
          (back to normal)
- your attire represents us to the
world.
          (pauses but no
          response from Igor)
And finally there is a list of slang
expressions not to be spoken in the
office. This last list is of course
forbidden to be memorized. Sign at
the bottom to indicate you've read
nothing.
          (calls out nearby
          entryway)
Mrs Peel! Mrs Peel! Come explain
the dental plan to Mr Poolicks.
          (to Igor)
Of course we have a medical plan,
too, but it is the dental plan we
expect you to use at our discretion.

We expect all employees to be right
in the teeth at all times.

> IGOR
> Right in which sense? In the
> political sense? Is that legal to
> demand that? You mean you expect me
> to be right in the teeth in some
> ethical sense? I don't understand
> but I want to please.

MRS PEEL comes from entryway near desk hopping on
one foot while trying to slip on her stiletto
heeled shoes using a pen for a horn. She is past
forty but still held in voluptuous shape by
supporting undergarments. Her intention is to
show off her jiggling and she succeeds in getting
on the second shoe only after coming to a stop
with her hand on Igor's shoulder, large breasts
in his face, the upheld pen the only thing
between them. Igor takes the pen from Mrs Peel
and furiously begins to sign the forms held on
his lap.

INSERT - LIVE ACTION

Real hand taking pen from near décolletage of
real breasts.

BACK TO SCENE

> MRS PEEL
> (to Denshag)
> Mr Denshag, your wife called to say
> that the doctors refuse to let her
> lose any more weight, even with the
> use of surgery.

Denshag returns to his desk chair.

>   DENSHAG
>   (again lost in bending
>   Fashion Doll to will)
>   But the cow is impossibly large.
>   She's always wanted twelve inches
>   from me. I've always wanted the
>   same from her.

Mrs Peel snatches pen to return Igor's attention
to her breasts.

INSERT - LIVE ACTION

Real manicured woman's hand returns pen to
décolletage of real breasts.

BACK TO SCENE

>   MRS PEEL
>   At IT FITS the individual is by
>   formal definition the primary unit
>   of privacy, so unlike some garment
>   companies, our code of decency is
>   not restricted to certain anatomical
>   areas.
>   (points to Denshag
>   playing obscenely
>   with doll)
>   Of course there may be times like
>   this which is one of those
>   unpleasant compromises in life based
>   wholly on financial necessity, in
>   desperation, as always, the blind
>   rule of authority perpetuating
>   itself against mere moral interests.

                         IGOR
                    (sensing need
                    to respond)
I like the dress on the statuette
very much.

                       MRS PEEL
It is a model for one of our actual
dresses made here. We sold seven
thousands of those just last year.
It comes with a mask.
          (puts fingers over
           face to make a mask)
I've worn the dress myself many
times.

                         IGOR
It's hard to tell where the plastic
of the doll leaves off and the
rubber of the skirt picks up.

                       MRS PEEL
In some matters of fashion much like
authority it's best to trust an
organ other than your eyes.
          (smiles with insinuation)
Igor? Is that a stage name? Igor?

                         IGOR
I only know my mother pushed me into
piano lessons for no stated
expectation.

                       MRS PEEL
Young expectant mothers must be more
careful when choosing names from
their television programs. They
must watch only the commercials if

        they mean to assure the boy born be
        like all the other boys.

Denshag disappears beneath his desk with the
doll. Mrs Peel takes up the chattering teeth
then motions for Igor to follow her over to the
raised kitchenette table. Mrs Peel sits on the
stool so she can exhibit her legs while fingering
the chattering teeth.

                    MRS PEEL
        Have you ever heard of the Panama
        Canal?

                    IGOR
        In reference to dentistry?

                    MRS PEEL
                (laughing naughtily)
        No. It's nothing wicked like that!
        It's in reference to coffins.
                (Igor stares blankly
                 at the teeth)
        You may recall that the men digging
        the Panama Canal were required to
        arrive for work with their own
        coffins. What with all the heat and
        malaria and typhoid, it made sense,
        right? And just so, it is natural
        that this company's executive
        officers like to believe that the
        work here is no less demanding than
        simply digging a hole in the jungle.
        It would hardly be worth paying
        people a salary otherwise.

                    IGOR
        So I have to buy my own coffin?

                    MRS PEEL
While other garment companies
subsidize the purchase of exercise
equipment, this company prefers to
subsidize an item that is certain to
be used, at least once.

                    IGOR
And coffins come under the dental
plan?

                    MRS PEEL
                  (offended)
It isn't kind that you should
believe the rumors about me so soon
upon employment. I've all my
fingers and I know exactly where
they belong at every hour of the
day.

INSERT - LIVE ACTION

Real manicured woman's hand of five fingers
wiggling fingers with pen now much like a human
finger making a sixth.

BACK TO SCENE

Denshag is suddenly beside kitchenette the doll
in his mouth. He gives a bellowing cough that
sails the doll into Mrs Peel who pretends not to
notice. The doll bounces to the floor.

                    DENSHAG
Mrs Peel, you had better get my
wife's doctors on the phone,
quickly, before they slip her a
breast implant.

Mrs Peel exits the entrance she entered. Denshag
approaches the kitchenette. TROLLY with Denshag
and Igor towards lectern.

                    DENSHAG
          This cubicle area is where the
          programmers work. You do know how
          to use an office chair, don't you,
          not just a piano bench? Here at IT
          FITS it isn't essential that work be
          stored in a cavity beneath your
          bottom.

                    IGOR
                 (finding no chairs)
          Chair?

                    DENSHAG
          I will take that to mean that any
          squeaking let off from your chair
          will be the ordinary groveling for
          business purposes.

They reach lectern where Denshag opens the
rotting ledger.

INSERT - LIVE ACTION

Real hands opening a rotted ledger bound in
leather.

BACK TO SCENE

                    DENSHAG
                 (continuing)
          Now let's see what number is
          available. Let's see. Let's see.
          Yes. I believe we will begin you

off adding the number six to other
numbers.

> IGOR

Just the number six?

> DENSHAG

Yes. For now I want you to
concentrate on what you can do with
the number six.

> IGOR
> (incredulous)

That seems awfully easy.

> DENSHAG
> (commanding and angry)

Listen up! The hard part is knowing
which numbers you want to add six to
because it's no good adding six to
just any number you come across.
You must be careful that the numbers
you add six to actually need six
added to them.

> IGOR
> (meekly)

And how will I know that?

> DENSHAG
> (in a rant)

Must I explain that IT FITS is based
within serial opportunity structures
that mirror hereditary instincts?
Must I explain even that? Here,
young man, you begin in the present
but only with an understanding
achieved from the past. First, the
overall purpose of computer
programming is to provide
information for use in making

economic decisions. Second,
computer programming is concerned
with quantitative information used
in making qualitative evaluations
when the competition of the global
economy hurries them into needing
sums, aggregates, congeries,
accruals, batches, clusters,
grosses, scores, tallies, and
totals. Third, although computer
programmers seem oriented towards
what has already occurred, this past
information must be relevant to
predictions for the future. This
last item explains the mystical
nature of computer programming.

Mrs Peel reenters without interrupting the rant.

                    DENSHAG
                  (continuing)
Yet there can be no argument in
favor of prime numbers, or even any
fixed algorithmic sequence, when the
failure of communism has once and
for all proven...

                    MRS PEEL
                (taking over the rant
                but turning it calm)
...that after a time you begin to
realize that the guarantees offered
by the company are not there to
protect any sense of integrity you
may have brought with you when
hired. The management is interested
only in integrities they themselves
define and administer. At the end
of the day any sort of sexual
humiliation is completely secondary

to the financial incertitude brought
about by living on a wage where the
means of production are controlled
by crude thoughts of trousers and
skirts entangled together in...

INSERT - DREAM SEQUENCE

Animated sequence of Igor rendered miniature,
alone in the IT FITS Information Technology
office except the Fashion Doll, the doll now
taller than him. He unstrings the chattering
teeth, giant teeth now in proportion to Igor,
into a long scarf he swirls about himself in a
dance like Loïe Fuller. The Fashion Doll
repeatedly steps back in repulsion almost as
though physically struck.

                    IGOR
               (meekly taking on
               calmed rant)
        ...the number six. The number to
     which my imagination is now
     committed now that I have abandoned
     musical scales. One. Two. Three.
     No longer rising. Three. Two.
     One. No longer falling. What is
     more? Six. The number that is the
     critical hour between five and seven
     each evening. A number rarely of
     import when gambling with cards or
     dice. Yet a number that is an
     aspiration to normalcy when attached
     to measurement in both feet and
     inches. The first for head height.
     The second employed for...the length
     of...a mathematical uncertainty.

The teeth retake their shape in a mouth that drops over Igor then bites him in half.

FADE OUT.

TELLER MACHINE
SECRETS

I have an unfading memory of being out at the airport 2:00 A.M. on the day after Valentine's day trying to test some software we had loaded back at the bank. The machine needed tightening. It was an old box without the paper journal rolling through all machines built the previous twenty years. This box especially enjoyed dispensing too much money that without a journal could never be charged back to the cardholder. Our new boss at the bank said the machine had dispensed an extra fifty grand the year before, and more the year before that, with numbers for other years discarded in a failure of due diligence, the new boss saying all this in a way that made it seem personal, the lost money an offense to his puritanical soul. In the airport, a man with the face of a brawler but his large body stuffed into a baby blue suit was using the top of the machine to write on a belated Valentine's card. *Darling. The proximity of so much hard cash here atop the money machine reminds me of your loving embrace. Was this fair paper made to write whore upon? You too are an apparatus to every wayfarer who punches your keys in desire for yet the same. One two three more. One two three more. What again is the name of the saint for travelers? Moor? Christopher? Jude? Easy?* I thought of the box as dispensing absolution.

"Do you suppose I could simply sweettalk the money out of this machine?"

This made Louisa laugh but with an aloofness appropriate to the late hour.

"The known event is two cancellations followed by a withdrawal over one hundred dollars."

She was quite imperious at having discovered the bad code in the programs unique to this automated teller machine at the airport. It wasn't clear to me at all that the old boss had coded the machine for his own use when on a bender but it seemed the implication. I only know nothing ever appeared in the newspapers concerning legal proceedings. The new boss was a decade younger than the old but managed to seem younger still behind a multitude of orchestrated twitches I suspected seemed most propelling to him when initially rehearsed. He announced he had been saved by Jesus Christ and from the very first meeting he was very keen on end dates for projects as though he were the calendar of the apocalypse. Of course like any good prognosticated end of times its calendar included no weekends off, the only termination the final termination, offered not even a scriptural day of rest. Damnation. Damnation. Damnation. Every single day.

"And after that anything could happen?"

"Not so loud."

Louisa and I were still in our coats in the chill of the airport near the entrance doors. Her coat had a white fur collar of sorts that grabbed at the ends of her shaggy blonde hair. I carefully picked one of the hairs as though reaching for a winter berry in a thorn shrub.

"I suppose around machines you cannot keep the ponytail you had when you were a girl."

"Too bad. I never had a ponytail."

I was meant to understand I was not charming her in the slightest wishing to give her ponytail a tug.

"Really? Always bobbed hair? And I thought I had a deprived childhood."

"I can see you suffered."

I was meant to understand I would never get away with coding a machine to give me money on the sly.

"Well, yeah, enough that I've ended up with a job that has me out in a fucking snowstorm in the middle of the night where all I can imagine to do is get on the next plane out, run away to the tropics, live on coconuts, play naked on the beach all day, burn myself raw on the black sand, tattoo myself with blood sacrifices, hurl myself blindly into a crashing surf, break myself, scar myself on the coral, disfigure myself with shark attacks, never put on clothes again, all just to make myself magnificently unemployable."

This made Louisa laugh aloofly again since she had given much thought to how I would never have been hired by anyone but the old boss.

"Certainly we would like to hire you young man, they will say at the future interviews, but we've had so many problems with naked savages before."

The cool laughter trailed off into something warmer but she kept her attention on the brawler still writing a card to his sweetheart.

"Sure, you laugh now, but six months after I'm gone, you will be flipping television channels, wired and tired one night, your pager having gone off constantly for four days, and there I will be in some documentary, happily naked, waving at the camera, wagging my freedom in the close-ups."

I was going too far grabbing my crotch in punk attitude but it didn't matter because there was never any sense she might yield.

"And you'll start sending me postcards begging to come join me. Come let me grow a ponytail with you, you will write, a ponytail all the way down to my ass."

"No. I'll be tired one morning like always, the pager having gone off constantly for four days, and open the newspaper to find they've hauled you off to jail, because some underage girl with a ponytail didn't want your hands on her."

I had brought Janice to the annual company party the weekend before because the rented hall had a good piano I could play. It wasn't the first time I had counted on improvising jazz to tumble a girl. Later Janice had nothing good to say about the party, most of the people from the bank arrogant dullards, Louisa brilliant only if reserve is mistaken for intelligence, the new boss especially gruesome, saved but saved for what Janice didn't want to imagine, especially didn't want to paint. The jazz had not been enough to get Janice into bed the night of the party.

"Ten seconds after which you'll be in a cab on the way to the airport, ripping off your clothes, throwing them out the window, off to rent my grass hut, that has just become available."

"I might. But no tropical island would be paradise unless you were in jail."

At three weeks into the job I had noticed my eyes burning at the end of each day with staring too hard at close words on the green tube. I was wearing the cheaters more often. Years before I had sworn off painting pictures, but one evening when the art center offered free admission, I saw a flyer for the classes taught in the low wing of building that bordered the parking lot, the nude model that night like all class nights fully visible from where I had the car, parking brake set because of the slope half deadly in winter ice. I paid though I had missed the first week chasing problems at work. I wanted something for my eyes at a distance and I surely received it because the crowded class, with everyone already committed to standing the same spot for fourteen weeks, left me shifting an easel about the far corner of the room, angling for a view. The easels were far too large for the small paintings being done and observing the model was like trying to look out to sea through the sailing masts at a marina. I felt restrained.

"Would you keep an eye on my things for a couple minutes?"

Janice too was at the back of the room after missing the first week. She had mentioned something about not being back in time from vacation so at first I assumed she was the daughter of one of the minister wives who crowded the front of the room. The class had three cliques. Besides the minister wives there were a couple women who illustrated home improvement articles for the popular magazine with its headquarters in town. Upon arrival the minister wives had placed me in the clique of old men who made minimal efforts at painting but always had much to whisper about the model. The wives had been chatting about the various religious retreats they intended to visit the coming summer, chatting with an extraordinary reticence on how they paid to get halfway around the world, as certain of their future rewards as the new boss back at work but with great sense they would receive theirs sooner.

"I have to swap out my contacts for my glasses."

The easels were so covered in charcoal dust Janice didn't dare play about with contacts in the studio. I watched her go off to the toilets the other end of the hallway and down a flight of stairs. It gave me time to poke a bit around her paint box. There were very expensive tubes of cadmium scarlet and cadmium orange never opened plus a handful of sable brushes obviously bought new for the class. There was nowhere in town selling supplies that fine. Later Janice would tell me she had bought the supplies on the way back home through

London from Egypt without knowing the model only kept the same pose for an hour. Only the magazine women were skilled enough to knock out a sketch that quickly in paint. I could have once. That night at the back of the room I mentioned how the easels appeared boats bobbing about some tropical paradise.

"My father owns a sailboat out on the lake."

"A lake?"

"What else is there?"

I did not press which lake since I knew it would be something private I wasn't supposed to learn existed. I thought about the sailboats on the Mississippi that look like feluccas working the Nile but never pretended a real day of labor. I had recognized the surname on the paint box put Janice somewhere among the richest family in town but for all I knew only the relatively poor cousins allowed their daughters out in the presence of nudity after dark. I was to learn much about recklessness from Janice. Janice had black hair with straight bangs but a long ponytail, her face extremely pale excepting where her lips always chapped, the strangely dropping skin raising color to the surface, making it unnecessary for her to wear paint, leaving it all for canvases she produced in quantity. That is a joke. Or maybe the next thought is the joke. Through those first weeks at work I had been mastering counting in the hexadecimal used in assembler language to represent numbers. **0 1 2 3 4 5 6 7 8 9 A B C D E F. F** is for fifteen. Janice was fifteen almost sixteen. Her figure was short but so curvaceous a couple of the horny old men found her worth a whisper too. The one asked me how long I had known the girl. I told him I would punch him if he tried talking to her but he went away uncertain how seriously to take the threat.

The strangely communal nature of the missionary women seemed to pervade all expectations.

"You draw really well."

"I am very out of practice."

"No. I mean you draw really really well."

At university I had once had a painting instructor who told me I would never be a great artist because it all came too easily for me. He could see I was already bored that second year at university studying painting and some sculpture. In truth I would have gone on painting if I had not been required to take an introductory art history course some semester when I should have been only painting. What I saw among a great many projected slides was that Derain first painted great Fauvist seascapes but finished his days painting imitation Corot countrysides. The art historian had tittered. That wouldn't have mattered except the painting instructor so doubtful of me was an old man who had studied with Derain at some point before the last world war. This oddly intimate connection to past painters put me right off my brushes like a politician trying to obfuscate his family tree peopled with molesters and imbeciles and hanged anarchists. I instead drifted towards cinema. It amused me cinema with all its claims for visual acuity couldn't get along without music shifting the emotions. After all I had been a small boy when all the new movies had jazz scores. I was attracted to the perversity of collaboration. Of course it is obvious now I could never have ruined my life becoming a computer programmer without first that attraction.

"Too bad your girl isn't the one with the money."

"She has a trust fund she doesn't talk about."

I had left Janice in my bed to come to the airport. She had chosen that evening for the first time to come to my apartment knowing full well she would be snowed in. She wanted the entire night even if I was off for work. I could get to the airport only because it was just a mile away down a straight flat road.

"Should we find a card for Mortenson?"

Mortenson was the new boss Louisa had been strangely fawning over for more than a month, laughing too hard at everything he said, rushing into his office for no good reason except to laugh more, keen to support his plans when others complained about the time being wasted, no one else about to document the system from end to end so the new boss could sound a wizard in management meetings. The new boss had been brought in with a mandate to bring projects in on time. At the end of every day he would ask how many hours I had left on a task as though I should, at least once, magically work a hundred hours into eight. I was always still working when he left for home.

"Did you meet his wife at the party?"

"She's gorgeous."

Mortenson was a broad-shouldered man who had attracted a wife even more blonde than Louisa but a wife practically mute in her timidity.

"Still I suppose you can go ahead with a card for Mortenson because his wife is too stupid to be able to read it."

Louisa gave me a sly smile that was the closest to approval I had ever seen from her. I poked a finger into the back of my mouth to make it a good mumble. I did not want that sly smile.

"I had the second gold crown put in at the start of this week."

"Great."

Louisa turned away only to find herself looking into the rack of Valentine cards at the airport shop. Her eyes filled with hearts. The rack ran down one entire aisle towards the refrigerated drinks and it reminded me I would have to wash my sheets again. It was a heart attack that had killed Louisa's mother ten days earlier when out shoveling snow.

"I told Doctor Brown about your mother."

Along the way I had learned the dentist Louisa had recommended had been her family dentist since her childhood. The dentist always asked after Louisa. He knew about her grade school refusal to eat beans then butter then anything but macaroni with cheese. She nearly ruined her teeth with vomiting when her mother insisted she eat everything on her plate. Doctor Brown even knew Louisa had never quite finished her community college degree in programming. But only with death did I recognize the dentist asked about Louisa in hope for conversation about the mother.

"He excused himself to go into a backroom to weep for almost an hour before he could compose himself."

The brawler had finally gone off, probably looking for liquor. Louisa proceeded with the first test against the machine while snow swept in across our shoes from the automatic doors at the airport. The doors sometimes didn't close for minutes. We worked maybe an hour shivering together the whole time. The teller machine no longer invalidly dispensed money on the known sequence of events, but while Louisa packed away her notes in her case, I was able to trick the machine half a dozen similar ways, robbing six hundred dollars barely trying. I looked at Louisa with the money held up like a winning card hand, and I think it was that gesture, not even the money, not even the late hour, that sank Louisa through the shoulders but still without bringing tears. She put a hand on my shoulder to hold herself up though she was right by the machine. She couldn't touch the machine again. Standing together in the opened automatic doors, I realized I could have taken Louisa off to bed right then, kept her the whole weekend probably, if Janice wasn't already there snug as a bug. It would be the only time I ever thought that genuinely possible with Louisa.

"You want a ride?"

Louisa drove some sort of utility vehicle she could shift into four-wheel drive.

"I'm not very far away."

For the first time she asked me where I lived, and when I told her, she laughed that I would live in apartments everyone knew got more police calls that any other in the city, outside public housing anyway, where no one even kept score. I told her I slept with three pistols.

"Buy something bigger with the six hundred dollars," she replied.

"You think that better than putting the money in the collection plate?"

I said it but I had already understood she wasn't going to tell anyone about the money so long as I didn't offer her any. Learning where I lived somehow assured her I was among the damned even without her having come to my bed to make judgement.

ROOMS WITHOUT
ROOM

A lake house isn't ever especially welcoming in a late spring with sickly thin ice still bordering the shoreline, the trees still bare, but Janice having mentioned my campaign work the previous fall put things almost right for a moment with her father. Of course I did not impress on meeting. The office lined to the ceiling with books almost overwhelmed me until I saw they were shelves of law books, histories of judges and governors and other land grabbers, the compendiums of social apologists long since forgotten, antiquated manuals on barn building and livestock breeding, illustrated volumes of the latest railroad passenger cars available for purchase, ledgers from long abandoned businesses five generations back, and most of all, bound copies of every newspaper the family company had ever published, including all the advertising supplements, as though there was still time to reword anything except the bargain prices of the past. The man handed me a book with a photograph of an unfortunate girl of perhaps fifteen embossed on the cover.

"This will be the one interesting to you."

Janice's father was a man unremarkable except for having large hands with black hair pushing forward from the wrists that made every gesture seem slightly invasive, a little threatening. He posed a finger at the corner of his eyebrow. It gave him a moustache. In the book handed me the photographs depicting white slavery of young women weren't so different in staging from the photographs in the book I could no longer find on writing for the silent movies. The maidens wore white linen. The villains wore waxed moustaches but longer than could be provided by wrists cheating their cuffs. The couches seemed awkward for the purpose. The dungeons were shabby theatrical sets. This too was a manual of sorts that probably taught much more about going into business than it intended.

"I've seen it before."

"Then you know what kind of severe laws were passed after this book was published in 1910?"

"On the telephone the congressman promised to be here no more than an hour late."

In 1910 the brisk trade had been in taking girls from Boston to Brazil but there was no point mocking the futility in laws against travelling girls across state lines. I had crossed no state lines. I had been programming far too many hours to let Janice drive us to Minneapolis to see the many good paintings always hanging there. A week earlier there had been a Caravaggio on special exhibit in Omaha Janice had gone to see alone and afterwards she would not even talk to me about the painting. Her lesson in history to me was I did not deserve to hear about what I could have seen myself.

"We hit a deer."

"The heavy snows this winter cut back on the hunting that usually thins them out."

Having just killed something seemed to make the war hero less fawning than I had seen him with other donors during the election that previous fall. Still he knew he had to fetch money on the run. Killing the deer had simply replaced the onerous sense of begging with an ephemeral sense of bloodlust. I was especially caught in headlights if not quite bloodied when the war hero introduced Alice as his chief of staff. The meeting had been arranged through the war hero's brother who everyone had expected to have that job. Certainly I had assumed the brother was in charge. I had telephoned the law offices where the campaign had been run and the brother had been quite accommodating but dissembling when I mentioned a new donor. Apparently I was out of touch with everything except the long hours programming that left even my sense of time passing perversely unlike the rest of the world. If anything it seemed desirable the meeting should start late.

"This is the number to call next time."

Alice handed me her business card with a wink the others did not see.

"Computer languages take a guy away from ordinary words of what goes on around everywhere else in the kitchens and the bathrooms and the bedrooms."

Alice didn't bother at that moment to understand what I meant but I knew she would think later about me now being a kind of regulated outsider in my own land. I had made my point. It was that estrangement that had made the shelves of books in the room so oppressive. Certainly it had been better when I was an untethered punk. I hadn't read anything but programming manuals since the start of the year and the simple weight of the slavery book had startled me that still I didn't know anything about what other people did for a living. I had given a couple of my poetry books to Janice with no requirement I ever get them back.

"A little summer beach reading?"

The war hero was now holding opened the book on white slavery but in his voice could already be heard his imagination fading.

"Your man here is dating my daughter though she is only fifteen."

Alice gave me a look but somehow my returned glance allowed her to reconcile this new criminality into my stated alienation. She remembered my hair once being spiked. She smiled. The congressman gave me his warrior face when the warrior sees an enemy far beyond range of any rifle and for a moment I thought perhaps it made some difference that Janice's father was not the owner of the big paper in Des Moines. The big paper had a joke about how for every story there had to be included an Iowa angle. World Comes To An End. Iowans Blame Second Coming. The dozen small regional papers the man with werewolf hands published would never report the end of the world. They were local news only, with no thought to ever crossing state lines no matter the pleasures promised. Anyway I do not know for certain Alice winked a signal to get rid of me. I was dismissed from the meeting with some implication I couldn't be trusted to watch even though I could be put in jail any time because of Janice.

"Your father thinks giving money to my congressman will buy me off too."

"From day one I thought he would just hand you one of his duffel bags full of small bills."

"He has duffel bags full of small bills?"

With a great enthusiasm Janice said she had something important to show me if I would take her in my new utility vehicle. Very shortly after that airport night I had bought something with four-wheel drive though I couldn't afford the payments. I had no choice. Emergencies at work had forced me out into bad snow a dozen or more times in just three months. I was lucky to have wrecked only my old car skidding into the ditch, though I never received a sense of deliverance from it, that coming away without a scratch. Out in the new vehicle Janice pointed me down one gravel road then another. Her father's house on the lake was so exclusive the nearest paved road was a mile off but we weren't headed to the paved road. We were the other direction down below the dam that made the lake. There the farm fields were covered in water all the way to the raised road and sometimes over the gravel where the road dipped. We saw deer standing in water within a patch of scrub pines. The road cut away from the river just before the first village below the dam, the road now asphalt, rising with a hill that was crowded over in newer homes cheaply built, the hill giving a sweeping view of the older spacious homes of the village now all underwater as much as several feet. It was perfect. I seem to remember there was in Paris a similar Monet the first time I ever saw one of Sisley's many paintings of flooded villages along the Seine. It is the Sisley that remains. I was a punk when first seeing those paintings after university but even then I recognized a natural destruction rising yet certain to recede described all that was to come. I saw my life in inundations. The easel I had a couple weeks earlier knocked together from scavenged lumber was in the utility vehicle and Janice had brought her beautifully polished paint box that opened into an easel of sorts, but without legs. Janice pointed down a gravel road the far side of the village where at first there seemed nothing but flood.

"We should live on a large barge when we move to Paris."

"And keep the curtains open for all the bateaux mouches trawling past tourists?"

"That'll sell some paintings."

I had noticed the houseboat Janice had brought us down beside didn't have a single curtain. The houseboat was alone on an acreage planted with sapling oaks so perhaps it mattered little once the trees had fully leafed. We stepped out of the utility vehicle into mud. The houseboat was reached from the last of the marginally solid ground with planks atop steel drums stretching forty yards out into what was now river not shoreline. Normally a single plank of twelve feet was all that was needed to board. The normal plank was the faded gray among the blonde new planks. The houseboat was still chained to its pier but the pier was almost entirely underwater and one of the chains pulled down, ever so slightly, a far corner of the boat.

"Who lives here?"

"How would I know?"

On the train my one time from London to Oxford I had seen houseboats on almost remote wooded curves of the Thames where the river seemed too narrow for navigation. I did not mention this recollection. I let Janice carry on with the pretense we were breaking and entering but I knew her mother was originally from London. Of course there had never really been a chance Oxford would accept me for graduate study. I went to Paris instead. Even on the train up to Oxford I had known it would be Paris instead.

"We don't need to go in to paint the river."

"All you have to do with these kind of handles with locks is jiggle them a little."

The door came open to her giving the handle a hard pull upwards with a twist. I had seen that done in trailer courts. But in talking together once about Paris Janice had laughingly listed all the places she had passed but never gone even in Des Moines. Railway yard. Drive-in theater. Strip club. Trailer court. Still I had been impressed she had been to a shooting range many times for the clay pigeons.

"How many duffel bags of money do you suppose it would take for a barge in Paris?"

From atop the houseboat the view of the village damned near could have been a painting from a hundred years earlier. Janice set her paint box on the railing that went around. I wasn't certain the roof of the old houseboat was still solid but I couldn't pass on painting the village. By the time I brought up my easel Janice was already penciling a preliminary sketch of her view. She had chosen not the nearest houses but those a bit farther up where the river must have normally curved but now ran straight. There was a car there with water higher than the windows. Janice drew the car in twice. A wicker loveseat resting atop porch railings on a nearby house meant the river had been even a foot higher at its worst. It made me want to paint quickly but I left beside me a smaller canvas in favor of a larger one I had been saving for whatever special came along.

"You're better than I'll ever be."

"Mostly it's just tricks anyone can learn."

After three hours I had almost finished the larger canvas and contemplation over the last touches to the darkening sky left me feeling the cold. Janice was down in the cabin of the boat after having abandoned her own painting a long time earlier. I wasn't sure how long. She had been behind me watching me paint the way she often had at the art studio. I had not missed her hand on my shoulder.

"Life is going to pass me right by too, isn't it?"

Down in the cabin it took me a second to realize Janice wasn't talking about me at all. She had brought me to the house of her mother to endow it with something she thought missing, missing even from her mother, in this houseboat without curtains. This missing thing wasn't art. It wasn't hope. There was money enough for all that. Still it was curious to know her mother taught history at one of the private colleges nearby, because there wasn't a book on the boat, not even a piece of paper far as I could tell, except for the grocery list taped to refrigerator on which there was scribbled a reminder for eggs. I imagined her father the newspaper publisher at his death speaking for his final word a forgotten reference to his boyhood never shared with his wife and daughter. Rosebud. No. Never a sled. It would be a memory of the book on white slavery he had been rereading closely all his life. He was a very successful man so had every right to an imagination that persevered.

"You aren't supposed to be that great in your teens."

"Remember my Robert Delaunay?"

Janice had a postcard of a superb Robert Delaunay garden painted when he was only nineteen.

"Let's cut the boat loose."

I had no doubt she had a key to the locks chaining the houseboat to the almost submerged pier, knew where the key was hidden anyway. She meant we should let free the boat before having sex on the cot that folded down from a wall inside the cabin. She was sitting on the cot while the propane burner heated water for the cocoa we had found in the one cupboard above the tiny sink. I watched the water boil with some notion we could sail across the little aluminum pot if I only chose. I had already put money down on an almost new camera that would be mine upon receiving payment from the war hero for introduction to a new donor. Already everything seemed possible to miniaturize into movie animation. On the boat there was only one spoon.

"If you cut us loose we'll smash up in the next dam."

"We won't drift that far."

"Girls with trust funds don't fake their own deaths."

Janice had often teased my job computer programming was an attempt to fake my own death. I had never dared tell her that at fifteen I had painted a startling good copy of that same Delaunay from an identical postcard. I had seen the actual painting at a museum when my mother took me along to one of her union events out east right on the ocean. It would be wrenching to admit. The old car I had wrecked that winter was the only thing of mine left from our mother's house my sisters hadn't been able to throw away. They had not had access to the title. It would be decades before I discovered the copied Delaunay had all along been hanging in the house of one of my sisters.

"I have something to tell you."

Ideally Janice would have revealed she was pregnant. I had plotted my moves wrong proving my connection to the congressman with the meeting. Her father putting the congressman under obligation meant it was now the business of the congressman to pull me into line. There would be no scandal. Alice would see to it. Only a quick but necessary marriage would change matters but how exactly did that go in the movie? Was it even in the movie? Perhaps it was only in the book where the bloke betters himself by learning accounting while a prisoner of war. Anyway there is somewhere he is considered a coward because he leaves the digging of escape tunnels to the public school officers, leaves the officers singing their school songs to the worms, is considered a coward because he loathes the Ruling Class even more than he loathes the Boche. I couldn't have been more than eight the first time I saw that movie Room At The Top on television. It's one of those with good jazz in it. But what single word best encompasses marrying the rich man's daughter you've gotten pregnant? It hardly matters since the day left me free for other business.

"In June my mother is taking me with her to Prague for a year."

"She is going there to teach?"

"Lecture anyway."

I hadn't even met her mother so never had a chance to twist favor. There was paint still on my hands. The painting from the roof was propped beside my knee and I left something blue along the handle of the toothbrush when I moved it out of my way at the sink when washing. The woman would know I had been there before pulling back her covers. I looked down at Janice now stretched out on the cot.

"In that first newspaper owned by my grandfather upstate..."

"Upriver. Great-grandfather."

"...in that first newspaper upriver in its early days it was too expensive to make an engraving for every important man who passed through town for an hour so grandfather would use the same portrait over and over until the copper plate wore out. No one seemed to mind. Important men would become more blurry through the year until finally just a smudge gave way to a new portrait the next visit. Only for women did there have to be a new portrait each time because important women were so seldom encountered the last plate could never be found for a second use."

I didn't mention that the music hall women who passed through town were known to have carried their own plates to assure a flattering likeness.

"You mean I should paint your mother's portrait?"

"Don't be stupid."

"You mean you want something else to take to Prague besides a baby?"

Janice laughed while pulling her blouse off over her head. "It's not for me."

She had drawn me nude twenty times in conté crayon, good drawings, one or two anyway, without ever moving onto paints. It was as though she were ready for many things in bed but not that. I had never even quickly sketched her nude because there was an unspoken understanding there mustn't be evidence acceptable in court. She had not signed her drawings. The houseboat was an impossible place to set up the easel, the path between the sink and armoire too narrow, nothing the other end of the room either without sticking a leg of the easel in the toilet. Instead I propped the small canvas panel, the one earlier set aside, on the short board that passed for kitchen table. Perhaps I should have more regretted having used the larger canvas for the flood. Janice rose to remove the rest of her clothes.

"I'll have to sit up for it not to be an ugly foreshortened pose."

"Whatever you want."

"You don't really care if you're a good painter, do you?"

Janice felt oddly rejected I wouldn't use her paint box with one of its blank canvas panels fitted into the lid. She insisted. I ignored her but of course Janice had never been entirely on board with the idea of getting pregnant. In all it seemed the economics weren't much different in that other musical I watched the afternoon before starting the programming job. I don't mean the musical about talking to animals that so dominated my thinking whenever in the cubicle writing more code. I don't mean the first musical from that day before starting the job. *Doctor Dolittle.* The one with Rex Harrison. In the houseboat I was thinking about the second of the three musicals. *An American In Paris.* The painter played by Gene

Kelly lives in a room so small the bed must be raised to the ceiling to put out the breakfast table. There isn't much to eat. But the painter is offered success by an older woman with a superb automobile driven by a chauffeur while the younger woman the painter madly loves is impoverished except for having great legs. Watching the movie before the job even started I had shouted at the screen for the painter to accept a comfortable drive to Biarritz over all that dancing on the Backlot. There had to be money. That was the economics. *Paint Your Wagon* but not your other. Standing with the flooded village at my back I knew I would not go on painting after Janice left for Prague. I had meant one night a week at the art center simply to rest my eyes and now there would be the camera. Every animal stays in my zoo because he likes it, claims Dr. Dolittle in one of the books about his voyages.

"How many times did you paint the redhead who came with the congressman?"

"I never got past quick sketches of her in poetry class."

I thought about the afternoon Alice removed her clothes for the painting then stretched across the almost dilapidated antique bed my mother kept for guests. It was a cold room in winter but for a couple hours each day there was strong light through double doors that let out onto the upper porch. The willow that in summer shaded the room nevertheless went on mottling the sunshine but with strange shadows mocking the skeleton beneath the flesh. Heavy snow pushed the light even brighter. There would be six afternoons for the painting. My mother was off with my sisters visiting family in even deeper snow farther north but Alice had made it clear she was not on the bed for anything but posing. She had paid me for a different flattery. Still I received no threat when I touched her to position her knee, took no repulsion because she could sense the painting mattered more even to me. Alice was nude but memory brought images of society paintings through my hands, a Sargent with an intricate white gown so captivating it spoke of skin, Joshua Reynolds with his portrait of the young woman in profile that gives over the image to fingers clutched upon the bosom of her dress but then peaks at her bare toes, the Fantin-Latour of a beautiful but constrained wife, no doubt a wife from good family, in paint grown so dark with age the varnishes now seemed to weep inner turmoil. The chenille bedspread I put in many shades a bluer gray to account for the bright lime I used about the eyes and down the lower thigh all the way to the foot. I had settled on Van Dongen and fetched the wool fisherman's cap from the embroidered chair where Alice had set her clothes. Alice had bought the cap recently in anticipation of Marseilles, Marseilles one of her many planned stops after Paris, with poetry taught by the nun recited from memory all along the route, all that poetry full of voyages. From under the cap Alice's short red hair twisted into the shadows of the willow that spread across one shoulder already a patchwork of freckles. The cap I made nine colors. Woman in a Hat. Why not steal? Van Dongen had cobbled his portrait with that title from Matisse so I was in very good company. Alice gave me a playful squeeze between the legs when admiring the finished painting but she would not kiss me.

"What rhymes with bullshit?" asked Janice.

It Fits. The white slavery book was keen to make illegal putting a prostitute in debt for the new clothes she was required to buy every couple of weeks. But everyone at the office except me had a house mortgage, everyone wore suits they couldn't afford but were required to wear, I wasn't the only one to buy an unaffordable vehicle meant for snow. Where was the difference? *Heaven is my judge, not I for love and duty, but seeming so for a peculiar end.* I mean it was redeeming beyond duty sometimes to imagine new computer instructions in that early assembler language. SODOM. The instructions of the assembler language were always given in acronyms. *Sort On Damnation Of Managers.* For just a little while then I imagined I coded the old poetic levels of hell with Dante confronting the three beasts. All these years later I have never seen another programming language so leant towards violence like that one so close its base nature, the actual language of the machine, the actual language overlaid with the most filamentous of translations, all blood and guts pushing through towards the shadows only poetry ever reached, the screams of zoo animals in the night. Later in my apartment I hung the little nude of Janice behind the poster for *Dr. Caligari.* I had signed it.

PERFORMANCE REVIEW

We were sitting alone together in his office for my performance review after the first six months. Over the years I would learn that it was standard practice at the bank to hire managers from somewhere far away so that the bank benefited from boldly innovative ideas already discredited everywhere except deep within the Cornbelt. Mortenson. With my fading memories of Paris leaving me some days little better than a patois, a slur, sludge of language mostly from poetry, I always mistranslated, but properly interpreted, the name to mean this manager was the favorite offspring of Death. *Le fils audacieux qui railla son front blanc.* The problem was it always seemed to be Louisa pursuing Mortenson. She laughed too hard at his quips and she acclaimed too quickly his strategies. The perversity on display left the other programmers with mouths agape like so many mummifications caught in eternal surprise by a volcanic ash. Obviously black is the traditional if not poetic color for death, the stalker, the reaper, the guide to the underworld. But what color could I saturate my animated movie to symbolize such a reversal? I mean about Louisa. Mortenson was a large but pallid man but obviously white is not only the color of virginity. There is Cowardice. There is Justice. The tricolor flag of Iowa is very much like the tricolor flag of France except the middle white stripe is wider in Iowa. In France the white symbolizes equality. At the bank in the software tracking project development we were all accorded the same number of hours in a day, it too being an equality, no matter our rank and abilities our sunsets and sunrises were the same. Of course the managers weren't on call all night long every night of the week. They were free to be pursued. In ancient times a stone was washed white to mark a joyful day but women behaving unchastely were no longer stoned to death even by stones without paint. *It is the cause. Yet I'll not shed her blood.*

"I was hired to bring order to this department's product development cycle."

"Setting arbitrary release dates always fails."

"You need to work with me toward goals."

Mortenson knew all about some of the new software tools just then coming along on personal computers to schedule projects, develop timelines, identify resources, identify conflicts, link task dependencies, project the end date. Louisa had fallen in love with Mortenson on first sight. *Is there not charms by which the property of youth and maidenhood may be abused?* I suspect she wanted an officer without even noticing she would never settle for less. She wished that heaven had made her such a man? Was that what she decided next time among the swimwear in the crypt? But to everyone else Mortenson's compulsion for calculating and re-calculating project deadlines was some memento mori that no one lives forever. Hallelujah. Hallelujah. But no one can be cast into the abyss until you get your own part of the digging completed. That was true time management in all its possible manifestations.

"The girls in grocery stores hate the new machines because it takes three very clumsy steps to submit the card into the system."

Mortenson was not concerned checkout girls disliked his means to riches.

"The last grocery I visited had two lanes entirely shut down."

I had not yet learned to lie through every tooth in a review but it didn't matter because Mortenson was dedicated to the talking points he had for our meeting. He had his papers in triplicate. He clutched his expensive pen. He had abandoned extemporaneous conversation with me some weeks ago though he still believed the only effective psychology was the psychology taught in business schools. Too bad it made matters in the workplace difficult that just any lunatic could read about winning through intimidation. It bothered him a great deal I had evidently read so much he knew nothing about, would never read, as though an unstructured conversation with me was for him too certain to degrade into patois.

"I need you to follow my lead in keeping staff meetings professional in every way, not just on track, but within boundaries you can observe in my own behavior, imitate if you will. I've only been here six months but I can see you clearly know the machines you program on very well. I need you need you to convey that knowledge to others in ways they can utilize for their own jobs. It isn't just that it isn't appropriate you curse all the time, shit, damn, fuck. Your face doesn't give you away. Then suddenly you are saying caustic things that seem to come out of nowhere."

He was reviewing my performance alright. At that time we were working on a big project to support debit cards. Everyone has a debit card now but back then there was such concern about how secure the cards would be I had taken to calling them deadbeat cards. Mortenson despised that. There had also been the assignment to edit names and addresses received at the bank against a file of commonly used vulgarities. Several times I slowly read out the file in some fashion that seemed I was confused by the words when not originated from my own mouth. It was great fun. I found one name already on file it took me a week to discover was an idiomatic expression suggesting you fuck your goat while the pigs watch. Still none of that mattered and the large raise Mortenson gave me I knew meant substantial theft from everyone else since the pot divided each year among the programmers was always roughly the same no matter how many more programmers were staffed. I stopped by Louisa's cubicle after the review.

"So how was it then?"

"San Francisco to Miami to Toronto in the same week."

I was meant to understand it had been exhausting. This was pretty hysterical since I was asking about sex but for Louisa the excitement was in the travel, some small feeling at being now a seasoned voyager, almost a rover. Mortenson had taken Louisa along in the tour of sister banks that might have interest in the kind of software we were writing. There must have been promises for more travel. There must have been no sex. I asked Louisa to describe the adventures though she wasn't keen that day to share experiences still being embraced close like secrets. She hated I came often to her cubicle to talk against the sin of boredom.

"No lotto wins? No bar fights? No shark attacks? No bull rides? No trips to jail? No smuggled drugs?"

She had turned back to the tube to type.

"Nothing at all. You must have the wrong woman."

"I'm sure I've got the right woman."

Louisa turned to look at me for the very first time with an unhesitant smile. It was stunning. She seemed suffused with the opportunities for sex she had refused but with graciousness that always seemed promise. She didn't understand my interest in her was like the pot for salary I wanted to keep from others by getting the biggest raise. Her virginity had become the center I surrounded with my hatred for managers and other programmers, for Louisa even, for everyone at the bank, for the foul righteousness quivering through conformity, for the emails that lied every third sentence, for the expectation I would embrace every falsehood, pretend anyway, against disbelief, knowing I was an ass to be discarded if I stayed long enough. I adored this guarded virginity that seemed an offense greater than cursing, greater than the vulgar word file edited against names, read and reread over the cubicle walls with shout, greater than anything I could imagine short of drawing blood. I could be reprimanded for cursing. Louise had to never slip once to remain in everyone's almost disbelieving esteem. She seemed magic.

"Did you get the new cash register working while I was away?"

Louisa knew no one could pretend bank business however successful surpassed travel for adventure. I turned away. Louisa snickered behind my back, amused that I would not talk to her about work when that is all she would ever offer, keen in her feelings, warming her through, that there was so much other withheld from many much better than me. I had no doubt Louisa had received a great deal of attention from more than Mortenson at the other banks. Mortenson snagged me outside Louisa's cubicle like a graverobber stumbling again over his tools in the dark.

"Mr. Tusk wants to see you."

For a moment I thought this meant the president of the bank wanted to congratulate me for the six months I had worked completing development that had overwhelmed the previous programmer who had sat in my cubicle. And more than another before that one too. I had made the bank a million dollars Mortenson had admitted in the review. It was probably actually five million. But in the corner office I instantly saw by the president's face he was not keen for greater fiscal revelation, was not keen to share the celebrations. There would be no trips to Biarritz with his hand on my knee. Instead the president berated me for all the foul language he had been told about. It seems that the hot little secretary no longer working for the president mentioned in her exit interview the week before that she was deeply disturbed by my language. The president seemed shocked that a small man would swear so openly. I looked too innocent for it. I did not qualify for it. It wasn't my right despite the promises in the state flag.

"She couldn't get rubber bands."

"What?"

"I need large rubber bands to hold together program listings but she couldn't order any because the bank has never ordered any before."

It probably helped that the president was clearly a bit bloated after lunch when he heard me ask how I was supposed to innovate computer applications while being stumped by rubber bands. He could feel himself unable to give chase. He needed a couple hours for the alcohol to be far enough past he could again be triumphantly domineering to the very tall senior executives he always hired to humiliate. I was not fired. There had been a moment where I certainly thought the game was to give me a grand review then terminate me. Instead there came a few days later a push to become a paperless office, that too being an innovative idea in 1989, one idea still waiting to be discredited, foresworn. I only know that for most people I have observed over the years it was easier to comprehend a large program flipping pages than flipping screens, as though on a glowing green screen IFTHENELSE underlay everything incomprehensible in the universe, a movie with an unhappy ending.

"I don't understand how such idiocy can be shrugged off just because the girl was pretty."

I considered bruiting about all that had been happening between Mortenson and the hot secretary but it would have undermined my attempt to appear ingenuous after so much language not patois. Fuck. Fuck. Fuck. Anyway Mortenson was too admired. A couple weeks earlier Mortenson had directed the programmers to enter the office building by the rear door past the dumpsters because our arrival in front each morning crowded the senior executives. The senior executives were all commendations. That first day I told Louisa the computer programmers were now expected to dive for raises being paid in garbage. Naturally Louisa was too proud with innocence to believe anything like that about herself so she called in sick for several days until Mortenson agreed to personally escort her through the front door each morning. Mortenson did seem to be screwing every woman in the bank. Little deaths. Certainly the hot little secretary had left the building through the back door thinking about various uses for rubber that had gone unheeded. I was again in Louisa's cubicle.

"He told me it is the highest score anyone here has received on a review."

"What makes you so special?" asked Louisa.

Louisa was so beautiful it was as if for her truth and insight coupled only with being desired so, it must be obvious, I couldn't be right about anything, being so undesirable, repugnant even most the time. I had expected more from conformity. A couple technicians who ran all the wiring were fired when they went to the labor board for not being paid overtime. From day one I was classified a professional based on an associate degree with no experience. I thought from all the things my mother had taught me I couldn't possibly be exempt from overtime. But on the telephone someone at the labor board told me that several years earlier under the first Reagan administration an attempt had failed to get programmers classified hourly employees, told me, in fact, only salesmen and computer programmers were completely unprotected by the law from abuse. Even the woman at the labor board seemed to believe the job called for a criminal response. It frequently crossed my thoughts I had access to the encryption keys to the new debit cards for the bank.

"Like all great men I stole my way to greatness."

Louisa laughed but I spoke the truth in a much more significant way than the division of salaries. The bank had the contract to run the cash registers for one of the grocery store chains spread across much the state and I had coded support for several new cash register configurations. This wasn't easy. For development purposes the bank shared a grossly obsolete mainframe with other banks merely running reports. There was nothing like a debugging tool that traced a program interactively line by line. Once a day a batch of mocked transactions ran to test code changes, but if the tester before you in the list had his transactions wrong, yours wouldn't run either. I didn't bother with those tests. It was possible to run actual transactions at one of the test cash registers so with that I beat my way through the code that had vanquished the programmers before me. The code was never the problem. The bigger obstacle was the registers wouldn't work without tape to print receipts and the previous programmers could never test much because there was never enough tape. Over and over the hot secretary who so dreaded anything like real work had denied ever having an appropriate purchase order number. The tape on the new machines was a different width to any ordered before. Like the programmers before me I wasn't about to spend money I didn't have on tape that was outrageously expensive unless bought in units of five thousand rolls. I know the programmer before me found a job elsewhere. Instead I simply walked out of a business supply store carrying a box of a hundred tapes with no one stopping me. From my size I didn't qualify to be a thief that bold but there I was all the same.

"I thought it was because you played piano."

"I haven't touched a piano in a while."

She was coaxing me to mention Janice but I acted ignorant. Louisa had somehow learned Janice was overseas so the very absence of Janice became yet more reason to talk about travel, another journey built around the implications of passion unrequited, even the fingertips unsoiled. Louisa was very keen to talk about travel so long as it were my secrets revealed. It was only much later I learned our dentist served Janice and both her parents too.

"Don't you miss playing for your little skirt?"

"She won't get much done to a waltz."

After work that day I went to a tavern I often went far enough from work I never saw anyone I knew. The owner there played jazz piano but only long after the sun went down. There had been evenings in winter with Janice along on a fake driver's license when I sometimes substituted at the ivories. President Tusk. I couldn't help laughing over the chords those cold nights. But in the long days of summer I sat on one of the stools in the window reading poetry from a book with French on one page and English the facing page. Only after the first drink did reading stop feeling like solving a puzzle within code. But it always stopped after the first drink so there was great incentive not to read anything less difficult. I needed away from code.

"I didn't know we were going to the library."

The young woman with the large idiot mocking me actually winced a bit, embarrassed as she sat at the table nearest the front window, but she giggled to please anyway. The other man laughed very loud. I was sitting swiveled sideways with my back against the wall because the sun coming in was too bright to face when reading. I looked at the two couples over the top of the book but from behind sunglasses. The men were large with college football bodies not yet gone to fat in the insurance business. The many insurance companies in town were so crowded with college athletes it left in question who pushed all the paper, unless, like here, the women were tagged along. The women were trim but tired even under the extra paint put on for a tavern expected to be darker than daylight. Perhaps fencers. Perhaps swimmers. Perhaps these women were dreamers not athletic at all.

"Let's all read the labels on our bottles."

The large idiot didn't know I had not settled into reading when he first drove his companions into the parking lot. I had just finished a set at the piano. The window faced the street. His luxury sedan was very new. The idiot thought it very funny when I bummed a cigarette from his girlfriend then only smoked a short length without inhaling. He read my lungs. He was a very professional insurance man. In the window I read the book for half an hour listening to sneering comments about poetry but did not wait for the tavern owner to take the piano for fear improvised music would herd the couples from the tavern. It wasn't even really dusk. But I wasn't painting now without Janice in the country so I didn't hesitate to spill the last of the turpentine jar over the paint rags. No one saw me slip under the new sedan with its grill facing a retaining wall of concrete blocks. It was of course an idea straight from the movies. *The Password is Courage*. What color is courage again? A rag of many colors taken for battle flag? I thought about how many passwords I had to have for all the different systems at the bank though here there would not be three tries to get it correct. Light the cigarette. Enfold it within the book of matches. Place the matches at the appropriate location and after a time the matches ignite. In those years cigarettes still burnt to the stub. I drove around the block until I saw smoke whiffing from the hood of the new luxury sedan then I stayed away until after the firetruck arrived. The burning made a nice glow in the evening sky and I braked for just a moment to read by the light.

"Je suis de mon cœur le vampire."

And that poem was all true enough because in the review Mortenson commented I never smiled.

RIGHT IN THE TEETH

FADE IN:

INT: IT FITS INFORMATION TECHNOLOGY OFFICE - NEW MORNING

Igor tentatively fumbles about the cubicles of the computer programmers.

INSERT - LIVE ACTION

Real fingers lifting tape on an ADDING MACHINE.

BACK TO SCENE

Igor continues exploring.

INSERT - LIVE ACTION

Real fingers clicking the beads of an ABACUS.

BACK TO SCENE

Igor approaches the lectern from its front.

INSERT - LIVE ACTION

Real fingers running over the upside-down numbers of the rotting ledger seen previously.

BACK TO SCENE

There is a bit of RHUBARB before PROGRAMMER I and PROGRAMMER II arrive through near entrance with fingers probing their mouths, consternation on their faces, perhaps some pain. Through all scenes they push before them like dance partners their wheeled cubicle chairs.

PROGRAMMER I
I think the hole in the back keeps
getting bigger but I'm no longer
certain it was ever a tooth.

PROGRAMMER II
Can you understand what I'm saying
over this whistling sound?

PROGRAMMER I
I never had fangs before.

PROGRAMMER II
Remind me never to let you kiss my
ass again however deserving.
        (pauses to feel tooth)
How did you like the new dental
assistant?

PROGRAMMER I
Her tongue has three colors like a
French flag.

PROGRAMMER II
The result of specialized but
constant use.

PROGRAMMER I
Meaning she's less fussy than the
last assistant.

PROGRAMMER II
You mean the one before the last
one, which, for a computer
programmer, can sometimes
mathematically be two before the
current one.

PROGRAMMER I
That bitch I never held in my arms
has three children now.

> PROGRAMMER I AND PROGRAMMER II
>   (together laughing)
> Think of the money we saved!

They notice Igor at last.

> PROGRAMMER I
> Look! A somnambulist leaving us a
> quarter for our teeth.

> PROGRAMMER II
> Even a somnambulist must not abuse
> the privileges of rank by reading
> upside-down.

> IGOR
> Mr Denshag has hired me to be a
> computer programmer.

> PROGRAMMER I
> Are you sure it was computer
> programming you were hired for?
> Upside-down?

> IGOR
> I've been assigned the task of
> adding the number six to other
> numbers.

> PROGRAMMER II
> Proof enough he'll never tumble the
> new dental assistant.

> IGOR
>   (sensing a
>   challenge)
> How's that?

PROGRAMMER II approaches the rotted
ledger and begins to carefully turn its
pages looking for lost treasure.

PROGRAMMER II
The number six is the most common
karmic affliction throughout the
harmonious planets. The number six
is indicative of failure in a
previous life to establish
fulfilling relations within a
family. You have failed to love.
You have failed to marry. You have
failed to produce children. You
have failed...

IGOR
(interrupting)
And dentistry will correct that?

PROGRAMMER II
A safe prosperity exists only if we
all act alike but without us able to
recognize each other.

IGOR
(sensing it all
stinks)
Will I recognize the police?

PROGRAMMER II
The police will occasionally conduct
raids, but for the most part, they
work in league with all computers,
ensuring the uninterrupted flow of
information about the past, because
the police exist to perpetuate the
status quo, and the status quo
cannot be defined, let alone
maintained, without economic
history, so and therefore and
whynot, in no economic sense can a
policeman be distinguished from a
computer programmer, excepting a
policeman is less inclined to share
his donuts in the middle of a crime
spree.

PROGRAMMER I
So just what is your expression
number?

IGOR
My what?

PROGRAMMER II
An expression number calculated from
the letters of your name is required
for employment. Not that we want to
know your name.

PROGRAMMER I
Destiny number, cornerstone number,
and secret passion numbers are
generally calculated for you
depending on the needs of the
company. Don't you know anything
about numerology? A computer
programmer?

IGOR
When do I meet the new dental
assistant?

PROGRAMMER I AND PROGRAMMER II
(together laughing)
Is that a six or a nine you are
looking at?

Mrs Peel appears exactly as before trying to get
her shoe over her heel with a pen.

MRS PEEL
In Tarot the number six is present
on the card of the lovers. But it
is really the story of the original
garden, the couple naked but
unashamed, before the fall. It
represents the choice the fool must
make to rebel against authority to
achieve knowledge.

> IGOR
> (calling to
> Mrs Peel)
> Sexual knowledge?

> MRS PEEL
> (very sternly)
> IT FITS company policy does not
> strictly require consenting
> employees to seek only knowledge,
> the inference of rebellion,
> invariably produced by a hormonal
> atmosphere, since knowledge even in
> partnership can result in something
> other than the usual
> misunderstandings that pass for
> ideal.

Mrs Peel again sits in the kitchenette. Her shoe
falls off to the floor with her foot in the air.

> IGOR
> Look. You have six toes!

> MRS PEEL
> (yet more sternly)
> Observations from computer
> programmers are like stains tracked
> into the bedroom on my own heels.

> IGOR
> And therefore...there is nothing I
> can add?

Programmer I and Programmer II are giggling
together until a familiar noise jolts them into
formality. Mrs Peel picks up her shoe.

> PROGRAMMER II
> Look busy but don't actually do
> anything. It's Chairman Povereese.

> IGOR
> Who?

CHAIRMAN POVEREESE, an absolutely huge man,
enters wearing a rather brash business suit, a
large elephant's mask entirely covering his head,
and a gold crown, the boss like a decadent
Babar.

                    PROGRAMMER II
          Our chairman of the board, you
          idiot.

Povereese pauses for a moment to brush his tusks
with a long-handled whisk broom he carries
against flies.

                    IGOR
                    (whispering)
          Why is he dressed like the king of
          the jungle?

                    PROGRAMMER II
                    (whispering)
          Sometimes being a stupid beast is
          the only way to remain faithful to
          capitalist principles.

Povereese lets out an elephant's trumpet while he
lumbers across to exit the opposite side of the
room.

                    PROGRAMMER II
                    (points at
                    Igor's mouth)
          Look at how even the most random
          effluence from a natural leader can
          facilitate valuable business
          secrets. Look!

                    IGOR
          What?

INSERT - LIVE ACTION

Real fingers pulling up real lip.

BACK TO SCENE

PROGRAMMER II
(pulls up
Igor's lip)
The number six tooth on a standard
dental chart is an upper right tooth
near the front.

IGOR
(little more
than a
gurgle)
Let go!

MRS PEEL
You two seem to be getting quite
chummy.

PROGRAMMER II
(to Mrs Peel)
Look at this!

MRS PEEL
Nothing I didn't see through a
keyhole when still a child.

PROGRAMMER II
He doesn't have a number six tooth.

IGOR
(painfully pulling
away)
That can't be right.
(emphatic but doubtful)
I can look in the mirror and see
there is no tooth missing.

PROGRAMMER II
You are examining your teeth within
reflection where memory creates an
image distorted from shame and
desire.

> MRS PEEL
> (obviously playing
> along)
> You must examine your teeth in the
> abstract.

Programmer II approaches Mrs Peel triumphantly.
He has anticipated her playing along.

> PROGRAMMER II
> (to Igor)
> You should listen. She was once the
> dental assistant here.
> (to Mrs Peel)
> I suggest that Programmer VI never
> again stand in front of a mirror
> unless you are there beside him to
> help find the hidden gap in his
> teeth.

Mrs Peel swings her shoe at Programmer II but he
has anticipated the attack so steps away putting
his chair between himself and her. Mrs Peel
stumbles but winds up safely seated in the chair.
Programmer II dances Mrs Peel about to her
consternation.

> PROGRAMMER II
> Of course, it will mean you'll have
> to share an apartment, a bed even,
> what with the profligacy of mirrors
> beyond business premises, the great
> shame of modern culture.

> IGOR
> (to Mrs Peel)
> I'll go buy a ladder right now to
> put a mirror over our bed.

Igor leaves in a dash. Mrs Peel leaps from
chair.

> MRS PEEL
> What the hell game are you playing?

                    PROGRAMMER II
        But you flirt with him. Why not
        take him on?

                      MRS PEEL
        But you flirt with him too!

                    PROGRAMMER II
        You cannot expect me to go on
        financially supporting you forever.

                      MRS PEEL
        You know perfectly well that in
        these times an attractive woman
        still cannot succeed without a
        menacing accomplice. I could be
        rich if I had a hulking brother. I
        only have you. Hands everywhere.
        Never hulking. But mother wouldn't
        waste yet another advanced medical
        procedure on making babies after she
        saw how you turned out.

A pause while Programmer II turns away
humiliated, slowly spinning his chair.

                      MRS PEEL
        Look at you. A computer programmer.
        And to think I've had my fingers in
        your throat. My own baby brother!

                    PROGRAMMER II
                     (dejected)
        More than fingers at play if you'd
        only remember.

Igor enters carrying a rickety old wooden ladder
upright against his shoulder, the sort of ladder
whose rungs are round rods, the sort of ladder
that narrows as it rises.

                       IGOR
        Look at the ladder I found. Imagine
        the waggish window washing stories

these old rods could tell! Could
there be a more perfect tool for
mounting objects atop a bed?

                    MRS PEEL
Theft from one's employer is seldom
the romantic beginning of every
lasting love story.

                    PROGRAMMER II
                    (sneaking in
                     comment)
And yet don't you sense a certain
appeal?

                    IGOR
Peel? Mrs Peel?

FADE OUT.

CAHIERS DU CINÉMA

Reds

In the movie *In The French Style* Jean Seberg goes from virgin to party girl so immediately without explanation that it leaves it obvious her later voiceover statement she slept beside the schoolboy, the boy who has passed for twenty-one, means more than having snoozed in a bitter cold hotel room. At least Janice wasn't a virgin. From the hotel window Seberg watches in the street below two drunken tramps who might be Didi and Gogo aimlessly crossing cobbles but the audience in response to the voiceover knows Seberg is done with waiting. Of course jazz is blamed. The scene cuts from Seberg and the schoolboy in the bed rented by the hour to a trumpet bell blowing hot jazz in a room full of dancers. Cutting to the bell has deep psychoanalytic inference that might make me take on memory of the Seberg movie *Lilith*, but it is impossible to think about a movie with Warren Beattie, even another movie about madness, without thinking about the movie *Reds* instead. I took my mother to see *Reds*. Didi and Gogo. With those names it is hard to imagine they are not waiting on Doctor Dolittle. Still what does Stanley Baker say to Jean Seberg? That she must not plead when he leaves her bed to jet around the world writing his newspaper articles, counting the corpses of soldiers in burnt villages, smelling out the next popular insurgency, interviewing the desert generals snatching rule, taking comfort where he finds it. Seberg says she will not plead and Baker says that makes her a gentleman. Being a gentleman is the only thing, he says. It is a deeply weird sexual confusion he grants her at that moment when they agree not to plead, a moment being Desdemona, and in the end, when Seberg has let her hair go back to natural brown to please the oral surgeon, it is Baker who pleads, who isn't granted the dignity of death, denied great ceremony before the battlements like Othello then entombment in the Kremlin wall like John Reed. I never got a chance to ask my old boss if Jean Seberg was a natural blonde. Probably it is better not to know so many things once movies are involved.

"It's too long now."

"It's too good to leave this far into it."

"Who are these people that keep interrupting?"

It was impossible for my mother to sit through a movie where the rooms depicted weren't kept tidy. She wouldn't even have come if someone at a union meeting the night before hadn't said the movie *Reds* spoke truth to power. On the way to the theater she had told me in great detail about recently cleaning the screened porch that was the gem of her old house. It was a couple days after Christmas but she had cleaned the unheated porch because on sunny days it was still where she sat, wrapped in a rug, as though in an open touring car from the salad days of Louise Bryant. Not that my mother had ever heard of Louise Bryant before. Nor John Reed. Nor Max Eastman. Nor Eugene O'Neill.

"I don't even remember the song they keep singing."

Lion bodies with heads of men like a character edited out of the play Robbie staged that same winter. Tzara. Yeats. Baudelaire. *Je trône dans l'azur comme un sphinx incompris.* In the end merely witness Henry Miller, the one I didn't read but was always encouraged to read when I was in Paris, who was actually witness to what except his whore of a wife while others chased revolution, I don't know, a wife Baudelaire would have understood anyway, understood even while firing a rifle from the barricades. In the theater I had to tell my mother to be quiet. I had been back from Paris a few days more than a week, so what was fresh in my head was reading Sartre on Baudelaire, especially the passage about 19th century belief that work would impose order on the universe where 18th century belief in reason had failed, because what really could be a more fatuous interpretation of Marx, if not Baudelaire too? I had been promised a job at the ketchup factory. In the theater my mother quieted into the 20th century where Sartre with his love of movies must have seen *À Nous La Liberté*. In *À Nous La Liberté* the little tramp Emile disrupts the factory assembly line of phonographs chasing the handkerchief of the blonde girl he loves but who loves another. In *Lilith* the incurably crazy girl played beautifully by Jean Seberg gives Warren Beatty her handkerchief like a damsel to a knight when Beatty mounts a horse for a contest lancing metal rings at full gallop, I shit you not, the scene incredibly moronic, two steps down from the jazz horn but with similar psychoanalytic implications. In the theater beside my mother my heart filled with rage when Warren Beatty standing on some stage assures the crowd that the workers of America are only waiting for Russian leadership. John Reed looks longingly to Louise Bryant in the crowd. She smiles back. In the newspapers publicizing the movie I had read Louise Bryant later enjoyed all the pleasures of artistic Paris in the 1920s married to a career American diplomat with a fine expense account. Chauffeurs. Servants. She was there with Hemingway. She was there with Fitzgerald. I imagined her rooms near the American embassy were very tidy indeed. I could not stomach that smile and I punched my mother in the face before grabbing her by the throat.

"The tooth commands I do my duty."

In the poster art for *Lilith* they made Seberg's hair red when it was obviously again blonde a year after ruining Stanley Baker, obvious in the first shots anyway, both movies black and white. The people at the countryside asylum are all from prominent families. Somewhere in the movie Lilith is said to have been institutionalized since age eighteen and it is hard not to then think *The French Style* is her delusion, the horror she recounts to others, in the same way the murders told in *Dr. Caligari* frame a world out of kilter, the buildings angled, the furniture tilted, the lovers tragically chosen. But this was not obvious to me before the years in the video store when I knew *Dr. Caligari* but none of the other movies about madness. Perhaps in *Lilith* the hair is genuinely red in the madhouse but in her imagination across Paris it is blonde.

"On page 113 of his book Sartre declares Baudelaire the man who says *no* but what does that mean after describing for pages a man who retains conventional morality in a need to condemn himself?"

The graduate student who said this in Iowa was substituting for the full professor some week the professor was off hiding, in Algiers perhaps, more likely Istanbul, certainly not Paris, since the point was to get far as possible from Sartre after teaching Camus to the university class on Existentialism. This particular graduate student was disparaged by his fellow graduate students for reading nothing but Sartre and comic books but the week had filled the others all with envy and loathing. This mocked guy was a born lecturer. By end of the week the class had doubled in size with students not actually enrolled. Still I noticed no one ever mentioned Sartre in his memoir of childhood played at being in movies but had at some age graduated from valiant hero to noble prisoner, burned at the stake, guillotined, then describes himself, completely unexpectedly, as a loose wench, a girl for the soldiers. Page 108. Perhaps it is better to remember that Picasso invented Cubism appropriating images he had seen at the cinema.

"You don't recall that in the movie Louise Bryant deserts a husband who is a dentist?"

"I don't recall that at all."

"You insist you chose the line about the devil from Baudelaire before attending the movie with your mother? Before you even thought to take your mother?"

La Dent. Serpent. Fang. Tooth. *A dans la cœur un Serpent jaune.* The snake who says *no.* I had attacked my mother in witness to the poetry of Baudelaire while leaving revolution to the movies. Then another movie about madness called *The Snake Pit* with its great technical shot from impossibly high of the crowded room of insane women dancing, screaming, laughing uncontrollably, the Russian woman on a soap box shouting for workers to unite, a political prisoner, the room an abyss, the shot one Baudelaire would have adored. The psychiatrist in the madhouse sat back when talking to me as though reclining but thought better of it. She remained upright no matter my stare. No matter how I played the somnambulist Cesare. In his diary on the making of *Othello*, Micheál MacLiammóir recounts Betsy Blair asleep on the plane to Morocco with head thrown back, mouth open, as though that too is preparation for playing Desdemona, no sillier than most American acting exercises, anyway, I think. Betsy Blair was married to Gene Kelly at the time, the great love of his live was Betsy Blair. To have a job I pushed my life through the songs of *An American*

In Paris but found I could often not think of Leslie Caron without thinking Betsy Blair instead. Why? Betsy Blair was a Red. Certified in *Red Channels*. That list of communists not to be hired had ruined her movie career before it hardly started simply because she believed too strongly in equal rights for black people. Desdemona. Orson Welles had had Betsy Blair dye her natural red hair blonde to play Desdemona. But Orson Welles shipped Betsy Blair off to Paris from Morocco without ever quite firing her because he realized she seemed too modern to play Desdemona, which means, I think, the Red showed through and through even in a film of black and white. Betsy Blair didn't need red hair. None of which is the weird part where Baudelaire's correspondences of color to music somehow becomes Surrealist coincidences. The weird part is Betsy Blair appeared later in a jazz version of *Othello* playing not Desdemona but the Emilia part, called Emily there, the wife of Patrick McGoohan's simpering Iago, a strange wife not telling Desdemona women should have the same right men have to chase sexual pleasure, not arguing equal rights in any fashion, no sign of the commie in this rather simpleminded wife who has sacrificed herself for a jazz husband. That movie too is in black and white. McGoohan does not run his wife through with a sword. Instead Betsy Blair shortly thereafter outside the movies married the director who in a couple years would make *Morgan! A Suitable Case for Treatment*. It takes my breath away, that particular coincidence. It is hard not to imagine there isn't lots of Betsy Blair somewhere in that movie too even though there is no magic handkerchief like the one Othello received from his mother. Instead the mother takes her son Morgan to place a wreath on the grave of Karl Marx. *N'es-tu pas l'oasis où je rêve, et le gourde où je hume à traits le vin du souvenir?* Insecurity has made you cunning, says Morgan to his wife. The biographies and diaries and memoirs never speculate what Orson Welles saw in *The Snake Pit* that made him cast Desdemona from a madhouse. Crime puts the human element back in, says Morgan to his wife. No. No. Unfortunately Betsy Blair doesn't play the Russian woman calling for revolution. In *The Snake Pit* Betsy Blair is seen the first time in a slightly tilted shot strangling another inmate. It is almost erotic. More than almost but none of the books mention it. How on earth can anyone miss the role reversal besides? Isn't she auditioning for Othello? *I am better but I still I am one of them*. I cannot count the times I quoted that line from *The Snake Pit* while sitting in my cubicle. Those first years in the cubicle I sometimes almost forgot it was Alice who kept red hair always on display. Alice never made a black and white movie.

"Don't you think it is enough that your mother leads a union she organized herself?" asked the doctor.

"There remain questions of doctrine."

Orson Welles once declared he would be staging a play with sets created by André Derain but it seems terribly unlikely Welles wanted bad Corots for a production of Marlowe's *Faustus* when what was called for was *Caligari*. How grows that family tree? How many degrees of separation does that path walked in artists put me from Welles? Three? Are they all rotting corpses found along a path in the same way Baudelaire wrote about seeing his mistress in a putrid animal carcass alive with maggots? It hardly matters since I saw Welles with my own eyes in the cemetery in Paris when I lived there. It was not so odd it might be a meeting in the movies. Maybe. In Truffaut's *Shoot The Piano Player*, before any of the principle characters are introduced, a man fleeing hoodlums runs straight into a light pole. The passerby who helps the injured man proceeds to recount how he married his wife because she was a virgin in a city with greater proportion of virgins than any other capital on the continent. Paris was not like that when I played the drum there. In the animation from my childhood watching television the dog that says only *no* is sent to obedience school but refuses to learn to say anything other than *no* until finally the instructor teaches the dog to say *no* in five different languages. It should have been that dog helped the minor character who has run into the lamppost. Also it is the perfect dog for Sartre to fail to name in his autobiography. He mentions having a dog in childhood only in passing. Page? I've lost that number but I remember he provides no name. In the television animation of my childhood there was first *Gumby* and then there was *Davy and Goliath*. In *Gumby* the dog who says *no* provides more guidance than all Goliath ever has to say to Davy about God. It is hard to imagine Baudelaire could find anything but an approvable vice in the dog that says *no* to everything though like Sartre he hated dogs. Still the dog might also have been merely a breed meant for companion to Louisa maintaining her virginity.

"Othello's handkerchief is a love charm sewn by his mother, who could predict the future besides cast spells, who had depths that cannot be explained within capitalist certitudes."

Baudelaire approved of unrequited love expressed in letters he never signed.

"It is the betrayal of this mother that causes Othello to strangle Desdemona."

Of course *Dr. Caligari* isn't the only German movie I've ever seen but my interest in other German movies seemed to exist for only a few years the same time I was at university because so many were shown in the student union. I saw *Berlin Alexanderplatz* but I cannot tell you one thing about the three or six hours I sat through. I also saw *Pandora's Box* for the first time though it was one everyone was surprised they couldn't find at the old distribution company where I once worked on the river. Louise Brooks. Lulu even. Lulu first drives a wealthy newspaper publisher to suicide then takes over the son who writes jazz songs. I remember two black dancers on stage. I remember Lulu dancing with a lesbian. I came away from *Woyzeck* knowing time in corporate America would have me eating nothing but peas with my ketchup because there would be no time for better. Later when on call every day all day all night through years at a time I have often thought the peas were the easy part.

"How many times have you seen the play actually staged?"

It only seemed common coincidence the psychiatrist at my madhouse was a Scotswoman. I was not surprised. It did not seem surrealistic. Still she tried to repress the stronger tones of her Edinburgh accent when around me because she could sense her very existence troubled me.

"Never."

The subplot added to the movie *The Quare Fellow* not in the play has McGoohan tumbling the wife of the man who is to hang. It is hard not to think of Iago lifted in the cage in the Welles version of *Othello*. In *The Quare Fellow* the man to be hanged has chopped his own brother into pieces with the kitchen cleaver after finding him in bed with the wife. The clever shone in the morning daybreak. In *Lilith* the love scene is overlaid with water reflecting sunlight like all those images in Baudelaire where the sun shimmers over the abyss, shimmers even over les femmes damnées, eblouissant rêve, allume le désir dans les regards des rustres, brilliant à travers leurs larmes, des boas luisants. What would you do if you found I had a greater talent for love than you thought? asks Lilith. The love scene cuts to the lesbian turning off the radio playing jazz because she is confident she comes next in line.

"Make the Moor thank me, love me and reward me, for making him egregiously an ass and practicing upon his peace and quiet even to madness."

"You know it all by heart?"

I first saw *The Tin Drum* back at university but the movie eliminates the encapsulating narrative of Little Oskar in the madhouse writing his memoirs. His doctor too is a woman. Charles Aznavour plays the shopkeeper who says Kaddish over of the grave of Oskar's dead mother. His shop is a toy store. He sells tin drums. I have watched *Shoot The Piano Player* over a hundred times but never once without thinking of the prayers over of the mother's grave. Still I think it more important that only in the novel does Oskar send his madhouse keeper with very specific instructions to purchase a ream of virgin paper on which to write his memoirs. He is tickled when the keeper recounts how the girl at the stationary shop blushed. Oskar knows what is what yet only the banging of his drum returns memory. I have nothing that returns memory except the movies and better still the songs from the movies. I read about tin drums but think of McGoohan at the end of the jazz *Othello* wailing on his drums with no one to blush since no one has lost a thing cherished. Betsy Blair says what to McGoohan? A prayer for forgiveness? Death to the generals? Be a gentleman? Nothing like that.

"It is a line originally written for Desdemona."

Early into *À Nous La Liberté*, the regimentation of a prison the convicts are desperate to escape becomes the same regimentation at a phonograph factory workers queue to accept just to have any job. The men wear numbers on their overalls in both places. Beatty works in the asylum because his dead mother was a nutter. And the mother looked much like Lilith. And for that matter looked much like Louisa. Nothing seems very far from McGoohan's imprisoning but drumless village where all names also have been taken away. In the jazz *Othello* McGoohan not once but twice looks into the night sky where there is thunder. The identical, and I mean very same, sound effect appears in the opening credits of *The Prisoner*, against a very similar sky, perhaps too identical except it is daylight. *Peut-on illumine un ciel bourbeux et noir?* And what 19th century certainty do the men of the 20th century in the factory with no view of the sky sing? About unrequited love letters that must be left unsigned? About chasing handkerchiefs caught in the wind? About the jazz their phonographs will play? No. Work will set us free. It is a line that ten years later would become the most notorious welcome to prisoners ever staged. Go! Go! Chase handkerchiefs. Go! *Get Out Your Handkerchiefs. Préparez Vos Mouchoirs.* And how old is the Parisian boy in that movie when he takes over his father's factories and his father's mistress? Thirteen? Fourteen? From which century is that couchmar? But anyway I am an obvious liar since in the very first episode of *The Prisoner* the bass drum carried by the village marching band is made prominent as it is made prominent in many episodes. McGoohan does not move to take it. In the credit sequence starting each *Prisoner* episode McGoohan launches into the dream state that becomes his imprisonment upon returning to his apartment after angrily quitting his job. He slams his resignation on the office desk of his superior. Does he absentmindedly leave behind an unsigned love letter to Betsy Blair instead? Wouldn't that be a shot from the barricades against work? More than a drum's complaint? The schemes of Iago?

ROBBIE AT REST

Robbie and I were sitting on wobbly chairs at a table in a tavern. I was thinking about how Gene Kelly maintained that being constrained from shooting *An American In Paris* actually in Paris was ever so fortunate. The tavern where Robbie had chosen to meet was meant to be some kind of traditional pub transplanted from the thistle or the shamrock, though the wainscoting was too new with shellac to register anything approaching authenticity behind the traditional lament being sung from the dais, accent from the backlot, everything in that tavern not quite the real thing. None of it felt especially fortunate. Robbie wanted me distracted with clumsy imitation so she didn't have to talk about her recent expedition to look at portraits held in private collections. Belgium. Austria. France. She wanted me very separate from those pictures. She feared my singular influence on pictures. Already she was miserable I had brought along the book from the Gauguin exhibit I had visited in Chicago on the drive to Ann Arbor. I had even bought the book hardcover to signal I now had the money for good books. Robbie was leafing through pages remembering the introductory art history class where I showed her lines from Mallarmé that seem to have been lifted from Gauguin's journal of Tahiti, only they can't have been since Noa Noa came after Mallarmé was dead, meaning Gauguin needed Mallarmé's words to fathom all that flesh, maybe even to distinguish one beach from another. It was just the sort of thing graduate students love. At the moment Robbie was pointing at one of the Gauguin reproductions in the book to distract my attention from the tall redhead on the dais in the tavern singing songs of rebellion. The rebellion came from within secondskin leather trousers. In my punk days I had owned similar trousers inappropriate to a sweltering evening the middle of summer but worn in a dare never to complain about the weather like everyone else.

"It is hotter than any night Ireland has ever blamed on the English."

Robbie was uncertain I wasn't talking about the nude she hovered her finger above. Perhaps she thought I was being deliberately conventional because she wasn't alone not wanting conversation about those portraits seen on her travels. Certainly I didn't want to be a portrait. With a voice that kept tumbling far from the peat and absent the firth, falling right into local sounds, the tall redhead sang a high soprano while thumping a bodhran so worn it almost compensated for the tavern being set for a movie musical. I mean the drum was the one believable prop. I was wondering if I might steal it. It wouldn't be until the next night I learned the two other women in the band there on the dais were much too genuine.

"Since when have you been wearing glasses?"

"Computer programming punishes the flesh in its own ways."

Robbie must have felt pity because she took from her purse the small gift she had brought back from her travels. It was miniature bagpipes, an antique souvenir toy smaller than my palm, a plaid bag of fabric with pipes silver tin. I was meant to understand there was great sentiment. She had been saving the toy for me for a long time. It was only much later it occurred to me Robbie had walked through the thistles of Scotland too on the recent travels but would never admit it. Innocent of deception I laid the toy on the open book then spun it above the nude as though it were a wheel foretelling everything except the weather. Movies can be shot day for night and winter for summer. It's done all the time. The weather always seems fortunate. Yes. Yes. *An American In Paris* was shot on the backlot.

"Isn't it a shame glasses don't put right everything you've seen before?"

"It plays if you give it a squeeze."

I laughed because I was thinking the same thing about the leather trousers. The bagpipes let out a few squeaking bars and for a moment I pictured my punk days as though memory alone might subvert the traditional military march the bagpipes played into yet another song of rebellion. In seven months computer programming I had learned not every insurgence goes on being sang after its failure.

"Do you know why a piper marches when he blows?"

Robbie must have known the answer to that old joke because she pretended not to hear. I needed other provocation.

"A whirlwind trip sounds like just enough distraction for the university here to rob you yet again when not looking."

"No. The conditions for my doctorate were established after that very bad start. I have my doctorate."

"You saw what then?"

"Emotional portraits."

Robbie knew I still championed painters who were never mentioned except in passing no matter the art history class in Iowa City. Robert Delaunay. Raoul Duffy. Alfred Sisley. The painting I kept returning to my year in Paris besides the Sisley floods was a Pissarro cityscape filled with snow. In Iowa City even Pissarro was mentioned only long enough to dismiss him for failing to embrace a mature style. In her class Robbie had shown slides of no more than six Pissarros before repeating the established denunciation. Now Robbie turned a page in the book and I ran my finger over reproduction while giving a little cough into the fist of my other hand holding the bagpipes. Robbie ignored the gesture.

"Emotional? Which is what? I haven't seen you in three years. A few postcards and two interrupted phone calls. There has to be something I haven't heard."

For the last hour Robbie had been disconcerting me with conversation cryptic with assumption I knew all her diary entries from the last few years. Her behavior had a weirdly political caress to it. There was that insidious way politics makes a listener behave through a slight ripple of fear. It was a conversational style I had experienced so many times at the union rallies my mother dragged me, but from Robbie it was delivered with an immediacy unprotected by labor union, an immediacy, an intimacy, echoing the nudes beneath our fingers. I did not want to be thinking about my mother.

"Well, you already know the worse thing was that when I arrived for the doctorate program they told me I had to earn a master's here first, but they didn't tell me that until I got here, so it was too late then to change my mind about coming."

"Wait. Wait. You never told me anything about that. All I ever heard about was that they put you straight into teaching classes at amateur wages. It wasn't enough that you already had your master's in art history from Iowa? What secrets do they alone possess here in Ann Arbor?"

"It's not quite like that."

Did they teach that Vincent Van Gogh painted only with his toes? Did they teach that Paul Gauguin went to Tahiti for a tan? Only singsong rhymes came to mind after exploitation was conceded. In Iowa City Robbie had taken her class to the university art museum. In those days the de Chirico was still billed as 1918 though it was in fact one of the many futurist fakes he painted after 1945 when he couldn't sell his truly awful paintings of horses who wished they knew Chagall instead. The same fiddle of a painter aping his earlier works turned up much later in *The Horse's Mouth* but the movie was clever enough to depict futility within the comedy. Perhaps de Chirico had read the novel. I knew that at some point after the war he had taught in Scotland among the bagpipes. The novel had been around a decade by then.

"D'où venon-nous? Que sommes-nous? Où allons-nous?"

"I know. I know. What the university did to me was idiotic and humiliating. Worse still was it worked out I didn't actually have to take the classes here for the master's degree."

"Are you saying you just had to purchase a second master's degree outright? Another master's degree in art history? Strange. Are their degrees available only in bulk?"

"I mean I was allowed to drop classes several times because my advisors kept hounding me to teach instead."

"Bastards. I would have told them to go fuck themselves. I've worked for bankers only half a year but you get to know quickly when the suits in charge are just being highwaymen. Stand and deliver! Work this weekend for free! Work every weekend, you silly peasant, pismire, because this is the only lawless room in a bank, we've got you before you've even taken out a mortgage on a house, before you've taken on any of the old bondage rules, growing family, growing debt, growing fat, those don't apply to you! We've got you for nothing!"

I looked over at the jukebox alight but not playing and for a moment I mistook it for a teller machine beckoning service like some kind of sea siren pulling me towards the shoals, without singing, the sound of money silent but insistent. I thought about the Monets I would never see. The Sisleys. The other Gauguins. The money would never be large enough for all that travel in pursuit of what proceeds the emotional portraits.

"How deep are you in debt now?"

"It doesn't matter. You know it doesn't get more prestigious than here, right? Every year there are a hundred applicants for each vacancy in my doctorate program. I've been very lucky."

"Well, yeah, yeah, yeah, that's what I thought about University of Iowa, too, that it was too damned good of a school not to deliver a career, somehow, even if it was never visible on the horizon, certainly never contractual, and never even hinted at in the required courses, all while I blew all my mother's money, all that savings scrimped in the belief in progress, all those delusions things would must go better for me than her even without a union. I figured out too late that money was the only reason they ever let me into the school. The degree got me nothing in return."

"Nobody ever gets a job with an undergraduate degree in, which was it? Theater? Cinema?"

"Phhfft. I could say that the teachers wouldn't even give me the time of day, but, in fact, that is the one thing the tuition did buy me. Bong. Bong goes the clock. I remember quite clearly how my academic advisor wouldn't see me until the exact minute of the appointment. Not a minute before. Never for a minute longer than scheduled. Evidently paid by the hour, the lucky bastard, for a salesman, which is all he was, since his advice, his only advice, was always that I needed to stay at the university another year. Spend more money! I see by your bank statement you still are quite intelligent. Stand and deliver in an essay of no fewer than two thousand words. Cleanly typed with small margins. Pockets turned out."

"How many paintings did you show even me? I mean besides the portraits of me right in front of me. Three? Four? You can't expect teachers to appreciate you for talents you won't exhibit."

She was keen to see the new paintings I had told her about but I was stalling. I couldn't help thinking about her ignoring even Pissarro. I fucking hated she had ignored Pissarro because everyone else ignored Pissarro.

"Ne travais jamais!"

Is that from Rimbaud? Is that from Baudelaire? I sat there running a finger over the rim of my whisky glass unable to remember from what poem I took that line I placed somewhere into all my paintings back at the university. Of course it was simply punk shouting down a future faking paintings from the past. I went on thinking about that Gene Kelly movie even though in that backlot tavern I never felt more enfeebled from having watched five thousand movies at the video rental store years before.

"What the hell kind of art education was that, anyway, drawing bodies posed forty feet away, far too far to see anything accurately, even with good eyes, with lighting from down low, pure Frankenstein's laboratory, I'm alive, I'm alive, because the graduate student babysitting the class, you couldn't call it teaching, the graduate student was too lazy to hang the spot lamp. Yes. Pure evil genius. Yes. Let's put the model far away as possible, tiny tiny in my field of vision, then tell me to draw larger, bolder, larger, big loose strokes, faster, cash cow, faster, piss away that paper, because we make our profit selling art supplies down at the student union."

Robbie took the glasses from my face without any sense it was a promise to undress me further once alone.

"You wear very strong lenses."

"They are only cheaters. Only for looking up close."

"So you could go on painting?"

"Only if my arms grew to fifteen feet."

The blonde waitress with ponytail finally delivered the steak fries I had ordered with the second round of the best single malt the tavern offered. The waitress was a student. I looked up into the close blur of her without the glasses when she handed me change for the twenty. One step farther back she came into focus.

"There is still other money not yet dispensed, the ancient money, a soldier's pay, because don't I look a soldier?"

"What?"

"Salt."

Robbie pushed over the shaker that had been on the table the whole time without my eyes noticing. The waitress left.

"What do you suppose she would have done if I had asked for sult from her rather than salt?"

It was too much the genuine old sod for Robbie to understand the tease with language. I thought about Orson Welles walking from Galway to Donegal leading an ass he had loaded with oils and canvas but then not painting a thing. On the ship over he had drawn portraits. Everyone had talked to him. This was all between the world wars the summer after all the economies in the world fell away but Welles had an inheritance probably something equivalent to what Baudelaire had received.

"Every guy I knew from high school joined the military because there was nothing else."

"Every single one?"

"Every single one with a prayer there would be a war before they were washed out for being useless."

Those guys never had a chance to go to Paris after a war like the character Gene Kelly plays in that movie. Those guys got nothing. Nulle. Robbie had taken my glasses at about the same time the singing about rebellion ceased though I didn't immediately make the connection.

"What did you do to piss off Louisa?"

"Not me."

I took back my glasses after the woman in the leather trousers had sat herself the opposite side of the table. It took me a moment to understand she was talking to Robbie about the waitress. In that backlot it seemed repetitive rather than cruel coincidence the waitress should have that name. What is Leslie Caron's name in the movie? Lise. Lisa sometimes Gene Kelly calls her but the movie ends before he comes around to calling her Lulu because the movie ends, now get this impossibility, without him ever having painted her in the nude. There is just the one portrait that seems to have come mostly from memory of the first meeting in the cellar braisserie filled with jazz. It isn't even an especially emotional portrait. If the story had spun along like a novel there is no doubt Lisa would have become Lulu once painted nude without ever having been seen naked. I hadn't been able to see any expression of displeasure when the waitress walked away without the tip I had forgotten to provide. I took off the glasses. Again I put back on the glasses. I wondered about a future encountering Louisa in ever so slightly different guises just to avoid being recognized an eternal return.

"She's a beautiful woman, don't you think?" the trousers asked me.

I slid over the book about Gauguin for the singer in leather trousers to see.

"The waitress? That's just a girl. She's little older than the naughty neighbor material Gauguin bedded in Tahiti. I mean when they would still let him touch, before the syphilis surfaced after he returned to Tahiti after a visit back to France, before the disease became obvious like a late line from Baudelaire. Those girls keeping distance put an end to the best paintings."

It had worked, pretending the leather trousers hadn't been talking about Robbie being a beautiful woman. We all looked towards the waitress now bending over near the jukebox after accidently dropping to the floor coins she meant for starting music. She will be mine when? Put money into what? Let me count and count and count. *And nothing shall content my soul till I be evened with him.* I wanted nothing to do with eternal returns trying to return a virginity that could only be lost once.

"And, at this moment, a girl posed ass up to heaven like that statue carved from logs Gauguin kept prominently in his front yard, his welcome to the house, a joke for the passersby. Quel horreur! Quel travais! Quel keister causing quite the scandal, since the statue depicted the local missionary bishop mounting his servant girl from behind, inexorably expanding the iconography of the presentation of the virgin beyond anything then known in contemporary art."

Robbie brought the book back to her side of the table as if to prove me an idiot.

"Which statue? That cannot be true. I've never encountered that story before and I read everything, absolutely everything, there was to read."

She meant she had read the lot when she was reading for her master degree in Impressionism and Post-Impressionism, the one from Iowa, not the one that didn't matter in Michigan, the one that was less than Gene Kelly and Leslie Caron dancing through the same history across a backlot.

"I've never seen that story either," said the trousers.

"You're one of Robbie's art historians too?"

Robbie explained that the redhaired singer in tight leather trousers was very much my own art historian. Before coming to Ann Arbor to work on a doctorate, the woman had been a curator at the museum in my hometown, the museum built from clamshell fortune, with its good Marie Laurencin and even better Utrillo, a genuinely great Utrillo, it should be noted. The woman in tight trousers had been at the museum at least some of the years I worked in the video store. I did not mention I hadn't stepped into that museum those years though at the table that night I had already thought about the Utrillo when thinking about Gene Kelly. In the movie the character Gene Kelly plays paints bad backlot Utrillos. How is love at first sight not nuts even in the movies? Anyway the story about the bishop wasn't in the Gauguin book from the exhibition. It was from an account written by a famous adventurer who lived his whole life sailing the south sea islands, some book I found when back from college searching for the book about writing for the silent movies, not a book an art historian would ever read, the one from the south seas lacking academic gravitas, like all days actually spent on the beach. I did not let go the idea of the beach.

"The best sculpture in Des Moines is this huge metal thing lying in a plaza downtown, three stories high and half a block long, that is a take on Robinson Crusoe's umbrella. The castaway Crusoe whose ship has sank, remember him?" I damned near mentioned the Buñuel movie. I damned near mentioned the Pissarro cityscape. "Only in Des Moines, this monumental sculpture that seems to be nothing about the city, not comment, a thing misplaced, it's just the skeleton of an umbrella. There isn't anything there to actually keep the snow off you. How perfect is that for the misery of the passersby?"

I was told to call the woman in leather trousers Widdershins though I also gathered it was actually the name of her band. I was left to wonder the given name of the woman just to bring me back home to the museum I didn't want to remember. Robbie had always been good about pulling me away from my own insights. It too was a thing graduate students very much love.

"I couldn't get Robbie to meet me in Chicago for the huge Gauguin exhibit there."

"Good for her."

If it was meant to be an insult I wasn't certain it was directed at me. Widdershins went on in a manner both professorial and unapologetic as though her name somehow protected her from conformity, made her a musician, a malcontent, perhaps even an outcast anywhere except the university. She spoke from the university. It is what I had heard from her voice even when taking on a traditional song. With her it was as though the university even more so than the tavern had its underworld all pots of gold beneath the floorboards. *Throw the beans out the window.* Anyway she brought to mind the wrong movie from that Sunday before work.

"It's strange to say but the arguments being fought within the discipline of art history have pretty much dispensed with the paintings, the profession having moved onto complexities and subtleties of its own making. I haven't gone to look at paintings to write something since I left the museum job when I had canvases at hand every day."

It took me a moment to understand Widdershins was saying Robbie had just travelled to look at paintings but had written everything she was going to write before leaving to look at paintings of the insane. There had perhaps been no viewing at all. There had perhaps not even been the expense of travel. There had perhaps been a month never leaving bed. I understood then the second master's degree and the doctorate to follow. How does it go in the wrong musical about the woman with two husbands? Gold is found digging some feller's grave. They fling out the body.

"I like that you're singing old songs of rebellion."

"Really?"

"With communism increasingly discredited, a worker has no choice but to seek other methods of resistance and retaliation and still more resistance from the past, the more distant past, before the rise of manifestos, before theories of the leisure class."

"The songs aren't that old."

"It doesn't matter so long as they seem that old."

I waved my hand towards one wall then another to approve the artificiality of the tavern with all its surfaces fresh with blarney. I could feel de Chirico in my fingertips. In my fist.

"You don't think anything new will come along?"

I laughed but did not mention computers in everyone's home was the new thing.

"I'm starting a new job in the fall that will lead to tenure."

"In Ann Arbor?"

Robbie wouldn't tell me where so I had to assume it was a little place with more farm girls. It was only much later it occurred to me she wanted me to be unable to ever find her.

"I would have gone on painting if I had known no one was ever going to look at them. It would have taken out the worry. Like tenure. Every seventh year a sabbatical not to look at paintings."

"And yet you changed to making movies though movies don't even exist except when projected like so many slides."

It was a line that stunned me for a moment with cascading memories of all that had gone wrong in the choices.

"I just got a raise after six months for acting less and less a savage."

Widdershins laughed while closing the Gauguin book.

"You're quite the savage."

"To them I seem one. How they love to note improvement in attitude! You've really restrained your language! People aren't so afraid of you! Here's some money to express our approval! They forget to even notice the programs I've written, failed to have written, didn't care to have written, stolen from elsewhere. Wasn't Gauguin told the same things when he was a stockbroker? Or haven't you ever read that either? Over the coming years I'll get paid greater and greater sums to think less and less but to behave more and more. It's real life alright."

Paint your wagon but not your canvas.

"With your two-year degree you make more than I will the next two years."

"I was better off studying programming with all the welfare women at a community college."

"More sex you mean."

"Why not more sex?"

"Don't you think it is possible those women were genuinely interested in bettering themselves when on welfare? It is a scapegoat's life that must be wholly escaped because the government machinery will not allow those lives to be improved incrementally, in any natural way, the way everyone else gets to prosper a step at a time. A college education can be an opportunity to those women."

"I wrote their programs for those women because the community college made a point not to flush those silly birds from the bush until it was absolutely unavoidable. The state money was too good not to tether them as long as possible no matter how obviously incompetent they might be. There wasn't a trainable bird in the bunch, not a homing pigeon, not a south seas parrot reciting the times tables."

I thought it prudent not to mention the instructors at the community college hadn't known a damned thing.

"So they instead graduated because you wrote their programs?"

"You got it."

"You thought you were being subversive?"

"Maybe at first. Ultimately it was just another career opportunity. What am I doing now but writing programs but for much less?"

The ones that never knock. Punk attitude. I could feel myself back in leather trousers.

"To those women in the college I smelled from money not yet earned."

This made both the women at the table laugh because every day they smelled so many much more sophisticated stinks at a university. But among the ten or so people I graduated with in computer programming that second year at community college, only three ever got programming jobs, with one of those having gone back to stripping, after what, maybe three months programming. I went to see her strip in this dive where the girls gave little completely nude lap dances for only five dollars. It was fun. She asked if I had seen a television documentary earlier than evening about elephants weeping over their dead. Only later did it occur to me that the stripper believed her own nakedness was primitive, adventurous, all about an intimate voiceover narrative, as much an escape as any voyage to the south seas. Perhaps she almost was a scratch and sniff picture left in some otherwise unread book on Gauguin. The night ended when she toddled off with a group of German businessmen visiting the tractor works. It was the same night I had dropped off Alice at the airport hotel.

ROBBIE ON PARADE

Robbie slept with Widdershins that hot night. The windows were all open but I went to sleep too tired from the drive to overhear a master and main exercise, my guest bed narrow, lonely, the house overlooking a ravine filled with scrub throwing pollen that awoke me before dawn with a swollen throat. I dozed. *Crows maundered into petrification.* In the late morning with sun high the window seemed a painting from a cursed landscape kept secret behind curtains. Robbie was long off to classes. Widdershins was just gone. It was further a widdershins house in that the owners lived in the basement while renting out the upper floors to graduate students. All the same I blissfully ignored the shouting at me from below for using hot water off schedule from the lease agreement. I did not worry their clothes were not cleaned. I flushed the toilet twice. *Probably thinking not to grow up is the brightest kind of maturity for us.* I was lord of the manor. Out on the street walking towards campus I thought about Ezra Pound trying to wheedle an advanced degree out of his university based on all he had published the previous year in London. The professors had laughed. It was their rejection wedded to pomposity I thought I could hear coming from the first of the university buildings I approached. There was a great grinding noise. *Hysterias, trench confessions, laughter out of dead bellies.* At least that patrician dandy Baudelaire in his youth had been clever enough to avoid the universities by repeatedly registering for classes to please a mother keen on her social position, but then never attended the lectures. Baudelaire had left his mornings free for writing poetry. I wished I had done the same. The noise coming from the first building turned out a worker sawing stone three stories up a wall because the alumni had donated yet another gargoyle to cap the rain gutters. The gargoyle looked like Pound. The concrete streets were already a chasing heat.

"Only my daughter won't be coming back from Singapore after all because the money's too good."

"But I know he has at least three girls waiting here."

"It was alright for a summer class but I wouldn't want to do it for a career."

I got lost along the way in confusion over the snatches of dialogue I overheard from the people on the street. Perhaps that morning any sound not a song of revolution was certain to discombobulate if not wrench. There was a park with a small bandstand where I caught the last few minutes of a hand puppet show put on for a crowd of children kept outdoors all summer in a daycare arrangement. The shaded sidewalks around were covered in chalk drawings that constrained in repeated squares seemed mostly desire for television. Burst water balloons fouled the grass everywhere. On the bandstand Punch had called in the Dentist to explain to Judy her new handbag could not eat her though of course the children knew that Punch had given Judy a live alligator not a real handbag for her birthday. Put money in thy purse if you dare. Off came the Dentist's arm. The children squealed. They wouldn't be stealing out of handbags again anytime too soon. I still had designs on the bodhran.

"That's the way to do it."

"Literature essays are idiotic. Could you write poetry simply from a list of rules without ever having read a poem?"

"Still they'll fire him for that just as though he had always been a fool rather than an international prize winner."

At the conclusion of the puppet show a group of the slightly older children were brought to the concrete slab before the stage. They rolled out old style tap boards made from maple slats strapped into a two-foot square like a window blind. The man leading the older children started music from a boombox. I got. A girl from the older children came forward in a twirl that became a tap dance. Rhythm. The girl was replaced by two of the other older children who proceeded through the very same steps but in unison. These two were boys. They were then joined by two girls to repeat the same steps yet again. I thought about computers always processing the same logic the same way. It is their value. I had never before thought it dance. Only when the first girl again joined with steps surpassing the others did conformity stop stretching far to the horizon.

"Who could ask for anything?"

"More."

I wondered if the first girl even owned a handbag.

"She teaches insights into Shakespeare that never crossed Shakespeare's own mind."

"Contempt is the sanctioned response to such sciolists but it gets things nowhere."

Again walking, I finally came across a bookstore rather than the university museum Robbie had suggested, because like Robbie, I too didn't want to look at more actual paintings, not this trip anyway what with Gauguin speaking only to the desperate fantasy. It was paintings tamed within books all the same and I searched among the books for anything speaking to the quotidian I knew. It certainly wasn't the Impressionists. The uniformity of industrial agriculture in Iowa precluded those images from personal reference. They were no better than butterflies at the end of summer. The Pop artists spoke like a drunk angry at a losing game with too much wagered. The Dutch interrupted their seascapes to talk about banking in terms otherwise a centuries old effluvium. I knew where I would end but I was happy for the search. Finally I opened the large German Expressionist book filled with men disfigured by the war now bringing the horror of their flesh to the streets and breadlines and cabarets, legless men on the corner among the diseased prostitutes, shattered artillerymen, with hands of sharpened red fingers, pressed naked together into the barrack showers, crippled men playing cards with their wooden legs almost indistinguishable from the table, an armless soldier before his old easel, trench soldiers whose gasmasks foretell fleshless skulls, then in the center of it all, always, a party of contorted jazz dancers immersed in corrupt pleasures, tap tap, perverse as somnambulists communicating with the dead in messages tapped from under the floorboards. I seemed the same back on the street. I seemed crippled. I had bought the book but back walking, perhaps because the book was tucked under my arm in a paper bag, the grotesque yet meager deformities from programming computers soon gave way to blankness, gave way to pain without expression. I was not a portrait. No one stared.

"Even when he dies his last words won't be his own."

"I wouldn't do it until he grabbed the back of my head."

"More and more it's like parsing failure from within works of genius."

That evening Robbie wanted ground where we interacted without speaking so she found a play the college theater was staging. The play was funny in a violent way though it was not a puppet show. It wasn't even a musical. Afterwards we walked over towards the same tavern from the night before with Robbie mostly keeping one step ahead so she had to turn her head to speak back at me. At first it was as though she meant to teach me how to walk the streets without hearing all the chatter. I was thinking I had already dug a tunnel into a bank from the basement of a funeral parlor.

"The story about the original production is an actress playing the nurse at some point in rehearsals complained that the jokes about the dead mother's dentures were abhorrent. I don't remember where I read this. The playwright showed the actress the dentures from his own dead mother. He actually always carried them in his pocket."

Robbie seemed keen on keeping her pace even but ahead. After all I had the program for the play in my hand for comfort. Robbie went on to tell me how the playwright was murdered with a hammer while sleeping, struck twenty times by his lover, the lover then swallowing pills to kill himself. I could feel her evasiveness by keeping one step ahead while speaking like a lecture that had been delivered many times. Her turning head was trying not to stare at what was left of me from the time at the university after having been at a bank. There seemed parts of me missing. I could still feel the heavy book of the Expressionist paintings beneath my arm though it was not there. It felt like a large sledge. Or an anchor. It was not there so it could be anything.

"Their bodies were found by a driver sent to fetch them."

"That sounds about right."

Death in the guise of chauffeur calls on a playwright murdered in a bedsitter. The hammer and the sickle. And isn't there something like that with a limousine transporting death in Cocteau's movie of Orpheus? I didn't explain all the associations going through my thoughts though I was keen to ask if Robbie believed the owners of funeral parlors lived in the basement while renting the upstairs to the dead. I did not ask. No one says if Joe Orton had his mother's teeth in his pocket when he was pummeled. It must have made for an interesting autopsy with those teeth like left over bits from within a computer not quite reassembled correctly. Aren't people always compared to computers now? I felt words from the play swirl past then through the images of the crippled soldiers while Robbie said it was cruel Joe Orton's few remaining relatives would not allow him to be buried with the lover who had killed him. I supposed the relatives thought it would be too theatrical. In the Orson Welles telling of Othello, Desdemona is marched off to the grave beside the Moor, her lord, her executioner, the man she wished she had been born because more than anything she wanted a death in combat. I did not speak that thought nor the thought of all those soldiers from opposing armies so often buried alive in the same trenches. Instead, because Robbie insisted on keeping one step ahead like Orpheus, the talk of burial put me in a tirade about having to buy my own chair at the bank just to have one that didn't squeak. Bought my own rubber bands. Bought my own calculator. Bought my own desk lamp. Bought my own teeth. Even on the street I never quite lost sense of being immured in the cubicle. I was shouting.

"Then when you get too old they expect you to walk off into the snow but you have to buy your own snow too."

"Stop it."

"Stop it? Stop it? I'll add it to the list of things I should stop. Everyone anymore seems to be telling me to stop something. There's no telling what I shouldn't do next. It. It. Stop it. Of course any lack of conventional moral choices on my part comes from being around computers too long. Invariably they are a moral impasse, computers, because they are binary, a set of switches, ones and zeros, on and off, yang and yin, light and dark, good and evil, heaven and hell. Still, there's no pleasing everyone, is there? Even two choices can be too many choices. You want machines to think for me? What was the name of that philosopher Ezra Pound followed about in those years in London? The one who argued all reality was only in his mind but was proven wrong when the trench mortar disintegrated him."

What was Rimbaud's name for his mother? *La Bouche d'Ombre*. Did he have her teeth? Rimbaud's father was only a captain so it had been easier to like his poems in that class with the nun when I first went to college. Still I was doomed to keep returning to the dandy Baudelaire who had famously stood on the barricades calling for the death of his stepfather, the general, second and much preferred husband his mother, Baudelaire holding a musket though he would have been better served with a hammer, like a lover. Hadn't his mother let the corpse of the first husband be disinterred? Thrown away because she hadn't paid rent on the grave? Of course I share with Baudelaire certain damnation. It is why I could not dismiss him. On the street I went on raging. Robbie and I were headed to the same tavern because I had drunk enough the night before to have forgotten there the book from the Gauguin exhibit. More likely I had left the book for another chance at the bodhran. I thought about the code I wrote but the bank owned without understanding beyond the money made. Controlling capital means profit without the burden of knowledge. That was a point Marx missed. At some point Robbie must have sussed I was angry to find her sleeping with someone else while I was left to churn through more thoughts about disfigurement. I arrived at the tavern alone.

"Where's Robbie?"

"She said you weren't singing tonight so turned off towards the house to find you."

I could see by the expression on Widdershins that Robbie was still a convincing liar. Widdershins and I were sitting at the same table from before but now with the two women who constituted the rest of the house band, the one playing pennywhistle and harp and mandolin, the other fiddle and concertina. I had met the women only in passing the night before. They were both my height but with slender bodies that somehow registered a barely withheld compression rather than slightness. That suggestion might have simply been their dirty clothes not much up from rags but tightly fitted. They might have been hungry women from the community college if not for the ferocity in their eyes. Punk eyes. Lots of mascara. My clothes were clean but I had only something just under twelve dollars in my pockets. I should have stolen the book that morning. It wasn't even hardcover. I could have gone to a money machine but couldn't imagine pulling the bank into the purchase of an art book, worse, pulling the bank into the vacation. My one credit card had reached its limit while in Chicago.

"In the bookstore today I saw a dictionary with words from the firths but not the highlands."

In the tavern I wanted the walls tilted and the doorways zigzagged and the shadows painted in place so they would not leave with the dawn. It was still the same backlot.

"Slàinte mhath, slàinte mhór."

The cleaner of the two women slammed back a shot of cheap vodka. It was not possible to imagine the women dancing jazz with bodies wailing.

"Widdershins. That was one word in it. I made a search to look it up."

The specialized dictionary I had browsed at the bookstore was of language recognized from reading verse long before the class with the obsessed nun. *Nine inch will please a lady.* No misunderstanding that. Yet Robbie Burns is a poet so imbued with belated respectability I was taught his poems when a schoolchild in winter rooms where radiators near wet corduroy smelled for heather through the mind. *Thou need na start awa sae hasty wi' bickerin brattle.* There was a time when I could recite that one. Now every now and then at the bank a mouse would dash through the cubicles on way to the lunch room, a field mouse reduced to lending practices, would dash past while I was coding a mortgage foreclosure application meant to take away the whole farm. Pick on someone your own size. *The present only toucheth thee.* There in Ann Arbor it was another scorching night.

"My sister Ailith says you're a fucking bastard until you buy us a round."

Ailith and Catriona. They had introduced themselves by describing all the places they had already travelled for their studies in anthropology, listing islands and outlands without the tattoos such women would now exhibit in validation, that tattooed woman from the video store so unique then, yet even without tattoos the effect seemed heated shadows over ruddy flesh, the short hair of the two musicians dyed black, bodies seeming to be waiting on yet more ink. Still Ailith and Catriona both spoke with Glaswegian accents so thick it was often impossible to comprehend just what emotion played across the face. It all seemed part of the act.

"In the Sunda Islands, Indonesia, mind, not the Hebrides, the natives once would stack twigs at the spot where a liar had been caught out, to show that they all knew she was a liar."

"Robbie is a terrible liar," claimed Widdershins.

I wondered what all Robbie got done with men without Widdershins discovering. I remembered Robbie in bed once telling me I was the first student she had ever fancied that far, far as the bed anyway, though perhaps not the only one fancied for purposes of her education. I suppose I was at least right to take her for thinking like a man. *The Knack.* The movie starts on the line of girls down the staircase waiting a turn. The full title of course is *The Knack And How To Get It.* It was a while before someone in class whispered I was the only man Robbie had ever been seen walking with on the street. I had not needed a whisper the night before to notice the tavern meant to be a conflation of Ireland into Scotland into Brigadoon was patronized entirely by women. *Empty your heart of its mortal dream.* That might seem unfair. *And How To Get It* is not part of its title when first a theatrical play. *The Knack* only. In the play but not so much the movie the young woman becomes dominant very quickly by crying the word rape for three pages to anything the men say.

"This one's a natural campfire builder."

There seemed to be some presumption that Robbie was absent because I had hurt her. The women were angry with me. Widdershins pointed my attention to the perfectly square sign near the perfectly plumb door proclaiming no unescorted male would be seated. That too tilted the backlot more towards Berlin than Glasgow but nothing gave in shape pictures from the Expressionist book. In The Knack the young woman crying rape has never been touched, not ever. It is like a diagnosis.

"My sister Ailith says there are unnatural reasons you won't buy us a round."

Catriona said this with a mocking American accent she took on as though translating for me.

"I'm already too much a banker to still concede anything to shrunken heads."

With gesture I somehow managed to imply something sexual like from a cabaret but the Glaswegians did not at all find that funny. To disarm my defenses Widdershins took away the bottle of beer I was drinking. Louisa. The same waitress from the night before interrupted to take my food order but everything on the menu I mentioned wasn't available. I asked if this was because it was late at only ten-thirty. Widdershins laughed sardonically then passed my beer to the other two women as though just once I were so beautiful I had been served first.

"No. The place is closing down for good at the end of the week so there is only what's left."

I think it was one of the Glaswegians not the waitress who told this but I don't remember. It somehow dazed me to be eating remnants poorly cooked because no one had reason still to give a damn. It seemed a scramble from the trenches. I thought about the last six months working on all that obsolete software at the bank. There seemed to be a connection I couldn't quite fathom but felt pulling at my skin through those images of disfigured men from the war. Loot in coffins. Mothers in coffins. Widdershins asked if she could have some of my fries. I think I said something about the place not accurately recreating the atmosphere it intended, fries not called chips like in a real pub, the language wrong even, as though that dictionary back at the bookstore were screaming in protest, shouting because I had not bought it too. I am shouted at by books all the time now.

"You think you know what we are talking about?"

"The cellar next the toilets even smells like Glasgow next the river."

"Glasgow has claimed vomit and urine exclusively for its own use?"

Widdershins put her hand on my arm to take my eyes off the twin sisters.

"You don't recognize me, do you?"

"From just last night?"

"I was in the video place where you worked all the time."

It took me a moment to remember her with the huge blonde woman who attracted all attention, the huge woman having hands that could palm a basketball on the run, wide shoulders over strong arms, an amazingly large head leonine in massive amounts of golden hair. One of the books I had browsed that morning had been collages of men in lion heads threatening prostrate maidens. Swords. Revolvers. Whips. It had seemed desperate fantasy no different from Gauguin if I squinted even a little to get past the comedy onto the judgements, the damnations, the strangulation of laughter. The huge woman had run a charity shop of some sort across the street from the video store and when she came for movies I never once failed to notice the huge woman was so proportionately perfect everyone found her expanse beautiful. Wasn't that Baudelaire's fantasy? To be a cat on the lap of a giant woman? Wasn't that what Orson Welles had written home from Ireland, that he was walking the road of the giants? I had forgotten all about the huge woman's girlfriend with the red hair. Still nothing tilted. There was nothing forthcoming from mere surprise.

"I remember now."

"I should have kept the assistant curator post back there since I haven't been able to get anything out of my doctorate."

I was about to ask what she had gone off to teach that morning if it wasn't a paying position when the understanding suddenly occurred to me she owned the tavern. She intended to follow to whatever job Robbie was off to take in a couple weeks. Of course it needed no genius to guess Widdershins wouldn't be closing the backlot if it turned profit. The charity shop had sold mostly baby clothes the huge woman had trouble folding with such large hands. I made one look around the tavern before turning open the Gauguin book to what I thought was the relevant passage.

"This is the part right after where Gauguin cannot convince the native governor of Tahiti that the artistic mission he's been sent on by the French government is not a cover for espionage."

"Is that more shit from the book you invented?"

"Life at Papeete soon became a burden. It was Europe – the Europe I had thought to shake off – and that under the aggravating circumstances of colonial snobbery, with its imitation, grotesque to the point of caricature, of civilization's customs, fashions, vices, and absurdities. Was I to have made this long journey only to find what I had fled?"

Catriona responded to Gauguin in his grave.

"Yeh fuckin' eejit. When Tahiti was first discovered, girls would trade their bodies to the sailors for iron nails, only the nails had to be larger in proportion to the girl's pulchritude. You know that word? A girl would hold up a length of stick to indicate the size of iron nail at which she priced her beauty."

"And a pile of sticks didn't necessarily prove every sailor was welcome."

"My sister says she thinks you're a dwarf."

"Do you remember that part where Gauguin writes about how the missionaries used to tattoo such girls with a special mark to shame them? But he never describes the mark. Can you tell me what it was?"

"You know the Scots women when transported by the English to the far ends of the earth for petty crimes were forced to whore for the sailors of their own prison and the sailors of any other passing ship that could catch up."

Rape. Rape. Rape. Catriona meant Tahiti and all those waters were close to paradise only long before Gauguin got there. If not for the children in the park perhaps my attempts to force past the backlot into Dr Caligari might have succeeded but the walls would not tilt. I remained married to those three movies seen on television before starting the job and especially married to *An American In Paris*. I thought about the scene where Gene Kelly with a checkered tablecloth over his head to make himself a woman dances with the guardian of the girl who would soon become the love of his life. *Evidently the man doesn't like jazz. What else is there?*

"Get off me."

My hand under the table couldn't block the roundhouse punch Ailith made at my ear when she glimpsed me feeling between the legs of the leather trousers that seemed my own. I went to the floor. I went to the floor with the leathers of Widdershins still so immediate on my fingers I didn't make a fist in response. The night before I had been trying to blow life into the bagpipes when clutched in my fist. But what painting again was it that Robbie had shown in class that was like that with the putti blowing in life? I had fallen madly in love with Robbie the first time I ever saw her. My head spun into its pain. The first missionaries arrived in Tahiti came on a ship named a word you can find in slang dictionaries, the name of the ship now slang for selling old merchandise as new merchandise, the true faith, but the same word passed my fingers that day in the bookstore dictionary, the Scots dictionary meant for childhood memories defining the word otherwise, the word there meaning gloomy and stupid and, in reference to soil, too infertile to produce a crop. No. Not Louisa. That wasn't the word. I thought about Robbie waiting in bed for Widdershins. In the madhouse I had with a length of rope not so different from ship rigging taken obtuse measurements of my height and breadth each morning on waking. *Sonsie pintle. Cock of the walk.* And still I had tried to hang myself.

ROBBIE SITS IN
JUDGEMENT

There is no end of choices for movies when taking on insanity. I suppose for a painter I ought have leaned towards *Spellbound* with its dream sequences designed by Salvador Dali but there isn't any other part of the movie worth seeing twice. Even with the nutter being played by Gregory Peck. Of course most would say the gold standard is *Cuckoo Nest*, working class man faces soulless authority, it being hard not for me to favor that too, but the year I spent confined for madness, I had a television that included an arts channel that frequently showed *Morgan!*. In that movie David Warner runs around in a gorilla suit frightening people until in the last shot the rising camera reveals he has planted a flowerbed at the madhouse in the design of a giant hammer and sickle. His mother has earlier berated him for betraying the working class by becoming a painter. My own mother was president of her union local but she had been too uneducated to ever embrace anything like communism. She liked crossword puzzles. I once had to give her the answer to the puzzle clue *Waiting On Lefty*. Odets. Unfortunately I never thought to keep my mother's teeth when she died, wasn't in a position to demand them from the madhouse if thought had come to mind, and anyway I had never paid close attention to Joe Orton because the movie made from the play *Loot* is a real stinker, the start a pathetic attempt to open up the play, then the timing of everything that follows seemingly perverted by the start. *Loot* is great only as a play. That insight perhaps explains a great deal what would happen the coming year at the bank. It was all performed with understanding I was under the inescapable influence of the three television movies.

"These paintings aren't what you did best."

I was finally getting around to showing Robbie the paintings I had been making with Janice over my shoulder. Robbie had wanted me in Ann Arbor only to the see the paintings, but there distantly facing each other from either end of the couch in her apartment, the paintings between us, Robbie felt disappointment I was not providing yet more impetus to her career. She needed me to be a madman somnambulist. That had been true right from the start between us. Here I thought it excessive for her to worry about publish or perish in a job she hadn't even started. We did not talk about the dozen or more times I had painted her nude before fucking back after her art history lectures when, because of Alice, some kind of enforced delay seemed a natural way about the brushes. Everything widdershins had gone into the paintings. Robbie had very much wanted to be pictured the succubus to my madness so of course eventually she altogether stopped the fucking to twist me past pleasure. It was after that I moved onto the cinema classes.

"Garbage in, Dada out?"

It was too much a programming joke to not go past Robbie in some wrong way.

"There's nothing here like that last you painted when taking my class, the pilot in leather helmet stepping from within a refrigerator filled with old church paintings, the refrigerator angled in shape like a coffin, that little bit of blood out of Christ's ribs from a spilled ketchup bottle, the baloney ring his halo."

A fighter pilot from above the trenches. It was myself painted in some futurist fashion as though I too had fought in the war before dada and surrealism and expressionism and all the other futilities that followed in rage. It was not surprising Robbie still failed to recognize me for the pilot behind goggles in the painting. She had never let me take off all my clothes. It was still a body worth forgetting, worth not looking back on. I remember her insistence to always be on top.

"You didn't like what I painted in the madhouse either."

"It was a hospital. Do you still not acknowledge all the good it did you?"

"It was simple enough art therapy. Paint a jug. Paint a flower. Paint a landscape. My lord! Don't all the drugs make the colors smell like vegetables? And I cannot remember the date of anything! Not even my own birthday! It is certainly a struggle to paint something that doesn't look crazy! Is that supposed to be a bird? Is it supposed to be a portrait of yourself? When will there come the day of capitulation when all paint brushes are hammered into birdcages? Perches! Cages! Perches! I think I might even have been Loplop for a while."

There are plenty of movies if you want to take on insanity though I was out from the madhouse three years before *Birdy* was released. I laughed myself so dizzy the first time I saw that one at the video store I vomited into the wastebasket below the cash register. *Une Semaine de Bonté* ends not with more men with lion heads but with a young woman, her veil clung to her weeping face, making an acrobatic flip over a pigeon. Loplop. That madman Max Ernst identified himself as Loplop though it was a name that could have come straight from *Doctor Dolittle*. I had looked at that in the bookstore then was surprised to see the expressionist book end with Beckman's painting of giant birds devouring men. A blue woman with blue hair is hatching from a giant egg. For a moment I supposed at the community college I too had been a bird of some sort without talons. Here I raged. I don't even remember it all.

"Enough," insisted Robbie.

"What good does any of this do now your thesis has been accepted?"

It was winter when I was first in the madhouse after coming home at the end of those seven months in Paris. The last night the arts channel was on the air before going out of business it showed *Morgan!* one last time, but the channel went blank just before that shot rising in the air over the flowerbed, as though it were a counter-revolutionary moment turned to white noise, like life since. I never have had a gorilla suit. But I did have the masks Robbie had sent me after her staging *The Gas Heart* at that college somewhere among the farmlands far to the west in Iowa. Robbie had counted on those masks to make trouble. I had taken to wearing the large bright red mouth on my head fairly frequently in the weeks before getting turfed at the video store by Mrs Apollonia Whitton. The full title of course is *Morgan! A Suitable Case For Treatment*. Far as I know there is no play where the title is simply *Morgan!*.

"You know only too well the art therapy developed by the group of doctors I wrote about continues to be used. The thesis is about madness inherent in contemporary painting. There is only so much to be said about the doctors since the doctors are far more known for their medical work, after they all left Scotland, than for the canvases they painted when working and teaching together in Edinburgh."

"In the madhouse I used to make wine in my cell using sugar and grape juice fermented in a sealed plastic bag. Merlot le Fou 1982."

It was too much a video store joke to not go past Robbie in some wrong way. Jean-Paul Belmondo is plenty nutty in that musical where he is always chasing around but never finding Jean Seberg. I think I had seen that one too on the arts channel. Definitely I had seen *The Knack And How To Get It* on that channel but it had been merely amusement without personal insight then. More important on that channel I had also seen a movie where the madman believes he can kill with his voice but later at the video store that movie proved so impossible to obtain its rarity undermined its believability. *The Shout*. I could rage but not shout. I was released from the madhouse in the next winter a week after the arts channel ceased broadcast.

"Maybe you would have gotten out sooner without wine."

Baudelaire in his last years stranded in Belgium so conflated the injustices done him he wrote his mother he considered himself to be in prison. It seems apparent that at the end of the road Baudelaire's correspondences of the senses becomes Rimbaud's derangement of the senses. Perhaps only sight and sound without confusion ever receive liberation. I got out of the madhouse by painting not one but three absolutely perfect small knockoffs of Renoir. My doctor was so pleased she kept the three pretty faces of imagined young girls. She had not looked like Ingrid Bergman, that doctor, not even looked like the doctor from the movie *Alfie*. Eleanor Bron. Pretty. Remember her from *Two For The Road* with an American accent not her own? *Children are mirrors of death*. That is a line from Sartre's autobiography. *'Ere, you can't be certain summink's there, can you, yet?* That is not from Sartre. *I'm one o' them as 'as done this to 'im*. That one is practically from Sartre but isn't. Obviously I'm making fun of the movie but perhaps not so obviously the play especially too. *Alfie* was another movie from the arts channel.

Anyway that doctor of mine, it had a face left other options than a cure.

"Are you joking?"

In the video store that day I brought in my friend with the tattoos, I was distinctly thinking not about marking south sea island whores but about the movie where Rod Steiger's skin illustrations, don't you ever call them tattoos, are windows into the future. I wanted change. In *The Illustrated Man* two children feed their parents to lions within their virtual reality room. I still think Mrs Apollonia Whitton should have had the dignity of dying from fear of lion biting rather than fear of lips kissing. She wasn't so much a prude away from her church friends. In her youth she had tried to be an actress. All the same I had never told Robbie how her mask caused Mrs Apollonia Whitton to drop dead when I jumped out of the shadows of the doorway that night she was taking the day's sales over to the bank. There on the couch I let that confession pass unmentioned. These were thoughts like children tapping at the window blind but still I couldn't make the walls tilt.

"There is an old movie where the parents of two malicious children plan to free the family from the effects of their computerized house by taking a vacation to Iowa because they think there are no computers there."

Robbie couldn't understand what I was talking about while my mind found its circles. And anyway I was fibbing. The reference to Iowa is in the book but not the movie. You see what I mean? Play better than movie? There I go again mocking Alfie talking to the camera. Paintings done from photographs rarely better those done from life. From memory it goes even worse. Still maybe it makes sense in some inversed way that watching too many movies becomes like tattoos on living skin.

"You knew all along the doctor at the madhouse was from Scotland, didn't you?"

"I knew after I called to check up on you."

"You knew before I ever got there."

"How would I know that?"

"That doctor told me you interviewed her for your thesis."

"She misunderstood when I called about how you were getting on."

That doctor in the madhouse had told me how when she was a student at the Royal Art Academy in the 1950s she had painted Sean Connery in the nude but he got sacked after the first week for trying to unionize the other models. It wasn't hard to imagine housewives all rushing off the husbands extra early without breakfast then forming a line up the stairs. The Knack and how to get cheese and butter. In business terms the career change to modelling was a lateral move since Connery had his clothes off all the time anyway. When I told my mother all this during one of her visits to the madhouse, the story for her was just another injustice in union suppression. My mother had never seen a Sean Connery movie.

"Anyway I painted several women like absinthe drinkers leaning far into their elbows on the table."

"Where are those canvases?"

"Taken from me for punishment over the wine."

There was actually only one great painting that year in the madhouse. Madness had glimpsed my future when my own thoughts struggled against just the next day. I had dreamt of a box in my future, dreamt myself sitting in a windowless cubicle seventy or eighty hours all hours of the week, with instructions that the Sunday concluding the one week vacation that year belonged to the office in its entirety, with some idea, I suppose, some underlying idea, that vacations precluded God. I had to get back to Des Moines the next day. In prison I painted the dream as myself trying to wrestle open a large immovable black box ten times my own size. I struggle. Women in business suits look on, timing me, glancing at their watches impatiently, dance cards dangling from strings attached to their wrists. But it was all too menacing for that Scottish doctor to see the allusion to Gauguin's painting of the Breton peasant women watching Jacob wrestle an angel.

"There is another thing I've been wanting to tell you about for your thesis. I've been working on new automated teller machines that speak an Edinburgh accent because some idiot somewhere in Indiana decided that was an accent everyone could understand. It scares children. It makes dogs bark. It reminds me so much of doctors I keep thinking my money comes only with a prescription."

"Now I know that's not true."

It was true though I knew she would never believe it. Speaking machines were very unusual back then. She would never believe it just as she and Widdershins in bed had concluded no Gauguin book by a sailor had ever been published. I still own my copy of that book too. Still Robbie was more comfortable now it wasn't possible I knew something she didn't already know.

"There are no other paintings? What's this one?"

"The one from the madhouse I painted of the girl who most days thought she was Joan of Arc. Did I never tell you about her?"

"Did you know the only known painting of Joan of Arc was also painted by a Scotsman?"

I looked that up later but the painting has never been identified so is presumed lost. I answered myself playing both parts over Robbie's consuming need to teach art history without the actual paintings.

"Girl. I lived in France on a student exchange program when I was only thirteen."

"Nutter. Really? I was about ten when my school offered French lessons on Saturdays but my mother wouldn't cough up the few dollars it cost. Public schools are supposed to be free. It was a matter of principle. How much French did you speak before you went there?"

"Girl. None at all. Nulle. And I didn't understand a word I heard that first month I was in Paris. Which was terrible because no one in the family I was living with spoke much English. I was very lonely. But then one morning I came down to breakfast and shocked everyone because I suddenly started speaking perfect French."

"Nutter. It had been delivered to you by an angel in a dream?"

"Girl. How else could it have happened? But not a dream."

"Nutter. Keep that to yourself."

Robbie didn't enjoy the story whatsoever though I had given it a theatrical interpretation especially when taking on the dialogue of the girl. Robbie took education too seriously to allow for angels.

"Couldn't you put all that imagination into painting?"

Jean Seberg? No. A picture of Maria Falconetti came to mind. Falconetti was Jeanne d'Arc in the famous silent movie that everyone thought was lost in its entire version until an old print was found a few years earlier than that summer in the closet of a lunatic asylum. I shit you not. *La Passion de Jeanne d'Arc.* That place I worked when I was a teenager had some fragmented version for rent. But where the hell else but the madhouse would you look for anything completely intact?

At least my first boss at the bank insisted that's how he left Jean Seberg.

"Imagination? I remain excluded from all life unless I capitulate to some form of slavery under supervisors who never see human nature in an employee's action. In business all action except that being exploited is believed an act of will. Supervisors are like savages who have never seen a photograph of themselves."

"It can't be all bad."

"No one here knows you come from a welfare family? You never told them the story about your mother sending you an unsigned Christmas card with a heating bill in it she needed you to pay? No. Even Widdershins doesn't know you've transformed yourself. Isn't that true?"

"I would appreciate you keeping it to yourself."

It was after all almost exactly the command from the first boss that first day at the bank I had been obeying all along. And the untouched oils of Orson Welles atop the ass were his virgin on the road heading towards a signaling though wandering star, heading towards a kind of miraculous birth, stardom in the Dublin theater of Micheál MacLiammóir. It's said MacLiammóir often went into trances when acting on stage. He claimed to read people's minds and in his memoir on the making of *Othello* he states he knew before Welles that Betsy Blair was too modern to play Desdemona. Who better for Welles to caste as Iago than a somnambulist who seemed all plough and stars but was nothing of the sort? I am not what I am. I cannot think of that tavern in Ann Arbor now without thinking of Micheál MacLiammóir. MacLiammóir was his own backlot with a face kept in greasepaint all hours of the day and night. Reporters from the newspapers politely called him artistic. He had been a successful child actor in England. And though he never touched a woman in his life, his real name was Alfie. There's another one for the bishops scribbling the testament of Hollywood.

"Widdershins doesn't even know my mother is still alive."

Against Nature. In her class Robbie had had us read a selection from *Against Nature* to explain all those canvases of the supernatural. And what then was the name for Robbie's pussy? *Against All Odds? Against All Flags? Against The Wind? Decision Against Time? Fantomas Against Fantomas? Atlas Against The Czar?* The movies provided no end of possibilities for love at first sight. Widdershins. Robbie had more to teach if only to prove she was far from the lap of her mother.

"Joan of Arc wasn't burnt at the stake because she heard angels speaking. Dressing like a man was against church law. What clothes do you suppose she modelled for the painting? Armor of course. But in prison the second she capitulated into the proper clothes she was raped by the English guards no longer afraid of God."

It was apparent Robbie was coaxing me to speak more openly about the madhouse since there seemed to be no painting that told the worst of the nights there. I could not have appeared that far from the worst of those nights with the bruised eye and the swollen lip the Glaswegians left me before I tired of the abuse. I am not sure now what sin I believed I needed to be absolved through such scourging. Capitulation. Degradation. In the tavern the bottle I swung had cost Ailith a tooth. That had made me laugh so hard about the false teeth foreseen in her future the other had backed away. All that painting Robbie nude had made me her creation in the way all somnambulists in a coffin must belong to somebody. Still I started gathering my paintings to put them back in the new utility vehicle. After the madhouse I had played that silent movie *Dr. Caligari* damned near every afternoon in the video store. I knew the rules of the game.

"Twelve hours a day at the office then working all hours of the night whenever the pager goes off means I cannot escape bringing to bed a stench of servitude."

She knew I was saying I wouldn't ever again want a fuck from her.

"You do understand, right, that the Gauguin show in Chicago was last year not last week?" asked Robbie. She picked up the Gauguin book I had brought to her couch with my own paintings. "Here in the front of your book. See. It gives the dates the show was hanging in Chicago. September through December."

No. I remembered it being two days ago I walked through the galleries when the guard told me I could not stop to draw. Everything suddenly seemed skewed but only within did things turn on angles not angels. I was appalled to notice the walls around me were unchanged. The light did not shift from bright. Only with concentration that seemed like pushing out from the cubicle could I recall being in Chicago to arrange with an advertising agency a commercial for the war hero. I could see the war hero standing in his hotel suite with his hair still wet from a shower. The walls there arched overhead with menace like a cathedral for the damned. Alice was in the room. Then suddenly I could see Alice with me in the galleries shoved along by the crowds so fast past the Gauguins we held hands to keep from being separated. Obviously in Ann Arbor I had been blocking another round of memories. Alice had bought me the hardback book for the exhibition because all exhibits anymore exit through the giftshop and now that book seems like some strange variation on Sartre writing about being and exits and no exits.

RIGHT IN THE TEETH

FADE IN:

INT: IT FITS INFORMATION TECHNOLOGY OFFICE — NEW MORNING

Mrs Peel and MISS CUMMERSUM, the busty new dental assistant, stand at the raised table preparing a lunch platter obviously not meant for themselves. There is a huge amount of food. Mrs Peel is slicing up a brain. Miss Cummersum's dental uniform is white, severe, but modestly fetishist with a few too many buttoned straps and white fishnet stockings deliberately torn.

> MRS PEEL
> He is suddenly very successful. You
> would, Miss Cummersum, be doing me a
> great favor if you would take the
> horny little dwarf off my hands. A
> woman at my age must not be seen
> keeping house with hunchbacks.
> Eventually everyone notices that my
> breasts aren't nearly so
> comparatively firm.

> MISS CUMMERSUM
> It isn't any easier for a young
> dental assistant whose experience
> with men is entirely limited to what
> gobs come out of their mouths. I'm
> not ready to move onto knowing their
> less immediate deformities.

                    MRS PEEL
It is perhaps not prudent to put off
knowing the other parts of a man too
long. I sometimes regret not having
ended my years as a dental assistant
with a - how shall I say it - a
rougher graduation. Instead I
dallied until forced from the
position because of troubles with my
hands.

Miss Cummersum pauses to regard Mrs Peel's hands
rapidly preparing the meats.

                  MISS CUMMERSUM
Troubles?

INSERT - LIVE ACTION

Real manicured woman's hand chopping real cow
brain.

BACK TO SCENE

                  MRS PEEL
After three years the dental
assistant here I had grown no fewer
than eighteen fingers on just this
one hand. I choked to death the last
man whose teeth I cleaned.

                  MISS CUMMERSOM
Husbands must eat what they are fed.

                  MRS PEEL
Technical vocations inevitably leave
a girl open to very loose
interpretations of what is normal.

                    MISS CUMMERSOM
I have been offered work fashion
modeling the new clothing line.

                       MRS PEEL
True. Modeling the clothes here at
IT FITS, by means of contraction and
constriction, did return my hands to
a photogenic ten fingers, but what
deformity are you seeking to
overcome?

                    MISS CUMMERSOM
Virginity.

                       MRS PEEL
True. That is perhaps the one
affliction most easily cured by
altering hem length. So why not
think again on the hunchback now he
is a success?

                    MISS CUMMERSUM
His primary bulge is at the wrong
end. And on the reverse side. I
think it would be more adventuresome
modelling.

                       MRS PEEL
Removing a leather corset only looks
like it requires eighteen fingers.

                    MISS CUMMERSUM
                     (points fingers
                      at mouth)
May I try just a taste?

                        MRS PEEL
        There's plenty.

But instead of taking a bit of food Miss
Cummersum takes Mrs Peel's fingers into her mouth
with some sense of seeking knowledge.

INSERT - LIVE ACTION

Real manicured woman's hand wiggling about a
young woman's mouth. The hand pulls away.

BACK TO SCENE

                        MRS PEEL
                  (regarding cold
                   cuts)
        Oh dear. Chairman Povereese abhors
        lunch meat over which career
        opportunities have been discussed.
        He can always taste it like so much
        bitter old Bolshevism.
                  (removes upper layer
                   of meats)
        In fact we had better pitch all this
        top stuff into the garbage.

Miss Cummersum has in fact gained knowledge for
she is now inexplicably wearing an extravagant
fetish outfit. Leather corset. Zippered skirt.
A single studded glove that covers only past the
knuckles. Slave buckles on wrists and ankles.
Her crotch a metal device like a snarl of savage
teeth. A dog chain around her neck hangs down
her back and drags across the floor. A mouth gag
ball hangs by its straps.

                    MISS CUMMERSOM
                    (spitting while
                    fingering own
                    teeth)
          This meat is for the chairman of the
          board?

                      MRS PEEL
          Eating meat is best reserved to
          those educated in slaughtering the
          weak.

Programmer I and Programmer II enter from
direction of the lectern. Miss Cummersum crosses
before the table in the strut of a fashion model.

                    PROGRAMMER I
          Do I hear a dog barking?

                    MISS CUMMERSUM
          Piss off. I'm not the dental
          assistant anymore. I'm free. Mrs
          Peel's fingers have changed my life.

                    PROGRAMMER II
          With only ten of them?

Miss Cummersum struggles to fit herself with the
mouth gag. Frustrated. Distracted. Finally she
instead tries to work a button that seems loose.

                    MISS CUMMERSUM
          The greatest imbalance of modern
          industrial justice is that buttons
          actually work from the outside.
          They work no matter where you happen
          to be. They work when intoxicated.

They work for unlicensed
practitioners. I fear they may
sometimes even work for hunchbacks.

MRS PEEL

Miss Cummersum has decided to become
a solitary simply because I asked
her to take on the hunchback.

PROGRAMMER II
(to Miss Cummersum)

Do you expect the hunchback to climb
into your clothes with you before
undressing you?

PROGRAMMER I

The least you could do is lift your
skirt to give us all a running
start.

MRS PEEL

A good rule of thumb is to leave
alone any girl too young to dress
herself.

Miss Cummersum interrupts with loud choking while
again struggling with the mouth gag.

MISS CUMMERSUM

I will demand of the hunchback that
he leaves untouched anything he
sees. There is no reason a man
contorted on his own terms shouldn't
be obedient to mine. Isn't that so?
At least his deformities aren't
based on common fiduciary
responsibilities. I think. That's
right? No? Perhaps it is just he

looks that way because his clothes
won't fit.

PROGRAMMER II

It was the economist John Maynard
Keyes who said that enterprise will
fade and die if the animal spirits
are dimmed.

MRS PEEL

Economists can make bark anything
except a dog.

Igor and Denshag enter past Denshag's desk with
Denshag having his arm draped awkwardly around
Igor's shoulders and hump.

DENSHAG

I always knew you'd be a great
success.

IGOR

I don't get it at all.

DENSHAG

Even our beloved chairman of the
board wishes to meet your mouth.
Just try not to intrude the rest of
yourself. No matter what else
happens. No matter how bent over
you find yourself. Legs akimbo.
Buttocks spread.

IGOR

But I don't even remember what
number it was you think is so
special all a sudden.

                    DENSHAG
This isn't some kind of magic trick
in where two people try to think of
the same number. This is the
numerological event of the kind one
normally associates with conquering
generals and eminent figures from
antiquity, with the rise of empires,
with leaps forward across the seas,
the subjugation of indigenous
peoples...
            (eyes Miss Cummersum)
The dental assistant! I don't dare
tell you the number now.
            (confidentially but
             hoarse with desire)
A silent tongue makes for a happy
life.

Denshag removes his arm from Igor's shoulders and
studies it to see if the hump has infected him.

                    IGOR
My whole life I've never overheard
anything private.

                    MRS PEEL
Already in his greatness he concedes
the privileges of his birth. Such
modesty!

                    IGOR
I suppose the number six normally
gets called out only to the heavens?
Even in a clothing company?

                    PROGRAMMER I
Into the cuffs.

                    PROGRAMMER II
     Into the linings.

                      MRS PEEL
     Into the pockets.

                   MISS CUMMERSUM
                  (to the fetish gag)
     Into the teeth.

                      DENSHAG
     Listen to those cheers from the
     workers now so far below you.

                       IGOR
     For me?

                      DENSHAG
     You cannot expect them to speak
     about you directly within earshot
     except to discuss what you are
     wearing though discussion about what
     you are wearing is now a requirement
     in their job descriptions. Dress
     well. No need to show them what
     you're made of. Don't stoop to
     that.

Denshag wistfully touches the fetish doll sitting
on his desk.

                      DENSHAG
     Isn't it amazing how all memory of
     my wife continues to shrink while
     the woman herself has become such a
     gigantic beast? You really must
     come to dinner some evening. I

can't begin to describe the horror
in watching that woman eat.

Everyone turns look towards a GREAT NOISE OF POMP
AND CIRCUMSTANCE, APPLAUSE, AND CYMBALS coming
from past the programming cubicles.

                    DENSHAG
         Here comes Chairman Povereese now.

Mrs Peel steps up to push Miss Cummersum towards
Igor.

                    MRS PEEL
         I would like you to meet Miss
         Cummersum.

                      IGOR
         Another woman? But did you not just
         cheer my success?

                    MRS PEEL
         IT FITS corporate policy includes a
         list of items that must never touch
         this kitchenette floor. The list
         has been alphabetized for employee
         convenience before being
         irreversibly encrypted under a login
         procedure that is too obsolete to be
         remembered. Forgetfulness is the
         means by which modern leadership
         secures the past.

                      IGOR
         You mean I have forgotten you
         already?

Igor immediately forgets Mrs Peel. He approaches
Miss Cummersum but his foot accidently catches on

the dog chain attached to her neck. She angrily
pulls the chain away.

> MISS CUMMERSUM
>
> The whole point of the leash is that
> there isn't anyone at the other end.
> The whole point of the mouth gag is
> there isn't anyone to accommodate
> even with small talk. The number
> six? It is too late to include me
> in your sums now that I'm dressed to
> be a solitary.

> IGOR
>
> Have you taken pills from the locked
> cabinet of the dental office? Are
> they poison enough to overcome my
> success? Am I to understand the
> pills are deadly only if obtained
> with a legal prescription?

> MISS CUMMERSUM
>
> You will suffocate me in my sleep if
> you are half the depraved monster
> your hump implies. Promise?

> MRS PEEL
>
> Miss Cummersum has pledged death
> before dishonor even though when in
> her mouth my fingers were crossed.

> IGOR
>
> I'm not certain computer programming
> has prepared me for a tragedian's
> night of comforts.

Chairman Povereese enters with a confusion of
WILD ANIMAL ROARS from somewhere back down the
hallway. The Chairman is this time wearing a

lion's mask with its mouth wide open and with
huge sabretooth fangs jutting from the jaw. He
wears the crown from before. Miss Cummersum
steps forward expecting to be sacrificed but the
Chairman pushes past her to drag Igor to the
floor like an animal killing its prey. Igor
screams.

FADE OUT

INVITATION TO DANCE

It was another weekend working at the bank again very much that third musical watched on television the weekend before starting the job. Gold fever. I kept humming the tunes. By that second summer I had so much gold in my mouth even Louisa commented on it when looking up at me from her cubicle chair. It was quite the claim, fit for claim jumping. But Louisa wasn't interested in my mouth beyond a certain amazement I would mortify myself in that way. Anyway Des Moines is a French town in name but has been forsaken by God since the monks were driven out to make way eventually for talking machines, in heaven and in orisons a city without name doomed to tumble into the pit, the pit being dug by all who slave there, every day right through the weekend, deep in their fevers. No Name City. Like the mining town in Paint Your Wagon. The mall is where the monastery stood. In fever at the bank over the last year I had several times put aside the real work to again create false addresses for false accounts on the bank that established what Des Moines had never possessed, a decadent French Quarter filled with jazz, whorehouses, opium dens, gambling rooms, a Storyville. *Throw the beans out the window.* Place des Coup de Matraque. Rue de Espoir Perdu. La Tour de Bouche Encore Sale. Henri-Georges Clouzot was receiving yet more poison pen letters at Boulevard La Belle Dame Sans Merci. In fever away from the bank deep into the night I worked on my claymation movie based on a storyboard I had drawn evenings at the laundromat based on a screenplay I had mostly written over lunch hours back the first summer at the bank. Even now I feel the completed movie is not much an exaggeration from life. After several false starts I scaled the plasticine characters to about eighteen inches to live in proportion with the three-inch nude figure so pleasing to Mr Denshag. Perhaps that nude of a very busty blonde woman found in the crypt of the church was meant to have habits and wimples quite unlike the fetish costumes I sewed for the movie. Certainly in scale to the plasticine figures it seemed a budget dress up doll. Perhaps it was meant to be Saint Apollonia. I had thought once to take the figures to work but before I could Mortenson ordered the cubicles reconfigured so much smaller there was never again room for the display of plasticine. Programmers took home their family photographs. Over a year I collected many doll house pieces for the movie, I thought the office desk made from real wood especially propitious, but sometimes the set would remind me that anyone who kept a child in a box as small as the cubicles for eight hours a day would go to prison, while a businessman who did the same with enough programmers walked away rich. The cubicles had shrunk more than once. By that second summer the cubicles were about the size of telephone booths, this at about the same time all the telephone booths were disappearing. The walls closed in. It was as though the shadows behind international capitalism perpetuated a certain allotment of small torturous spaces without which anarchy would prevail. The walls closed in again. In my experience there was not room for both a programmer and a prayer at the same moment in cubicles that small.

"Tag. You're it."

The little blonde girl squealed in a run away from my cubicle down towards that of her mother. The bank had pushed a cadre of technical writers into the programmer area at the end of the first phase of the debit card development. The little girl's mother was a pretty but slight woman who had the ambulance called for her every couple weeks when she again toppled over from her diabetes. The woman wrote good technical documents without knowing the name of a single poet and the little girl was soon back when I didn't chase.

"What songs do you know?"

"You are my sunshine."

She sang. There wasn't a window in the enormous room. Louisa laughed so the little girl ran away again towards her mother.

"You wanted a jazz song from her, didn't you?"

"It's no worse than that I started piano with a passion for show tunes. Luck Be a Lady. Surrey with the Fringe On Top. I Got Rhythm. Experimentation playing Favorite Things leads to ruination playing Manteca."

It was too much a jazz joke for Louisa to understand it. She had never heard Manteca, let alone smoked it, and that absence, so like the writer without poetry, made me imagine Louisa falling over to the floor with the words to *I Can't Say No* looped on her medical bracelet. I laughed to myself.

"Did you ever get a piano for your apartment?"

Louisa was persistent to know how I lived in the three steps from the bedroom to the kitchen of the large new apartment I couldn't afford. She thought the only purpose behind a spare bedroom was to raise children.

"The church up the road from me has a piano in the basement they let me play."

This worried her because she knew the only church near my apartment was pastored by a man of faith wearing a business suit, as though prayer were legal recourse against all the heavens, whatever god was handy, for not honoring contractual obligations. To Louisa that church seemed part of the banking system.

"Is it ever in tune?"

I worked from life yet I could not fathom trying to make a movie about what exactly encompassed me because there seemed no way past depicting working class degradation to depicting working class resistence. *400 Blows. Metropolis.* Of course I understood well enough that in most movies the working class serve for comic characters. Because of the comedy *Modern Times* is not substantially different politically from *Ma and Pa Kettle Back On The Farm*. Then in *On The Waterfront* Marlon Brando wears more eye shadow that Eva Marie Saint. How is that not comic? If Karl Malden had been the method actor he claimed, he would have slapped Brando right down the dock, like a real priest, slapped him all the way into the river, scrubbed that face over the side of the dock. It is hard to escape, the comedy. At the tavern where I sometimes played jazz even I would sometimes improvise around the melody to *Lydia The Tattooed Lady* because it is a funny song I never quite lose. I recognize London had it right for a moment with *The Taste of Honey* but Richard Burton stuck himself into *Look Back In Anger* like Prince Hamlet pushing a barrow. *Long Distance Runner. Saturday Night Sunday Morning. A Kind of Loving.* Those movies have it right too I suppose but it isn't my life. The nonsense about Richard Burton playing jazz trumpet isn't even in the play. Here the dramatic movies allow working class resistance only if the protagonist is insane. *Taxi Driver.* Later there was *Fight Club.* Too often movies are just another opportunity to watch the same rich people kill each other in under two hours. *Othello.* There couldn't have been a better idea than that? I kept thinking there must be more than that ancient depicting working class cunning. But what else was there?

"Are you coming dancing later?"

"If yet more shit doesn't come down on me."

All the programmers were there Saturday cleaning up the odds after another big release for debit cards, a program crashing here, there, a display on a terminal goofed with misspelling, a stutter. No one had been to sleep but after a few quiet hours there were plans to celebrate at a hotel that overlooked a finger of the small lakes that cut through the southern part of the city. Mortenson had gone home hours and hours before but Louisa could not help herself speaking about his generosity.

"He is buying the first round later."

"I would rather we had spent the night in bed."

I never let anything I said to Louisa be a direct proposition since it was her preservation not despoiling that genuinely interested me. Still sometimes I could not help but give her words subject to interpretation like some modernist poem incomprehensible while all the same charming by daring. I yawned. Louisa turned back to her tube without promising me a dance but after a couple hours sleep at my apartment I went over to the hotel. In vain I looked for a piano near the dancefloor in the hotel bar. I looked though I knew there would no longer be one because the area where the bandstand should be was more tables. Recorded music was blaring mostly drums of no imagination.

"They built the hotel around an old ballroom but only the floor and the back wall and the ceiling remain the same."

"How can you tell that?"

"I have a picture of the ballroom in an old jazz book full of photographs."

Mortenson believed me for a moment until he started having doubts anyone would ever have published the picture

book with nothing but the jazz bands I kept describing. I had
stolen the book from the community college for a graduation
present to myself. Mortenson had a business degree and it
profoundly limited his take on history. The book was published
in 1955. Would I have become a jazz musician if I had
encountered the book earlier in life? Perhaps. But by the time I
stole the book the word jazz on the binding had completely
faded away. The Pictorial History of Nothingness. Of course I
might never have made a movie if not for that library book
teaching how to write screenplays for the silent movies long
after there weren't silent movies. It was the first time I ever
thought about making a movie, the time I found that book. A
still tongue makes a happy life.

"There was never a ballroom here."

Louisa condemning me for fabrication placated Mortenson's
need to monetize what had passed into lost memory. She was
wrong but in some sense even for me opinion from Louisa
carried weight for more reason than she had lived in Des
Moines all her life. She knew about lost venues. Her father had
closed movie theaters in town one after the other the last few
years. Perhaps the first gossip I had ever heard from the other
programmers at the bank included comment Louisa remained
a virgin only because her father was manager at the drive-in
where everyone else went to see paradise by more than the
dashboard light.

"You look like a French woman."

"What?"

"You look like a French woman with that scarf around your
neck."

I was letting her know everyone knew she had arrived in
Mortenson's car with marks on her neck. The jazz version of
Othello is some stilted tale where no one dies, as though jazz

makes everyone too cool to die, from violence anyway, certainly never from evil schemes. That movie ends with bruises visible on the neck of the Desdemona character in the shot before she walks off with her Moor towards St Paul's just the other side of the river. Where is the angry young man? Richard Burton? Anyone? This London one goes wrong with Patrick McGoohan playing Iago a sniveling and fawning failure so unlike the cunning bastard from the play he should remain. Yet in its way it is a fine movie. It has appearances by Charlie Mingus and Dave Brubeck playing and Richard Attenborough in the Roderigo character runs up to Johnny Dankworth to express disappointment Cleo couldn't come to the party. I had never even heard of Johnny Dankworth and Cleo Laine until seeing the movie in the video store on a pirate tape I quickly wore out with reruns. Cassio is a marijuana hophead McGoohan ruins by turning him on when out on the roof of the refurbished warehouse where the jazz party is being held. Manteca! It is the only scene this drummer Iago shows menace above frustration. Iago is named Johnny Cousin in the movie and McGoohan should have played it more like his similarly named John Drake from *Danger Man* later transformed into the same character, but without name at all, in the television series The Prisoner. I am not what I am. In *The Prisoner*, Number 6 repeatedly has cunning plans to escape the village where he is held among a kind of holiday camp conformity, the discreet charms of acquiescent. *A still tongue makes a happy life*, that is a line from the show. Mortenson would have taken away my name for a number too if he had known it might still my foul language and all that sarcasm.

"Come dancing."

"We do lots of dancing."

Mortenson seemed to be trying to explain history first repeats itself in tragedy then in farce especially when it involves businessmen dancing. Louisa pulled Mortenson out onto the dancefloor. Passing through the jazz party for a single line of dialogue is Carol White all pretty in bleached hair but uncredited in this first movie just as she would be in her last when some movie long after her death appropriated footage from her best movie. *Poor Cow*. Unacknowledged. *Poor Cow*. There's another London one that gets the working class right but the book is even better. Carol White goes unremembered like one of the jazz musicians in the book with its faded binding. The jazz movie ends with McGoohan banging at the drums he won't let anyone else touch after telling Betsy Blair, his wife, he doesn't love her nor love anything else, there is no love for Johnny Cousin. That is Iago?

"Did you count the hickeys on her neck?" asked one of the programmers.

Keeping time too is counting. The other programmers knew I kept keen interest in Louisa without understanding that concupiscence served to keep me even farther from Louisa than they were allowed. A couple weeks earlier one of them had tried to get a rise out of me by asking if I had noticed Louisa now had breast implants. I have never known a worse bunch of liars. You have to be able to code extremely well to create functional logic but remain deceitful.

"Always be a drummer on the stage not a drummer in front of the stage."

"Say again?"

"Drummers are the mirror of death."

The programmers laughed because the programmers were used to me saying the most incomprehensible fragments lifted from the movies. *Je suis un cimetière abhorré de la lune*. In the same poem is the word *boiteuse* but it doesn't actually mean a female merchant of boxes the way I liked to think it. Think it about Louisa. The Welles movie begins with the funeral procession of the Moor and Desdemona, with shots of the cage hung from the castle wall where Iago will be left to die, the movie at the end leaving out the most important line from the play. *Cold. Cold my girl. Even like thy chastity.* No. Not that one. This one. *For this slave, if there be any cunning cruelty that can torment him much and hold him long, it shall be his.* That would be a cubicle no bigger than the castle cage in which I went on for thirty years. For all it matters Carol White was in a movie with Orson Welles too but I don't remember her having a scene with him. In that one the characters are all rich. *We'll Never Forget What's His Name.* That black ragtime player probably thought getting his picture taken was all in fun.

"You're turn."

"No thanks."

Louisa seemed genuinely disappointed I would not dance with her but I couldn't come near her because of the scarf. Mortenson laughed at me for being bashful behind such a foul mouth. He didn't need to understand a single thing. I wouldn't follow him. The table had gone almost dry and the curvaceous waitress with the dissipated frown was nowhere to be seen so Mortenson went off for beer. Probably he would have taken me to the roof to hop me up if he thought the despondency with which I was regarding Louisa meant I would overdose. I shrugged a gambler's shrug knowing what cards I held. I would have danced with Louisa had I believed it was a genuine request without a kind of mocking behind it. All these years later I still regret declining. All these years later I hate that scarf for all it meant that night even though I certainly got my revenge thanks to the very same scarf. Its evil twin anyway. Like all the other evil twins in the movies.

"Drunk? And speak parrot?"

That we should with joy, pleasure, revel, and applause transform ourselves into beasts. Cassio. Doctor Dolittle. For a moment I might have been either. The waitress did not understand except to understand I was buying last round before closing. Mortenson and Louisa had long left by then.

"Whip me such honest knaves."

The other programmers laughed because the waitress with a frown over a revealing blouse seemed just the waitress to own whips though she was yet another blonde with a ponytail. Igor Iago. It is a singsong name like another beast of burden with two heads from *Doctor Dolittle*. But the older I get the more I find the movies have left behind important secrets in the books. I read books now. I never watch movies. In *Doctor Dolittle* the greatest fighter of the Popsipetel people on the floating island is named Big Teeth. He is mentioned then never seen again though there is a great battle three pages onward. This is not unlike *Othello* where in the very first lines Cassio is described being damned with a fair wife, but the wife never makes an appearance, is never mentioned again throughout the play. Apparently the wife is off being sensible the whole time so needs never be given a name however fair she might be. Could we not at least expect a number be given the rank of her beauty? I am left to my own imagination whether Big Teeth was given that name because he ate his prisoners.

"Lulu's going down on him in the car every night after work."

"I've seen that too."

The worst liars. In the jazz movie instead of a handkerchief there is a cigarette case Iago uses to convince the Moor against

Desdemona. Not much is made of the cigarette case. Instead the Iago character named Johnny Cousin doctors a tape recording so Cassio speaking of his black girlfriend instead speaks about afternoons in bed with the Desdemona character. The recording not the cigarette case instigates the jealousy. In *Morgan!*, David Warner tells Vanessa Redgrave that anxiety has made her cunning, Warner a painter who doesn't paint talking to his rich wife, then noticing his wife has been wearing a diaphanous scarf while out with her new lover, he adds, I would say even devious if I did not love you. I almost forgot that scarf. How is that not Betsy Blair all those times she cheated on Jerry Mulligan? I mean Gene Kelly. Were there handkerchiefs? Scarfs? In her autobiography Betsy Blair describes at least some of the other men she was tumbling about under chasing her rights to be like a man. Was there some reason Louisa asked me to dance I simply will never know? Morgan dons a gorilla suit to make himself invincible. The movie cuts to King Kong showing his teeth. I suppose I should have known Johnny Dankworth from his having done the music for that movie about madness but there aren't four bars of jazz in it. I know. I know. But I didn't see those early episodes of *The Avengers* where Dankworth did the wailing jazz theme until years after Louisa wanted her own vengeance against me. At some point at the end in *Morgan!*, in the garden of the hammer and sickle, Vanessa Redgrave gives out a laugh unrestrained, conquering, the way Louisa burned into hearts when she laughed. A few days after the night at the club by the lake came the rumor that Mortenson was getting a divorce. In the movie *Morgan!* in that one laugh you can glimpse a gold tooth far to the back of Vanessa Redgrave's mouth though the movie is black and white. I can only imagine what she ate for supper that night.

DOROTHEA
AT SEA

In the madhouse I couldn't get away from that one movie. Even now there often seems more imposing itself. In *Morgan!* when he tells his mother he is seeing a psychiatrist she tells him she hopes it will make a man of him, this shortly after calling him a class traitor and shortly before feeding him porridge, apparently his comfort food. My own mother sat across from me that first February day I was allowed visitors telling me the tomatoes had done especially well that fall but they had long been gone. Anyway she had not been allowed to bring food. I think she yet again mentioned being grand marshal back in the Labor Day parade again since in years without elections there never showed a politician. When my mother said that I looked around for politicians among the other patients. It had been especially crushing that last fall because the Reagan landslide had driven into hiding anyone with a red opinion. Red flag. Black flag. At the madhouse was the first time I had ever noticed my mother had partials uneven with her few remaining real teeth, like the cobblestone street I had lived above in Paris, cobblestones being a favored weapon of the revolution, my place in Paris being just around the corner from where they once decapitated admirals and bishops and ladies of fine family. So the famous song said anyway. The one sung by Juliette Greco about the time she was the girlfriend of Miles Davis. Yes. Yes. The one written by Sartre as though for Desdemona. I hope it makes a man out of you. But that bloody street was no longer cobblestone even in my time there and that seemed opportunity missed, something offkey. I had been still in Paris on Labor Day.

"Why are you talking about Paris again?"

She meant why was I so crazy I was talking incessantly about cobblestones without pause to catch my breath. I imagined even the footprints of radicals couldn't be found in the dust left by the parade she had marshalled. I was overcome envisioning the parade on cobblestones.

"Would you rather I sang about it?"

There must be a thousand stupid songs about Paris appropriate for the madhouse. But the music in *Morgan!* that throws you off if you're American isn't chanson française, musette, not even jazz, but the frequent repetition of a tune that makes you remember nothing except perhaps a scraggly and forlorn Christmas tree from the cartoons, makes you remember your childhood. *O Tannenbaum.* Few Americans now know the tune was lifted for *The Red Flag.* What else is that Morgan's mother says? Your father wanted to wave the red flag over the rubble of Buckingham Palace. *Though cowards flinch and traitors sneer we'll keep the red flag flying here.* In the library of the madhouse there was a book that said that song remains the official anthem of the English labor movement. I was surprised I could find that out. Anyway the song was why there was no jazz in the movie. It wasn't the only infiltration. There was in fact a shockingly large amount of communist and anarchist literature that seemed to have been smuggled past the locked doors of the madhouse. In this country *The Red Flag* was the first song in the *Industrial Workers of the World Songbook* and the copy that had once belonged to my mother's father had long sat unnoticed among the extra blankets and linens in a trunk at the foot of her bed. Maybe it wasn't the first song.

All that trunk and my mother's teeth too were thrown out by my sisters while I was locked away. I was furloughed a couple hours for my mother's funeral and I remember that in the casket my mother's closed mouth seemed oddly caved. An abyss. A pothole at least. I assume *The Red Flag* is now pushed beneath the linen if not the soil in England too.

"You sign your paintings with your logon?"

Dorothea stepped about the room naked looking at the paintings I had done while with Janice. On the paintings I had shortened my signature to the eight characters used for logging onto the computer at the bank. Even now with passwords one hundred and two hundred characters long it is still possible to imagine the user name reduced to nothing, a thumb press, an eye scan, a tongue lick, a tooth nibble, all an algorithm that has rendered you to a number after all. Dorothea moved around the room like an ancient prophet bringing down walls by circling with a trumpet blowing passwords. The apartment came with a cabinet meant for china that instead I used for tiers of diorama created from the flotsam and gimcracks and figurines always being collected with some thought to animate them in a movie. The bishop was there mounting from behind his servant girl from the church crypt. Dorothea wrongly believed she had me figured.

"She's never going to be yours you know."

"What makes you think I want her?"

"You talk about her when there is nothing to talk about her."

I suppose in some sense Louisa was just a cobblestone street within an echo of madness. It was obvious Dorothea understood in ways I couldn't but special knowledge must be expected from a nun especially once no longer a nun. She was astonishingly beautiful for someone not much younger than

my mother, her body preserved all those years a bride of
Christ like in a tomb, perhaps not so emaciated now she was
no longer a nun proving faith through denial, seven years
pleasure having added subtle curves within her tall figure. She
towered over me. Her teeth were flawless except for one
snaggletooth that seemed to express her doubts. I suspected
she had had a great deal of work done on her teeth since
abandoning the church.

"I'm a good sailor."

"I don't even know how to swim."

"Really? Because I always sense an undertow in the holy
water."

"Is that all you sense?"

That spring I had bought a small catboat from an operations
manager who had landed a better job in a desert five states
away. The marina hadn't been keen to rent me the slip since
there was a waiting list, but I threatened to sink the catboat
right where it was docked, then spend the summer scuba
diving the wreck, stealing from others what I could not find in
sunken treasure. I retained the slip. The woman at the marina
office had seen pirates at the lake before. Dorothea looked out
over the water from the catboat.

"Do you come out here every Sunday?"

"It gets me out of pager range."

"Shouldn't you stay within pager range if you are on call?"

"I am always on call."

"Always?"

"Sounds a familiar level of expected devotion?"

Dorothea didn't laugh but instead looked down into the
murky lake water.

"Prayer is more difficult than programming."

The operations manager had sold me the catboat for only a hundred dollars because he had so wanted the hell away from the corn fields. I supposed I would find other reasons for his flight if I dug into it. There was often trouble for me too when I wasn't responsive to the pager while off sailing. Mortenson had written me up once. Whenever a storm came through Mortenson would guffaw I was making the bank rich yet another day it was too dangerous to sail.

"It is the damned animation that makes me so skilled at programming, those little increments of movement between shutter releases, the next photograph, the next photograph, shifting the plasticine clay, building in slow repetitions towards the illusion of movement, it is the very same writing computer code."

"I think you'd find yourself skilled at anything you attempted."

"But not poetry of course."

I laughed at myself. Dorothea had seen the figures on their set built in the spare bedroom of the larger apartment where I now lived, but she had been more keen to talk about the masks from Robbie's production of *The Gas Heart*, the masks not entirely unlike things Dorothea had seen at religious fêtes in Spain when she was first a young nun, before all that poetry had been memorized, most of it anyway. I had stretched naked on the bed wearing the foam rubber mask of the eye in the glaring insight of the somnambulist. I then stood. *With heads uncovered swear we all to bear it onward till we fall.* I had stood there swearing to the red flag while wearing a mask because it seemed just the thing, sex if not liberty, at least the pleasures of the poor, a sing-a-long, if we can't just shoot the bastards. Dorothea ruined six hours of work by picking up one of the plasticine figures. It was the one meant to resemble her.

"Et le vent ouvert aux allusions mathématiques."

"They are like the stained glass figures I still sometimes dream start to scurry like rats after communion wafers."

"I can tell you the word for teeth does not appear even once in Rimbaud's Une Saison En Enfer."

"And now absence is what you judge important in a text?"

I didn't tell her that the word for teeth appears so often in Lautréamont's *Les Chants de Maldoror* the book should be assigned at dental colleges. Dorothea no longer wanted to talk poetry. It didn't matter a pope's fart to her if I now knew more than she knew about the poems she had taught my first year in college. I was quiet. I recited no further verse. I did not want Dorothea to regret landing me the programming job. I wanted larger responses than regret from Dorothea but at the same time thought it was a goof to be screwing someone so important at the bank. Dorothea was the communications director. She had been talking directly to God so long that she was if anything overqualified to be talking to the newspaper and television reporters.

"We don't hear anything more about Peters."

"You aren't supposed to hear anything more."

From within the mask of the eye I had been confessing how I stole from the lawyers the poster of *Dr. Caligari* because it had originally hung in the film distribution company where I had worked during high school. I had swept floors. The poster had hung on a bare brick wall near the drafting board where I sometimes drew advertisements. Everything in that bankrupted company had auctioned for pennies but I had been too busy that winter at university painting to bother with movies. I hadn't thought about the poster and I hadn't yet seen myself in it. It only seemed important enough to steal after campaigning for the war hero. At work Peters was an accountant who had been caught embezzling small amounts the bank pretended were large amounts. Ten thousand? Twenty thousand? I would never know exactly because Dorothea never spoke out of turn. But she never spoke about poetry at all and her silence on poetry was itself a falsehood given with straight face. I knew the poems continued to churn through her thoughts into her judgements. I knew she measured every business falsehood she presented to the public in metric feet. I was a somnambulist who could see everything within her soul except her death. It was even pretty certain she could swim.

"The bank wants a pretense there never is temptation?"

"Do you actually have the clear credit card encryption keys to the bank?"

"And the seven hundred affiliated banks."

She paused in thought while I let out the sail a bit more against the falling breeze.

"That has to be worth at least five million dollars in Hong Kong."

Hong Kong was the center for card fraud that year with fake cards running losses even to our distant bank. The generosity of the machine out at the airport remained a business secret I certainly did not share with Dorothea. This was a year before the underworlds across the seas began using fake debit cards to buy medical supplies easily sold on the black markets, but still with debit cards, there was a certain anticipation, a certain foregleam, that theft would be easily within reach, a real chance, the ruination of capitalism even. I had first mentioned the encryption keys the night before while pouring wine that I knew was also a key to something but something not locked away at all securely any longer.

"Show us your breasts."

Dorothea was being shouted at by a large man in a passing fishing boat who cut his engine to be heard.

"Show us your cock first."

The large man stood in his boat to zip down his fly. The other man in the boat held out his beer can to Dorothea as though we weren't six feet too far for a reach. The two men were tanked. Unfortunately the breeze had now died so there was no just sailing away from the manhood on display. Uncircumcised. Spotted. He held his thick penis our direction while letting out a stream. I noticed his jeans were still wet the knees down from pulling his boat off its trailer, a common enough sight on the water, but here with all the urine it seemed to be claim he was the giant who had filled the lake.

"You call that live bait?"

"What better you got?"

The large man stared me down though I hadn't spoken. I let a short length of sail line droop over my fist in commentary. The insult would come to the large man later perhaps many times when the next woman asked to be tied to the bed. At the moment he persisted giving Dorothea all he had to admire though only the fish were jumping. Dorothea pursed her lips the way she might have parsing a poem seen before but not quite remembered. I thought I could hear other monsters beneath the water.

"I see you're still an idiot."

"I see you're still a bitch."

It was only after the breeze came up enough for me to sail us away that I thought more about the other man, the one holding out the beer can as though no distance was too great. He had been very relaxed. It was only after the breeze came up I realized it wasn't merely because he had seen the large man drunkenly expose himself many times before. It was the satisfaction I had seen in the mirror myself that morning before leaving for the lake. This other man had had his trousers rolled up and I don't know how he managed it but his strong calves still sleek from having been wet seemed to expose him even more than any pecker. I sailed close to a bank of cattails and other weeds where the fishermen could not come without fouling their propeller.

"It was only after I was no longer Sister Agnes that I looked back in recognition that all the people I had known were much more stupid than I had thought at the time."

"I remember you always thought all the students were stupid."

"You have no business being a computer programmer."

"You still think Alice should have been a nun?"

She did not answer so I knew she included foremost herself in the list of those who were more stupid in the past.

"Tell me about the man in the bow of the fishing boat passing you the beer."

From that Dorothea understood I knew she had in the past slept with the man holding the beer all the while being wildly desired by the larger man holding his cock. It must have been some time ago because she shrugged her shoulders. Anything recent she wouldn't have acknowledged at all. In bed I could see how she wanted passion but passion spotlighted at a distance otherwise within shadows. It excited her I so wanted Louisa. She sensed in it a poetry I couldn't escape. But we both understood we were soldiers where the trenches could be survived only by forgetting the comforts of home, by just not giving a damn. She dared not remember poetry. She understood I was that soldier who didn't care if he lived the night because after all Louisa would not remain a virgin forever. I had seen Dorothea did not always enjoy being in my bed. At times it almost tormented her. Anyway, the sailboat was again becalmed most of an hour, with us making only some fifty yards along the shore carried by the uncertain current of the lake, passing odd patches of picnic grounds cut into the scrub trees, the grass there beside the plank tables spiny but mowed. Suddenly I tacked for the marina at a sustained rise of breeze that surprised by quickly becoming a storm rolling off the prairie.

"The bookstore is on the drive back."

I was to drop Dorothea at the restaurant where she had left her own car the night before.

"It can't be worse than looking at all the goose shit along the shore."

Dorothea laughed because we had spent the last hour whispering rude comments about the sunburnt families in the picnic grounds, the fat little girls dodging the goose shit thrown by the fat little boys in love, the fat women reading romances, the fat men fishing for fish thrown back into the lake dead at the end of the day. At the bookstore it was raining too ferociously to get out of the car. The light blurred. There was a very old woman standing with her little dog beneath the overhang of the strip mall looking into the sky for something much less than salvation but still receiving less than asked. I was surprised when Dorothea pulled me into a kiss with a hand between my legs. I might have known I was her surrogate for another man. *Paint Your Wagon*. In that musical about two husbands, after Lee Marvin walks off, after the credits when the music drones along unending, Clint Eastwood must strangle Jean Seberg to prove his rectitude to those who have built the church, a school, the courthouse that all went unnoticed until the taverns collapsed. It is the true ending that comes after the music. Kill the slut. I hope it makes a man of you. I put my hand gently on Dorothea's throat. In *The French Style* Jean Seberg is a painter who is shocked to discover her first Parisian lover is merely a schoolboy. Her hand between my legs made me certain Dorothea's next lover would be younger still but all the same I was content it wouldn't be the next week. *Alfie.* It was the plot from the movie *Alfie.* Still there would be time for genuine failure. The best scene in *The French Style* is where the mother who had lived in Paris in the 1920s tells her daughter she has no remaining talent for painting because she has fucked it all away with too many men.

"Middle West."

We were in the bookstore near the maps.

"What?"

"Do you ever say Middle West?"

"Midwest."

"You know it shortened only after it became easy to fly over the whole thing without seeing one stalk of corn."

"You think so?"

"After the trains were gone Iowa didn't rank more than one word for description."

She didn't laugh. Dorothea agreed without acknowledgment in the way she once had when teaching poetry, like all those books about poetry discussing stresses, then never marking the stresses in the examples, as though determined not to share the deeper knowledge, as though determined not to move beyond generalizations into misstep. Those books too prepared me for computer programming. Dorothea must have known I could never escape Iowa and in time could only be described by misshaped contractions. She pointed over towards the poetry shelves.

"Try harder than the picture books."

She meant I shouldn't waste my time on the many shelves of movie books, usually all photographs, always the same nonsense text, Fred Astaire at first much less famous than his beautiful sister, Charlie Chaplin with another underaged girl, John Wayne stuck in low budget westerns like Humphrey Bogart not recognizing gold at his feet, Bette Davis punching a drunken Errol Flynn and damned near knocking him cold, Gary Cooper fucking six times a night but unable to keep up with Clara Bow without pauses for a hootch run, Orson Welles directing the greatest movie ever made yet within ten years having to empty his own pockets to finance *Othello*, the texts all the same stories with small variations, never fading. Eventually the stories of Hollywood will have to be codified into a single testament that never changes but it remains difficult imagining the bishops capable of such work.

"Did you know Louise Brooks was in a John Wayne movie?"

"Who is Louise Brooks?"

Lulu in Hollywood but even without that explanation Dorothea understood I was trying to talk about Louisa because I was among movie books. I thought about the scene where Lulu dances a wild jazz for her extremely repellant old benefactor who scolds she has forgotten everything he taught her. He is a kind of ancient dwarf. He travels with a circus strongman. Dorothea pushed me on the shoulder. Dorothea pushed me on the back. Then she left me before the final steps to the poetry shelves because she had foresworn poetry to hold a job she must struggle not to despise. She went to look at the sailing manuals as though to prove I could have caught the wind at any time if I had simply prayed harder. We might not have been rained on. It seemed shockingly lonely standing among the Rimbaud and the Whitman and the Ginsberg and the Stevens and the Frost and the Plath and the Cummings and

Neruda and Keats and Burns and all the others no one wants for testament. The truth is the IWW songbook came with lyrics but no sheet music. *Come dungeons dark or gallows grim. This song shall be our parting hymn.* If there were a movement now significant enough to have its own songbook, it would be a jazz fake book, with all lyrics so known they wouldn't need to be included. *Quel philosophe. Quel poète. Je n'aime pas la poésie.* My boat too had been chased by sailors wanting sex. But what name do you call a wind where the heart dissipates even when finally the sails take full? *Mariah* won't do. *Blancs Manteaux?* I could see I wanted a very different song at the end.

RAISE THE RED FLAG

It was another hard weekend working on something so all important it pushed aside the debit card project. I remember that diverting task only in certain fragments of code, a bubble sort, a new file keyed on credit card expiration date, and one idea that didn't last the morning, the idea that the cubicles were groynes that protected the bank from all that was offshore, pressing against us in rising tides, never certain if what was weighing against the walls wasn't a higher truth, wasn't even insurgence. That is a joke. It had been obvious for some time upper management directives more often were made to assert authority than pursue wealth. But Mortenson too was always advocating change though the bank's systems were fifteen years obsolete. He had learned in business school change was a tenant that could justify his position even if it were change without reason. On obsolete systems this was more like trying to rewrite history by goofing dialogue over an old gladiator movie with the sound turned off. It lacked even the dignity other people's money brings to most any situation.

"What's your name today?"

The little blonde girl was again running the aisles too beautiful not to tease.

"Loplop."

The little girl laughed.

"And your name is Lulu?"

In *The Quare Fellow*, in the play anyway, perhaps the movie too now stopping to think of it again, the prisoners pound metal against the water pipes in protest while the fellow is

197

being hanged, the fellow has who killed his wife, the poor one, not the rich one, not a Moorish general in sight. In Des Moines that morning so much typing of the other programmers sickened me with nausea at the thought there was a scaffold waiting for me, as though the typing were the pipes being banged, a protest gone unheeded. *Dans le rue des Blancs Monteaux*. That morning I felt a hood rather than mask over my head. In *The Quare Fellow* there is a long scene of the prisoners digging the grave for the man about to be hanged and the other programmers digging my grave was a dream that recurred whenever Louisa came from shadow around an oblique form, past a sharp tilting angle, into a twisting cityscape that was always Paris passing for Dublin, the early morning dreams free from borders, McGoohan sometimes both Doctor Syn and Doctor Caligari, masked in stitches, commanding Louisa in her virginal trance. But nothing killed me and nothing killed me and nothing killed me. Even Louisa looked at the little girl wondering if her own cares were misplaced.

"Oubli oubli Lulu."

I sang maybe four more lines imitating Charles Aznavour singing over my grave while placing my fingers on the desk where the chords would be on a piano.

"What song is that?"

"Go ask your mother."

The little girl ran off to her mother who was again working the weekend despite having given notice. Louisa turned back to her tube though a moment earlier she had complained she couldn't finish her work on the audit reports until I finished mine on the transaction interface. That morning her tube was at best a crystal ball. The work left her trapped into coming to lunch when I threatened not to return at all if she made me go alone. It was not the first time I had discovered unfinished work could be used for a hammer. I had been hammered many times while leaving the sickle to Mortenson. But it was the first I had used work to get something from Louisa and only did it then because she couldn't even give me a smile on first encountering each other that morning. Louisa had arrived to find me talking to the mother of the little girl.

"It's a good thing I've quitting before I get fired for telling them to fuck off."

"It's the same everywhere else."

"That can't be true."

Louisa argued everywhere was the same only because she had never liked the woman from the technical writers. The mother of the little girl had heard much better stories about work from her own parents and of course she hoped for more than an expanding void for her daughter and the children not yet born. The last few days she had been even more fragile than usual, almost ill. Weeks ago Louisa had scratched more updates to the technical manuals on paper but text processing on the old mainframe was always at best like untangling fishing nets filled with a rotted catch. The woman dreaded retyping all the technical manuals yet a third time. I suggested she lose the updates and in response she had given me a very unchaste kiss.

"Okay but you have to pay for my lunch then," said Louisa.

The restaurant down the street was vaguely the orient without ever stating for white people its country of origin. There must have been an immigrant community who knew. Just before the cash register there were videos for rent in a language unidentified but the rather salacious covers seemed more than atmosphere for the diners. The covers of nearly naked girls looked roughly handled. Still white people lunched there because there was an almost addictive salad dressing quite unlike anything Des Moines had known before. The rice and meats were fine. But everyone came for the salad dressing that for the locals more often seemed shocking than pleasing. Around the room were faces wondering what all they had missed in life. On the other hand I felt myself on the scaffold remembering intensely some taste I had meant to search out again, the hood over my head slit for the priest to anoint the temples, but without salvation, nothing coming through the slit but more sounds of typing.

"How'd you like the guys from Concord?"

"I doubt they can deliver on that many promises."

"Wasn't it funny how excited they became when I told them Des Moines has the second largest concentration of insurance companies in the country?"

This technical company out of Concord Connecticut provided insurance payments from a personal computer at a time almost no one was yet doing payments from home. The programmers from Concord were brought out to discuss providing frontend to the mortgage payment system because there was nothing yet at the bank interfacing to external users except the teller machines and the registers at grocery stores. There wasn't really the Internet yet. The personal computer would dial the bank on a telephone line. The bank officers were already talking about taking credit card payments if we could get the mortgage payments to work.

"They only acted excited so you would continue believing they were ignorant about what they've known all along."

"That can't be true."

Louisa scoffed but wasn't at all pleased to understand the programmers from Concord had played her. She gave me a hard look because the visitors weren't there themselves to receive all her cascading suspicions. She wondered about me and the technical writer mother of the little girl. That morning I had had my hand on the woman's flank.

"That tall woman over there is the state senator in the newspapers."

"The one from the scandal?"

Just a few weeks earlier the tall woman dining had been photographed with the war hero congressman in the hotel room where he died from a heart attack while wearing nothing but one red sock. *Fan the flames of discontent.* At the funeral of the war hero I had stood behind the crowd sketching the large family tomb built a hundred years before, winged angels, a Canterbury cross each wall, the stone all beautifully rusticated. *D'avoir sa croix et son tombeau?* I answered Baudelaire every day. *J'irai cracher sur vos tombes.* Later over drinks that day of the funeral Alice had said she was going back to acting in movies overseas, there was a movie in Tokyo they wanted her in, but there was one shooting in Berlin too that was the better part but worse pay. It had been nice to finally see Alice again with her face scrubbed. I was now sketching Louisa on the legal pad she had brought to write out more plans for work.

"That's good."

"You think so?"

"I mean, not like your doodles in meetings."

"Those are deliberate."

It startled Louisa I would ever make ugly drawings for consumption by managers so she chose to believe I was being my usual sarcastic self. But it trapped her thoughts. I did not explain to her the war hero in one sock might still be alive if the painting over the hotel bed hadn't been meant to drive him away before noon checkout. He might have lived if not so hurried. From reports in the newspapers I had learned it was the same hotel from the weekend on the campaign I perhaps

wanted to rewrite. Alice. Gauguin. I wondered if his other sock
had been black. I brought me back to thinking again how that
morning was the last time I would see the mother with her
little girl. After the kiss I had suggested the best hours of day
to meet without her husband becoming suspicious were the
hours from 5 to 7. I had learned that from Agnes Varda at the
movies but had never attempted seducing a married woman in
all those years since the video rental store on the river. In my
hands the slender mother of the little girl seemed especially
frail but I had her half undressed before she abruptly decided
she could do better back home. Then she hesitated. Then she
stretched onto the bed. The mother of the little girl had very
much liked to hear love poems she had never heard before.

"From now on we are going to call ourselves engineers."

It was another staff meeting where anything could happen
in the next half hour.

"I don't have a degree in engineering."

None of the other programmers had more than some
associate degree. I tell a lie. There was a fellow with a bachelor
of science degree proved so worthless he had gone back to a
community college to get an associate degree. I considered that
to have renounced right to call himself an engineer. Anyway he
was incompetent. Being a worthless programmer often made
him the center of much conflict without him ever quite
understanding his superior education would never constitute
qualifications. But how to get all that on a business card?

"You should be proud you do the work of an engineer,"
Mortenson had insisted.

"If I really get to choose the accreditation printed on my
business cards then I choose mad scientist."

The waitress who brought our meal was so especially
beautiful with her shining long black hair that Louisa couldn't

stop looking though she was careful to turn away before it became obvious staring.

"Wouldn't it be something to be like her?"

I put my hand close enough to Louisa across the table she had to abandon the waitress.

"I wasn't thinking that."

"The fact we can project ourselves into what might have been is proof we are free agents."

I was mocking Mortenson with thoughts from Sartre now the days were getting too long for Agnes Varda to procure temptations.

"It's what makes you a pain in the ass."

"I would choose evil genius for my business card but whole the point of a business card is to make yourself seem extraordinary while making yourself seem affordable."

The salad dressing we had come to enjoy together seemed especially stinging across my tongue because it would not linger. At the checkout register Louisa looked over the rack of salacious movies to imagine herself the waitress one last moment. The waitress was if anything even better looking than the inviting girls on the videos. It was odd watching Louisa overwhelmed with regret wormed from shame she was not free to do what she wished with her own beauty. I look into a mirror and it is blank, says the Mouth in the play Robbie staged, which registers now a reveal the mouth is vampire, a meaning it could not first have held but simply one time has given it, given it that rather than mere mortality. At the register there was a mirror where people could check their teeth for any lingering salad. I would have gladly paid the check double if Louisa had glanced into the mirror but she went on staring at the videos in trying not to look again at the waitress. There was something so dreamlike to her behavior I could not immediately return to my cubicle after again sensing my grave dug by the other programmers. Out on the street I gripped Louisa by the upper arm.

"We have another stop."

"You aren't going to finish your programs today, are you?"

"Is it surprising I enjoy keeping you waiting?"

Again she knew I was talking about Mortenson but probably did not know I was thinking about the mother of the little girl. In the movie *Cléo de 5 à 7*, the beautiful singer wanders the streets of Paris waiting on the results of medical tests, waiting to learn if she has cancer, though she already knows because at a tarot reading that begins the movie, she turns up the death card. I was thinking about the mother of the little girl, knowing she was quitting her job because her health was failing, but trying very hard to imagine Louisa the panicked singer instead, very blonde, her figure stopping traffic when she crosses the street up near Notre-Dame cathedral, erratically breaking into tears in the café. She wails into the wall of mirror behind her seat. But it is the mirror she stops before at the bottom of the stairs in the building of the fortune teller that matters, that is remembered. Into that mirror she declares she is alive so long as she is beautiful. *Être laid. C'est ça, la mort.* I thought that could be Louisa too thinking only if she were ugly would it be death. She otherwise could not fear its embrace. Reinterpreted in patois the line from the movie had made me laugh and laugh other times when hearing Louisa talking over the walls of the cubicles. Laid. That too seemed a joke.

"I like my job."

"You can love your dog, you can love your cat, but don't love your job because it will never love you back."

I led Louisa a turn away from the return to the bank down a street that was all small brick buildings barely maintained. This was the far end of downtown. We passed a couple doors that clearly no longer opened. There was a shop with its windows bricked over. A couple mechanics in especially filthy overalls were arguing under a car hood at a little garage where seven perhaps eight cars were packed about it, old cars, every last one a beater. Here there were no restaurants. Here there were not even any taverns. We were the only people on sidewalks where the grass grew spindles between the many heaving cracks. There was a fabric store with a window full of knitting needles. There was a butcher shop. And then there was the shop I had been to many times.

"What is this place?"

"Every flag you could ask for. Even the red and the black."

"The what?"

The entryway between the two sets of doors had walls covered in small flags the size of kerchiefs, the flags under glass like the lobby cards in an old movie theater entrance, all colorful images advertising next week's excitement if you found no adventure in this week's feature, found nothing to rally around, nothing to die for. The tall state senator had been talking to the woman lunching with her about what movie to take their men to see that night. Their voices were bitter with compromise and their beds went cold over the salad. What did Antoine Roquentin write about his cinema? Around him people sat waiting for the screen to dream for them? I have often wondered if the desire to make movies was simply a desperate reaction against relinquishing freedom to the movies watched. If only Sartre had thought to have a flag instead of a business card. They could have used his flags for tablecloths down the street at his café, pulled them over their heads to dance, that café the place I had once drank most evenings too though it was a long walk to my apartment.

"I don't recognize many."

"You can see from here they keep the Confederate flags at the rear so you have to walk through the whole shop to get to them."

"Like milk."

The walls were covered in flags of all sizes though the exceptionally large flags were hung from the ceiling in a loop at the center of the shop. At front around the cash register hung a very great many stars and stripes so no one could question loyalties even to capitalism. The back wall was the oddball flags not even necessarily for a country that ever existed. State flags. College flags. Team flags. The shorter wall one side was the western world flags. England. Norway. France. The shorter wall the other side was everywhere else. Australia. South Africa. India. I took Louisa through the large flags hanging at the center of the shop like walking a maze where to make your way you must push aside branches. Embraced by flags I stopped to kiss Louisa for the first time.

"You don't belong here at all, do you?"

"I do."

In my voice I could not keep out the bitter compromise I had heard from the senator. Louisa noticed. Perhaps the only thing she cherished from me was the echo I so often made to her own phrasing like any good jazz man behind the soloist. I think she would have kissed a second time if she had not heard I might imitate just any voice in passing. I could feel Janice wanting into my voice. I could feel Dorothea wanting into my voice. I could feel even the mother of the little girl wanting into my voice but no further. I held up the last of the flags when we stepped from the maze because it felt as though we were stepping from an ocean crossing. The kiss somehow left us disembarking.

"France."

"I bet they don't sell many of those."

I had had to special order the large flag from the Soviet Union though that empire would not fall for another year. The flag came from Belarus. In *Morgan!* the hammer and sickle hang in the back window of the station wagon David Warner is living in after Vanessa Redgrave has kicked him out of her house. At first that summer the hammer and sickle had hung in my apartment opposite *Dr. Caligari* but I had to roll the flag on hot days so the thermostat would read correctly for the air conditioner. Lately landlords had been threatening to evict me because I was using the flag for a patio door curtain. *Anything can happen. Anything can happen.* That is the maddening revelation that comes to Antoine Roquentin when he realizes there is no God causing the world. *Anything can happen in the next half hour.* That is the maddening revelation made by a puppet on strings in the opening credits to a show they televised weekends when I was a little boy. Among the little boys in class it was only the second most popular show of puppets on strings but the phrase was in the opening credits so we knew it by heart. We repeated it endlessly. *Anything can happen in the next half hour.* We all played at being puppets on strings with understanding it meant our actions were all determined. Even some of the girls played at surrendering freedom to strings.

"Don't ever kiss me again."

"I would never want more than that from you."

"Just don't."

It had been a mistake to include Sartre in my reading everything about Baudelaire because there had been so much ancillary reading necessary to understanding Sartre. I read *La Nausée* the first time in Paris. Sartre had been dead more than a year by the time I got to Paris but there were still flowers found on his tomb every day. I was devoted to poetry. Baudelaire through Aragon. In Paris I might have found more similarities between those two poets if I had then known what slaves they made themselves to their women. But instead I read Sartre then Céline because he was quoted on the jacket of the Sartre novel then back again to more Sartre. I experienced a great nothingness in Paris but I don't believe it was an existential nothingness.

"I was only kissing the oriental waitress in you."

"Asshole."

It is hard to calculate how much bad faith an exotic waitress is enacting when the beautiful virgin longs to take her place.

"Have you ever seen the movie The Snows of Kilimanjaro?"

"My father let me into every movie in every one of the theaters he managed no matter how old you were supposed to be."

"This would be years before that."

"Then no."

Sartre contended a choice was made at the age of seven or eight or nine that became the principle lived from then forward. For Sartre Baudelaire at eight chose to be the damned poet when his beloved mother remarried an important man. His tomb in the same cimetière as Sartre is a minor addition to the glory given the stepfather. There is a cenotaph honoring Baudelaire the other side of the cimetière, without corpse, and I wondered if that wasn't what gave Sartre the idea that Baudelaire tried to be two men, being two in death, already. What happened to me at eight? My mother had the dog put down because she wanted a cleaner house. But there was one other thing at the appropriate age.

"In that Kilimanjaro movie there is a shot of Ava Gardner and Gregory Peck walking along the Seine on the south bank coming towards the back of Notre-Dame. They kiss. I was about eight the first time I saw that on television. It was the most beautiful place on earth. I thought the same when I finally got there to see for myself though I was alone."

"Can you lend me a tape?"

Louisa asked often how I lived so knew I kept tapes to all my favorite movies, but never knew I never watched the tapes, usually never even opened them. I preferred to remember the movies when seen in the video store. The ability to imagine what is not the case is proof I am not subject to the determinism of a puppet on strings? Men always get the lives they deserve? The parents they deserve? Perhaps if Sartre had learned to play instead of just listen to jazz he wouldn't have been so keen to inspire his own miseries in other people. Emotions are a form of behavior deliberately chosen? I too knew what it meant to be relieved of freedom against my will. *Pour soi en soi?* In one of the *Dolittle* books it says a dog asks questions with its nose. In Sartre dogs have merely essence, like rocks, but the dog my mother put down understood at least fifty words, a variety not only imperatives, while my one understanding was which bark was a call to be let in the house. Louisa was fingering a display of silk flags meant to be worn for scarfs.

"I'll buy you one if you let me have the neckerchief you are wearing."

It was this display of scarfs I had especially brought Louisa to see.

"I like the one I am wearing."

"A change will do you good."

Where does Sartre ever reconcile all this with Marx's contention that we are controlled by economic forces? Wage slavery is capitalism's bulwark against existential freedom. Who has the time? In the novel Antoine Roquentin can afford to be nauseous because he has private means. What the hell could I care about the problems of anyone with independent income? Roquentin feels the overwhelming absurdity of his existence only to immediately imagine raping a little girl. What is so transcendent? How is that not always like the rich? In my cubicle that summer I kept hung a printout of Picasso's assessment of my life. *Les ordinateurs sont inutiles. Ils nous donnent que les réponses.* Would Sartre have given me useful questions rather than useless answers had I arrived in Paris years sooner? I am sorry I only kissed Louisa the one time but it all seemed much more imperative when I imagined her with a wasting disease. I do not feel it was determined. Anyway Sartre didn't understand Baudelaire because he didn't understand poetry and on meeting I would have stood a good five inches higher than Sartre and anyway in Paris I had read Sartre called someone an engineer when he meant to be especially insulting.

"I'm taking that taxi."

Outside the flag store Louisa had caught the attention of some passing taximan without making effort. She dashed off without looking back. In the movie about waiting for death the singer is in a taxi listening to herself yé-yé on the radio when the automobile is attacked by art students wearing masks, growling, shouting, thumping the fenders, making the singer laugh. On the radio it is a pop tune not especially awful. Later when the singer leaves her loft apartment to again wander the streets, dressed in black but wearing a new scarf, she passes a small child pounding something quite like jazz out of a toy piano. It is better than what was on the radio.

RIGHT IN THE TEETH

FADE IN:

INT: IT FITS INFORMATION TECHNOLOGY OFFICE - NEW
MORNING

A nude Miss Cummersum appears to be a bluebird
hatching from a huge egg until the egg splits
into body parts that eventually resolve into
Igor. On the floor Igor is now wearing the white
dental assistant's dress Miss Cummersum was
wearing earlier but the dress has been enhanced
with many of the accessories from the fetish
dress Miss Cummersum was wearing later. Leather
corset. The single studded glove that covers
only past the knuckles. Slave buckles on wrists
and ankles. His crotch the metal device like a
snarl of savage teeth but with an extravagant red
tongue too. Most important his hump is now on
his chest. The misplacement of hump seems to
enforce some idea he remains egg. Miss Cummersum
stands over him with toes trapped in the teeth of
the metal device. She finally now has the fetish
gag ball firmly in her mouth. She is nude but
painted blue. Denshag and Chairman Povereese
stand to one side as though not to dirty their
shoes with real work. Chairman Povereese is now
a rhinoceros. He still wears his crown.

                    DENSHAG
          Yes. I have them pose like this
          every casual Friday to remind the
          other workers there will come

                    211

Monday. Of course the blue woman
represents all that has gone
unrequited through the workweek.

Povereese lets off roar.

>   DENSHAG
>   (to Igor)
> Explain to Chairman Povereese how
> this very little number of yours
> quintessentially defines a confined
> abstinence, restrained, abstinence
> held certain within restraints even
> without pledges to obedience,
> explain that abstinence within
> restraint is now the guiding
> principle of the modern masses, such
> a small number, your number,
> untouched but submissive to the
> economic hegemony of our garment
> company, to all our corporate might.

>   IGOR
>   (coming up on
>   elbow)
> Look. I've shared a bed with the
> most desirable woman in this...

>   DENSHAG
>   (interrupting)
> No! Wider!

>   IGOR
>   (incomprehensible
>   with mouth wide
>   open)
> Look. I've shared a bed with the
> most desirable woman in this...

Povereese roars before charging across the room in exit.

> IGOR
>
> Once again I have a job tickling the ivories but never once did I expect hourly wages to migrate my hump to the other side of my torso. Should I have seen that coming? Am I not a somnambulist in service to the number six? Certainly it is very much a time of incertitude. What would an economist predict?

Denshag goes to his desk to play with the Fashion Doll. Life is somehow normal. Programmer I and Programmer II enter and take the exact place of Povereese and Denshag overlooking Igor.

> PROGRAMMER II
> (aside)
> There's only so few gratifying ways you can defile a body when it is only playing dead.

> PROGRAMMER I
> (aside)
> And you can't count on any of them even with a computer.

> PROGRAMMER II
> Hunchback. Hunchfront I mean. What do you think you're doing on a floor meant only for irremovable stains? Surely humiliating my sister should be enough for any...man...one... one thing. Why strive for immortality?

The two programmers approach to each slap a hand
on the backend of Miss Cummersum. She squeals
and her body stretches wildly towards the ceiling
like a rubber band but her toes are held so she
snaps back with a twang.

The two programmers sit in their chairs to make
it easier on themselves.

> PROGRAMMER I
> Don't let us disturb your work, Miss
> Cummersum.

> PROGRAMMER II
> But it is imperative computer
> programmers not be hindered from
> solving the questions left by
> economists.

> PROGRAMMER I AND PROGRAMMER II
> Is there elasticity along a demand
> curve?

The programmers prod Miss Cummersum so violently
from behind her pelvis stretches forwards to fill
the screen before snapping back. Mrs Peel
enters, again putting on her shoe with a pen,
pushing aside the programmers who are sent
spinning in their chairs. The programmers come
to a stop away from Miss Cummersum.

> MRS PEEL
> Even the most successful men are
> eventually undone by their bodies.

> IGOR
> Whose bodies? Their own bodies?

                        MRS PEEL
        Has this not yet occurred to you
        that dentistry is about correcting
        physical failure?

                        IGOR
        But only from the top lip to the
        bottom lip.

                        MRS PEEL
        A mouth is not always that small a
        place when push comes to shove. You
        wear the second skin your skin
        abides but have you learned nothing
        from your shoes?

Igor sets about trying to work the fit of one of
his own heels without shifting Miss Cummersum.
He is wearing the torn stockings. The stiletto
heels from the fetish costume simply will not
give way.

                        IGOR
        A little resistance from my toes to
        shoes means my mouth has gone wrong?
        A common odor perhaps misplaced in
        location? Mouth seeming foot? Even
        when all the other clothes indicate
        I am now the dental assistant?

                      PROGRAMMER II
        You are just a little programming
        irregularity.

                      PROGRAMMER I
        A rounding error.

PROGRAMMER II
A branch and waltz through core.

PROGRAMMER I AND PROGRAMMER II
Dead code!

IGOR
(beseeching
Mrs Peel)
Certainly I am not dead!

PROGRAMMER I
Dead.

PROGRAMMER II
Dead.

PROGRAMMER I
Dead.

PROGRAMMER II
Dead.

MRS PEEL
If I taught him nothing else in this
life I taught him how to wear heels
without ever quite having them on.
How else better to define being
master of his own fate?

IGOR
Don't think I won't get it on once
no one is watching.

PROGRAMMER I
Rape.

                    PROGRAMMER II
        Rape.

                    PROGRAMMER I
        Rape.

                    PROGRAMMER II
        Rape.

                    MRS PEEL
        It's too late to say I never gave
        you nothing from below the waist.

                    PROGRAMMER II
        Why encourage him to cast his mind
        that far. He's already looking up
        from his childhood like all men of
        genius. No need to draw him a map.

CLOSEUP on the fetish ball in the mouth
of Miss Cummersum as it suddenly begins
to crack open like an egg.

FULL ON scene when from the egg comes
an impossibly large winged dog that
circles the room three times before
flying off.

                    WINGED DOG
        No! No! No! No! No! No! No! No! No!
        No!

                    MISS CUMMERSUM
                    (mouth freed)
        I expected more from being the
        symbol of nature than giving birth
        to a dog that is already an angel.

                    IGOR
Who would not want a mouth speaking
the judgements of men against
heaven?

                    MRS PEEL
Imagine all the loving things people
say over even their most contrary
dead dogs that will never be said
over a hunchback.

                    IGOR
                 (panicked)
And just how did I die if I'm so
dead?

                    MRS PEEL
                (sentimentally
                  to no one)
A dental assistant must recognize
blood events by the company she
keeps.

                    IGOR
                 (astonished
                  and repulsed)
You mean I must menstruate?

                    MRS PEEL
It might help if you think of it in
terms of workflow.

                    PROGRAMMER II
Abstinence is a subversion of
capitalism only within an
unregulated number sequence
representing immortality.
              (feels about his teeth)

Virginity simply mustn't be allowed
to go on so long as that.
        (removes finger from mouth
        so it will be understood
        he is speaking importance)
This woman isn't especially tall.
Or blue. But already everything
down to a mouth giving birth to
mythology she serves only the
company.   It is inevitable company
ownership will extend closer to the
floor every year she works here
standing atop all that nature
abhors.

                PROGRAMMER I
A vacuum? A mop? A dust cloth?
How is that for you, baby, does it
make you feel clean?

                MISS CUMMERSUM
                (to Igor)
Why do you encourage them? Getting
back to nature does not mean nature
should only be approached from the
rear.
        (rubs own bottom)
I can always find another job
eventually since eventuality is what
remains of the promises of a land
made independent by revolutionaries
but now ruled by insincere smiles.

                IGOR
Do you want me to predict how long
it will take? It just now occurred
to me I will never be free until I'm
dead. I am dead. So dead. In fact
I am the somnambulist now for all

those buried beneath this forbidden
floor.

PROGRAMMER I

Should we pull the gold out of his
teeth?

PROGRAMMER II
(to Igor)

I bet you didn't see that one coming
either.

Denshag is still at his desk where the
Fashion Doll dances with her
handkerchief to a rhythm kept by the
chattering teeth. They both move in
the jerks and clatter of windup toys.

DENSHAG
(only now looking up
from Fashion Doll)

Perhaps it is time for answers to
the economic questions John Maynard
Keyes wished he had lived long
enough to speak.

PROGRAMMER II

The questions? The answers? Speak
which?

IGOR
(in trance of a
séance speaks
over the
toy clatter)

All measurements are invariably a
dog chasing its own tail since the
act of measurement has itself a cost
that must be recognized. This is

both the bestial and hindsight
nature of economics within
information technology. Computers
are testaments to repetition. That
is to say, all assessments of
personal worth are invariably wrong
until a second dog comes along to
sniff your bottom, which in turn
requires a third dog to...just say
no?

FADE OUT.

CAHIERS DU CINÉMA

An American In Paris

Of course I recognize *The Bride Wore Black* is an attempt by François Truffaut to provide an alternative ending to *An American In Paris*. The American Jerry Mulligan is remade a Frenchman named Fergus so perhaps not French at all, more likely from Irish ancestry like Mulligan, but a famous painter anyway, the very thing Jerry Mulligan is never going to be once he sexually rejects Nina Foch, the Milo character. Her money is the only path for his success painting knockoffs of Utrillo. Whenever I watch the musical I am always reminded of Derain painting his awful Corots. But Fergus being a famous painter means in this telling he does not reject the money of any of the rich women who cross his path. His being famous means he has never danced through any history of painting in his imagination with Leslie Caron. He loves no one. He is Johnny Cousin. None of this is particularly obvious so Truffaut made the other possible ending to *An American In Paris* a decade later in *The Man Who Loved Women*. Charles Denner plays an almost identical character in both movies though called Morane in the second movie to push even closer to the Mulligan character with assonance in the name. In *The Bride Wore Black* all the five men Jeanne Moreau plots to kill are heartless seducers of women. In that movie Fergus tells how he follows women in the street but is overwhelmed when there are too many to ever have them all. He tells how he hates when a man not a woman sits next to him on the train. In *The Man Who Loved Women* he speaks from the grave how he never had any male friends. Morane knows the rules of the game. Fergus knows the rules of the game. In *The Bride Wore Black* Fergus hides Jeanne Moreau behind the door while he makes an arrangement understood to be a liaison with the superb redhead model. It is the game but then Fergus paints Moreau in a costume of the goddess of chastity. *I'll have some proof. Her name that was as fresh as Diana's visage is now as black and begrimed as my own face.* It is hard not to hear those lines spoken by Othello while Jeanne Moreau poses with the bow and arrow of the immortal virgin huntress. The Julie character Moreau plays is meant to be pure since her revenge is against those five drinking buddies who accidently kill her groom her only love her childhood love on their wedding day. The groom dies on the steps of the church. Julie remains untouched but Fergus removes her shoes to draw her feet bare. In *The Man Who Loved Women* a similar reference to dance not danced is made when from the grave Morane looks up the skirts of all his old lovers to admire one last time their legs. And that's just it, isn't it? Because in *The Man Who Loved Women* only after writing his memoires of seduction, only after years chasing women in the street, years of ogling girls in the park, of chatting up every waitress, every shop clerk, by a chance meeting Morane realizes he became a seducer after being rejected by a woman. That's right, Leslie Caron. Who else would it be? It must have been love at first sight. All the books about movies say Truffaut was the only director in France who would give Leslie Caron a job. Why? Because the character Lise had surmounted everyone like that ballet dance through history that redefined everything to itself without actually looking at the paintings. Even Jean Seberg peddling newspapers had not freed the men of France, and perhaps all the men of the world thinking of France, from memory of Leslie Caron. No drumming could get past her. No one otherwise left breathless. But in *The Man Who Loved Women* there are no bad paintings displaying the economics of the situation. Morane works with miniatures. He is the man who did not take money from the rich woman so has been reduced to designing oil tankers with a wave machine that creates motion something not entirely unlike bedroom undulations. He is merely an engineer. There remains no easel in his apartment full of crime novels.

"You can't insert that if you expect the customer to get the idea."

"Lulu, I didn't study cinema for nothing."

"You can't."

"It's a great shot."

"You can't."

"Whose idea was it to flash advertising on the machines anyway?"

"From way up."

"And grocery stores want this shit for their teller machines?"

Truffaut wrote an introduction to Andre Bazin's book on Orson Welles but the book isn't much and Truffaut knocked off the introduction on a plane headed for Los Angeles. In the book Welles is quoted that he throws away everything he paints but perhaps someday will paint something good enough to keep. I have no hope for anything but the strange sense of loss over my own destroyed paintings becoming an essential sense of loss. I need it to replace other memories. What in that destruction can be my last words? Word? Bazin argues that one of the great themes in Welles is the nostalgia for childhood, arguing it is even his fundamental project, in the sense Sartre meant, the existentialist sense, though Sartre more famously dismissed *Citizen Kane* for not being true cinema because it looked to the past rather than the present. In some tortured way I suppose that means the ideas of Baudelaire can never be cinema. Still, in Micheál MacLiammóir's diaries on the making of *Othello* he describes the cistern where one of the fight scenes takes place as satanic genius, a place to breed toads and armadillos, the setting for an unwritten masterpiece by Baudelaire. After reading that, I have never been able to watch *Othello* without thinking it all Baudelaire, because what is Desdemona strangled dead on her wedding sheets but a story of lost innocence? She blames herself. Who does that but those who have found innocence a punishment?

"And for the new machines at the cinema complexes so you should like that."

"Even at the drive-in for the last show?"

"Not there."

I had been to the drive-in one time with Janis just to give the backseat of the utility vehicle some work outside winter. She was just back from Europe. It was the last time I saw her.

"No advertisements for the condoms available for purchase next to the toilets?"

In interviews Sartre was never certain he had actually written the piece on Welles published under his name years before. Of course he knew he wrote it, liar, what a bad liar. But by then, when questioned, Sartre knew Bazin, knew Bazin had important things to say about the découpage in *Citizen Kane* reinventing the nature of cinema, the editing no longer the standard breaks between long shot, close up, medium shot, but something stranger shot from down low with all the shots compressed into one, usually through movement of the actors, sometimes through arrangement of the décor. Sartre knew to keep quiet. Bazin calls the low angle an infernal vision but doesn't he miss the point? How does he get to Baudelaire watching *The Magnificent Ambersons*? I mean, in the novel the Joseph Cotton character goes to work in the mines but I don't remember that being in the movie. Isn't the low angle the viewpoint of a child? What happened to Welles at seven or eight? That Sartre might have answered instead if he hadn't been living with his widowed mother all through his most famous years, always his shoes needing to be tied, his nose to be wiped with his mother's handkerchief. It was her apartment.

"My father has chosen a family movie for the last show."

"What movie?"

"His favorite."

I would never have loved Louisa so much if I hadn't known she was raised in the movie theaters her father managed for some corporation, operated in ever decreasing fortune, the drive-in now sold off for a big box store and a row of shops, the last of the cinemascope theaters recently razed to build a sports arena, the most crumbling theater near a college campus given over to showing queer movies, then that theater too torn down when the leaking roof ruined the screen, like a money shot. I programmed each day hoping every line coded would be ephemeral.

"I bet the shops they put up instead remain empty."

"Do you think destruction is more tolerable if it is meaningless?"

Jeanne Moreau pushes her first victim off a balcony when he reaches to retrieve her scarf that has blown away. They are at a party. It becomes a strange riff on *Othello* that the kerchief with its magic should finally serve rather than betray its mistress. It is no accident that Jerry Mulligan has his ballet fantasy about the history of painting while standing on a balcony overlooking backlot Montmartre, no accident, he intends to finish the dance with a final leap. *Seek though rather to be hanged in compassing thy joy than to be drowned and go without her.* Are we really to believe it is love at first sight for Jerry Mulligan because Lise personifies everything he loves about Paris? Doesn't Lise in his ballet fantasy personify the actual canvas of certain paintings? What the painter has touched? I have many times watched the movie that way. Anyway there are lots of women in the ballet dancing with flowing scarfs. But by that weekend before first going to the bank I could not help notice that in the movie Lise's wealthy guardian makes it quite clear her knees have remained coupled despite all their corybantic hopping. Her virginity is made a central issue. And so it is all obvious and yet in her autobiography Betsy Blair at an old age still questions why Gene Kelly wanted to marry her when she was but a girl more than ten years younger than himself. Did she never see the damned movie? Wasn't she the virgin she claimed? When Betsy Blair left Gene Kelly to live in the real Paris she found herself a very handsome actor her own age, perhaps even a few years younger than herself, but the autograph I have from her in her autobiography does not scream of knowledge gained, there is nothing bold about it. Obviously Jeanne Moreau kills the Fergus character simply by releasing the arrow from the drawn bow. The audience sees that coming a mile away yet all the same it is the best painter's death ever filmed.

"I think trying to persuade people to spend their money for anything less than sex constitutes a perversion."

"So you don't watch movies on television anymore?"

"Doesn't your father always show advertisements before the movie trailers now?"

Louisa couldn't deny her father had been reduced to shilling things other than fantasy, other even than popcorn, but from her attitude Louisa clearly did not believe it affected the bloodlines, it trailed no curse. I too have no male friends. But the name Oscar Levant stumbles about in my mind until it becomes Oskar Bronski perhaps Matzerath so this abuse of observation passing for synchronicity becomes another way *An American In Paris* surmounts all other possibilities. It is all strings. Oskar too is uncertain who is his father. Like Baudelaire, Sartre had a hated stepfather. The mother of Orson Welles simultaneously kept two men Welles called daddy not father. I keep clear of drums but there are always more drums. I have not longed for a drum since that beating in the pub with the bodhran silent on the table over my battered head.

"Those things don't actually pay that much."

With years passing I found daydreams of defenestration could no longer find political inspiration from within the cubicle while the possibilities of sexual insistence never arrived. I no longer have a cubicle. Louisa has tried to kill me many times now she no longer works at the bank. How does the third of the five victims die in *The Bride Wore Black*? I am perhaps afraid to remember. For a second victim Jeanne Moreau poisons the wine of the short ugly man who claims to never have luck with women. Moreau knows he is a liar because now she too is a kind of somnambulist, being a virgin goddess. I never take the attempts on my life to the police since the final man is killed by Jeanne Moreau in prison with his own breakfast knife. She is in prison for killing Fergus after being identified by the police from the mural Fergus has made of her over his bed. The mural over the bed is his claim from the grave to have had her virginity. It happens off screen, the final stabbing. The camera trollies with Jeanne Moreau pushing the breakfast cart towards the iron doors of the cells in the men's wing of the prison. Louisa is more than clever enough to succeed through some similar scheme. The auditors at the bank have never liked the look of me, always contumacious, a possessor of outside interests, leaving little doubt there exists a plan for my imprisonment in the files of human resources just waiting for me to slam a resignation letter on the desk of some manager, just waiting for me to declare my freedom. In that movie in that final scene none of the men are banging protest on the water pipes but there is execution all the same.

"I bought a television but I've not watched anything on cable since the first weekend I brought it home."

"Because all the commercials were selling sex? Or none of them?"

The men of France could not reject Leslie Carson in the same way that man who runs into the light pole at the start of *Shoot The Piano Player* must marry his wife to prove she is a virgin. This insignificant character to the plot is keen to find he has not been fooled all his life, desperate to prove the world is not a sordid nothingness waiting to take the soul, the character of Baudelaire, you see, always writing about light but finding damnation. Isn't that almost the plot of one of the other great working class movies from the London of my childhood? How does that one start? With a spotlit dog running along the street to a jazz score by Sonny Rollins so good it makes any movie since without jazz seem beside the point. The dog arrives to where Alfie is having it off with a married woman in a parked car. The story Alfie tells about the woman somehow doesn't feel so different from the man running into the lamppost in the fog. Alfie says she is on her way out because she wants him to meet her husband. It. Notoriously he refers to women as *it* rather than *her.* Alfie chases a kind of innocence that would not occur to Moran or Fergus because they are damned with a singular obsession for that one perfect woman. Baudelaire suffered the same. But then even Alfie trips up thinking he has found the perfect woman in a rich older woman. It breaks him.

"So the last movie is actually going to be An American In Paris?"

"It isn't one you can quote? You don't sing the songs in the shower? I'm pretty sure I've heard you. You trying to tell me now you don't want to be Gene Kelly? Eh, Kelly?"

She meant she had heard me over the walls of cubicles singing songs from the movie but Louisa could never understand it is the right of a wage slave to speak against the job. Alfie gets caught whistling. *Never be cheerful on a job if you're doing a fiddle.* It should have been a line in all subsequent editions of *The Industrial Workers of the World Songbook* beginning on the first page then repeated on the last. Of course all this acquiescence to the movies becomes gratification for the bourgeoisie, things being cleaned up, since in the play the movie is based on, Alfie drives a lorry before becoming a chauffeur driving a limousine, maybe even drives the coal truck Bill Naughton drove before becoming a playwright, having to scrub hands in olive oil each night to remove the dust ground into the skin. Imagine Alfie finding the body of Joe Orton. Then imagine the movie retold in a series of black handprints revealed below the waist. How's that for *Othello* played by Welles?

"I have a good voice but I've never tried to take it to the piano in public."

"Why not?"

"I prefer to keep my motivations secret."

"Not that I've seen."

Rover, isn't that what McGoohan and company on the set called the weather balloon that chases down recalcitrant prisoners in that last show where McGoohan is a number not a name? That anyway is what all the testaments about the show claim. The weather balloon covers a man's face but becomes not just strangulation. It becomes mask. For the longest time I didn't notice that the white rubber pressing over the screaming faces was meant to be a death mask taken from the living. Still it seems a sensation experienced a thousand times in the cubicle. The balloon becomes all the technology that strangles the jazz in poetry and the madness of painting and the voice that shouts *no thanks*. I am no longer certain every year a wage slave isn't meant to be celebrated in a death mask given to record the horror of it. I do not mean to say I completely appreciate Truffaut's insistence woman must destroy man with chasing if not worse. McGoohan overcome by the balloon looks surprisingly like the death mask of Baudelaire, at least how it should have looked. That death mask is a museum piece like a painting. They haul it out for the tourists.

"You've seen less than you like to pretend."

Louisa stood silent for a moment watching the teller machine play a commercial for retirement investment we hadn't yet applied with sound. It was the first teller machine we had ever seen that could play video.

"I was lucky to get in under the pension scheme before they froze it."

"I didn't get under it."

"So why are you here?"

There certainly was a horror in finding a poised career forcibly redefined within three televised musicals, yet perhaps it might have triumphed if other movies, the ones seen long before, hadn't kept intruding through the work hours, the intrusions delusive, implying loss of innocence but perhaps more accurately revealing a lack of faith. I see now that perhaps my enslavement has all been because the somnambulist and the poet never became a single mind in rebellion. Was I supposed to make a choice? Was I supposed to make a choice which of the three movies would dominate the cubicle? Each morning even now I sing the songs from those three movies in the shower but the sanctified water never once has become ablution. They call the wind what? No name? What number? No. I had no choice that might have mattered. Virgin unpursued. Virgin pursued. The auctioned woman with two new husbands. Where is her lasting celebration she has palate for both sweet and sour? What animal does a girl choose to become after she goes untouched by both sport and frailty when wanting to be a man? What shocking dance of modern painting does Lise dance through once Jerry has her? How many times does she return to dance the next paintings and the next paintings and all the other successes of someone else? For work I remained kept in a box all day like the somnambulist from the movie of stilted walls but when presented to the audience there came from my tongue across my teeth only talk about the weather. There was no meter. There were no rhymes. It wasn't even the passerby with the virgin wife who ran into the lamppost. I was much less.

AT THE ART
CENTER

No one knew how all the many pieces of the old computer system fit together, the code I mean, everyone always having to pause to look up this, make an educated guess at that, meaning anything new was cobbled together like an alligator said to be a purse. Each line of code inserted likely broke something somewhere else much farther along the complexity of processes. It didn't help no one making decisions ever knew what he was talking about. I don't just mean management was forever creating meaningless projects to make work for the weekends. It was even more often the case the bosses excused their own lapses in decision knowing the programmers could simply be forced to work harder later to accommodate corrections claimed to be inspiration. Never underestimate mismanagement. I was that Sunday afternoon ignoring some especially egregious lapses in management by sitting in the café of the art center drinking tea over a piece of cheesecake. I had been to work that morning. I planned to get out on the catboat sometime later that day.

> It is never unreasonable you still insist on
> remaining untouched in that way but it is
> equally never unreasonable to argue there are
> other ways to please. The bed was clean. I do
> not know what you think you smelled. Of

course you must never spend the night since
you feel that way about the early hours.

I had stolen the love letter from her cubicle before Louisa
ever saw it. Her cubicle like all the cubicles was overflowing
with printed programs and printed reports and all sorts of
other printed documents so an envelope gone missing for
weeks would be no surprise. Perhaps Mortenson would feel his
crotch heaving him into unsteady footing for the week he
waited for Louisa to speak of the letter. Perhaps later after an
argument Louisa would snicker another letter had not come
email because Mortenson had habit of addressing electronic
mail to the wrong employee, the wrong bank branch, the
wrong government, the wrong universe, pledging love to the
most unappreciative recipients. Still it was becoming
uncomfortable picturing Louisa alone with a boss who begs to
take her orders long into the night. All night long. The letter
made it clear Mortenson like death itself was always in more
hurry than those pursued.

"I rewrote the essay three times but I couldn't convince
myself they were great paintings."

"He hangs in every museum."

"Not here."

"What would you say if we donated ours?"

"I didn't argue he wasn't historically significant."

It became dreamlike the more the schoolgirl with her family
at the next table recited her essay in phrases carelessly
plagiarized from Baudelaire. Discovering a logic of light and
shade. Suggestive colors. Red and green together producing a
monochrome. There were three daughters perhaps all in high
school, the oldest, the one with her long red hair braided,
perhaps in her first year of college, the middle daughter the

quiet one, her blonde hair streaked red much like the mother, tall like her mother too, then the youngest perhaps not yet in high school, perhaps advanced an extra year since she was the smartest, almost genius from everything I'd heard about her, gorgeous like her sisters but her red hair cut short because she was supposed to be the boy the parents hunted on the third adventure. They were richly dressed. The father athletic like a runner was in a better suit than ever seen daily at the bank. The girls were in deep cobalt blue dresses that left the glory of color to the mother dressed in a viridian casually vibrant under the sunshine coming through the windows that looked out onto the courtyard fountain. It amused me the family would walk over to the art center from St Augustin's after Mass. They were the most beautiful ménage I had even seen. I had not seen them together before, had only ever before seen for certain the mother and the youngest daughter, and then not together, yet because the luncheon was at the art center shimmering with prayer, it seemed as though I could taste them in my tea. I tried to imagine the temptation of St Anthony Baudelaire kept hung in his room when he even had a room. It was the mother grilling the eldest daughter.

I have not forgotten we will be married soon.

I tried to ignore the letter. The more they talked the more certain I became the Delacroix the lunching family owned must be a fake. It was merely a matter of honor, that painting. The mother mentioned parents they all knew who promised no inheritance beyond an education and the faces of the girls fell away like viewing purgatory rendered in artist oils on the way to lower levels of oil burning in hell. But then the father pulled his daughters away to safety talking about the dogs bred on the acres they owned somewhere south of the city. Sunday afternoons earlier in the year were always spent selling puppies so wasn't it nice to get to the art center instead?

"You would have gotten a better grade if you had typed your essay."

"It wasn't required."

"You would have gotten a better grade anyway."

"It's a trick?"

The first time I entered the art center I expected to find it curtained in portraits of the early pioneers and their ever more prosperous descendants. Instead I walked past the Henri Matisse and the Roy Lichtenstein remembering how on the Titanic the orchestra launched into a ragtime number just when the water reached their feet. *Freeze in hell you rich bastards. Die with my noise in your ears.* I had thought that once before walking through a gallery of Astor portraits. Instead that first time at the art center I saw a very delicate pencil portrait of a young woman I never again saw hanging. Burnes-Jones. Long after all that Raphaelite nonsense tried to return beauty to myth against modernity. I looked across the table noticing how much the quiet daughter resembled that portrait. It was too much. I imagined the early portraits meant to be hanging all darkened with time into shrouds hiding regrets. In the later portraits by van Dongen the pioneer descendants stood assured they were too rich to ever be scalped.

"You walk into a room upright if you want others to listen."

I turned instead to the discounted book I had bought at the museum giftshop on my way to the café. Downstairs next the toilets was a large window looking onto steel bookcases crammed tight with art folios the ordinary crowd were left to envy but never touch. Apparently the view was meant to work the sphincter because I never saw anyone enter that library. On a Sunday the toilets had a line waiting.. Anyway the books sold in the giftshop were not academic. I had bought the Beatrice Wood autobiography to read her claim she was the model for Roché's Kathe. Nonsense. In both the movie and the novel Kathe resembles an ancient bust carved in marble. But in Truffaut's movie of *Jules et Jim* the foot race takes place on a Paris bridge with Jeanne Moreau dressed in men's clothes, a moustache penciled over her lip and like all successful men cheating the start call so she carries the race. In the novel by Henri-Pierre Roché the race occurs frequently, repeatedly, through Cimetière Montparnasse past the cenotaph of Baudelaire. Kathe passes for a man on the street only the one time without a race occurring that same night. I love the movie but did I prefer the novel to the movie even then? I must have. In the café I leafed through the autobiography reading how Beatrice Wood was terribly poor though born to wealth. I could not empathize. They had servants, her family. They sent their daughter to a debutante ball. Even now I always watch when the Truffaut movie pops up though it is the novel that seems to have existence. This too is nonsense of course. Sartre was wrong about songs sitting outside mere being. He was writing before people started talking about lost jazz recordings. Sartre had no concept for extinction. For him a recording no longer available in Paris was found still in the provinces.

"I am not sorry I took the class but it's mostly memorizing dates as though death and birth matters more than the paintings and sculptures."

"Do they teach every change was a change for the better?"

"It all matters if it's on the test."

They laughed in a strange unison that meant family but to other ears seemed rehearsed. In flipping pages, I saw the family at the next table somehow start taking on the incremented movements of the plasticine figures I used in the animated movie I was making, the father shifting elbows a breath each time I glanced, the eldest daughter straightening her collar with fingers that seemed numbed with hesitation, barely moving within each moment.

"Anything could happen."

The boyish daughter said this the moment I found the same words in Beatrice Wood. I could not be certain I hadn't put the words in her mouth, the daughter. They are distinctly there in the book. Baudelaire wrote that Flaubert put the mind of a man into the body of Madame Bovary chasing sex. Beatrice Wood remained friends with Henri-Pierre Roché until his death though she broke with him romantically when he admitted he was sleeping with her friends. He seduced every passing virgin. The scene in *The Man Who Loved Women* where the secretary prudishly refuses to continue typing the memoir actually happened in real life when Truffaut had Roché's journals typed. In my new book Beatrice was soon chasing sex without love as if she had caught it for a disease. *Their ills instruct us so.* Good for her in heavenly light or otherwise. I read but wandered in thought. In *Jules et Jim*, the character Roché makes himself, Jim, breaks his engagement to Kathe then spends three seasons sick in his childhood bed, tended by his mother. Sartre moved in with his mother the day after his stepfather was buried. Baudelaire's mother wrote syphilitic Baudelaire to not even think he was moving in after his stepfather, the general, the hero of Lyon, was buried. Probably Sartre believed he had one up on Baudelaire at least in accommodations. The day I was released from the madhouse, my sisters put me in a hotel suite with instructions to soak hours in the hot tub provided, the jets set high, wanting me scoured before I came near, even to the front steps of our dead mother's house with *for sale* signs planted near the sidewalk. Baudelaire longed to be Flaubert in the house of his childhood with an adoring mother. Sartre was delivered the reality of that dream. I soaked for three days then found the job at the video store that probably would have been the job in the ketchup factory if I hadn't felt so clean for a moment.

"What are you going to have?"

"The iced tea here you can see through like a watercolor wash."

These were different voices screeching like old birds. I looked up to find the perfect family had gone without me making their movements, not rising, not steps, certainly not in notion there were hours to spend elsewhere. I gave up the table and wandered towards the front gallery thinking I would just leave for the catboat but was instead surprised to find I had caught up.

"I think maybe I see you all the time coming over the trail across the bridge from the railroad tracks."

"I am not jumping trains."

"No. You study piano. Isn't that you?"

"How do you know that?"

The boyish daughter did not remember I had seen her once at the house of the woman who let me sometimes play jazz in the tavern she owned. The woman gave piano lessons. The girl saw me so often on the park trail she couldn't differentiate the memories into that one with me dashing off with sheet music under one arm and the wild chords of Horace Silver shining in my eyes. The boyish daughter was probably thirteen but even the oldest daughter with her plagiarisms and sarcasms smelled sweet with virginity. I held the Beatrice Wood book under one arm and my eyes in search wondered if I couldn't seduce all three sisters before moving onto what mattered deep in my damnation, mattered to liberty, mattered to movement free from the restrained increments of indifferent birth.

"Look at those tailored clothes."

In Sartre Roquentin tells the autodidact that young people standing before a painting fake their joy. But this painting was not from the paintings Roquentin sees in the Bouville museum of the great men of the last generation. It was not a pioneer painting. Here the three daughters stood before the Singer Sargent where the two children are exquisitely dressed but miserable in appearance. The painting overwhelms with feelings of constraint and torture. They are still growing. They might have just stepped from a shared bedroom becoming increasingly crowded. Roquentin realizes in the portraits of the great men there is not one who failed to leave children. It is their right. Even in the one painting he has come especially to see, Roquentin finds a man with children, though Roquentin has learned the man was almost a dwarf, painted though with reduced furniture to appear the same in size as the other men of the great generation, the men who built the port city, the men who must have laughed when reading the scandal sheet that called the dwarf a louse in a president's beard. In business the dwarf was remembered a strike breaker. Of course Sartre is writing what he himself would have become had he gone into business, become a general, at the very least become a stepfather asserting his rights. The three daughters now appeared to move more naturally, but with stops, as though movement in my editor where I could run the film backwards should I choose. Without certain future they could not escape me.

"But look at how unhappy they are."

"Posing."

"It had to be more than that."

"Posing."

"There is no reason to think the mother has beaten this little girl."

"You only have to look at her to know," I insisted.

The letters of Baudelaire to his mother are like that old comedy where all a poet's poems are requests for money, his greatest poem being, of course, the one that asks for loan of a preposterously large sum. It is a comedy bankers sometimes recount over their whiskeys paid from the expense account. But Baudelaire's letters to his mother survive only because he was forever asking for money. If he had only written the discovery of a new painter of great talent, had written the *correspondances* of senses cause perfumes to register red, had written all works of art express an elusive love for beauty, if he had written only those things his mother would never have felt her bourgeois values so violated the letters had to be kept in evidence. He wrote lunatic spleen. The raging letters became an accountancy matter. Still his mother invited him to live with her once *Les Fleurs du Mal* was accepted a great book even under prosecution for indecency. Even that mother.

"Why do you think her mother beat her?"

I thought it would be the boyish daughter but here it came the eldest daughter asking, demanding as though she would write it down.

"For listening to jazz."

The boyish daughter thought this especially funny.

"I practice two hours every day."

The boyish daughter said this to her quiet sister so conspiratorially the eldest sister gave her a shove four steps down the gallery. She meant to get her sisters away. At the same time the eldest sister gave me a glare meant to command me not to follow. Berthe Morisot played piano for Baudelaire during his final illness. There was no jazz yet. I only know it was not his own voice last in his ears since the paralysis brought on by syphilis had robbed his speech, the poetry, had taken his shout. Early in life his mother had sent him on a sea voyage to rid herself the embarrassment of such a son. It is recorded he helped save from floundering the ship full of passengers who wouldn't speak to him. Perhaps he thought differently on that heroism after seeing a negress publicly whipped when the ship was stopped at some island. He had prayed the ship would sink after all then abandoned his voyage fearing his prayers would be answered. Was it memory of screams from the negress last in his ears? That would have been close enough to jazz for a dying man.

"I'm nineteen."

"You think a banker should care?"

Those sisters were very attracted that I should see in them an abuse from their mother. The eldest daughter told me her age because she could see sweep across my face the disappointment that she not her youngest sister had sought me out alone. Perhaps she believed she saw relief.

"How old do you suppose Marie-Louise Pailleron had to be before she ever heard jazz? I mean once there even was jazz. Forty?"

Baudelaire writing about *correspondances* in the arts somehow missed the fervid correspondence of condemnation.

"She became some kind of poet, didn't she? Maybe a journalist?"

"You mean despite the beatings?"

It was the mad recognizing the mad that made me so want the youngest sister. Instead I led the eldest sister down to that library across from the toilets where the window was blocked with a view of academic art folios seldom if ever opened. I had keys. Back among the racks the eldest daughter lifted her skirt to reveal she had taken communion without wearing underpants. I remembered a year about that same age never taking communion without bringing something stolen. Lifting the leg of the eldest daughter with my trousers unzipped seemed somehow very similar when that heeled shoe rode the love letter in my rear pocket.

"Did you even pay?"

"I not only paid with credit card before the start of the year I've already paid the credit card bill."

The mother in the family was administrator of the art classes at the center. I was in her office the one time the previous winter when I arrived for the figure painting class, the class where I met Janice, only to be told I wasn't enrolled. The woman was accusatory. I tried to imagine impoverished artists slipping into the class without paying but instead I kept seeing Gully Jimpson in the face of Alec Guinness trying to wheedle his old canvas from Sara Monday. *The Horse's Mouth* was quite true to the novel in a condensed fashion. Sara Monday has kept the painting of herself in the bath to remember how it once was to be beautiful. In the office the mother of the family searched through a stack of forms before concluding without doubt I had never paid. While she was searching I stole her keys. The mother in the family had kept her maiden name for professional reasons, kept the name of her famous ancestor Delacroix but now was forever angry to find she was merely a bookkeeper. She scanned a stack of forms but it was of absolute importance to the mother in the family there should be no form proving my payment. She skipped over mine. There was no arguing with her because it would have been arguing against her memory of once being very beautiful. I paid a second time. The teller machine at the airport could always be fiddled into supporting the arts another round.

"You're good."

"Were you standing on my new book the whole time?"

The eldest daughter giggled but took her hand away from my shoulder. She meant I painted fine. She meant that more than a year before she had seen my painting in the hallway outside her mother's office where the student works were exhibited each term. It had been a sensation. Remembered. I mean I had recreated the lost painting of me wrestling with the large black box. That swindle against progress a success that hadn't mattered the slightest since Janice left. But one of the businesswomen keeping time had clearly been a portrait of the mother of the three daughters. The eldest had been another a good fuck the painting had gotten me. I still wanted the youngest daughter but only if I could have the silent daughter first. Intensely I wanted to revolt a typist but the computer programmer in me wanted matters to occur in appropriate sequence. A countdown. A branch and count.

"I think I saw your father once before today too."

"You bought a dog?"

It wasn't until the moment I was first inside the eldest daughter it occurred to me her father must no longer be a banker. I envied all the more. I loved the family all the more knowing the father had retired young into a profession with larger cages. It did not stop me from wanting the mother condemned before she was no longer at all beautiful. I would paint her again. I longed to ask if I might someday the light was good the same way all the ambitious artists who passed through the art center knew to ask to paint her if they wanted ahead, wanted in some upcoming show, wanted to be the paid visiting artist. I would seem like all the others. But the painting from my hands would not provide the pleasures of the poor, Sara Monday remembering life when it was still the warm bath of youth. I would paint the still beautiful mother a deformed monster, nude of course, at a table beating her screaming daughters across an afterchurch luncheon carved from the husband's corpse. The dogs would watch with bemusement like they do in the all the old Dutch tavern paintings.

"There was a conference of bankers meeting to describe new financial transactions run from teller machines, potential transactions anyway, the meeting occurring high in one of the buildings downtown because they wanted to look down like rulers, gods, only it was all fogged in, they saw nothing but their own emptiness reflected in the walls of glass."

The eldest daughter was quiet for a moment then put her hand inside the trousers I hadn't yet zipped.

"You are not a banker."

"I was there to advise on technical matters."

"You advised them to jump?"

"It is as difficult to imagine a mother without maternal love as a light without heat."

"What?"

"A bit more from Baudelaire you might find useful."

I never actually put hands on any of those three girls. It is amazing the hallucinations provoked standing too long before a painting even when the girl in the painting is clothed to the chin. Marie-Louise Pailleron. It is not my fault there are no paintings of great men hanging in the upper halls at the art center. I would have preferred it. Had Des Moines never produced even one great man? I had made it only into the lowest halls down next the toilets. What then were my rights if not to leave behind children? Of course all this was some years before light without heat became common outside calculators but perhaps all anticipations found through desire served this current modernity so absent the call to sainthood. If the St Anthony Baudelaire hung still exists I have never seen even a photograph. It was painted by his father. If the father had lived Baudelaire might very well have been just another academic painter whose angels cast down their eyes to not look up the skirts of the rising Virgin. Better not to know. What is that Othello says? *Better all the pioneers had her so long as I never knew?* Iowa is full of the descendants of pioneers who took everything they could put hands on. I am merely one of their number and I have read but never quite believed Baudelaire thought talking to a dog a satanic whim, talking with dogs something the father of the beautiful family must have done many times, all day and night, like a meeting at the crossroads, like Dr. Dolittle howling at the moon.

MUDVILLE

All week in the jacket pocket over my chest I had carried a letter from Alice, which I might have read in the tavern again before the music started, but instead I avoided the letter with its poem by browsing the tall shelves of jazz books the woman who owned the tavern had recently added to a narrow blank wall. It was unclear if the books both new and sorely used were for sale. I thought they were important decoration. Before sitting down at her piano, the tavern owner told me the bookcase stood where, when she first bought the place, there had been two pinball machines that had struggled to keep jazz rhythm but came close, maybe ragtime. The owner had laughed at her own joke. In the letter Alice was mostly laughing at herself for having been forced to return to film acting after the death of the war hero. She had a part in the countryside wearing a stifling wig that smelled from the last actress to wear it. The period costume included a long dress under a wide hat with a peacock feather. The letter went on to describe a German television series that seemed merely a variation on *Jules and Jim* with much more emphasis on the world war trenches. Two men. One woman. Gold fever of a sort if you include the desire not to perish when shoveling past corpses. Alice was happy her own money could again mean something other than politics. But the letter made me brood on how I had briefly adopted conservative politics simply to desecrate a dead mother who had failed even to consider the possibility of a worker revolution. Honey, the letter began.

"Treat it gentle?"

"You know, if you could play soprano saxophone I could give you regular work."

I ignored the woman who owned the tavern to continue reading from Sydney Bechet's autobiography. I had never before seen the book. At least this tavern didn't have televisions on every wall, but it made me wonder what kind of people would ever see Alice in the wide hat, thinking about something I heard when living in Paris, that television was meant for children to outgrow. No. I heard that in a movie. Still I imagined fat hausfraus consuming vast quantities of herring and clams and squid and eel while watching television. A picture of Beethoven on one wall. A picture of Hitler on the opposite wall. No longer watching television I was instead reading all the usual suspects between slipping back to Baudelaire on the very worst nights after a savaging day. I first read Allen Ginsburg and Gregory Corso and Jack Kerouac all trying to sound like that soprano horn. Then I stepped towards Paris to read Ezra Pound and Hilda Doolittle but Hilda didn't speak to animals and not to me either. Mina Loy. E.E. Cummings. Wallace Stevens. I reread a few of Edna St Vincent Millay's translations of Baudelaire that I had read the first time after locating the building that had once been the hotel where Millay had lived in Paris. Had it still been a hotel? Had I tried to get the same room? I don't remember. I had gone to Paris with a long list of addresses and a map covered in numbered circles correlated to the list. I suppose everyone uses their cellphone now to track down the past. Of course I reread Apollinaire. Soupault. Verlaine. Mallarmé brought on the most confusing dreams about 370 assembler code that shuffled order in search of paths I could not fathom. You could do that in assembler. I mean it was possible to physically alter the behavior of one instruction with another instruction. That has been disallowed in all subsequent computer languages. The alter was to the machine language itself in memory and the poetry of Mallarmé seemed to make the same physical changes across printed lines forming dreams. I somehow ended up with an original edition of Amy Lowell poems. None of those poets were the poet come to read his works that night at the tavern.

"Most places you cannot get in the door without a master's degree."

"But you have one, no?" It was only a guess.

"I only taught for a year," responded the poet.

For the moment he was like a pedigreed dog with its hair shaved in some way that made the breed hard to identify. I had to pull back from that thought because there was too much to like about him to be so dismissive. The poet was scrawny with a pale scraggly beard nothing like the trimmed facial hair of the academic poets so far come to the tavern. He looked starved. I liked he had worked in bowling alleys and car washes and county fairs before getting some certificate that had him working in a medical lab running tests for venereal disease. Perhaps he looked tubercular too. He had got the certificate after the advanced degree as though literature were a malady he had sought to cure from his lungs and all points lower. I first wondered if at work he wore a cotton mask all day then envisioned a hangman's hood.

"I'm nothing. Ask anyone with an education," I said to the poet.

His howling was not my howling. His anger held onto life in a way not possible within my abyss of shadows. My heart had been eaten. He spoke of cultures grown in the medical lab as flowers of the modern evils but he meant it for at least a wink if not a laugh. Still it was fun that night to play piano behind the poetry. It wasn't entirely unlike any other time being the rhythm section when the saxophone took the break. The woman who owned the tavern usually played for the poets she brought in to read but she seemed to understand I needed to be kept away from the new shelves of books until they became just something else that no longer mattered within all my unexpressed rages. The owner had given the piano over to me for the reading.

"The only time I ever write good poetry is immediately after I travel."

He meant he kept to the road. I wanted to describe sketching while travelling though I had not once gone anywhere beyond Iowa since leaving Paris. No. The drive to see Robbie. Anyway it was a backlot performance on my part too and for the first time in a long time I played piano without ever having seen a computer. I knew no passwords. I knew only the language taught by my mother. Behind that poetry I was not who I was.

"I write before I've even showered, when I'm still exhausted by the flight, sometimes even when still in the car though I've arrived, preferably not entirely sober."

I remember the man but not a word of the poetry he recited except I remember that the poems repeatedly evoked a longing for early morning before the crowds bustled. It seemed a miscalculation this poet had put himself in the middle of the tall corn fields throwing their stifling humidity at high summer. If anything nearby could offer him inspiration it would have been the gleaned fields barren until spring planting, but that was months away. I was perhaps trying to imagine him hungover. It seemed I would never stop imagining how other people did their jobs.

"This one I wrote after failing to outrun a hurricane that had chased me up the coast."

I doubt the owner of the tavern ever took to bed any of the poets she had been bringing in to read since that spring but she did expect the poets, having paid for their time, to give her their complete attention after the reading. No. There was no desire to be perhaps written into a poem that might last forever. The owner of the tavern had recorded three albums when much younger, rather good albums with a quartet, so she had herself carried through time in inflexible order though the albums were long since out of print, the albums when bought used merely scratches competing across vinyl. I had them all. Now I am even older than the owner was then perhaps I must conclude she merely wanted from the poets a close attention to all she had to say. She had become verbose once her voice was no good for singing. She never shut up. Most nights between songs at the piano in the tavern she could drive customers out with ceaseless chatter. I doubt she ever liked me very much. I always twirled my own thoughts.

"That is a nice melody you were playing behind me."

"Si Tu Voir Ma Mere."

"What's that again?"

He hadn't travelled that far. The poet was part of some scene raving on the coasts that merged poetry into hip hop music. I knew that music. It was all the poetry of all the ages pressed into a tin drum to express anger. I did not bother. It was never good poetry. It was seldom good drumming. *Un ordre inflexible les fait naitre et les détruit.* Is there any line from Sartre that sounds more like Baudelaire? I clearly remembered walking silently on the way back to my apartment through early morning Paris with a tin drum I had played through the night on a march across the city. I had always felt a poem in that but I had never written it. For years in a school composition book I kept the first lines of the poems I meant to write should the despair of life ever ease enough for me to see purpose beyond futility. Perhaps they were poems I would write should I travel. But the poet from afar seemed more perturbed than confused to find his words accompanied by something more than a driving rhythm. He sensed only competition.

"It's too pretty."

He meant the music assuaged his anger.

"Really? I was trying to play it like a disinterred corpse."

Probably I meant I had been overturning the chords like two men overturning skulls full of gold teeth while deepening their trench with a shared shovel. We were sitting at the bar between the first and planned second reading. I had the Sydney Bechet open to the page before the photographs then turned a page earlier to capture the thread of thought. The first photograph was Bechet dressed as a little girl in the way all baby boys were photographed in those days. In text Bechet was on about even in his old age still not comprehending why so many great *musicianers* ended in the madhouse. Down in New Orleans Sydney Bechet's mother had spoken to him only in French. The movie with the line about television being for children had been in that language with some sense it couldn't have been any other.

"I need poetry to be something other than complaint."

"You want love poems?"

"Baudelaire wrote in vengeance against his mother."

The poet liked me better after the second reading because behind him instead of playing more Bechet I had played chords that almost seemed Thelonius Monk pieces with all their slanted edges and odd angles coming to rough stops. Bechet did not live long enough to see Thelonius Monk go mad. But this poet could imagine in the music what he wanted from the street, that claim to early morning a reeling anticipation of the rush about to come, the cacophony, feet dodging feet then knees colliding, the shoulder forever giving way, elbows thrown into the eyes, the rush never in step on crossing at the lights, ahead of the beat, a demand, a demand, the inevitable sidewalk scaffolding like so many lairs built from scarecrows, in the lair the monster of the craving of the crowd, all mouth.

0000EC 9120 31EE	001EE	TM PLSTRI1,PLWTCVV	MESSAGE REQUIRES CVV?
0000F0 47E0 8100	00118	BNO IABU710	NO – MEANS YOU DONE
0000F4 9017 3000	00000	STM RG1,RG7,PLSWSVR	SAVE REGISTERS
		ENTRC IABW	CALCULATE CVV
000100 45E0 80F0	00108	BAL R14,IABU700	LIBERATE THIS ONE?

The light shifted with more night entering the tavern in the shape of passing time. The piano keys had begun to coruscate though they were silent below the fingers of the owner of the tavern chatting not playing to gather her audience. The lights behind the bar were again fogged blue. This was another night in the years when people were still free to smoke in the taverns. The poet with his cigarette was standing beside the piano not pulling the words into verse but into the mathematics he sensed about him, these couples and companions sitting at the tables around the tavern, out from their offices but never safe from the fogs they themselves now emitted, the fog taking to the lights like an insect hatching, a swarm of moths, all mobbing their few hours to live. They knew how to make claims, that crowd. They were miners. Every day they too overturned the dead for gold. I thought about the tune that plays in the movie while the bull running amok knocks every saloon of the mining town over into the mud. Picasso must have loved that scene. Earlier behind the poet I had improvised around the chord progressions in that tune to sound like

Monk. *The Gospel of No Name City*. It must have been a carking torture to that old boss of mine to see Jean Seberg presented with two husbands when he had known her a virgin. Having two husbands must also be a kind of insurance against so many mishaps. There could never be a wasted life. It would only be a matter of time before I saw that show with Alice pursued by two German soldiers. That anticipation left a bad taste. I always made a point to never swallow anything the day before a visit to the dentist just so if the fingers went sideways there was nothing to bring upwards. But the beer went down anyway when I tipped the bottle to my lips. I was surprised. Still I was waiting in the abyss while the rest rushed towards their false lights. I worked by wit and not by witchcraft.

"You think my couch will be comfortable for the night?"

"What else you got?"

Among the insurance crowd I noticed a large man whose suit seemed blue but flashed green occasionally to prove everyone else a liar. He would live forever. It was his right because he compiles the longevity charts. Under the table he had his hand up the thigh of a woman who wasn't his to touch. The woman looked away as though expecting any moment to be called for something but she wasn't quite sure for what. I doubted it would be a religious calling. I light a cigarette and see myself in the mirrors in the cubbyholes formed by any absence of a bottle on the shelves behind the bar. Drink me. Drink me. And how does Roquentin recognize himself in the mirror? Not his face. His red hair. At the far end of the bar sits Doctor Brown because he cannot keep away from jazz but wants far as he can from all the drinkers out of the insurance offices. For college that same year I was born he spent the year in Paris among the last of the Zazous like an anthropology student. The wrinkles across his forehead and around his mouth do not fool me into recognizing experience when I know it is only acquisition. In worldly matters it is more significant to notice the very tall very skinny young waitress working the bar always dresses to exhibit breasts she doesn't have. Absence does not define her experience. Gossip in abundance provides her a raucous history that does not give way. She dyes her blonde hair red but only at the tips so she echoes those artillery soldiers standing naked in the barracks showers with their sharp fingers all bloody. Still she is nothing like a painting. She takes from whatever crosses her path. Sitting at her bar it is difficult to not be pulled into her dreams. The skinny waitress pauses to imagine the bottle in her hand before serving Doctor Brown another. The bottle pleads. It is its right. The waitress can taste the whisky even while it pours. She has given the doctor his lolling tongue. I am almost pulled into being huge globular breasts but I am waiting so have all manner of resistance and the practice of a damned slave. That's it. I know the rules of the game. I smile but feel myself rebuked by the piano keys not under my hands because I am remembering not what I improvised moments ago but what I read in the letter some hours earlier. I am pushing against time. Doctor Brown does not get to dismiss me for a madman. I press down my hands. Like sinking into muck my fingers from both hands merge into the dark wood of the top of the bar where many rings of beer glisten so much tidal pool with the sea out. The cigarette is left in its ashtray like a buoy run aground over where my fingers have been submerged. The tide too sits out for only a few hours but the surf that returns will be their surf not my surf. The tides are charted too. For a moment I have no hands but the letter calls like a sea siren being transported by prison ship to the ends of the earth. A ship pursued. *This song for mariners and all their ships.*

"I have only the one bed."

In jazz time can be reversed in some ways but it isn't necessarily adventure. It is at best call and response. The proprietress began to play after laughing away more need for words for the first time in a very long time. She was soon improvising but there was never any chord that surprised me, I saw each uncharted movement long before it was taken, each regular as machine logic, certain to flow the same each time, the certainty of a bank, the repetition of pennies accumulated the one atop the other without cascade, in the playing a regimentation that might seem different from the last but was always the same if it could be predicted. The proprietress did not play one note not in my head first. I cannot say the same had been true about her albums but I no longer even have a phonograph to listen. Sartre had not foreseen the possibility of no phonographs. I like the photographs on the album covers when the owner of the tavern was younger than I was when I knew her. Music cannot be abstracted into perpetuity because it tries so hard to be ephemeral.

```
0000D4 D503 3314 3654 0033C 0067C    CLC   CVVEXP(4),=4X'40'    EXPIRE DATE SPACE?
0000DA 4780 32D0    002F8            BE    IABW820             YES – MAJOR ERROR
0000DE D503 3314 3658 0033C 00680    CLC   CVVEXP(4),=4X'00'    EXPIRE DATE LOW VAL?
0000E4 4780 32D0    002F8            BE    IABW820             YES – MAJOR ERROR
0000E8 D501 3316 3664 0033E 0068C    CLC   CVVEXP+2(2),=2C'0'   EXPIRE MNTH INVALID?
0000EE 4780 32D0    002F8            BE    IABW820             YES – MAJOR ERROR
0000F2 F224 338F 3314 003B7 0033C    PACK  PLSWK00(3),CVVEXP(5) PACK THIS DOWN
0000F8 D201 3424 338F 0044C 003B7    MVC   PLSWKEX(2),PLWWK00   MOVE EXP CVV CALC
```

Some of these days you'll miss me honey. Only of course Alice never missed me at all beyond whatever odd sentiment of displacement caused her to write me letters with poems those very few times over many years. Displacement. This many bytes from the base address. It was perhaps the most damning word that played each day through programming in that old assembler language. Displacement. The word I'll utter at my death. Assembler code was printed with the machine language to the left but a translation to the right. It was not unlike my book of *Les Fleurs du Mal.* Had the letter smelled of perfume? I now wanted my hand on the letter in the jacket pocket but fingers if they even were fingers now seemed insufficient. I tried hard to find scent but the cigarette smoke pulled my brain. The couples at their table seemed to be so many cripples and whores and diseased passed occasionally in the foreground by the owner of the tavern in her red dress, the poet in his tight trousers. A woman laughs so loud her mouth seems frozen open. A man pulls at his ear to be certain it still is there. A woman waves her napkin through the cigarette smoke. A man sucks in his belly in response to a woman turning her head towards more arrivals at the tavern door. A tracking shot like the second hand on my watch. The couples are cheating at cards. There are hands under the table for all reasons. There was now no one at the piano. My own hands were still lost within the flotsam of the bar. I thought about how in animated movies the character can always extract his own plasticine from what he has violently merged, pull himself free from a stumble beneath a steamroller, from a plunge into the picket fence, from a smashup against the moon. Like sex? Right? No. I only ever received poems from Alice damning the social conventions in our old hometown. There is one where the sisters walking poodles in the park do not know their way of thinking is the way of thinking taught from the pioneer schoolmistress whose bronze statue is now wet in fresh piss. Alice kept her arrivals to herself.

0001C4 D707 3340 3504 00368 0052C		XC	EBW016(8),PLSWKB2	RESULT TO PLSWKB2
0001CA 4160 32F1	00319	LA	RG6,CVVKEY1	ADDRESS KEY 1
0001CE 5060 3334	0035C	ST	RG6,EBW004	FIRST VALUE ENCRYPT
0001D2 4160 3340	00368	LA	RG6,EBW016	
0001D6 5060 3338	00360	ST	RG6,EBW008	NEXT VALUE TO ENCRYPT
0001E0 4180 3330	00358	LA	RG8,EBW000	POINT AT PARM LIST
0001E4 45B0 329E	002C6	BAL	R11,CALLDES	DO DES ROUTINE

I had imagined the proprietress often not in bed but in a cemetery looking over the grave of Charlie Parker. Dig this! His is the jazz grave nearest Des Moines, if you get out the maps to start circling the addresses, the grave being down in Kansas City, though of course even a grave isn't permanent, so circle in pencil. The inner front cover of the book of Amy Lowell poems is stamped with the name of the original owner. It was once a college book belonging to the daughter of a man who had gotten very rich in Des Moines building a trucking empire. Amy Lowell had independent means. I have long lost track of Janice after she moved to first one coast then the other. There are no letters from Janice. Dorothea simply left without farewell. And now that the bank has moved finally to a server environment, every line of assembler code I ever wrote has been irreparably lost but without granting me complete deniability I ever coded one damned thing. It was some time before I realized the shelf of jazz books in the tavern was the personal collection of the proprietress. She was putting yet more words she felt part of herself on display. I am now choked with all of Alice's poems. Still I might someday get around to reading the Amy Lowell book. I am like a thousand letters gone unmailed.

THE WRAP PARTY

There was one quite fitting response to Picasso dismissing computers for only providing answers. *Questions are a burden to others. Answers a prison for oneself.* Picasso lived long enough to have seen that too on television if perhaps he set aside drinking himself blind one evening a week. That show had probably made Picasso remember his harlequins but perhaps just perhaps even Picasso wondered how *Danger Man* begat *Secret Agent Man* begat *The Prisoner* with Patrick McGoohan struggling so hard to be in revolt after having been such a simpering Iago. The answering quote is from *The Prisoner*. In the premiere episode of *Danger Man*, the trouble shooter played by McGoohan solves the murder of a bank president who has stolen a crate of gold, the story told so fast its nonsense hardly registers, any fool given a breath knowing a bank president gets far richer than any crate of gold by stealing from the small depositors, the farmers, the pensioned widows, the dispensable employees, a few dollars here, a few pounds there, it all adds up. The wife's lover has killed the banker. The wife is never fêted the true hero of the story in her own time but the years circle back on new media, the glory of rebellion so often found if not sought only in reminisce, anything can happen, video tapes begat digital video discs begat streaming. It is an eternal return. *I follow to serve my turn upon him.* But perhaps I was already acting in accordance with memory. I had again refused to give Dorothea the encryption keys to the credit cards for the hundreds of bank branches that used the central software.

"You promised."

"When you show me your plane ticket for leaving the country."

"I will drive across the border."

"Paris."

"Never Paris."

She meant we mustn't ever see each other again once she had the encryption keys.

"Drive all that way alone?"

Dorothea understood I was nudging but she did not answer. The apartment I couldn't afford had a superb long living room with a bare white wall on one short side that took movies very well. The projector was clattering but Dorothea had become deadened to the noise over the couple hours watching my animation repeated times, while I never heard the projector, its knobs and loops and light holding me but the rhythm of the spinning celluloid always so quickly internalized I had to concentrate to notice its play against the overdubbed soundtrack. I stood at the projector threading the excerpted sequence without ever entirely shifting my attention off Dorothea posed naked on the futon. I was remembering brushes mixing yellow ochre into a touch of vermillion, and other times hints of green umber, to make flesh on linen canvas in the guest bedroom of my mother's house. My hands knew their way around the projector without concentration. In the novel about his tin drum evoking memory, little Oskar decides to grow but only manages to ruin his ability to break glass with a scream, he breaks his shout and in doing so cuts himself off from his own greatness. Still women are passionately attracted to the hump he grows on his back. I kept on my clothes.

"You were the only programmer at the party?"

"Mortenson only invited his banker peers and a few old college friends who must have been peers in some way too."

I meant Mortenson would not have invited to his bachelor party any old college friend who had risen too high above him. The banker peers were from the bank and from several other banks around the city and points farther. I continued to fuss with the leader to the excerpt while Dorothea stared forward at the empty white square for the moment projected. My recounting the party troubled Dorothea because for her the true story in *Othello* wasn't the jealous Moor murdering innocent Desdemona but the whore Bianca misused so cavalierly by the patrician Cassio. *Tis the strumpet's plague to beguile many and be beguiled by one*. I couldn't have been more pleased she had her own problems with Mortenson.

"But you were there."

"Just to show movies on and off through the party."

Because of Louisa the best man had arranged the party far from the bank at a new tavern that sold itself for showing movies rather than sports and more sports and yet more sports on its large televisions. Louisa was keen to help her father in this new venture now all the genuine movie theaters he had managed his whole life were shuttered for good. It was a big deal to Louisa because her father owned the tavern not just managed the tavern. Louisa had even been there to introduce me. Her father was a mustached man in a rather extravagantly shiny suit that almost made him a circus master, but the latest law against pornographic videos had made the taverner, within the showman, so warry he would not run the cassette tapes himself, wouldn't touch them, turned away even from looking at them. He pointed me towards the machine so dark under the bar it might have been a virgin unwilling to fuck with the lights on. It was a good machine all the same. The first clip started and Louisa quickly left the tavern with some sense the bride must not see as well as not be seen before the wedding. Her father pretended not to see that too. The best man was some weasel I only knew from the bank's company meetings where twice a year large ideas were promulgated to the entire staff with no sincerity even a few of the words would prove wise. When recruiting me to provide the movies, he had stood in my cubicle all management arrogance cloaked within roguish manner because he hadn't the imagination except to assume a fellow interested in movies must be foremost interested in watching women kneeled and tumbled and spread. Under some sense of duress I created highlight reels for the party. I still had numerous addresses to movie distributors from my days in the video store but none of these were necessary. There was a place tucked away three steps into an alley only one block over from the flag shop where new releases cost dearly but even the bawdiest smut from twenty years ago and earlier went cheap. *Behind The Green Door.* Nudist volleyball games from the 1950s. *Baby Face. Inside Misty Beethoven.* A strange revenge movie where several naked women with beehive hair wrestle in turns in the backseat of a large convertible over possession of a ragdoll into which they stick needles. That one didn't even come with a title except for something invented for the box. *Debbie Does Dallas. The Devil In Miss Jones.* A couple tapes from the salad restaurant. I owned no equipment to edit video but it was summer so no one questioned me when I walked into the communications department at the college where Janice's mother still taught. I went in wearing my threadbare jacket with patches at the elbows I always wore to the bank. The college had had an excellent video editor.

"Did you hire the stripper too?"

"There is a corkboard covered in pink index cards in the shop where I bought the movies."

"The cards were for strippers?"

"The cards were for anything you want."

"And buttered popcorn too?"

Dorothea had quite enjoyed my new movie about teeth, still in its rough cut, though by the second showing if not right from the first she must have recognized herself portrayed. Mrs Peel. After all she had seen the figure before. Had touched it. Had felt herself in it. There had been rumors about Dorothea and not her brother but a brother of some order those years before back at the Catholic college, so looking at Dorothea naked, her far knee raised, I could only hear jazz not poetry in her past. *Monk's Dream.* I had crudely scored my movie with jazz I had written that perhaps also was too much a highlights reel without the force of genuine imagination. I knew I would eventually go back to the college to use the multitrack recording equipment I had seen there. *Ascensuer Pour L'Échafaud? Dentistry to the Gallows? Workin'? Cookin'? Quarin'?* I had played the trumpet solos myself. Take that Miles Davis. It was impossible to imagine Louisa would ever marry Mortenson though the wedding was meant for the very next morning. I knew I perhaps could stop the wedding simply by giving Dorothea the encryption keys. At least Dorothea was certain Mortenson would take the encryption keys on a run.

"You couldn't have shown that movie."

"No. I showed the excerpt I'm about to show you but not any at all that you just watched again."

I turned off the light on the projector and the room was dark except for ambient light snaking through the curtain of the balcony door. The reel I was putting up was the handkerchief dance I shot for the movie without ever having it in the screenplay, that is, until later, when in rewrite I gave over the Loïe Fuller dance to Igor reduced to doll. The original handkerchief dance presents Miss Cummersum losing layer after layer of fetish clothes merged into the great arch of scarf swirling about the ever more naked body. Of course the scarf the fetish clothes become is the scarf Mortenson gave Louisa. Of course I knew Mortenson had given the same scarf to Dorothea probably even before he gave it to Louisa. Of course. Of course. The flag was of St Kitts with its two large stars on a diagonal stripe of black cornered one side red the other green. I took Louisa to the flag shop that one weekend after lunch so she would recognize the scarf she was wearing was a flag. She had seen her scarf in the display of other silk scarfs that moment I offered to buy her another in swap. I had pretended not to notice there was one among the scarfs the very same. I offered her love by presenting her proof of betrayal. Because of course Dorothea had worn the scarf to work too and women can be trusted to notice what other women are wearing. Louisa had understood it was the perfect flag for a man intent on two women of extremely different experience.

"What did he say?"

Dorothea asked this about half through the dance after yet more chains and collars appeared on Miss Cummersum only to be taken into the swirling scarf rendered in plasticine. Through the dance Miss Cummersum looked ever more like Louisa. I had so especially enjoyed animating the chains and collars and scarf the scene ran to six minutes. The scarf eventually knots into a ragdoll like in the strange pornography of the women in the backseat, the ragdoll poked full of knitting needles being something of a man, something in a suit and hat anyway. It is a very different understanding of history and all that has passed on television.

"There was an hour where he never seemed to stop laughing."

"At this?"

"This was the start of it."

"There was cocaine?"

I was especially pleased with the excerpt because in the wall of mirrors behind Miss Cummersum there appears to be dancing a real woman completely nude without a scarf. It was a miraculous double exposure. Mortenson could only have thought it was Louisa seen from the backside, couldn't have been certain it wasn't her anyway, not after having watched me doodle Louisa a hundred times in meetings, face, figure, hands, torso, one time the feet in sandals. I knew Louisa had complained to Mortenson about it. Then a couple weeks earlier I had brought my movie camera to the company picnic because I needed everyone to think there had been at least one night Louisa let herself in front of the camera in whatever manner directed. It didn't matter Louisa had tried so hard to ignore the camera. Every man and perhaps every woman at the picnic had thought about the backside of Louisa. I gave it to the movie. No one from the bank would ever recognize it wasn't Louisa in that old footage of Janice. Anyway everyone would get the connection to Louisa no matter what because the wall of mirrors in the movie are round distorting mirrors exactly like the automobile side mirror Louisa had long kept on the tube in her cubicle. I had said let's do masks. Janice had said let me be the mouth. I had learned from the old jazz movie of *Othello* to count on more than a handkerchief within the cunning plans. But Mortenson hadn't made any of the connections before he passed out.

"Show it again."

The animation had been shot so fast across four days calling in sick it played like improvisation.

"Really?"

"Rewind it and show it again."

I thought Dorothea meant to spot it wasn't Louisa in the mirrors at all but when I started the excerpt again she stood. She started with a twirl. The movements she made coalesced with the projection onto her nude body, the animation of Miss Cummersum plus the boogaloo of Janice, together the dancers forming a trinity that was three but one flaunting before the gates of an abyss. I stood there knowing Dorothea was making it impossible for me to ever reinsert the excerpt into the teeth movie. In *An American In Paris* the long ballet at the end is famous for being shot against images from paintings by Dufy and Renoir and Rousseau and Lautrec. Van Gogh. Utrillo. It is the history of the greatest paintings ever made but in her dance Dorothea presented me with every painting I had ever thought but failed to paint. Oils and canvases and brushes seemed to fall away from my hands like too many women on the street. It nearly caused me to give over the encryption keys because it made it more important than ever that Louisa remain a virgin. The honeymoon was to be in St Kitts.

"Rewind it and show it again."

I want possession. Even now I want to shoot that live layer over the other two dancers, the backside nude in the mirrors becomes wildly distorted in mirrors from the funhouse, Miss Cummersum with her chains is within a proscenium with a large hand, my hand, pulling back a curtain, then this new nude facing forward, older, body nearing its turn to sag, then the dancing foreground body becoming what is distorted when the mirrors give way to paintings, arms merging before again separating, legs in step, I got, I got, the ballet, letting Dorothea eventually become the jazz dancer surrounded by the maimed, the prostitutes, the perverted survivors of the trenches. But I cannot bring myself to use the computers I now have at home that would easily provide such sophisticated overlays.

"I've seen enough."

Dorothea tipped over the projector to hinder pursuit when she rushed for the balcony door because she understood the projector was more important to me. I had never painted Dorothea. No portrait. No nude. I would rescue the projector first. Still I caught Dorothea with both arms around her waist to pull her back into the apartment. I had never asked her about the other guy who left her at the alter the weekend before I started the job. Nevertheless I knew she couldn't handle a second disappointment. She hit me several times in the face before I managed to almost make her laugh.

"At least put on your clothes, won't you, please? This is too respectable a building for jumping naked."

Dorothea would have made it off the balcony railing if the bunched hammer and sickle curtain on the sliding door hadn't slowed her a moment while I hoisted the projector back onto its end table. Highly indignant, in performance anyway, I proceeded to recount who lived in the luxury apartment complex, in the penthouse the man who owned the not one but twenty-three restaurant franchises, he had food delivered numerous times a day, kept time on it, the entire first floor the woman whose late husband had built the malls, she went to auctions but bid only to drive up prices, throwing away anything she accidently won, directly above us the only son of the richest farmer in the state, his pink running shoes not allowed near the fields, pig shit too valuable, the son too visible, the three spinster sisters across the hall who were always bringing home stray cats, but only for a couple days, then throwing out the cat again. I recounted the insipid ways they had all attempted suicide and Dorothea again almost laughed but suddenly I did not want that laugh.

"You understand Mortenson has authority to the encryption keys himself."

Dorothea didn't answer though everyone knew Mortenson could barely log into the computer without written instructions taped to the tube. I wanted to quote *Othello*. *If though wilt needs damn thyself.* But I knew Baudelaire would better push Dorothea towards vengeance against this man she loved though feared to look on. The wedding was the next morning. It made sense after all that if I had failed to instigate *Othello* I might still fall back on *The Tin Drum*. And how did that go? Oskar is in the madhouse for a murder eventually proven to be committed by one woman against another over a man they both loved. Oskar was guilty only of obsession with the dead woman. Why not make that my revenge? Anything can happen. It had long been apparent to the somnambulist in me that Dorothea longed for the poetry she had abandoned each time she herself was abandoned. I quoted from Baudelaire several lines from the one about a monk that begins *les cloîtres anciens sur leurs grandes murailles.*

"You think I'm damned?"

"What do you suppose the bank would think if they saw this apartment?"

It was best to leave Dorothea believe I was embezzling to pay for an apartment that was in truth where Janice's father had kept his longtime mistress until providing her golden parachute penthouse accommodations four hundred miles away overlooking Lake Michigan. I had often tried to imagine the jazz ballet that had shifted out the mistress. Battement développé. Battement fondu. Battlement breached. It was the apartment still reeking of sex, despite deep cleaning, that had pulled off Dorothea's clothes so quickly every time she stopped over. I had not touched her that night. No. Janice's father did not come see me at the apartment. The father left me live there because he knew it was the one apartment his daughter would never accede to visit, not ever, Janice so loathed that mistress she knew all about, knew her addresses, knew her shoe size, knew her breasts size, the mistress for Janice the city's true Storyville. For an instant I very much wanted to take off my clothes too but what more could follow the ballet of my own damnation?

"You're an innocent all the same."

I did not ask how I was innocent because I knew that in quoting even Baudelaire I provided all necessary proof. I had worked in the cubicle long enough to know real damnation is a cage with something like bars that pass light only to make shadow. The real answer to Picasso is that his comment on computers went untranslated in the cubicle. No one cared what gibberish he had said. No one remembered that story about Gertrude Stein being halted on the road to Paris at the end of the Occupation, the time the Resistance fighters let her and her Alice proceed on only after seeing the Picasso in the backseat of the car. I mean that no one thought Picasso was still a passport to liberation. The trick was for the death that freed me from the cubicle not be my own.

"You want more wine?"

Dorothea who had once been a nun laughed very hard now.

"No. I don't want wine."

I did not ask how I was innocent because I knew that in making animated movies I provided all necessary proof. Mortenson could not see betrayal in what for him were merely cartoons though a couple other bankers and especially the best man had pissed themselves seeing what was intended. In my head I could hear Robbie ask about a slide projected on the wall for her lecture. Who is the hero in this painting? Robbie asked but no one answered the obvious because it was decades too late for the politics. *Is it the guards painted so nobly? I contend it is the prisoner about to be hanged, no?* It did not occur to Dorothea that should the police ever search all I owned the movie about teeth contained nothing like the confession expected from a madman. How could there be? How could there hint treachery in an animated movie so like what is remembered from childhood? Wasn't I Orson Welles at last looking up from down low my whole life? The police would hear no drum in the projector. The forgotten thing about those first Patrick McGoohan shows is the background music is sometimes very good improvised jazz that spools past faster even than the stories race to their endings. I deliberately kept the movie about teeth the length of those first shows. I tried for the same jazz. I played the drums for the jazz over the animation too.

"You should put your clothes on before you catch cold."

"It's a hundred outside."

"The central air conditioning is very good in this apartment."

"Turn it lower."

Dorothea meant to make the room sex temperature.

"I will only end up talking about Louisa just like the other times."

I could feel the refusal rushing into the quickening of her heart and into the heat of her hands, one hand now on my face no longer a fist, the hand of an old woman but with the fight not entirely gone out of it. It was a matter of direction. Cut. This time try to hit your mark but with your head turned a little away from the camera. Cut. Cut. I am sure my obsession with Louisa mattered much less to Dorothea than that Louisa remained a virgin in a world now otherwise completely soiled. Still standing there grappled, it suddenly occurred to me that Dorothea had never noticed Louisa wearing the same scarf, because like some character from Truffaut, she had no women friends, not since the convent, certainly wanted none of that again. The movie excerpt I meant to enrage Mortenson had instead enraged Dorothea. I did not have to suggest she murder Louisa. It was enough to make it impossible to run away with Mortenson by withholding the encryption keys. It was enough to have pulled her away from the balcony. At that moment I did not have to speak about my own intensions for revenge against the wrongs done me because a woman puts so many things in her purse besides money.

THE BRIDE WORE
BLACK

The last admonition Mortenson ever gave was the Friday before his wedding and it was the damnedest thing any manager ever said to me though so much has been said since. The project I was working on had no clear design. The details coming down from a higher manager were vague ellipses, blatant contradictions bordering on daring, fantasies of grandeur quickly bloated, historical inaccuracies seemingly politically motivated, more misunderstandings of simple mathematics, and finally blind belief in customer gullibility. The details changed every day. I coded what I thought best and in the end I wrote a document summarizing the features to the new application. The upper manager railed that not only did the application not remotely work as expected but somehow so subverted his directions they could never be restated. It hardly mattered. It was at best never going to be more than an idiotic application. Then Mortenson gave me shit for not including in my summary document all the things the application didn't do. I about fell off my chair guffawing at the notion I would spend the next thirty years of my career doing nothing but listing all the things the application didn't do. It did not give a view of Paris from soiled sheets in Ménilmontant. It did not swear in the voice of a mime. It did not run foot races with the ghost of Baudelaire past flowers indifferent rather than evil because even the worms in Montparnasse cimetière have long moved on to others. Begin in Paris then spend the next thirty years describing all the things the application didn't do until finally you find yourself in Iowa. It did not ask what the hell good was a showgoat if you weren't worshipping the devil.

"You should try this first."

"I don't know."

The virgins sitting near me in the burger restaurant might solve their embarrassments before dark but at the moment were uncertain they should pull a fountain drink through a plastic straw. Mennonite. Amish. I could not say. They hadn't changed from farm clothes though Louisa had often told stories about such teenagers riding horses only to where they kept their motorcycles hidden in the sheds of some old quarry or other. Her father had long ago left for Des Moines but this was her hometown in southern Iowa with its one crossed main street where the highway slowed speed. The burger restaurant was on the highway. The Catholic church sat on the one main street that crossed the highway, the church sitting back from the street, though it was obvious the church cemetery had been cut into more than once to widen the asphalt, make way for the living. Headstones pressed against the cross street seemed the dead struggling to break away from unfulfilled paradise even if only to become sidewalk. Tread on me. The narrow sidewalk was old red paving bricks that almost certainly had once been the road. I had already seen inside the church it was too dark to film the wedding without lights but the priest had long ordered there be no lights. It was his standing order. I had my camera in a large leather satchel on the chair opposite where I sat eating some kind of pork cooked so solid it made one of my gold teeth ache. The burger restaurant was the only chain place in the town but where it was on the highway there galloped new construction expanding the town with a strip of shops and a new gas station and a monstrous grocery store. Even I could feel threat in its modernity. It must have been overwhelming to the virgins. The virgins were trying not to listen to the two behind the service counter.

"Are you going to go back to college anyway?"

"I think I'm going back to take the lab job."

"The one killing dogs?"

"I would take care of the dogs between the experiments."

"Awful."

"The dogs will be kind to me."

"Stay here and I'll be kind to you."

The virgins could feel the interchangeability of their flesh with that of the boy and girl their same age working the counter. But I felt isolated to the point they all seemed beckoned somehow in flickering light from the cross street where all the churches were unevenly rowed like a constellation of dim stars. There were five churches. I was not beckoned. Even in the cemetery outside the Catholic church talking to Louisa I sensed too little brightness for my camera to shoot the wedding though the sun was mostly out. There were huge shade trees. The stone church had a fine bell tower that cast shadows. Atop the table I fingered the light meter I had brought like it was a saint's medallion rubbed too smooth for further answers. It seemed an irremediable damnation to have failed to stop the wedding. Mortenson was paying me very handsomely to photograph the wedding but he had been drunk at the bachelor party when hiring me. He had made it a command. I pressed the trigger on the camera to capture the virgins without taking the camera from its satchel.

"It's too sweet."

"But isn't all the ice wonderful?"

Louisa had been wearing shorts and a shirt that exposed her midriff as though she were already half stripped to step into her white wedding bed. We were under several large trees only a few feet from the grave of her mother. I had found her standing there after talking to the priest. I had hoped to find her corpse there already feeding maggots like the inspirations of any other poet out for a stroll.

"The priest has made it impossible to shoot."

"You can play the organ instead."

"Jazz organ? I could play Green Onions when you walk the aisle?"

Standing outside the church Louisa merely smiled because she knew better than to suggest anything I might be compelled to violently contradict. She knew when I was angry. No doubt the arranged organist had offered something traditional but the reason for her absence seemed so extraordinary that it must carry into the ceremony. The woman was lost in a cave after going out spelunking the day before. I shit you not. Louisa had told me this with no sense of irony the woman might have been looking for pathways to hell otherwise unavailable in that remote part of the state. There are at least a couple parks in Iowa that feature caves.

"Remember the cartoons when we were little called Davy and Goliath?"

"Everyone remembers those but they were Protestant not Catholic."

In the premiere episode of *Davy and Goliath*, Davy becomes lost in a cave where he is threatened with falling into an abyss equal those frequently threatening Baudelaire in the *Fleurs du Mal* poems, the abyss of damnation. Earlier the family father explains to Davy that God looks after us all so, God willing, he will be back at work at the office come Monday morning, which is an insane prayer, perversely unpoetic in seeking mercy, since even the punishing God envisioned by Baudelaire never once baited with grace only to switch with wage slavery. All the same God looks after Davy in the cave. But is it an insane prayer to want Picasso to have seen both *The Prisoner* and *Davy and Goliath* on his television? Was it impossible for a painter to have seen all what I had seen? Nonsense. There was no escaping my own abyss from having watched too seriously too much on screens. I did not want amusement. *Computers are useless. They only provide answers.* I stood beside Louisa knowing I would never be anything but a computer programmer though the image she presented among the stones in the cemetery was overwhelmingly demanding all there could be given. It was a cruel thing she had asked me to photograph her wedding after Mortenson had second more sober thoughts.

"Do I get to sing at the wedding too?"

"Couldn't you save it for the reception?"

I made a very fine riff of scat singing. In response Louisa laughed that great rather low rumble of laughter that caught at every man who ever heard. It promised enormous pleasures but only at the end of a long cave through which no one had ever found his way. In that premiere episode the dog Goliath declines eating overbaked cookies because his teeth aren't what they used to be. Louisa flashed her perfect teeth. Perhaps it was her light I sensed circling others in the restaurant because once again I understood with remorse there was no escape from having chosen to live according to three musicals. Go talk to the animals. Go dance with the painters. I was born under a wandering star. Now keep the fuck away. Go! Go!

"You two look like you're on a crime spree."

The virgin couple laughed but only because I had brought out the movie camera before advising their afternoon. They understood technology so little but knew a camera could lead to fantasy otherwise prohibited. At least they were not aware the camera did not record sound. In *The Tin Drum* the somnambulist sleeping with little Oskar is a dwarf woman so indeterminate of age she might be eighteen and she might be eighty. Oskar is a teenager. I was that woman to these two teenaged virgins many generations from the fatherland but still subject to the same propensities. Perhaps I was indeterminate in sex to these virgins too. They wanted to hear nothing from the dead but because they were virgins they could tell I spoke from the abyss.

"Can you not envision death with his scythe leading a procession of brides?"

Again the virgins laughed but they knew what I meant without ever having seen the movie I was thinking about. In the cemetery that morning Louisa had said there were so often concurrent weddings at the churches that it was known to the locals as the *procession of brides*, brides coming out to the church steps all up and down the cross street, at the same moment brides in twos and threes and sometimes even from all five churches, coming out to mix their sacred vows into a confusion, crowds mingling, bouquets caught by the wrong bridesmaids, screams of hilarity. Louisa had also said she had spoken to Mortenson that morning. I loathed hearing that. It meant Dorothea had not killed Mortenson either, after I had so counted on her to drive down to this little town to kill Louisa, her rival, had not done a thing, certainly had not damned herself. There was a clever. When Dorothea left my apartment the night before she had taken with her a very fine square blade from the massive kitchen knife block forgotten by the newspaper man's mistress so pampered she need never cut anything herself ever again. I left the virgins to their ice.

"Father, I have been relegated to the organ."

I was a second time back at the church but the priest was uncertain he should let me play the organ. I had not shaved that morning. I smelled. It was very hot again even before noon and I had not washed the sweat from the long day before. There was even on me the faint smell of Dorothea wanting a fuck. Finally the priest made me audition with certainty this dirty little man would stumble over everything attempted. Naturally I couldn't be certain Dorothea hadn't turned the clever on her own throat. At that speculation I played the first sacred song come to mind but I cannot now recall which one arrived from my fingers in response to a day over which I floundered in all schemes. In front of the priest I could not remain a somnambulist though blood struggled within me to keep hold. I must assume the priest was a virgin too. Three songs later the priest was satisfied with my performance. I did not know what gospel the stained-glass window nearest the organ was meant to depict but these two figures peering into a starlit sky somehow became entwined into the future that stretched out before me like the desert presented in blue glass spliced with lead.

"Don't be nervous."

"Have the windows ever moved as though come to life?"

"You don't have to play that swell."

The priest laughed at his own joke because it seemed enough he would bless the marriage. I felt the need for the windows to be animated beyond static pose, perhaps make their way to the abyss, giving the statues of the saints in the church, even the Madonna with child, a shove over the ledge for refusing to move, leaving only the crucified Christ rigid with hopelessness because he was nailed in place. The priest shuffled on. The windows remained where they had been placed. I left the church with a sickening disappointment that took my stomach and loins now the head again gathered no light even from windows. Down two churches a bride and groom were leaving the first of six weddings scheduled across the churches that day. In the rice under their feet they sensed nothing but abundance.

"Do you know him?"

"Do you suppose he's getting married too?"

In the little town there were sidewalks only before the five churches and two short rows of commercial buildings. Homes sat on huge lots with large gardens. Of course the temptation when walking a small town is to believe all you see is the same every week with slight variations, as though life itself were a regulated series of motions that over a year becomes a single illusion of gesture presented to heaven, animated, the prayer for thanks, the prayer for forgiveness. I knew I was upsetting the heavens. I carried the camera raised to my eye, ready, because when real people are involved, what is a movie with its multiple takes but an insistence on singular rather than aggregate perfection? When real people are involved only the best take is shown praise. The grass being mowed would not be the same grass next mow though the man mowing might limp the same foot. The baby crying might try not to grow the next week but the tears would differ. The pretty young mother glanced into the camera before looking down at her daughter without offering comfort. Could that seem telling a second time? Older children bicycling past waved for their pictures but I did not pull the trigger. I walked on through the narrow side streets. A woman who stood arguing about money with a man just arrived in a truck raised her palm over her face turned in profile. Each day is infinitely variable once put to film but for these people in their small town only one thing needed to be different. I needed them to remember me walking their town elsewhere at the time the churches all caught fire.

"I've walked about, seen all there is to see."

"She ain't ready for another half an hour."

I had stopped outside the house belonging to Louisa's grandmother. The old woman was not the first I had passed still about a garden though the day had grown a sky thick in stifling haze. The sense of wanting to be finished with work filled the town but because the highway that ran through the center of everything never slowed, if anything grew more crowded, the dust could not settle into rest, the light kept at sparkles, tires rumbled, the dogs even barked. It was perhaps paint drying I smelled. The old woman could have been from any of a dozen Van Goghs of harvesters seeming dull brown when bent over in the field of tumbling reds and twirling yellows that in museums passes for beauty. I had seen this at the Courtauld. I had seen this at the Phillips. I had seen this at the Metropolitan. I had seen so much first on slides in a classroom that afterwards the actual paintings never were quite enough to keep me away from movies.

"Louisa doesn't know she is beautiful."

"Of course she does."

I didn't have to ask why Louisa didn't want help dressing for the wedding. She never asked help. Perhaps I caught a glimpse of her nude passing an upper window with too sheer a curtain. I looked away. I recounted for the old woman the time a few programmers went for a drink after an especially turbulent day at work that had stretched into the dark. All the barmen rushed to serve Louisa. A waitress greeted her with a pat on the forearm. The owner left his kitchen long enough to tell Louisa the fish she liked so well was especially fresh. I thought something was being sold and I thought this all the more so when Louisa said she didn't understand why the staff were always welcoming towards her since she had never spent more than a few dollars at the place. The other programmers were too tired to take this ingenuousness without becoming angry. It was impossible to not see it for coquetry in a woman who had solved the programming problem we had all chased for hours. On leaving to sit elsewhere one of the other programmers took the beer that had been poured for Louisa before anyone else was served. He took the beer without her daring to resist the theft, threat in that man's eye. Louisa did not want to wear the beer. I slid my glass towards her but Louisa refused the beer because she accepted solicitation only from those she believed warranted nothing in return. She did not sense herself on sale. The grandmother in brown skirts lent on her rake after adding a few more colorful stalks to a pile in an ash pit.

"She sure doesn't care when she goes ignored."

"Louisa cares about not having things taken more than about not having things given."

The grandmother went on to talk about toys that Louisa still kept at her house. The toys should have unreeled through my head into animation but there was nothing forever providing Louisa nude at a window as though in a mirror. I already regretted not capturing that window on film though the programmer who had taken the beer did not last long at the job. He had left the beer undrunk on his table and every so often had called over to Louisa to look at the full glass no one had touched. The fire alarm finally sounded.

"Aren't you going to the wedding?"

"Louisa wouldn't being having the wedding here if I weren't here."

"Your late husband was the banker in town?"

"Louisa has always had to make her own way."

I wondered who had run through the family money. I wondered. Still the old woman could sense me pulling forth somnambulist insinuations only because I spoke through the fire alarm calling to the volunteers. The wail made all speech revelatory. I could tell the old woman objected to Mortenson having been married before though he had married at a government office before a judge. The priest hadn't objected. I had seen no sign of Dorothea in my walk around town and it seemed unlikely she could have gotten into the house past this old woman. Then I saw the clever not far from my feet in the garden.

"Is that your clever?"

"Never seen it before."

The old woman didn't know you couldn't be a liar against a somnambulist.

"Can I have it?"

"You have very small hands."

Only then did I pull the trigger on the camera but Louisa did not come back to the window. I still have that reel. The old woman went into the house to tell Louisa she had met the tiny man Louisa had mentioned was also in love with her. Now the old woman could only agree with Louisa that Mortenson was a smarter choice. The old woman would put on her church dress for the wedding though the fire alarm had told to stay in the garden. I suppose my voice too had said to stay in the garden yet when I arrived back at the street of churches there were no brides rushing out in flames. The wedding party from the church at the far end of the street was out on the sidewalk with the bride sitting on the hood of a sports car where she could feel her wedding sheets slipping out from under with threat never to return. Her sports car had tin cans strung off the back for a departing drum. Her church belched smoke. In front of me the church that mattered was engulfed in flame. There was enough light in it now for anything.

"Where's Louisa?"

I had not seen Mortenson approach. I panned the camera towards the smoke rising in the sky to finish the shot of the five burning churches. I panned while listing for Mortenson the things the new application did not do. It did not make brides faithful. It did not optionally yes or no bypass flooding the ceremony of innocence. It was never a chastity belt. Having stepped forward a few steps to peer into the church, Mortenson turned to look back into the camera, aghast and terrified, then he swore something at me in his rush into the church, something unrecorded, forgotten like the man himself. I cannot picture him now except in that film of him swearing. That is amusing, because if I had not always seemed too small to be anything but harmless, punishment against me for using foul language would have been made all along, intensely for his own pleasure at first, then with termination of employment that included blackball against all other job opportunities. Had Louisa come into the garden the night before? Had Dorothea made a swipe at her? The footage of Mortenson rushing into the burning church is on the same reel as the old woman in her garden but there is also the footage of Louisa shouting at me the last time through the soundlessness of a movie over all of which has been added only a siren that seems very far away. Firemen are running about. People are telling the fireman some idiot ran into the church for no good reason since even the priest kept his distance. No one seems to question that the doors to the church had been propped open to create a draft. No one seems to have noticed the scarf tied to the neck of the statue of the Madonna with her child. The scarf had after all worked its magic on its own. It needed no film. By the end of the reel Louisa is there in her wedding dress standing across the road from the church with the tears on her cheeks glimmering in the flames resurgent.

"You bastard."

I have inserted a white title card so her words won't be lost in alarm however distant before at the very end of the reel dogs howl in the foreground. The movie comes back from the card to Louisa swatting at the camera as though it is a late season wasp. A few hours afterwards there were so many cameras the virgins from the restaurant forgot to even mention mine that had directed them to dance right into the hells offered by the neighborhood caves. There had been quite a crime spree just as I had suggested. Thirteen dead and that didn't count Mortenson. The virgins did not deny burning the churches. Nice kids. Later no one believed a word when the virgins wrote their murders into a poem one line at a time in exchanged letters posted with stamps. I am there in the first line of the first stanza. Then there again in the second line. I am there in the last of their lines hundreds of lines later. I am the devil.

INTIMATE JOURNALS

In the novel one of the visitors to little Oskar in the madhouse brings a King Oliver record with promise to elucidate its relationship to Karl Marx. Unfortunately nothing more is said on the matter. Then it all goes circles with the Scottish doctor from the village where I was kept because what is on television but *A Fine Madness* with Sean Connery taking off his clothes with every woman who hires him to shampoo her rugs. It is quite the symbol of resistance against convention. Of course I have a hard time buying it. Still he shampoos rugs and he is the most working class of poets blocked on his second book. His wife is a waitress. He stands on street corners debating poetry. He attacks the society women who have hired him to read. Of course the epic poem he is struggling to write is completely backlot so better it never happen. Fun all the same. Then the refined doctor in charge at the hospital schemes to give Connery a lobotomy after Connery has it off with the doctor's wife in the huge hot tub used for treating patients. More deep cleaning but here the rich scheme, so that much is not backlot. Shit. I remembered the movie more or less but I completely forgot Jean Seberg plays the doctor's wife. How many doctors does she marry to escape being a painter in *The French Style*? Oral surgeon. Psychiatrist. Where is the movie with the chiropodist? The pathologist? Where are all the other nightmares of Lilith? The psychiatrist in charge is always Caligari too? Right? I have a copy of the novel around here somewhere.

Freedom is what you do with what has been done to you. I suppose that is the sort of nonsense Sartre couldn't help declaiming given he spent his time a prisoner of war writing love letters. In *La Nausée* the autodidact tells how when a prisoner of war late in the war the prisoners were gathered into a hangar so crowded there was almost suffocation. Then suddenly in the crush the autodidact felt enormous joy and all these two hundred men were his brothers. I never felt that in cubicle life even when the cubicles shrank to punishment chambers nor when after the cubicles shrank beyond sight later when the open office was small tables with men genuinely put shoulder to shoulder like buried soldiers and next to me the boy six foot eight would shower me with snot through his ceaseless winter head colds. Later the autodidact would sneak into the hangar alone to remember his joy. I want no memories of cubicles. I eat my chicken cold. *Il n'est pas necessaire que je sois avec quequ'un.*

In *Doctor Dolittle*, the second book but the first movie, the doctor proves to a court he can talk to animals by calling to the witness stand the dog of the judge, who is quite certain the doctor is mad, beyond eccentric. The dog testifies to what bawdy shanty the judge was singing the night before when coming home drunk. The judge is humiliated but does not admit the song has long been creating in him an existential crisis built with nausea. After all the story takes place before jazz. The little boy witnessing the adventures of Dolittle seems always to be that surly boy in the Sargent painting back in Des Moines. And anyway the whole problem with the testimony of dogs is it is hard to imagine one not testifying its owner is mad. Trousers? Television? Tea? There are few dogs that find sense in any of that so it is just as well quotes from dogs are not reciprocated for our tombstones.

I can buy jazz too cheaply these days, nine classic albums squeezed onto four disks, questionable sound quality, a clown car. But that's the best music arrives now, with the bebop falling out so many horns honking so many red noses dented so many large shoes tripping, though those same large shoes once upon a time were too hip for anything but envy, the shoes I could never hope to fill. The pamphlet included with the music returns nothing from those smoky nights except the titles and a few remaining photographs. Anything you cannot glean from the photographs? Go get from the laptop. Go get from the tablet. Go get from the cellphone. Go! Freedom is what you do with what little is left for you. Honk! Slap! Throw a pie! Throw the bucket of confetti! The comedy always comes back into it.

I have not crossed the river but I bought a flatscreen television when back here the first day here from Des Moines. I am now the box. I am the clown car. Drunk, from atop my roof I can see across the river right to the street where Charlie Parker came for white women. It is perhaps still a hunting ground. But the welfare women I once knew living on this same street or nearly this same street where I now live have long since disappeared into other economics mistaken for freedom, roofs that don't leak over the bed, toilets that flush on the first try, successes like that, mistaken for manhood.

I let his obsolete bebop roar heave over me like a crowd on bleachers while I for another year on thirty work for the bank but now just do teller machine support in the branches fifty miles all directions. Things are so centralized anymore. Before the 370 assembler code went away entirely they rebranded the mainframe the legacy system as though it would someday be left to the children to squander, but all that computer code was more like the family farmhouse the grown children leave to weather, rot, beckon the night winds. Computer code like mother's jewels discovered to be paste. Computer code like father's most weirdly shaped tools, the ones no one knows any longer what they were meant to do. Computer code like the valuable landscape hung in the living room everyone even back in the day whispered had been done by numbers it was so ugly. No. I don't mean bebop numbers though there was plenty clownish to be found in all that code. It was testimony to the incompetence of so many who had worked through it.

I turn on the television downstairs while eating my lunch. *I Want To Live*. Susan Hayward was not so unlike Louisa in size and here in black and white even the hair seems almost alike. She is just finished fucking. Music comes from below. Moments earlier in the movie there in the movie in the jazz club downstairs is Gerry Mulligan young and lean like a blade working the reed. It makes me laugh, the name. Live but don't grow old. Refuse her one offer to dance. I had to go back to work at the office I keep upstairs. I don't remember how they kill Susan Hayward before the credits. Cyanide? Merciful. Electric chair? The skin stinks the same from working on computers. The keyboard subtle through the fingers learned to be swift but never swift enough to evade the currents that accumulate in debilitating atoms like so many whole notes split impossibly small by Charlie Parker.

In the play about the Moor, a play of seemingly months of events compressed into days, not too surprisingly there is an expression of impatience. *Go to, farewell*. It is an impatience never heard on the street now. I have had thirty years of impatience. Freedom is what you do to put money enough in your purse. The rest can wait like two tramps seen only from a hotel window.

Go! The jazz call to impatience on the street. Jack Kerouac had stood at the back of the room field hollering Go! while Allen Ginsberg read his dog *Howl* to an audience the first time.

What television rerun do I also remember Gerry Mulligan in? *It Takes a Thief?* No. The half hour before that. *Run For Your Life*. Go! But I'm only thirty miles north of my mother's old house so it doesn't bother me the backlot was trying to pass for Barcelona in that episode. Was that the cliffhanger episode? Ben Gazzara saying I love you to Claudine Longet but I'm dying just like everyone else only much sooner. Go! Rushing like bebop I don't recall though I am at the bottom of the clowns in the car where memory serves many purposes. No. It does not serve prophecy anymore. That is a woman's thought all the way to faith. A clown's thought? Appetite. All the way to a second breakfast then followed with lunch. Susan Hayward leaps from bed with a laugh that too is not so different from Louisa.

Jean Seberg could not free the men of the world from thought of Leslie Caron but she came damned close. Claudine Longet never stood a chance. I imagine Louisa turning me into the police who will shoot me dead. *Qu'est-ce que c'est 'dégueulasse'?* That closing line from *Breathless* takes the mind right back to Sartre, doesn't it? *La Nausée*. I think about the virginity of Louisa every day.

The beautiful mulatto girl at the branch nearest here carries her own desperation in number of customers the bank expects her to push through each day. She sits in a cubicle opening new accounts. I tell how once at the main bank the police opened the safety deposit box of a notorious nutter only to find nothing but dentures belonging to his victims. I am too old now for the mulatto girl to listen to my tall tales. Instead the girl complains the new software for certificates of deposits is too complex to get anything right the first try. I reward myself with the desperation of the mulatto girl though it is merely conversation going no further. I am not there to take the break. I tell her I am just there to upgrade some other software on the interactive teller machine that had failed installing remotely. I cannot help her. I had meant not to get near her at all.

In Des Moines at the art center now, for a long time really, there sits a piece that is three vacuum cleaners stacked, like canisters of film, the tales not just held within but sucked from without, clean behind the Matisse, sweep under the Sargent, it becomes the image for all life there, rising like a cornstalk, its predecessor, but without interest in the sun, without concern for the rain, it wants dust from all who approach it, the dust of your skin, your soul, the pioneer portraits, any other stupid thing you've got. A dog asks questions with its nose but that's just another line in the *Dr. Dolittle* book that didn't make the movie. A dog might chase answers but never a vacuum cleaner. I am the same. I am a happy tongue.

Thousands of years ago the pyramids promised not only the pharaohs immortality but the priests too. I should just put on a movie. At least three months now since Susan Hayward but on one of the regular channels there is a commercial for expectant young women who have jumped from their fucking. I shout that every expectant mother must remember watching only the commercials on television assures it will be born a boy with business sense. The problem is I was right at nineteen in that poetry class when no one at that age is supposed to be right about anything and certainly never in a poetry class. I knew what was coming. At the bank and all its branches everyone makes pretense, forcing themselves to propagate known falsehoods, aggrandizing themselves by exploiting others, demanding all others believe on pain of inquisition, the rules of the game having become not rules of the church, not that, though the only difference is the absence of the central promise, the central flimflam, the promise of immortality. The slaves are again not promised eternal life. That's how it was in the time of the pharaohs, no heavenly salvation for the slaves. Capitalism has looked into the far past for the oppression too now Marx doesn't matter.

There has not been a meaningful raise in my wages in ten years. I approach retirement with some sense 401K was once the name of a gang of German war criminals escaped to unknown lands. My disk of *All Night Long* with Betsy Blair is a German disk that is always trying to slip out of the English language version. I sometimes think the gang is headed by the mother of the war hero. Anyway I have decided the bank now must accept great risk since I have been forced into risk for so long. I test nothing I do. Eventually some glitch will cost the bank in corrupted accounts, hacked withdrawals, weeks of inaccessibility, fallout from ruined reputation, nationalization of branches in foreign lands, but it seems unlikely the bank will ever lose the four or five billion it must lose to match my 401K losses, in proportion. I would still have to be in the central code for that but I am far way in more ways than distance.

Now from the window in my bedroom turned office I watch the crows fly over the little children in the school next door, the children oblivious to the crows, the crows missing nothing.

In it I see Vincent Van Gogh though it is only Edward Gorey. Most days I try not to see paintings in it at all. The crows want the moment while the worms celebrate each graduation from the school.

In *The Quare Fellow* the rich man of the two men sentenced to hang is reprieved. Of course. One of the prisoners jokes there is a certain dignity to beating a wife to death with the silver head of a walking stick but at no point do the prisoners discuss the head of the walking stick. A body might expect them to take keener interest in the tools of their trade. I wonder. Was it the head of a lion? The head of a dog? I've tried to read the play again but I can never get past this question about the walking stick. Was it the figure of an angel the hand was meant to grasp? The first time I ever saw Orson Welles in *Othello* I mistook the lines at the end about a woman's labor pains to be Othello describing his own pain. I mistook him to be suffering a couvade, morning nausea, mourning nothing. I mistook him wishing he were a woman. It was only later when reading the play I understood Othello is in fact speaking of Desdemona but the play isn't better for it. In the madhouse too there was a very large rich man once an athlete free to do whatever pleased.

Of course Baudelaire was just another poet with private means until taken under control of the courts, forever a numbered prisoner, so he wouldn't squander. He lived his life after that injunction in cheap hotels when not so poor he begged the floor from friends, anywhere to sleep, bummed money from Delacroix though no close friend, my mind confusing lines from Henry Miller into Baudelaire's intimate journals, Baudelaire saying ecstasy is a number, I shit you not, the best Miller line when he excoriates his mother for an obsession with cleanliness from which Paris has freed him, what he does with what was done to him. Fuck the vacuum cleaners rising to the sky like office buildings. But why do I tolerate even a prisoner with private means? Because though his father was excused being a priest by a revolutionary government executing priests it is unclear if the father was ever defrocked by the church. His father was always priest. In that Baudelaire found himself ineluctably damned. My own mother never remarried after leaving the father of my sisters and never provided the name of the priest who fathered me because what is a name anyway when there are numbers to take its place? Her entire life she only ever slept with two men. One. Two. It is like the credits from *The Prisoner* with its thunder effect over the weather balloon.

On the web I find an obituary of the madman who in the community college years studying programming often demanded a ride because the bus made him late for work. He was in a couple of my classes but he was careful never to sit near. I had business with women. He understood. The donut shop where I dropped him was not far from the apartment I then rented so I knew the madman could be found for hours at a time sitting at the street window, some character from a painting, obvious stuff but not unappealing, women and broken men crowding the Edward Hoppers. The madman had no job. He didn't even seem to understand the donuts were fried there through the night not come early afternoon following classes when the remaining donuts were already stale. I think the shop girls must have given him the stale donuts for free. His job was to eat the leftovers. I find in the obituary his birthday is my birthday. I had forgotten we once got drunk together to celebrate our birthdays but I can no longer be surprised by anything read. Instead I am surprised to find his doppelganger sitting on a park bench wearing some kind of hooded pullover so I will never be sure it wasn't a ghost. The thick massed hair. The beard left wild. I had not forgotten he used to live summers in one of the park ravines because the basement room his parents gave him they gave him with conditions. I live near that park now. I again pull the dog away from a used condom.

"He's a handsome dog."
"I just had her fur sheared for the summer."
"He looks like a fighter."

It seemed important to the ghost to question the sex of the dog. Was it true when the madman told me his father was the general over on the arsenal island? Of course not. Would Baudelaire with his stepfather a general have taunted me over the sex of my dog? Fuck. Maybe. Anyway I have seen the obituary a few days too late to attend the services and no one goes visits the dead at the national cemetery now the security is tighter than an international airport. Out by the bridge I have seen officers with guns drawn. They check your criminal record. They examine your anus. The officers don't want the sort of visitors who might pocket the ghosts.

There are so many shootings in the neighborhood now it is difficult to imagine even Sartre could spot revolutionary morality in it.

And what is the sex of your weather balloon? In *The Prisoner* there is an episode where the warders of the village use a brain scan into the prisoner's dreams to learn his secrets. But again any fool given a breath knows that misses the truth. Warders want far away from the distortions and disruptions of an evening with *Dr. Caligari*, the streets uneven, the post office so many leaning birdhouses, the somnolent women prophetic in only disturbing ways, without touch. There are easier means to extract secrets from the prisoners. Don't you want to be normal? they ask.

Didn't Sartre launch such balloons during his time in the meteorological army unit before captured by the Germans? In Paris I went to the pet cimetière to see Rin Tin Tin. In the autobiography of his childhood Sartre recounts walking through the same large cimetière appalled that the epitaphs carved in stone were in every way indistinguishable from the maxims once spoken by his grandfather. He is accompanied by an American friend so similarly offended the friend kicks the ear off a concrete dog. What American friend would that be? Jean Seberg from No Name City? Eddy Considine from Alphaville? Sartre also gives no name to the dog he owns a few pages later in the autobiography though this in a book repeatedly stating the importance of names. In the autobiography he several times calls himself a dog entertaining his grandfather. A poodle. Sartre could only wish to have been that adorable. In a close reading it becomes obvious everyone in the family preferred the dog begging belly rubs to the boy quoting books he was too young to understand. Sartre wrote an entire philosophy around wanting to be the dog but unable to become the dog. Existence. Essence. Being. Nothingness. Six. In failing to talk to the animals Sartre became the evil shadow to *Doctor Dolittle*. Perhaps we were to understand that the weather balloon in The Prisoner represents Sartre? Sartre probably recognized himself when he saw the show. There. That's it. None of this is greater idiocy than what Sartre wrote about Baudelaire.

Curiously Sartre's description of himself precociously reciting literature he was too young to understand, giving performance, is entirely like the biographies describe Orson Welles at the same age, already a showman, not especially bright in any other way.

The new software at the bank that sits atop only the capital of the old can create emails impossible to tell from the real thing, the nature of contemporary spam requiring perfect deceit, by hook or by crook. The latest chief executive at the bank has a beautiful wife he has not yet traded for trophy. Curiously I saw the wife here in the hinterlands when she attended a party for members only at the museum back downriver near my mother's old house. The members were celebrating a traveling exhibit as though they had come to delineate the history of impressionism with everything but dance. I slipped into the party without paying. The wife was slender, small though with six grown daughters, far better educated than Louisa with all the misjudgments in scale that can produce, profoundly attractive all the same. Her rhythms seemed the same. This lawyer in speaking about Sisley and Caillebotte seemed just a little ahead of the beat the way Louisa once threw words over the cubicle walls. There was a slight southern accent quite unlike Louisa but then the headquarters of the bank after the last merger is now in Atlanta, isn't it? I saw one of the curators make a pass. The line to make a pass at the wife went right down the stairs three stories like the line formed in the same museum downriver months later that last day to see the loans from the Musée d'Orsay. *Keep moving and keep your remarks in the visitor book to a single word.*

In *The Snows of Kilimanjaro* Susan Hayward plays the second wife of the writer with the gangrenous leg too far out on the savannah to get treatment. Gregory Peck plays the writer who with each new woman in his life always found a next one richer than the last. He is a writer who knows his business. Still he blames the money for ruining him but only because with vultures flying overhead he has left so many things unwritten. He has never had a woman quite rich enough to make true all the stories. He remembers giving more for the money when he didn't love than when he did. It has been performance. He hit his spots. He has made his means by other than writing. No. No. All that is in the Hemingway story not the movie. *She's a splendid woman by all standards. Maybe if I close my eyes she'll go away. Par la griffe et la dent féroce de la femme.* Anyway Susan Hayward is content to be outliving the failed bastard.

Of course the wife of the chief executive was Louisa though it took me a long time afterwards to believe it really was Louisa. I already knew. I mean I knew all along. Other programmers back in the day had left in my cubicle several copies of the same newspaper clipping of Louisa marrying the rising executive. He wasn't at our bank then. One of the paintings on display not from the d'Orsay was a Sisley flooded village Louisa owned with her chief executive from the bank. I mean I knew Louisa would be at the party because she owned a painting. I had gone to see for myself this eternal return but the paintings seemed to make it so impossible, as though the great paintings of Impressionism were the tilted walls, the angled streets with lampposts twisted in curls, the moon shining only for a tide never to return to beaches of stones that stain green in an otherwise black and white night. I did not let Louisa even see me though I longed for that dance.

RIGHT IN THE TEETH

FADE IN:

INT: IT FITS INFORMATION TECHNOLOGY OFFICE - NEW
MORNING

At the programmer desks there are the two chairs
but in the chairs are male mannequin torsos
wearing the suit jackets and ties previously worn
by Programmer I and Programmer II. Denshag
stands behind his desk holding his Fetish Doll
now dressed in mourning black with veil. In
front of this desk, one foot atop the child's
school chair, stands the Chairman, now headless,
his crown hanging from rope about his neck like
the fetish gag. Igor sits at the kitchen table
still in the uniform of a dental assistant but
now the uniform is completely covered with blood.
His face and hands are spotless. On the table is
the rotting ledger. He tosses SIX LARGE COINS
onto the ledger out from a COFFEE MUG that reads
"You want it WHEN?"

INSERT - LIVE ACTION

Real hands returning the coins to the coffee mug
then tossing them again.

BACK TO SCENE

     DENSHAG
  Of course Chinese women are by
  nature just a lot smaller in

                    stature. Tiny. And tinier still.
                    Traditionally barely visible. There
                    just isn't anything the average
                    seamstress in our great country can
                    stop eating to compete with that.
                    What else can we do? Pull their
                    teeth? We have the technology but
                    not the pluck. Is that the right
                    word? Now? Even for teeth? I used
                    to know the right word but economic
                    conditions change so quickly they
                    are hard to accurately describe even
                    to yourself.

Denshag pauses for a response from Chairman
Povereese that will never come. Large black
beetles crawl out from the neck onto the crown.
Igor looks at the beetles before tossing the
coins again as though believing he has brought
the beetles into being with prognostication.

                              DENSHAG
                    Of course I appreciate fully that
                    the only reasonable response is to
                    move all manufacturing overseas
                    where they speak a different tongue.
                            (to Igor abstractly)
                    Of course obesity has become a
                    fundamental freedom in this country,
                    merging with the old freedoms to
                    become the new freedom, the only
                    freedom, the obscene freedom of
                    speaking with your mouth full.

Denshag drags a coffin from behind his desk, a
rough wooden coffin of traditional design with
corners widened at the shoulders, the coffin
tapering at the feet. On the lid of the coffin

there is a very nice brass plate with his name.
From the coffin he removes a dressed mannequin
torso he places in his own chair. Of course the
mannequin is dressed in exactly the same jacket
and tie. Denshag then exits past the kitchenette
table still dragging the coffin. He drops the
Fetish Doll on the table while passing.

INSERT - LIVE ACTION

Real hands dropping a doll on the table among the
coins.

BACK TO SCENE

Mrs Peel now stands beside the table without
having entered. She wears the costume of an
ancient Chinese empress, long gown in intricate
pattern, no sign of feet, pen holding her hair in
place. Beneath one arm she carries the head of a
bull. With a grunt She shifts the head to
beneath the other arm to stand closer the table.

> MRS PEEL
> I see bleeding has convinced you
> once again you can never die.

> IGOR
> The problem with tossing the I Ching
> is that the results of six tossed
> coins always add up to exactly the
> same dollar value, whereas the toss
> itself is what seems different, just
> for the moment, like a jazz riff
> lost in cigarette smoke.

> MRS PEEL
> The I Ching is not an instrument,
> jazz or financial.

                    IGOR
Can a dental assistant fulfill the
job description without instruments?
Without mouths?

                  MRS PEEL
Everyone knows you don't need
computer programmers predicting the
future once the company merely
plunders the past.

                    IGOR
And pushing production overseas is a
plundering of the past?

                  MRS PEEL
Ask around.
        (motioning to headless
         torsos)
How is that, baby, does that do
what?
        (lowers hand)
The wealth of previous generations
is the only money left in an
exiguous present.

                    IGOR
But can prophecy actually be
restrained simply by making the past
no longer safe from the present?
Don't the beetles and worms eat even
without teeth?

                  MRS PEEL
The costs of legacy systems must be
kept within reason if not
probability.

                    IGOR
                 (paging ledger)
One head. Five tails. That
means...
         (reading)
Stripping away.
         (not reading)
I should never have left Miss
Cummersum a solitary. I should have
been happy to take her to bed even
when all I wanted was you. My
success gave me rights. Still it
was wrong to demand her clothes
without fair exchange.
         (reading)
Stripping away makes it unbeneficial
to travel.

                 MRS PEEL
I hardly think it astounding that
the I Ching correctly predicts the
humiliations of modern airline
travel for anyone dressed below
first class.

                    IGOR
Prophecy cannot reach a billionaire?

                 MRS PEEL
Don't let someone with more than six
coins make you feel inadequately
dressed.

                    IGOR
I hate this new job but I suppose
any job is better than no job.

MRS PEEL

Those without humps recognize change
is opportunity. Even loose change.

IGOR

Have you seen Miss Cummersum?

MRS PEEL

She chose lesser humiliations than
you.

IGOR

Could I have married her? A virgin?
Could I have ever believed she was a
virgin? I seem to remember reading
something once when I was a computer
programmer about the law of averages
assuring six tossed monkeys must
eventually land ass downwards.
Anything can happen?

MRS PEEL

Darwin had scars that proved
otherwise.

IGOR

Perhaps a financial incentive must
always be in play.

MRS PEEL

The criminality of teaching monkeys
to use money is beyond the
imagination but well within the
experience of any business leader.
Of course with only six monkeys you
get only tossed heads and tails. It
would take at least seven monkeys to

establish an effective banking
system.

                    IGOR
                  (reading)
Yang cannot overcome Yin at this
point because Yin rises now like
stripping a wedding bed of its legs.

                  MRS PEEL
Money always strips the wedding bed
in the end. Because no virgin steps
from eggshells or even clamshells
blown in from the sea without
breaking something the salesman said
would last forever and a day. Is
that not more than menstrual blood
staining you? And yet your own
blood?

                    IGOR
                (still reading)
You must not go anywhere distant
thinking you can apply great
strength upon arrival.

                  MRS PEEL
Good advice for any honeymooner but
sometimes even for honeymooners
success is merely thrust upon you.

Igor tosses the coins again but this time out of
the cup flies blood.

                    IGOR
                 (waves hands
                  over bloody
                  bloody dress)
Without breaking a sweat?

                    MRS PEEL
Better than without removing a
stitch.

                      IGOR
I don't believe you but still love
you.

                    MRS PEEL
Why torture yourself with your own
misshapen expectations about love
when you have been entrusted with so
much responsibility? Not every man
is left alone with six coins he can
call his own from 9 to 5. Even if
then denied 5 to 7.

                      IGOR
Am I alone?

                    MRS PEEL
You must be now I am management.
          (Wags fingers like
           metronome)
I... work... work... work... work...
work... work.
          (Fumbles with fingers
           uncertainly)
Six words! So many! I shall miss
the days when work was one word with
meaningless repetitions leading up
to the weekends.

                      IGOR
Help.

MRS PEEL

Or like that, some similar vulgarity
pleasant only to the tongue.
Remember my tongue?

IGOR

Am I alone with all possible results
dictated by a book translated from a
language I will never know? Aren't
the legs of a wedding bed meant to
dance? At least bump and grind?

MRS PEEL

In modern economics only capital is
allowed to move freely, move freely
across the bed even, pleasured by
mirrors, regarding only itself. You
have proven very astute at
anticipating business developments
even before these tricks with coins.
But don't anticipate unnatural
events with every new blood moon.

IGOR

Perhaps if I throw only five coins.

MRS PEEL

Straight from the wedding bed into
embezzlement?

IGOR

I could throw the sixth into a
fountain for a wish.

MRS PEEL

I once had a husband who had a
similar faith in other waters after

I refused to ever again sleep with
him.

                    IGOR

Husband?

                  MRS PEEL

Of course husband. My name is Mrs
Peel. Remember?

                    IGOR

Everyone said Mrs Peel was just an
honorary title, a fashion statement.

                  MRS PEEL

My husband drowned but not in a
fountain. Probably not. And yet
wouldn't it be poetic to think so?
The police returned to me only his
wallet. Soaked clean through was
that wallet. A lovely memento mori
all the same. His pockets full of
stones still I was so beloved he
left room in his wallet for a
picture of me among the presidents
on the fifties and hundreds and
twenties.

                    IGOR

But not any singles?

                  MRS PEEL

I certainly couldn't still be called
married despite having the wallet to
put under my pillow. It never has
dried properly. What do you make of
that?

                    IGOR
You would never have to question
where I was nights.

                  MRS PEEL
You cannot have me by becoming more
like me.

                    IGOR
I knew conformity would never keep
its promise.

                  MRS PEEL
And yet here you are six times
richer than before.

                    IGOR
Is there no way left to break free
from wage slavery?

                  MRS PEEL
Embezzlement will always seem
honorable given the obscene
alternatives you are faced with
daily.

                    IGOR
You admit that? Without objection?

                  MRS PEEL
I must object that your stolen coins
have heads and tails. This is not
acceptable. It is expressly against
the sexual harassment policy of IT
FITS to exclude the torso in favor
of more evidently earthy appendages.
Heads? Tails? Is that all you've
got?

                    IGOR
               (gestures at
               mannequins)
     I doubt they'll much mind.

                  MRS PEEL
     Better give me the coins before you
     cross the line.

                    IGOR
               (sweeps coins
               close to chest)
     A give back? Management demands a
     give back? Never ever. Never. To
     the barricades! The worker's flag
     is deepest red! Union! Union!
     Strike! Strike! Strike!

Suddenly eight or nine identical figures of Igor
come marching through the room led by a piper
whose bagpipes are perhaps a little undersized.
The marchers wear kilts but are otherwise
ordinary hunchbacks. They pass through the room
quickly becoming ghosts that fade away before
reaching the exit. Their disappearance with
fading music again leaves it possible to hear
Igor shouting with futility.

                    IGOR
     Strike! Strike! Strike! Strike!

Mrs Peel snatches the coins then shoves them into
the shouting mouth to silence it, fingers deep
down Igor's throat, thrusting, wiggling like a
search for pleasure among the teeth.

INSERT LIVE ACTION

Real hand thrusting into a real mouth but the
image is layered so the fingers multiply to
eighteen.

                        MRS PEEL
                         (V.O)
            Never ever to the barricades?
            Union? You call for union? Won't
            this do for union? With me striking
            right against your teeth? With the
            taste of me in every flavor ever
            after? Put money in your what? Put
            what in your what? Put what? Put
            what of me into what?

FADE OUT.

ALICE FROM 5 TO 7

I was walking a dark street when my name was called by what seemed at first a voice but might have been a light. I could feel all my senses mixed in confusion. There was somewhere ahead a café I had known in my youth but there was no telling if it was still a going concern. It was after midnight. Behind me the streets were lit with gas lamps flaring in the barely controlled rhythm of my breathing. In the dark I stumbled on cobblestones. Finally I came to the café but there was no longer a door. I leaned my nose against the window. From a wineglass the lone waitress in the lone spotlight poured the salt meant for me. The waitress was the wineglass. The wineglass was the waitress. Within the mathematics I could smell salt because I had my nose against glass that maybe was no longer the window. Then I was awakened when the plane hit turbulence several hours into the flight. It was my first vacation with travel in years so out went savings for a better than cheap airplane seat only to find myself still pressed too close among businessmen. They left me alone only because the book on my lap wasn't one of the finance tomes the others all seemed to be reading in conquest. I mean it wasn't like reading poetry in the tavern. The businessmen in first class understood a book was made great only when great men read it. I saw it was an observation Sartre might have given Roquentin though I was uncertain I wasn't thinking this only because of the dream. All the same I awoke again quite surprised Alice had invited me to visit Paris. A few weeks earlier I had called Alice on her birthday perhaps because I knew it was not the thing an actress would appreciate but she had in fact found it funny I would dare. In the past I had almost never found Alice at home when I called. We had talked only a few times over very many years.

"Do you pay extra for international calls?"

"Nowadays it's neither here nor there to the bank."

"You're calling me from a bank?"

I had not intended to be the man writing his sweetheart atop the teller machine but perhaps there was no escaping it once the airport was involved. Anyway there had been the airplane full of businessmen and then I had waited in Paris more than four whole days without seeing Alice. She hadn't felt well enough to meet the previous days. The fifth day was another afternoon in Paris in April with a sky that wanted to sparkle, like always in Paris, there being good reason Baudelaire could never stop writing about reflections from the daylight before the inevitable afternoon shower, all reflet et éblouissant et clarté. It was not madness. In Iowa the best days were so sharply clear they seemed to fill shadows with work that must be done before the shadow gives way. It hardly mattered anymore. There wasn't a shadow in Alice's apartment when she finally had me come around. The windows had no curtains.

"Baudelaire actually wrote his first poems here?"

"Three or four doors up the street at the top of the building."

"Close enough."

The apartment was right on the Seine so the water made games with the sunshine that surprised. The room was very bright. Alice offered me a glass of white wine with some wink that we were drinking the very best she had racked over the years. The first glass went quickly but I again smelled salt. Alice and I had not been in the same room together since the cup of coffee after the funeral of the war hero. *Musicianer*. I bussed Alice on the cheek before going to sit at her piano to play the tune practiced just for her. *A practice of arts inhibited and out of warrant*. It was the theme played over her scenes in one of the few movies she starred. I wished I had written it. In the movie there is a scene where Alice sings what seems improvised words to the theme. One of the jazz magazines that no longer existed had long ago run a photograph of the pianist who had written the theme for the movie. The publicity photograph was him with his arm around Alice's waist such that his large, very black hand posed on her hip. They weren't lovers for long. Alice was never given credit for the lyrics to the theme that had sold a million copies.

"You should have written one yourself."

"Would you have known it was original?"

"That guy beat me all the time, you know."

She had never told me that but there was no point quibbling in a room so bright. I switched to a tune I still thought was the best I had ever composed. It swings more than a little. It's a tune written for the teeth movie but so pleasing I could never bring myself to use it for something that from its very nature reverberated childishness, something that seemed childish even through all the dark comedy against the job. Anyway, because the tune never made it over the movie, it could no longer be thought a tune about Louisa, not with certainty anyway. *Oubli Oubli Lulu*. I had purloined much from that one for my tune. I began to play and Alice brought out our past.

"I'm amazed you have them."

"You didn't know I stole them from you?"

"I thought I forgot them in that office with the filthy floor I had been told to clean."

Alice had brought out the risqué deck of cards we had played with all those years before. They were still like new. They can't have been opened often since that night of the television crew. But instead of dealing out a hand onto the piano Alice dealt out a kind of tarot fit only for a minor actress. It was near a traditional cross spread but stopped before the thirteenth card. I had not known Alice to be superstitious. She was at least guaranteed no death card among the cheesecake but at one corner of the reading was the joker I had given tattoos. It seemed to bother Alice a great deal something of me would impose itself into a reading. She didn't want anything immediate to the day.

"This card indicates there will eventually be difficulties with money."

Alice was predicting into her distant future. It occurred to me the laughing blonde portraying the queen of diamonds had never once yet worried where her next jewels were coming from. *Les Jeux Sont Fait* is after all a gambler's call. Just glancing about I was overwhelmed the apartment was so very luxurious despite the absence of curtains. Years before Alice had written me she needed another movie because the apartment had depleted the trust fund. The baby grand I was playing did not even slightly crowd the room and the furniture was especially attractive woods brought out of Stockholm and probably from as distant as St Peterburg. There were a couple antique Italian pieces that belonged in a museum. There were no books. The only set of shelves in the room were filled with mementos of the western shot in Spain and the mobster picture shot in England and the comedy about tourists caught up in Rome that summer from a while back before the movie was made when it looked like revolution in the streets. There were eyeglasses and wigs and gloves and shoes and hats and drinking mugs of yore and a paste crown historically accurate and a diadem all metals from outer space. There were teacups and champagne glasses and all sorts of ashtrays. There was a false moustache attached to the stem of a tobacco pipe in remembrance of a favorite leading man who had died before the picture completed shooting. There were fine sable paint brushes thick with dry colors. There were field glasses. There was a horse pistol. There was some portion of a shark's jaw. There was a ukulele with only one string that had been played in the best of her war movies only with all the strings. There was the bloodstained broadsword from when she had been a highwaywoman. There was a rubber bull's ear placed before her montera. There was that sword too. There were no awards.

"This card indicates heartbreak lasting a hundred full moons."

She even glanced into a mirror to check her makeup before we left the apartment. I remembered having to bring my own bookcases those three or four years in the apartment the newspaperman had once provided his mistress. Kept women must not read. Still every few years Alice had sent me an especially good poem she could never have written without books around somehow. Baudelaire had kept his books in a trunk so all his ideas seemed born from his own flesh. It seemed a scheme applicable for kept women. Of course Alice only ever sent me the poems about the hometown she claimed she hadn't visited since young.

"You sure you wouldn't be more comfortable here?"

"It has to be a hotel."

"You never think about buying curtains?"

"I pitched the old dingy ones but haven't found anything new I like at all."

It wasn't just she was now afraid of the dark. Alice had for many years juggled at least three wealthy men at the same time so it had become habit to worry someone peeking through windows might make a farce. But the last wealthy man had stopped dropping around. Alice was alone, and though she had been unwell all week, her vanity remained determined we would go to bed in belated celebration of her birthday, even if it were only me with money saved over the years but nothing like riches. At the very least I would help her recall all she had overcome in our hometown, our little dirty river town. The plan that afternoon was we would go to bed before sunset, before Alice got too fatigued, before I wanted sleep because all days now seemed long on my eyes even when not travelling. We were old. On my third try switching hotels each night I had found a room with especially good curtains that kept out all the Boulevard Montparnasse. Actually the hotel was at the start of the street below the boulevard more or less angled off behind Café du Dôme. It would be a long walk.

"We need to get a taxi."

"Walk me at least to the Panthéon."

I didn't want to fight crowds of tourists for a taxi but there was no arguing her out of the walk. Crossing the island Alice led the way when the sidewalk narrowed to one but at those moments she held my hand to keep balance. I took from her a leather bag meant to be purse but was if anything even larger than the satchel stolen from me in the airport. The bag was very heavy. Alice no longer let loose my hand after we reached the bridge taking us over to Rue Cardinal Lemoine. But I had been long enough out of Des Moines by then there was no urge to allow that particular coincidence to intrude into my thoughts. Awake there was no mixing senses with the past.

Only with a feeling of great distance did I remember being on the street the first time.

"That time living in Paris I almost got an apartment in this building here because the landlord claimed the piano in the main room there had been left behind by Bud Powell."

"That doesn't seem likely."

"Why not? Right up where we are headed they have a plaque up on the building where the landlord told Hemingway his writing room was where Verlaine died."

"You think there will someday be a plaque for Bud Powell?"

"Why not crazy Bud Powell too?"

I didn't believe a word of it but there was no reason to make Alice feel defeated. After all landlords must be good for something. *Le passé, c'est un luxe de propriétaire.* Alice pulled me through a dodge of traffic to get to the other side of the street since we had to cross at some point anyway but then we got off course up rue Monge. There was a shop she wanted to browse. It was an elegant place filled with expensive hats and the usual other accessories. Inside Alice picked through a display of foulards but there was no mistaking any of them for flags. Yet it was strange. We were being looked down on by a wall of framed photographs of all the celebrities claimed to have patronized the shop. I supposed the photographs were something like flags of all the nations that had conquered Paris. Then I saw there was a photograph of Alice on the wall from back that one year she sang in clubs after that movie theme became so popular. *To hell with Bud Powell. Look at me.* It was that same summer I had been in Paris. I had seen Alice sing that theme at the Theatre Champs Elysée on a joint bill with several other more traditional singers. Her recording of *Sous Les Ponts De Paris* was almost a second hit on the radio. At the show that one night Alice had introduced me to the pianist then sharing her apartment. In *La Nausée* the genuine old blues record Roquentin so likes hearing for the negress singing is in fact a white woman singing. Sartre got that one wrong too.

"What do you think about this?"

Alice had put a diaphanous red foulard first around her shoulders like a shawl that accentuated her breasts but now she pulled the foulard over her face.

"You think it will make it easier for you to remember what I used to look like?"

She meant would it be easier for me to come to bed but there had been no hesitation on display. I was not the one who had delayed. The foulard slipped a little.

"Look, it's her."

I held up the book I had bought to pass a couple hours nearby the Île Saint-Louis before meeting. I had ended up on the island itself again in the famous glacier that is in all the tourist books but never seemed to have many tourists. I had been there an hour every afternoon to read some other book purchased just for that afternoon. Every afternoon I had been trying to be nearer Alice. Now it was a pain to have the new book for the long walk but from the weight of Alice's leather bag I knew there would never be invitation again to the apartment. I mean there was no leaving the book behind with the idea to come back to steal something better. I held up the book to one of the photographs on the wall.

"It might be her."

The glamour shot on the wall was not clearly the woman on the back of the autobiography with her leg hoisted in the street to fit her shoe.

"It's her alright."

"What's the book?"

I turned the binding towards Alice.

"The memoirs of the late Betsy Blair."

"Why does that name sound familiar?"

"She was almost Desdemona in the Orson Welles movie of Othello."

I did not mention Betsy Blair remains mostly remembered if remembered for a movie where an ugly man finally finds love. It's not as though I might have taken Ernest Borgnine in a fight. And anyway it had been a long time since I had thought about Gene Kelly dancing about a backlot Paris. It had been a long time since I had felt compelled to think about Gene Kelly at all so it had been almost a shock to find the book by Betsy Blair. I had bought the book expecting more bad dreams.

"And so that's what you felt compelled to choose at Shakespeare and Company?"

"It's signed."

"How can you be sure it's hers, the signature?"

"In his memoires, Pablo Neruda describes being run out of Venice by the Carabinieri for his politics, describing the town as the birthplace of Desdemona, as though to him she was absolutely real, mentioning her but not one of the many admirers met at his poetry reading."

"You still read poetry all the time even though you never write a poem?"

"What else is there?"

I might have said something about the movies Alice had acted in because the treasures that wall of photographs had pursued were no longer for sale there in the shop. I might have mentioned paintings. In the same paragraph Neruda mentions Canaletto as though the painter is from the same verse as Desdemona and Othello. I had other things to mention but suddenly I could not be kind though I had come a long way to be kind.

"Later on Betsy Blair was Emilia not Desdemona in the jazz version of Othello."

"So that's why you tracked down her book?"

"In the jazz version Iago is played by Patrick McGoohan."

"I worked with him once on a movie but you remember that, don't you?"

"Of course."

Of course I remembered not a movie but a television episode where Alice with no more than eight lines played an innocent woman on trial while McGoohan played the corrupt judge. Of course this show was decades after *The Prisoner*. The character of the defense attorney was the star of the television series. There is always another defense attorney. Alice preferred to remember that work a movie since we were long past age when truth in recollection mattered. The only thing the wall in front of us demanded was a week of kindness.

"A while back I bought that movie of Othello McGoohan directed that everyone has long thought was lost."

"How was it lost?"

"The rock opera."

"Same thing but with more body hair."

Perhaps Alice had seen stills from that opera shot in the New Mexico desert with an Iago who wears a leather vest open to all his chest. Perhaps McGoohan had shown Alice the movie at his home after a crowded wrap party for the television episode. It is hard to believe Patrick McGoohan found purpose in not one but two versions of *Othello* until the scene in the opera where the hillbilly Michael Cassio gets drunk. And where is the shirtless Iago? Behind the drum kit thumping his victory. It could be McGoohan playing Johnny Cousin from the earlier movie except in that movie all the men wear shark suits and all the women wear evening dresses. I did not mention that this Desdemona looked less like Betsy Blair than like blonde Jean Seberg. McGoohan cast another redhead for Emilia.

"I like that Welles movie except it is obvious the actress playing Desdemona has been dubbed over by somebody else."

With time I had come to view every Jean Seberg movie just another nightmare from the madhouse in Lilith. *In The French Style*. Her *Joan of Arc* the one I met in my own madhouse. *A Fine Madness* not so different really from *Dr. Caligari*. Even *Paint Your Wagon* with her two husbands seemed dubbed over with nightmare. Seberg too was hanging on the wall in the shop. And on the wall there was a photograph of Orson Welles from back in the days the shop still sold hats for men. In his memoir of shooting *Othello*, Micheál MacLiammóir praises Orson Welles for making Iago an evil man rather than the Mephistopheles in so many productions.

"In the rock opera Iago sings he is both Iago and Satan."

"I am not what I am. Sung in duet."

Two husbands. Two Baudelaires said Sartre. I laughed then unwrapped the foulard the rest of the way because it wasn't funny at all. Suddenly what came to mind, stumbling me in a kind of suffocation, were the masks Robbie had sent me after her production of the play with giant nose, giant ear, giant lips all in foam rubber, seeing the masks in my mind still hanging like correspondences of the senses off the headboard to my bed though they had long been put to the trash, the masks so long unworn having rotted across the years all the same.

"Haven't you played a dual personality in a movie too?"

"Hasn't every actress?"

Alice let me buy the foulard for her because there had been no gift brought to the apartment. It had seemed silly to buy something in Paris after the jar of antique buttons from home had been lost in the transfer of airplanes in Atlanta together with the digital camera and at least one change of clothes also in my favorite old leather satchel. I had overpacked every bit of luggage I owned with some idea there might be a long stay in Paris. There is no longer the option to shoot on real film. There are no development labs. There is no film stock. I keep a digital camera but it is not the same so I go years at a time without animating a thing I never complete anyway. On my first day in Paris I had gone to a very good camera store on the Boulevard des Filles du Calvaire but the name of the street so put me off there was no buying a replacement camera. Alice was still beautiful. I saw that for myself.

"Back to Cardinal Lemoine?"

We were again on the street.

"It is the best way."

"It's too steep for you to walk."

"I want the climb."

She meant me to understand this in some sexual way too but instead of leaning in for a kiss I thought about all the times Louisa had tried to murder me since I left her a virgin on her wedding day. I was in the hospital three days after the brakes on my utility vehicle went bad out on the highway. That was the first time. I was in the hospital only a few hours the time I bought a dinner at the grocery store but left it out of my sight while searching shelves for an imported chardonnay. It was the first of seven times I have since had my stomach pumped. I have a shoulder that has never been right since a shove down the stone stairs outside the library left me unconscious on the winter ice. The police didn't want to believe something lawless could happen at a library. I now have a reputation for accidents. Alice and I climbed the street then went onto the Place Contrescarpe past the plaque commemorating where

Hemingway first lived in Paris. Of course Louisa had never come back to programming in the cubicles. I kept her nameplate but someone else had already swiped that mirror mounted on her computer terminal.

"We're off course again."

"I want another look down rue Mouffetard."

The street seemed even steeper than the one we had just climbed as though we were finding different levels to an abyss. It is terribly easy to snooker a boy only eight. Seeing *The Snows Of Kilimanjaro* for the first time again years later in the video store I was appalled to find it was merely a backlot movie with good second unit shots done on location. There is a very fine recreation of 1920s Paris in Place Contrescarpe. But in one scene Gregory Peck sits under yet more backlot Utrillos listening to a saxophone solo in a room crowded with what seems to be existentialists sitting entranced if not drugged on the floor. That scene cuts to worse. In the foreground of the second unit shot onto the rear of Notre-Dame there is a gas lamp clearly brought along from the props department. It was that lamp multiplied into my dream on the airplane. In the shot the distant couple walking the Seine are only something like Gregory Peck and Ava Gardner. At eight I had been perverted. But then in the video store after viewing it a hundred times the shot onto Notre-Dame became genius because the shot left matters free for the couple to be anyone at all walking up that most beautiful spot in all the history of all the world. Anything could happen.

"Did the keys stick on the piano Bud Powell left behind?"

Alice was still unhappy I had mentioned Bud Powell getting a plaque someday. We had turned back towards the Panthéon but became so busy talking we passed the plaque for Verlaine without ever seeing it. It was important to miss that plaque.

Along the way I touched Alice at the neck but only to touch the foulard. The scarf made me think about the Loïe Fuller dance in my movie with its mirrors so passing for Louisa. I still thought too often about Louisa. Alice too loved to talk about movies.

"That isn't actually Loïe Fuller in that movie."

"Of course it is."

"The Lumière brothers saved a buck filming a copycat."

"The distribution company I worked for when I was a teenager always rented that one out as Loïe Fuller."

"F is for Fake."

All the books about Paris so much always alike too should someday be a single testament decided by bishops. There are books that state it is not actually the building where Verlaine died. Of course Verlaine had to die somewhere. There is always the family tomb in the Cimetière des Batignolles if it becomes important to prove he's for certain dead. I thought about a couple days earlier when I went to the café down the street from where Sartre had lived with his mother but the table there with the brass plaque stating it had been Sartre's favorite table was not the table the waiters had pointed out back in the months when I lived in Paris after university.

"Bist du dort gewesen?"

"Es tut mir leid, daß ich dich je getroffen habe."

"Paß auf deine Zähne auf."

Surprisingly the Place du Panthéon was more crowded with Germans than the expected Chinese. Alice was very pleased. It was as if she were waiting her turn to be called in front of the camera to deliver her big scene. She stopped to talk to a couple women our own age then stopped to talk to a group that was probably a university excursion then finally we were in the taxi that took us around the Jardin du Luxembourg the side of the

Senate buildings. There wasn't one war cripple among those two hundred Germans. Things had moved on. The guidebooks tell all about the buildings that are no longer across from the Senate. Once there was a hotel where Fitzgerald had landed and Faulkner had lived for an entire year. Once there was a restaurant called Foyot's that everyone with enough money to get into the place later wrote about but still the place was torn down. It is the same route shot from inside the taxi the singer rides in *Cléo de 5 à 7* but it's hard to say how much still then existed even back then. Dates aren't often accurately recorded even on computers. The guidebooks rarely concern themselves with where the movie stars passed if writers have passed. I prefer books now. Alice rested her head on my shoulder.

"Sei nicht böse auf mich, Schatz."

"Did you talk to them about sex?"

This made Alice laugh very hard but she took her head away.

"Et le jour n'est pas plus pur que le fond de nos pensées."

I cannot remember now exactly how often Alice quoted Verlaine before I left Paris. *Elle parle et ses dents font un miroitement.* Anyway the elevator in my hotel was one of those old contraptions that squeeze hard together even two small people. It gave Alice the giggles to take us up to the top then then back down to the right floor. Still we didn't kiss. I had a hand on her ass and still we didn't kiss. Inside the elevator it smelled of cheeses, bought dearly, overwhelming the much fainter scent of baguette bought too late in the day. It was a tourist smell. I thought it preferable to the flashy businessmen stink on the airplane but suddenly I was that stink. I had thought again about Louisa. Alice must have noticed.

"You know I'm not good for sex anymore, don't you?"

"I figured."

"And you aren't angry I brought you all the way to Paris anyway?"

Alice was sitting on the bed in my room with one shoe off before she offered to please me without being pleased. She was exhausted from the walk so was slow to see there was no anger. Finally she smiled when she saw I was wearing one red sock and one black sock like all those years dressed for work dreaming revolution. I took off her other shoe then rolled her on her side to not face the window. Even the very good curtains didn't keep out all the light. Alice was sleeping with a slight wheeze in her breathing before I joined her on the bed. I had her leather bag set between us and I took out a stack of papers but could barely make out the top poem in the darkened room. I knew I would never make love with Alice. I had known that back in the office of the lawyers that week before the 1988 elections when the television crew visited. I had known it for more than thirty years and that knowledge swept about me like flowing curtains snatching all light, like scarfs swirled into shrouds, like a handkerchief pulled from my pants because there was nothing else on offer but a sight gag pending a hilarious pratfall. In the rock opera Iago pulls the handkerchief from his trousers as though bringing out his penis. I'm sure that must have given everyone in the theater a good laugh. Alice rolled towards me.

"I want you to keep my poems."

"I have enough money to stay in Paris long as you want me."

"I have someone hired to take care of me for that."

Alice fell back to sleep with her hand reached past her leather bag to rest on my thigh. She had taken off the new scarf too. And her skirt. I thought about the rather prim Manet painting that may or may not be portrait of the Jeanne who had been Baudelaire's mulatto whore. I thought about my painting of Alice nude that hung with prominence in the apartment with all that light on it. I wondered what would become of that painting. Finally I tried not to think like a banker. Instead I thought about the children brought by their grandparents to the glacier where I had sat reading about Betsy Blair dancing in the chorus line, the Parisian children sitting across from me polite in degree that seemed improbable, more quiet than if those boys had come in masks. They had never sniffed a girl's bicycle seat. They had never hidden broken breakfast plates in their bookbags to dispose at school. They have never stolen a typewriter. Certainly they had never almost set the apartment on fire burning a candle for Verlaine. But wasn't it Baudelaire in the movie? No. Balzac. The one with his statue in all the museums bulging at the crotch. It seemed those children knew Truffaut was long dead buried all the way out in Montmartre with no desire any longer even to peer up the passing skirts. I sat there without moving just to have Alice's hand on my thigh. After something no more than twenty minutes Alice was standing.

"I need to go home now. Will you come with me?"

I didn't understand. Alice dressed while I put on my shoes and poured cognac from a bottle bought a couple days earlier into a flask brought from home. Alice had asked if I didn't have anything to drink. We took a drink off the bottle before leaving. On the way out the door I brushed my hand over my new book but I didn't understand why I should do that. Out on the street Alice insisted we walk past the cemetery to the farther Métro station. We passed the flask back and forth.

"It's really close if we just go up to Vivin."

"No. It has always been very unlucky for me there."

In the movie the superstitious singer meets a young soldier on his way back to combat against freedom fighters but I was nothing like a soldier even in my prime. Together they go to the hospital to learn the lab results the singer has been waiting on all day. But we were not going to chance into any doctor zipping past in his convertible sportscar anywhere near the Raspail Métro station. The diagnosis was certain and the ancient l'hopital Saint-Vincent-de-Paul right there had been abandoned indifferently for at least a few years. Anyway it had been an obstetrics hospital. *Children are mirrors of death*. Alice and I walked the long wall of the Cimetière Montparnasse and Alice let me know it wasn't a doctor she sought going to the farther station.

"Everyone is told this cemetery is full but you can still get a place if you know the right people."

Alice was telling me she had a plot for herself near Jean Seberg to not go on residing so close to Baudelaire. The cemetery was bolted for the night. We were passing a spot in the stone wall probably just the other side from where Sartre is buried. If today you Google the cemetery you will be arrowed the spot where Sartre is buried. There rests his immortality. On the map there is no mention of Baudelaire. All the same that evening I did not want to talk about a spot for Alice. Vincent de Paul claimed to have been sold into slavery after being captured by sea pirates. It seems to me he had simply read the bits where Othello tells Desdemona about his early life. Anyway in those times the claim must have seemed good as any to explain a year shut away with madness.

"It was Orson Welles."

"Who started the fire?"

"Long dead."

"Who signed your book?"

"No. Who pissed on that tin drum in this cimetière because my face was the wrong face, like I had put on the wrong mask in a modern tragedy imitating the ancients, an eye instead of a mouth."

I had walked this same street the night I flailed the tin drum Alice had sent from Berlin. It must have seemed great fun back then to send me a tin drum. In the morning I had written the last poem I ever wrote, then much later I had come across the river from my apartment in the Marais on a march all the way to the cimetière in Montparnasse, slapping the sticks on the tin every so often, though it was the middle of the night, before settling on a roll leading to an improvised crash on crash every seventh step. I had been reading *La Nausée* all that day. I was seeking adventure. I now remember myself being the groveling Iago but this was before I had seen that movie with Patrick McGoohan hammering the drums while Betsy Blair walks away with nothing to say about revolution. Now in memory it is sometimes Alice walking away. But didn't I pass that last year at the university convinced little Oskar had insight, that the world was so corrupt the only meaningful response was to never grow, to bang a drum in anger instead? I had gone to see *The Tin Drum* the three times it was shown at the university union. A little later I had read the novel instead of studying for a philosophy exam. After all I was small. Then that night long ago I drummed right to the grave of Jean-Paul Sartre but stopped short because there stood a large man facing the stone. The man kept his cock in hand long after his bladder was empty. I kept a slow rhythm on the tin. The drumming helped the large man find yet more for the stone but instead of the same aim he walked over.

"You mean he pissed on our drum?"

"That's the one."

"And it was really Orson Welles?"

I knew Alice must have met Orson Welles at more than one party but she had never been in a movie with him. She had seen him in the television commercials like the rest of us. My mother's father's house where I had spent most school vacations was just a couple streets over from where Welles was born in Kenosha. It was a tumbledown house in a row built for factory workers my grandfather bought after the bank took the farm. He worked in a factory then. Welles was born in a mansion built on a fortune made brewing beer. It was no accident in the commercials in old age he sold champagne. It was family business. On YouTube now you can watch Orson Welles very drunkenly struggle to film one of those commercials. I looked at Alice and I wanted to live in that bright apartment overlooking the Seine if even for only a few months accompanying despair. I have never been happy with anywhere I've lived. Over the years I had too many times hinted in my letters to Alice about horrors at the madhouse. Probably I had even been repetitious since I had always doubted she ever bothered to read very many of the letters. Her voice was suddenly in sorrow for all those things men had done to her.

"Why would he piss on the drum?"

"Our drum."

"Our drum."

"I had arrived the ghost of Sartre."

This made Alice laugh with cynicism new to her that day so it took me a few moments to catch up to her introspections. Alice slapped her hand on the stone wall several times in rhythm to our steps. I reminded Alice that at the end of *The Tin Drum*, the book but not the movie, little Oskar becomes rich drumming a jazz that returns people so vividly to their childhoods they weep uncontrollably.

"You think Orson Welles pissed on Sartre because you drummed up his childhood?"

Tin. Tin. Roquentin. Rin Tin Tin. Didn't the studio head famously say Rin Tin Tin was the best actor on the lot? That's another for the bishops. Roquentin on his last day in Bouville sits in the library reading a newspaper article about a man whose life is saved by his dog. The boys the lecherous autodidact approaches know they are not allowed Baudelaire because the librarian has marked the book binding with a red cross. The library has many forbidden books marked that way. The autodidact strokes the open palm of the smaller boy but Sartre does not say if the stroke too was in the shape of a cross. I would never have thought to put Louisa's scarf on the statue of the Madonna if little Oskar had not so many times in the large book and once in the movie tried to make the accompanying statue of the infant Jesus play the tin drum. Oskar would hang the drum on the statue. Only in the book does the statue of Jesus come alive to bang the drum in memory of childhood before the cross. We can all guess what happened to Jesus at eight.

"Engineer."

"What?"

"What I said to Orson Welles when he pissed on the drum."

"Our drum."

"Our drum."

"He wasn't an engineer though."

"Not on his business cards anyway."

About the time we approached the station at Boulevard Raspail I was thinking about cubicles. I had thought about cubicles every time on the crowded Métro the last few days when crossing then crossing back the city. I had Alice's hand in mine and I thought about that painting of me wrestling boxes that had been so successful it had put Janis in my bed. I wondered if the grubby poet from the tavern might just might introduce me to his publisher. It seemed unlikely. Still I knew there would be drumming in some of the love poems that filled the leather bag. Then over the next block at the entrance to the station Alice was suddenly superstitious from being close to the cemetery so wouldn't go down the stairs. Alice said there was a taxi rank at the next far corner but we didn't have to go that way at all because an available taxi pulled over for Alice before she had even signaled. We were even five steps back from the curb. It seemed magical. The huge black man driving let out a rumbling guffaw when Alice gave him her address, saying he already knew the address, then he went behind the cemetery and made other circles I couldn't follow until we were back to Boulevard Raspail, except now headed towards the river. Alice did not question it. There was an overpowering sense the man knew exactly what he was doing come each light and each obstruction and each pedestrian. Still Alice remained uneasy about the cemetery so had to find something other to talk about herself.

"I never played Desdemona again after that college production."

I had sat in the front row for all the performances of that college production. It hardly matters Betsy Blair was a redhead too since everything she ever made was shot black and white. Welles had had her hair colored blonde for Desdemona. I sometimes forget that. *Rencontre á Paris*. I have never found that movie even among the pirates but isn't that the only one with Betsy Blair in color? I mean before she grew old. I no longer look. I know IMDB now will tell me if the movie really is in color but I don't want to know either way. Even the cover on the memoir was in black and white though with some overlaid tinting to make the hair somewhat red. The taxi was soon on Boulevard Saint Germain headed in a direct shot towards Cardinal Lemoine. The huge black man switched from French to perfect English after hearing Alice speak to me some more.

"Notre-Dame is burning."

The driver pointed out his window at the great plume of smoke coming over the arrondissement though he seemed to know we were not rushing to gawk a fire. He said he had driven past when there was just the first smoke almost an hour earlier. There had been no firemen then but things were closed off now. The station at Saint Michel was closed but he thought probably we knew that since he had seen me step first towards the station on Raspail before turning away.

"Everyone there says it is all going up for sure."

Hasn't that African got any piety at all? You would think it was a line from *Othello* but it is one of Ava Gardner's lines to Gregory Peck from the Kilimanjaro movie. Alice asked about Pont de la Tournelle and the driver said the texts on his cellphone warned the bridge was packed with people the traffic had to inch through. Alice insisted the driver put us off on Saint Germaine the near side of Cardinal Lemoine. The driver insisted he swing us about whatever path he had in mind to get onto Cardinal Lemoine. Alice flashed money to make the huge black man stop. In his face I saw a hurt I didn't understand except to understand it was very important to this man to get Alice to her door. Perhaps he remembered her from the movies, from that hit record of the theme. Then it suddenly occurred to me the man had many times given Alice a lift home from whatever hospital it was where she saw her doctor. Alice didn't want me to know the driver was a man she hired all the time. Of course he remembered the address. The driver couldn't have been much younger than us and for the first time in my life I thought I understood the workings to someone else's job but I understood not just because I had seen the man drive. I looked twice before certain the driver wasn't that pianist I met only the once. Still maybe it was him.

"They aren't containing it."

Alice and I were crossing to the bridge.

"No. It's going to be destroyed."

The fire was just licking the spire. The sidewalk before the bridge was also very crowded and I deflected an elbow before it could catch Alice in the eye. There were people kneeling. One was a nun. I pushed us past hordes milling about but I wasn't trying to get Alice home and Alice knew it. There was a very fat man hard to dodge because he kept dropping packages all wrapped alike in glittering green paper. I remember at that point I looked upwards towards Sacré-Cœur because I knew that after far more than a hundred years the workers finally would be gathered there to ask for the forgiveness Sacré-Cœur had been built to demand. Fifty thousand executions of Communards could not satiate the rich so the church had been built to demand the poor plead for their souls. Earlier in Lyon General Aupick had left enough of the striking silk weavers live that the rich did not go without silk. His was the mathematics of true heroism. His mathematics was the stuff of medals on the chest. I tried to think only about the past but the fire at the cathedral stretched every one of my failures into the present. I could see there was no getting down the quai under to the other side of the Pont de l'Archevêché right next the cathedral. The police had it cordoned off. Alice and I were at the top of the stairs leading down to the quai Tournelle.

"Are you going down?"

"Do you think you can get home on your own from here?"

I finally understood we had left the hotel room only because Alice had remembered her poems but forgotten to bring her opiates.

"I'm going where you go, honey."

We found we could get down the stairs if we kept close to the wall of the embankment. We finished the flask at the bottom of the stairs.

"There is a real opera of course. Othello."

"There is a ballet too."

"Up in Ménilmontant the street mimes perform it."

"And the preschoolers perform it in Montmartre."

"And the panhandlers perform it in front of the Arc de Triomphe."

Everyone but the bloody working class performs *Othello*. We were making up nonsense to assuage the pain from what we were seeing before us. Most everyone else had out a cellphone to distance themselves from the fire in an aggregate perfection of photography. Alice and I might have laughed at our joke of all the world struggling to perform *Othello* but the crowd on the steps would have beaten us to death. There were women weeping. There were men weeping. There seemed there no genuine protection from anything even worse. I could feel the deaths of every shoulder we slipped past now we were down the steps. Every breast. Every cock. It was the cacophony of feet dodging feet before colliding that the poet from the tavern had so wanted kept from his mornings. I could feel the flesh begging to be buried but being offered no grave. They were hearts in the dark abyss. It was the monster of the crowd craving absolution the rich could never imagine. The crowd could all be burnt for virgins at the stake but it would not help, nothing would be saved. They knew the rules of the game. The cellphones could not make souvenirs of this hell. I had expected to glimpse Louisa stalking me the day before when on a walk to visit my old apartment. I had not seen her. I had kept thinking I would be stabbed when passing among some throng of tourists. In his rock opera Patrick McGoohan has Iago stab Othello to death. Could he have gotten it more wrong? In the Shakespeare the whole point is Iago makes dolts out of his superiors in rank. And it is easy. He easily pulls them into his practice, his plot. There is no meaning to any of it if Iago is simply going to stab Othello anyway, making Iago what, exactly the Quare Fellow? There wasn't another church Louisa might have burned that could have mattered to me. Of course she had not stalked me. She was still clever.

"I can't stomach much more of this, not without bringing up the cognac."

"A ruined cathedral might actually make the island more romantic," said Alice.

I kept pulling us forward though I knew we could not get to that second unit spot from *The Snows of Kilimanjaro* because there were policemen. I don't really know if people were already singing hymns like in the television reports from later that night but I like to remember us walking through a singing crowd. In so many movies the cut is from romance to jazz but the Kilimanjaro movie cuts from the saxophone player straight to that perfect spot behind the cathedral. Certainly at that moment if never before I understood why I played jazz even though long ago in the video store I had laughed that the jazz played in the movie was 1950s cool rather than 1920s hot. The movie presented no memory people had once danced to jazz. If at eight my lungs hadn't proven too small to play even a child's saxophone, after months trying, I would surely have later played tenor saxophone right into that shot from the movie beside the cathedral but back some way from the rose window, long ago in youth conflating the jazz right into the romance, maybe even had the saxophone along to do it right then again, right there in front of the fire. Instead I had played the tin drum there on my march that one night. All the same, at that moment on the quai with Alice holding my hand, I wanted correspondences between the senses to keep farther from what seemed revenge against me. I wanted something other than drumming. I wanted an orchestra. April. Paris. One more time. After all that is Johnny Hodges blowing backlot jazz in the movie. I ached to have played saxophone. My face must have shown its horror at all my failures because Alice suddenly felt a terrible responsibility for bringing me to Paris only to see the cathedral destroyed.

"You know that drum actually was one of the ones used in the movie."

"I always believed the note you included with the drum."

"I was always helping you out."

"The drum didn't survive."

"I got you that job managing the video store."

"No."

"You knew Apollonia Whitton was my aunt."

I didn't remember that. For obvious cause I had blocked that memory too but the job through the war hero I remembered too damned well. I especially remembered the fascist mother of those two lawyers. And it had never been difficult to guess how the computer programming job had come through Dorothea. Alice had placed a telephone call that had started out talk about poetry. Of course Dorothea had always denied there had been any call but denied it always with something near singing in her voice. I was insisted I accept the coincidence. Yes. Alice had arranged every job of my adult life. Yet on the quai this summation of my personal experience with capitalism seemed so inconsequential my mind wandered instead about La Présidente, Madame Sabatier, another Apollonia, Apollonie this one, who Baudelaire had loved from afar but never quite anonymously. He turned away years later when she finally offered herself to him. Baudelaire needed for his poetry a love out of reach that was perhaps tumbled with other darker sexual inhibitions as well. Saint Apollonia is the patron saint of dentistry because all her teeth were pulled in her martyrdom. Suddenly for the first time I remembered Apollonia Whitton had spasmed a few moments on the steps before the bank night deposit when frightened by a mask of a mouth. Then I could not think of Apollonia Whitton without thinking about the statue of Apollonie Sabatier writhing in orgasm. She didn't need a plaque. That statue is still exhibited in the d'Orsay for everyone to see. Alice had acted in similar scenes where there is shown no actual sex but there arrives an orgasm played to the sheets and sometimes even the obscured bedroom mirror. One of the movies was shown for months in the theaters then seemingly forever on cable. I had seen Alice in orgasm so many times she seemed turned to a museum piece with it. There on the quai I tried to believe it did not matter especially we hadn't had our *hour of love, of worldly matters, and direction* before parting. It seemed a joke from the mouth of Orson Welles. Movies. Direction. Even the bishops so dignified in their miters while writing the testament of cinema would snicker up their sleeves at that one.

"Let's go."

We had made our way to the policemen stopping people from going forward.

"I can't watch anymore but I can't leave."

"That's not what I meant."

Alice squeezed my hand and pulled me gently towards the fire.

"We'll get arrested."

"Haven't you ever been arrested?"

"Never."

"Imagine how famous my grave will become when I die in a prison cell."

Raise the red flag. Raise the cage holding Iago. Alice ran past the policemen and I ran after her and she didn't have a moustache penciled above her lip while chasing down the quai and she ran with no scheme to murder me even once we were in the same prison together. She was not Jeanne Moreau. She was as innocent of Françoise Truffaut as those children in the glacier. Gene Kelly had two left feet. Leslie Carson had never been born. We ran laughing and I caught her hand when we reached the spot. It was very hot there. The fire had climbed the spire now. I caught her hand and she let herself be whiplashed back into my arms and she put my hand on her diseased breast and she put her hand on the back of my neck while giving me the deepest kiss of my life that lasted until the policemen caught up.

It was not Ava Gardner. It was certainly not Gregory Peck.

Still it was the most beautiful spot in all the history of all the world and it is gone forever no matter how I frame it now.

ABOUT THE AUTHOR

Gary McClintock lives in Illinois near the banks of the Mississippi River. He graduated from the University of Iowa. This is his third novel.